Reactions From Ja   ᴅ**ᴇᴀders**

These reactions are as written. The
a Japanese person making their be:
language, !

GW00771089

m

A must-read for all Japan fans. Could even a Japanese writer portray contemporary Japan so realistically and poignantly? When you finish reading this, you will surely be a fan of Miko — a hikikomori girl trying to break out the harsh working system in Japan. And not only that, but it also has the perfect balance of pain, laugh and tears. Once you start reading, you won't be able to stop turning the pages. It is a gem of a book that I, as a Japanese, am confident to recommend. It exposes social problems in Japan that are never visible from the outside. Join a little girl and her cute cat on a journey into Japanese real society!
Yui Miyamoto

Very well written shedding lights on Japan's social issues. I think Japanese people would love this book because it feels validating to know people are aware of their issues in Japanese society. It was a feel good book. Awesome details and descriptions of Japanese words! Additionally, the culture of shame is sadly very true. I hope many Japanese people read this and see how silly it is to think that shame is worse than death.
Miki Umesaki

If you are feeling sad, this novel will make you happy like eating chocolate. It will resonate whatever circumstances you find yourself in, it will help you to motivate yourself and discover your true purpose. It will help you get out of your comfort zone and find purpose to fulfil your life and be happy. Self-doubt can go away as you see Miko's way of living. I recommend reading The Hikikomori to get smiles and happiness.
Kyoko Aoki

This is a strange feeling. It is set in Japan, where I live, but something is different. It is not the fake Japan of old Hollywood movies, but rather like a parallel world just a step away. Although real social problems are described, they are not heavy, and on the contrary, there is a light and fluttering feeling of flight. If you can understand the tightness that many Japanese people feel in order to feel secure, you will feel a great sense of liberation with the characters in this world after reading this book. I hope this story will spark interest in Japan and the Japanese people.
Fumio Sayo

The Hikikomori depicts the social problems that modern Japan is facing... The Hikikomori is certainly a powerful piece of work. The author has successfully made it both socially conscious and entertaining. I would recommend this novel especially to young and middle-aged Japanese, as well as to readers from other countries who are interested in Japan.
Yumiko Hashimoto

At first, I encouraged Miko almost prayerfully. However, the roles were reversed as the story went on and I was the one encouraged by her courageous and intelligent actions. I enjoyed the car rides, experiencing the various locations and feeling different emotions of her family and strangers. The author was successful in transcribing Miko's innocent voice from her heart completely, with help from Fluffy Kitty. I hope more people will be encouraged by Miko!
Rika Otsu

My heart was full of positivity by reading your novel.
I realized that it is important to take action to solve problems, rather than just sit back and watch the problems that arise in society.
I sincerely wanted to be a humble, kind, and strong person like Miko.
When I finished reading your novel, I felt confident and motivated to live positively.
I am so glad I was able to read this book this summer!!
Yuna Otani

THE
Hikikomori

by
Mark Vrankovich

The Hikikomori
Copyright © 2022 Mark Vrankovich
All rights reserved.

The moral right of the author has been asserted.

No part of this publication may be reproduced, distributed, or transmitted in any form or by any means, including photocopying, recording, or other electronic or mechanical methods, without the prior written permission of the author, except as permitted by copyright law. For permission requests, use correspondence information below.

This is a work of fiction. The characters in this novel are the product of the author's imagination and do not represent any actual persons living or dead. The institutions and organizations mentioned in this novel are either the product of the author's imagination, or if real, used fictitiously without any attempt to describe actual conduct.

ISBN: 978-0-473-63422-3

First Published 2022

Graphics by Gavin Manson

Correspondence:
inquiry@thehikikomori.com

Address all physical correspondence to:
The Hikikomori
PO Box 105-212
Auckland 1143
New Zealand

Website:
www.TheHikikomori.com

Facebook:
https://www.facebook.com/TheHikikomoriNovel

V1.0.4

For The People of Japan

The feminine Japanese name

Miko

is pronounced phonetically as

mee-co

Ten-year-old Miko Nishimura walked the forest path each morning on her way to the school bus.

Located in snowy Aomori Prefecture at the northern tip of Japan's largest home island, Honshu, the forest's ancient name "Negai To Nageki" cannot be translated precisely into English.

Roughly it means the place for wishing and lamenting. However, some Japanese scholars argue the forest's name is better rendered as the statement, 'a wish is also a lament'.

But little Miko was unaware of the scholarly debates about the forest.

Miko jingled as she walked because her mother tied a bell around her to scare away the forest bears.

On the long bus trip into Goshogawara, Miko would untie the bell and bury it deep in her schoolbag. So its jingle didn't reveal she was from the country. The city students made fun of people from the country.

This day Miko was paying careful attention to where she stepped. It had rained last night, making the trail muddy. She didn't want to get mud on her school shoes, or, worse, slip over and splatter mud on her school skirt.

Her school was strict on proper presentation, and so her uniform had to be clean to avoid her parents getting an angry teacher's note.

Miko came to a circular clearing. A blue pool of chilly sky floated above, contained within the circle of the old tree tops. High on the clearing's western side, shavings of early morning sun painted a bright-green crescent across the tops of the trees.

She skipped around the muddy patches out into the middle of the clearing. There she pulled out a plastic bag to feed her bird friends.

Miko shook out the white crumbs she had scraped from her mother's *shokupan* breakfast loaf.

Her father had toast and honey this morning, leaving his empty plate covered in crumbs. Miko had brushed those in too.

Doves flew from the branches. The bush warblers landed and hopped along, only to be passed by the golden Japanese quail running from the forest.

Miko was careful to ensure the pigeons didn't bully the other birds. Under Miko's watch, each bird got an equal share of the crumbs.

She liked to draw pictures, and most of her drawings were of her bird friends.

Miko waved goodbye, setting off from the clearing back along the forest path. The muddy puddles spread wider in the shade of the trees, so she concentrated hard on where to step.

Each day, as she passed a bent pine tree that curved upwards from the path's berm, Miko prayed.

Please please can I have a friend. Just one. Please.

Most other students had friends. So Miko was envious.

She knew envy was a bad emotion. But even when she tried, Miko couldn't stop being envious of people who had friends.

There must be a secret to making a friend.

Miko wanted to ask someone with friends to tell her the secret, but she feared talking to people she didn't know.

Once when she was five, playing alone at a windy playground, there was a girl in a pink dress with a yellow ribbon perched at the top of the slide, and a group of six boys and girls rushing across the playground.

The group stopped to watch the girl slide down.

At the bottom of the slide, they talked excitedly with her, waving their arms in the air like monkeys swinging across branches and pointing towards the jungle gym.

One of the girls linked arms with her, and the seven of them raced off together.

As they went the girl's face beamed with joy.

Miko wondered if that was how it worked. So ever since, when Miko saw a group of children approaching, she secretly hoped they would decide to link arms and make her their friend too.

A trio of wet pine needles fell, landing on Miko's head.

She picked the fresh smelling needles from her hair and used her fingers to comb her hair back into shape. Miko needed to have tidy hair to avoid being scolded by her teachers. It was hard because her hair was naturally a little messy.

There were strict rules at Miko's school regarding hair. Every girl's hair had to be black. No other colors were allowed without a doctor's certificate or a certificate from the school.

Most of the unfortunate girls with non-black hair dyed their hair black to avoid being picked on by others, even if they had a certificate.

Miko was pleased her hair was naturally black. Her mother cut it into a bob-cut that didn't go far below her chin. Miko thought her hair's straight fringe and straight sides made it seem like she was wearing a lower case n on her head.

Miko approached the creaky wooden bridge over the rapids. The forest stream was heavy with melted snow and recent rain racing down off the slopes of Mount Iwaki, swashing and hissing over the rocks.

The noise from the rushing water was why the black bear didn't hear Miko's bell.

Normally, forest bears move away if they hear humans. However, if the person gets too close, they attack.

A bush hid the bear from sight.

As Miko passed the bush, the bear came into view.

At the same moment the hundred and ten kilogram bear caught sight of Miko.

Startled, the black bear snarled, swinging around and lashing out with its claws. Missing Miko's stomach by less than a hand's width.

Miko didn't scream.

She ran.

Her running further enraged the bear. With a growl it bounded after her.

Miko ran as fast as her ten-year-old legs allowed. She ran through the forest, zipping between two closely spaced trees.

She never knew, but the two trees made the bear take a detour, which opened the distance between her and her snarling pursuer. If it had not been for those trees Miko would have died only a few meters away from where she met the bear.

From behind came the lumbering thumpty-thump paw falls of the monster. The bear snarled. It breathed out in harsh rushes, matching the sound of the steam engine that had visited the railway museum.

The animal's unbridled fury burned across her back, like a blowtorch on her soul.

The bear was gaining fast. Miko ran straight out onto the forest road. The target-fixated animal plowed through the bushes and emerged right behind her.

It took another swipe with its paw and grazed Miko's right shoulder, spinning her around in the middle of the road as it clawed her school backpack.

There was a man on a motorbike. With a familiar face, wearing a white bowling ball style helmet.

The man yelled at the bear and forced his way between Miko and the animal. He made loud barking sounds with his motorbike's engine.

The bear hesitated. Then it turned, and ran back into the forest.

Miko kept running.

The man called after her.

Miko kept running because of the terror gripping her young heart. Animals had always been her friends. The world had gone wrong.

She ran through the forest, branches whipping at her tear-stained face and mud covering her shoes and socks and skirt.

She crossed back over the road. A distant shout came from the motorbike man.

Miko ran and ran. To the forest trail. Along the trail back to the end of her street. Then up the hill to her house.

As soon as Miko saw her house, she started yelling, "*Okaachan!*

Okaachan! Okaachan!", which means Mummy.

Miko didn't stop calling until her mother burst out of their front door, her frantic pace and wide eyes resonating with the terror in her child's voice.

Her mother scooped Miko up into her arms.

"My little love! What is it?"

"A bear! A bear!" Miko said, grasping the folds of her mother's apron and dress to pull her closer.

Suddenly, her mother took her hand from behind Miko's back. Her hand was red with blood.

She yelled, "Miko!"

In a frenzy, she put Miko down. Spinning her around to inspect her shoulder.

The sight of the blood and her mother's reaction electrified Miko's horror.

For a moment she felt faint.

There was the roar of an engine accelerating up the hill, and brakes squealing and gravel crunching under tires.

"Is she OK?" the motorbike man demanded.

"No!" Miko's mother cried.

"A bear chased her out of the forest."

"Please take us to Tsugaru Hospital Takahashi-san!"

Miko was squeezed between the man's back and her mother's front as the man drove them to the city hospital.

The man smelled of fish because he was Isamu Takahashi, the local fish seller.

Miko's clawed shoulder stung like her scraped knee had, back when she was six and a wheel came off her pink trike. Her parents kept complaining she rode her trike too fast, but the truth was Miko couldn't make the three-wheeled machine go fast enough.

Except this pain was more widespread and more throbbing.

Green trees and endless rice paddies rushed by the spluttering motorbike.

They rode through Sad Town with its weather-beaten town hall covered in flaking rust-red paint.

Sad Town was a nickname given because there were no children in the town anymore. In the past the school bus had stopped outside its town hall. Now the school bus drove straight through.

More rice paddies zipped by, replaced with buildings and cars and noisy trucks as they entered the city.

At the hospital came good news. The bear's claws had done most of their damage to Miko's thick duffel school jacket. Its claws had shredded the woolen material, but the cuts on Miko's shoulder were not deep.

The doctor fixed her up with a few stitches and a mean injection that made her cry.

The doctor reminded Miko of kid's TV host Kōichi Yamadera, but with more sensible hair. He looked genuinely upset when Miko cried.

"It's going to be OK, Miko," the doctor said. "I'm sorry it hurt. You are a very lucky girl."

Later, Miko's father came rushing in. Her father traveled by bus to work, so the owner of the construction company had driven him into the city.

While the doctor talked, her father stroked Miko's hair and clasped her hand like it was precious.

That her father held her hand made Miko realize how dangerous the situation had been. He had only held her hand when she was little and not after.

When her father heard of Mr. Takahashi's actions, he went out into the corridor. Through the internal glass window Miko saw him bowing low, many times, to Mr. Takahashi.

Miko's family and relatives bought their fish from Mr. Takahashi's fish stall from that day on.

Isamu Takahashi didn't know it, but the story of him saving Miko would lead to many people choosing to buy their fish from him, and within a year he would have enough saved to put a deposit on a small shop.

Owning his own shop had been Isamu's private dream since he first started selling fish at his father's fish stall back in 1986. Every day since, for twelve years, Isamu had imagined arranging his iced window displays, and chatting to customers while wrapping their fresh fish in his own shop.

Miko's doctor decided she should stay one night in hospital so they could observe her.

Her father had gone out to buy something, while her mother sat in a chair by Miko's hospital bed.

It was after 1 pm when through the thick hospital walls came the squealing and roaring and popping hisses from Uncle Ken's taxi. He was a taxi driver in the city of Sendai and it hadn't taken him long to drive the big 350-kilometer distance from Sendai to Goshogawara.

Uncle Ken arrived, breathing hard. Seeing Miko sitting up in bed, his concerned expression turned into a grin.

"Not too bad, eh? My favorite squeaky dwarf will survive."

Miko's mother gave him a paper cup of water. He gulped it down and then sat on the bed next to Miko.

"The doctor said she will heal up fine," Miko's mother said.

"What about inside here, Chika?" Uncle Ken said, messing up Miko's bob-cut hair. "This type of experience doesn't exit easily from a young mind."

"Akio-san said the same thing."

Miko's father returned, exchanging a relieved look with his twin brother.

Her father was carrying a fluffy white cat soft-toy, the size of a loaf of bread.

"Miko, I found a friend for you," her father said, giving Miko the toy cat. "What will you name him?"

Miko considered this important question extra carefully.

The cat had a fat body, little feet, a long white fluffy tail, and a cute face that suggested it was very smug about something it had just done.

"Fluffy Kitty," Miko announced, officially.

"An excellent name," Uncle Ken said.

At her father's signal, her mother and uncle joined her father outside in the corridor with Mr. Takahashi. Where they started an adult discussion. Leaving Miko alone in the room.

The hospital smelled of cleaning chemicals and starched bedsheets, but for a moment Miko tasted in the back of her nose the sweet warmth of freshly made candyfloss.

"Hello, Miko," said Fluffy Kitty.

"Hello, Fluffy Kitty."

"I'll be your friend, Miko," said Fluffy Kitty, and looked very smug about it.

The bear attack made Miko not want to leave her house.

Unfortunately, she still needed to go to school.

But no longer could she make herself walk through the forest. It was too scary a place now.

Many policemen and firemen had searched for days, but found no trace of the dangerous animal. And for several weeks after their search ended, her father had taken long walks in the forest and not seen the bear either.

So he suggested Miko should try walking to school like she used to, because he was sure the bear had moved away.

At his suggestion Miko had curled up into a ball and started shaking. So her father never made that suggestion again.

The rear of her parents' house bordered on the forest, and that was as close as Miko would go.

Each morning before school, she fed her bird friends at the edge of the trees, while keeping a wary eye out for bear-shaped shadows in the woods.

Her father bought a used Suzuki Alto microcar from his work colleague's grandmother. Her mother used the tiny white car to drive Miko to the bus stop each morning, and would be there waiting for when Miko's bus returned in the late afternoon.

"This is an excellent arrangement, Miko," Fluffy Kitty said, his smug face peering out the unzipped top of Miko's schoolbag. "You will never get mud on your shoes again."

"Yes, I am a lucky person," Miko whispered.

As the bus rattled along, Miko finished applying a ring of Sock Touch glue above her ankles to keep her socks up. "And no more dumb jingle jingle bell either."

Miko was a talented student who loved books. Reading took her to impossible places. Like visiting the penguins in Antarctica.

Books also let her imagine doing impossible things, like piloting a spacecraft down onto the moon.

Miko's readings seeded her mind with new information, allowing her to grow many kinds of fascinating theories.

The school bus turned the corner into Sad Town.

Sun, rain, or snow, each school day the old people from the town gathered to wait at the disused bus stop outside the rusty red hall.

The gray figures waved to the children as their bus passed.

Miko and the other children waved back, which made the old people smile.

Once their school bus had passed, the children would turn their attention back to themselves.

Everyone, except Miko.

Because, as the bus pulled away, the old people's waves slowed. Then their hands and smiles fell.

Those shrinking figures stood forlorn like bent statues, staring at the back of the bus. Until the bus turned around a small hill and Miko couldn't see them anymore.

At that turn, each day without fail, Miko's heart seemed to say,
Something isn't right with this world.

Sad Town used to have its own school. But the lack of children meant its school had been closed. The countryside children who once traveled into Sad Town now passed through to Goshogawara on the school bus.

This arrangement was unusual, since school buses are rare in Japan. In Japan, most children live near enough to a school to walk or cycle. Even young children travel to and from school by themselves.

But school buses were becoming more common, as Japan's falling birth rate created more abandoned ghost schools.

After Sad Town, the bus passed a lone pine tree that grew not far outside the town's boundary. At this new point each day, Miko prayed for a friend.

Please please please, can I have a human friend? Just one friend. It would be nice to have a friend to talk to. I have lots of things to say, so I promise she will not get bored.

Miko didn't tell Fluffy Kitty she prayed this. Because while he was her first talking friend—her bird friends from the forest only squeaked and chirped—Miko very much wanted a human friend too.

She only prayed for one friend, since she didn't want to seem greedy. But Miko's secret fantasy was having more than one friend, with her being an important member of their friendship group.

So, to avoid seeming greedy, she planned on being sneaky about it. She would first pray for one friend, and once that friend was secured, then she would ask for the others.

But the friend-making secret never revealed itself to her.

Instead, the most attention she got was from bullies.

Bullying was a constant feature of Miko's school life.

She feared school days, but didn't want to disappoint her parents by refusing to go. Her parents liked it when she did well in school.

So Miko didn't pretend to be sick. Instead, she went to school each day and tried her best.

Miko didn't tell anyone about the bullying because she was ashamed of being bullied, and didn't want to burden other people with her problems.

Walking across the bridge from the bus stop Miko arrived at the school gate.

There was only one teacher in sight. The teacher had her back turned, talking to a group of students at the far end of the courtyard.

Shige Takeda and her five friends got up from their seats.

Seeing them, Miko wished she had super-jet shoes so she could race right past them, faster than they could ever run.

"Where are you going?" Shige asked. She grabbed Miko's arm and swung Miko around into her friends.

Shige's friends surrounded Miko. They tugged at her jacket, pulling it in different directions. They put their hands into the jacket's pockets and searched for items.

Because Miko's parents couldn't afford to buy new pencils and writing pads, Miko clutched her schoolbag to her chest to stop the bullies taking anything.

From the outside it looked like a friend huddle with Miko at the center.

"Why do you come to school, Miko? You're so stupid."

"Shouldn't you be helping your parents on the farm?"

Miko kept still and silent. Talking encouraged them. Struggling was an excuse for them to increase their cruelty, like a dog shaking a panicked rabbit in its mouth.

The pinching started. With fingers and thumbs like pliers through her clothes, they took a strong purchase on Miko's skin. Teeth clenched and muscles trembling, they twisted hard.

Then came the sewing pins they hid in their jacket sleeves. They jabbed Miko's arms and thighs and bottom with the pins. Miko couldn't predict from which direction the sharp pain would come.

Her yelps and tears delighted the bullies.

This was Miko's typical reception when she arrived at school.

However, it wasn't the physical pain that hurt the most. It was their emotional daggers.

Whereas boys fight with their fists, girls fight with their tongues, and these female bullies were experts at spitting poison words.

Through terms of exhaustive experimentation they had pinpointed Miko's emotional weak points, and were diligent in applying their knowledge. Savoring her pain with their gleeful eyes and crooked-teeth smirks.

"What a revolting face you have, Miko."

"Miko the pig face."

"Why did you come? We know someone as pig-ugly as you will never succeed."

"Can you imagine her parents' disgust when she was born?"

"What shame they must feel being out in public with such a deformed child."

"Miko, the boys are scared of you. Shunsuke told me the boys call you 'the girl who doesn't need a Halloween mask'."

Miko never understood the true reason behind their remarks. Miko was prettier than they were, and these delinquent girls were jealous. Their insecurity made them work hard at pulling Miko down to their level.

Miko had a little face, broad and round, an upturned button nose, strong cheekbones, and two big bright coffee-colored eyes. Her mouth was wide and expressive, which delighted people when she smiled. In a society where cuteness in girls is highly prized, Miko was zipping along in the top quadrant.

But Miko couldn't conceive in her heart that people, even mean bullies, would lie about such an important aspect of a person.

What they spoke into her each relentless day solidified like burning lava in her soul. Becoming black and as hard as rock.

And so slowly, her young years passed.

Endured rather than enjoyed.

Eleven years old, twelve years, then thirteen.

At age fourteen, no boy had ever confessed to her, when many other girls were winning confessions.

This was proof enough. Ugly girls didn't get boyfriends.

So when Miko walked with her parents she kept her head down, to avoid causing them discomfort.

Soon she went everywhere with her head lowered so as not to disturb others with her unpleasant appearance.

In Japan, much more than in the rest of the world, it is expected that you will consider others. So Miko felt it was her duty to protect her fellow Japanese by hiding her disturbing face.

Accepting the reality of her unattractiveness, Miko fell in love with a fictional boy called Ren Matsuda.

Ren featured in her favorite manga comic, *Hidden Stealth Ninja*. Ren wanted to become Hidden Stealth Ninja's sidekick. However, he could never locate his desired master.

What Ren didn't realize was that Hidden Stealth Ninja was already using him as his sidekick. Ren just kept missing the clues. Such was the skill of Hidden Stealth Ninja.

Miko often imagined holding Ren's hand. She wrote "I Love Ren" and drew a heart on the inside of her pencil case. On the inside, so no one could see her confession.

Miko knew Ren was not a real person. But in a way that was good, because then Ren couldn't reject her. Besides, she wasn't the only student in love with a manga or anime character. It was OK to have a manga character as your first crush.

But the bullying affected Miko at a deeper level.

Miko couldn't grasp what wrong actions she had performed to deserve the bullying. Her heart told her people should be her friends. Even the bullies. But her heart had also said animals should be her friends, and the bear had attacked her.

So Miko came to realize it wasn't something she had done. Instead, it was something she was.

Miko was bullied because something was inherently wrong with Miko Nishimura. She didn't express this belief consciously, but as a wordless truth that grew in her subconscious. Potent, but without form.

However, there was one area where she was defiant. The bullies ordered Miko to follow their made-up rules or face punishment.

For example, Miko was not allowed to drink from the water fountains, if a bully wanted Miko's spot in a line Miko had to give up her spot, and there were many playground seats they instructed Miko not to use. Miko called these instructions "Bully Rules".

She hated the bully rules and refused to obey. The bullies punished her infractions as soon as the teachers were out of sight. But despite the physical pain, Miko couldn't bring herself to submit.

When Miko hammered her mind into a spot, there it stayed.

Miko's criteria for evaluating rules were simple. If good people made the rules, then she would obey them. If bad people made the rules, then she would ignore them. Bullies were bad people. So their rules were invalid.

One of the worst bullying incidents happened in 2003, when Miko was fifteen.

This significant event occurred near her school, on a bridge that crosses over the Kyuto river, which runs through the middle of Goshogawara.

After school Miko had to cross the bridge to get to her bus stop, but big Moe and her two friends were waiting.

There was another bridge, down by the noodle shop south of the school, but there wasn't enough time to go that far. If Miko was late, she would miss the bus and her mother would have to drive into the city to collect her.

Miko couldn't let that happen, because her mother was not a confident driver.

"Be brave," Fluffy Kitty said.

"I wish Uncle Ken was here with his taxi."

Miko crossed the road. So she could walk by on the other side of the bridge from the bullies. But the three bullies crossed over too.

On the bridge there was a warm wind rushing down the river.

"Hey, Bear Food. Where you going?"

Miko looked around. There were no teachers in sight, and only a few other kids back by the school gate or at the bus stop over the bridge.

"I asked you where you're going, country girl," Moe said, blocking Miko's way.

"Home," Miko said.

"Bear Food wants to go home to her rice farmer parents."

The two other girls snickered.

"I've heard her parents keep her out in the pigsty, because she has a pig's face."

"I've heard that too," one of Moe's friends said.

"What can pig face do?" Moe said, her face showing disgust. "Stop wasting our time and go back to where you came from."

The insults went on for about a minute.

Then Moe punched Miko in the stomach.

Miko doubled over. The deep pain made worse by being unexpected.

"She's crying!" Moe said.

Laughter came from her friends.

Miko's schoolbag was being pulled.

"What's this?" Moe said. "She has a plush toy."

Miko looked up.

Moe had Fluffy Kitty clasped tightly in her fat hand.

"Give him back!"

"Maybe he wants to go swimming," Moe said. She made like she was throwing Fluffy Kitty over the metal railing into the river below.

Miko screamed. Then realized her mistake. Moe grinned an evil grin. Now the bully knew how important Fluffy Kitty was.

"Miko! I'm scared. Help me," Fluffy Kitty said.

Miko knew in her heart that Moe would throw Fluffy Kitty into the river. The horror of losing Fluffy Kitty drove her to do what she did.

Miko swung her schoolbag. Catching the bully full on the side of her face. The heavy library books inside making a solid whack sound, like a baseball hitting a wooden bat.

Moe crumpled. Her head donging on the metal railing as she fell.

Her two friends stared down wide eyed at their lifeless leader.

Miko grabbed Fluffy Kitty from Moe's hand and ran past the bullies. She ran as fast as she could go. All the way to the bus stop.

She got on to the bus, rushed to the back, and kneeled on the crimson fabric bench seat to watch out the rear window.

"Is she moving?" Fluffy Kitty said.

"Yes," Miko said.

Moe was sitting up against the bridge's railing.

The bully put a hand up to the railing to pull herself up, but her hand flopped back down. Moe's two friends were talking rapidly to her, pulling at her jacket and occasionally glancing fiercely at Miko's bus.

"I'm in trouble," Miko said.

"You saved me. You're my best friend," Fluffy Kitty said.

Miko hugged Fluffy Kitty very tightly.

Miko's mother said she knew something was wrong as soon as Miko got off the bus.

When Miko's father got home, he listened to his wife. He came into Miko's room and asked her to repeat her story and show him the bruise on her stomach.

He said something under his breath, which Miko couldn't understand, but it had a male power that frightened her.

Her father paced out on the deck with the phone, having a long adult talk with Uncle Ken in Sendai.

After homework, dinner, and family-time watching their favorite shows, Miko went to bed.

In the silence of the night, Miko lay awake cuddling Fluffy Kitty and wondering what punishment the school was going to dish out. It was her word against Moe and her two friends. Would the police be involved?

As a distraction, she switched on the portable black and white Panasonic TV set on her bedside table. Purchased secondhand after their wedding, it was her parents' first TV—gray plastic with a suitcase carry handle.

The old set could only find one channel, and sometimes, depending on the weather, the picture rolled upwards. It whined as it warmed up. Miko turned the volume down.

A news show featured a speech given by gray-haired Chairman Ikari. Chairman of the vast Ikari Conglomerate and head of the country's most powerful *keiretsu*.[†]

Miko knew of Chairman Ikari; he was one of the most significant people in Japan. The dark-suited chairman was warning about the business risks of deflation to a crowd of suited men.

How does someone become so powerful they can change the course of the country?

To Miko, even with all her reading, that path was incomprehensibly unknowable.

He must have many friends, unlike me. And when he enters a room people will notice him, also unlike me.

---

† A keiretsu is a business association. While a single big business has a lot of power, many big businesses working together (as a keiretsu) increase immensely the power and influence they can wield.

Fifteen-year-old Miko perceived keenly the gulf between herself and the Chairman. It was as if she were standing amidst the crags of a low valley, and he high on the peak of a distant mountain.

Am I Japan's most insignificant person?

Miko was not jealous of Chairman Ikari. Instead, she was struck by the stark distance between them.

The books I read are about significant people. Insignificant people, like me, don't have books written about them. We are born, and we live, and we die outside the pages of books. And no one remembers us. Chairman Ikari will be remembered. He is a great man.

Miko switched off the TV. The picture shrank to a bright white dot in the center of the screen.

She swept the back of her hand across the TV's glass tube. The static electricity crackled and made little flashes as it tickled her hand.

In the dark room the screen's bright dot took a long time to fade.

"Try to sleep," Fluffy Kitty said. "I'm sure what you're imagining will happen tomorrow is worse than what will actually happen. You'll just get a scolding. Nothing more."

Miko closed her eyes and tried.

But the worries from the bridge event had crowded into the rollicking train carriage of her mind, and they were refusing to get off at any of the stations.

Fluffy Kitty started purring.

In the distance came squealing and roaring and popping hisses. The sound grew louder and louder until it reached a crescendo outside their house in one long tire squeal.

Soon through the walls came the sound of Mother and Father and Uncle Ken talking in the living room.

Miko couldn't tell what they were saying, but after a while the soothing sounds of her family's muffled voices and her cat's purring allowed her to fall asleep.

The next day, Uncle Ken drove Miko and her father to school.

In the morning there had been a phone call from the school requesting a parental meeting, which was fine with her father and Uncle Ken because last night they had decided to make their own meeting.

Miko sat outside the principal's office while her father and Uncle Ken went inside. Her schoolbag, where Fluffy Kitty was hidden, on her lap. Her left hand reaching inside and holding his paw.

The drab waiting room smelled of discipline.

Miko examined the white-faced clock high on the opposite wall for a clue.

When Miko was little she imagined the clock hands formed a mouth, convincing herself the saddest parts of the day were when the clock read around twenty minutes past eight and forty minutes past four, because the clock's mouth was frowning.

Whereas the happiest parts of the day were near fifty minutes past two and ten minutes past ten, when the clock's mouth made a big smile.

Miko had taught her father how to interpret clocks. Afterwards he complained that when he checked the time, the first thing he saw was a happy or sad face.

But in this instant, the clock's big hand was pointing at twelve and the little hand at nine, which resembled a wry smile. Meaning the wall clock held no predictive power for this scary meeting. Since a wry smile could mean either a good or bad outcome.

Moe, it turned out, was in the hospital under observation for concussion.

Moe's lanky father arrived with an angry face.

He was an office worker for a stationery supply firm. He carried a brown leather diary with loose papers peeking out between its pages like lettuce in a hamburger.

"You are Miko?"

Miko squeezed Fluffy Kitty's paw tighter and nodded.

His stance deflated.

"You're no bully," he said.

He went into the meeting. Closing the principal's door firmly behind him.

Miko listened for raised voices. Staying absolutely still, in case her moving might somehow trigger an argument.

But there was no yelling.

After half an hour, the four men emerged.

Moe's father bowed to everyone, including Miko.

"I am sorry for what happened. I did not raise my daughter correctly. I am to blame. Please forgive me."

To understand Miko's story it is important, although we'll never meet him again, to follow Moe's father for a short while.

Moe's father walked back to his workplace with his head hung low. The instant he had seen the frightened girl Miko sitting in the waiting room, he knew his daughter had lied to him.

He had failed as a parent.

Some Japanese men would blame their wife, since mothers spend the most time raising children. But he would not do that. He loved his wife and knew how hard she struggled with Moe.

No, it was his fault. He would visit his wife and daughter at the hospital this evening and apologize to them both.

Arriving at work he went to his gray low-walled cubicle. But before he could sit down, his boss summoned him.

What have I done wrong now?

I have no energy for being yelled at.

He went into his boss's corner office and stood at rigid attention.

"Hara has moved up," his boss said. "So I am promoting you to manager. You will take his place as head of distribution. Get yourself settled in his old office, and tomorrow when Hara is back, he will conduct a handover."

Even after eighteen years of working for this company, his promotion was a surprise. Promotions were rare. People tended to stay in the position they were hired, with replacements brought in from outside.

Moe's father had often daydreamed of becoming a manager. A manager with his very own office.

But never for a moment had he believed his secret wish would actually happen.

The extra money would solve many of his family's problems.

Soon Moe's father sat in his new office, behind a timeworn red pine desk. No more cubicle life for him. He had a door he could shut and a nice view over the river.

And so his day turned out to be both sad and happy.

After the meeting, Miko's father decided Miko could have the day off school.

The three went for ice creams and then drove to pick up Miko's mother before going for a scenic drive in Uncle Ken's taxi.

They visited Tachineputa Museum with its giant paper festive floats, each as tall as a four-story building and glowing with luminescent colors.

At Lake Jūsan they drove over the wooden bridge to Nakajima Island and, because no one else was around to disapprove, pretended to be pirates on the wooden jungle gym boat that had a metal slide spiraling out of its bow.

Driving back over the bridge, they ate locally made apple pie at the picnic tables by the lake's shore.

They also visited the Fuji and Wisteria waterfalls near the Oda River. Near the water plumes the path was a bit slippery, but worth the effort.

The Wisteria waterfall reminded Miko of author Osamu Dazai, a famous olden times writer who, like Miko, was also from Aomori Prefecture. Osamu had dreamed of riding a bicycle to see a waterfall "framed in summer leaves" just like this one.

Listening to the adults talk, Miko gathered the meeting with the school principal had been trending towards becoming explosive, until Moe's father arrived and did the opposite of what they expected.

He had admitted Moe's story of Miko bullying Moe was inconceivable, and he was having trouble raising his daughter.

Miko's father suspected he couldn't share his concerns with any of the people he knew, and so took the opportunity with strangers to speak his mind.

Miko liked the way Uncle Ken's taxi smelled of warm oil and how it rumbled when it idled. She imagined Uncle Ken's messy hairstyle was caused by spending so much time inside his vibrating taxi.

She hoped one day Uncle Ken would let her drive his taxi. When she was bigger, of course.

Miko often drew pictures of this daydream. In these drawings, the taxi's passenger seats were filled with the future friends she prayed for.

"I should be able to charge a bit more in Tokyo," Uncle Ken said. He was moving from Sendai to Tokyo. "I'll start the fare meter with my Tokyo rates. Let's see how much today's trip would cost."

"Tokyo sounds like a scary place," Miko said.

"Busy, not scary. When you visit, I promise to take you on the swan boats at Inokashira Park."

"I like that idea," Miko said. She had often imagined pedaling a pretty swan boat around a lake.

Miko enjoyed the long drive.

She had her parents and Uncle Ken trapped, so she could tell them her latest theories. This was much better than her fallback strategy of writing essays no one else ever wanted to read.

Miko found reading books generated many ideas in her mind. But those ideas desired to be set free, and so, to be kind, she had to let them run around in other peoples' minds too.

If she had friends, then they'd be the ones listening to her ideas. But since she didn't, her family would have to act as substitutes.

Miko knew her theories, about why world cultures operate in certain ways, the future of space exploration, or why the photos of ancient Egyptian pharaohs surrounded by hieroglyphics reminded her of Japanese TV, bored her family. But it benefited the ideas themselves to be talked about, and explaining them helped her discover more about the ideas too.

Besides, it had been her parents' decision to have a daughter, so they had to expect an amount of suffering.

"Tell us one of your jokes," Miko's father said.

Miko was not fooled. He was trying to distract her from her task.

"I'm sorry, Father. I don't have any."

"You used to make up jokes when you were little."

It was true. Miko used to invent jokes on the spot about the situations they were in, like shopping or watching TV.

But that was before the bear attack. After the attack, she wasn't able to.

"I'm sorry, Father. I believe I have lost that ability. But the good news is I have been reading many library books and have lots of interesting facts and ideas. That's better than making up jokes, don't you think?"

Her father made a groan. But this was expected. Miko wasn't about to let his disinterest sidetrack her.

Reading a book about the history of Japan's fishing industry had given her an idea about how hundreds of years of the practice had influenced

Japan's culture.

It is highly likely Father will enjoy hearing this idea.

Half way through the trip, Miko couldn't believe the red glowing number displayed on the taxi's fare meter.

"You'll be rich, Uncle Ken," Miko said. "That is as much money as Father and Mother need for their cherished dream of cruising to the tropical islands and down to the land of the kiwi bird."

"Yes. Almost enough," Miko's mother said. "Maybe with these profits, Ken, you can finally get married."

Everyone laughed, including Fluffy Kitty. Uncle Ken was married to his work. "No time for love," he would say.

However, Miko stopped laughing early, because in the rear vision mirror her uncle's eyes were sad.

"Let's ponder the beginning of a romantic relationship. Allow me to reveal to you its true nature," Uncle Ken said. "It is that serendipitous moment when two stalkers begin stalking each other."

Miko's parents informed Uncle Ken they found his humorous statement both funny and insulting at the same time.

Miko had read the dictionary. She knew what 'serendipitous' and 'stalker' meant. So she laughed too.

However, Miko was convinced Uncle Ken had used his joke to deflect some inner sadness. She decided to ask her parents about her deduction.

As the day rumbled by, Miko was pleased to be with her family. They made a good show of not caring how she looked.

Her principal had promised a teacher would start patrolling near the bridge, but in her heart Miko knew the bullying wouldn't stop.

Twice before, Miko had seen bullied children stand up for themselves. Afterwards, the bullies had left those brave children alone.

But Miko understood that wasn't going to happen for her. In fact she knew, although she didn't know how, that the bullying was going to get worse.

Miko wished she didn't have to go to school. She wished she could stay home, where it was safe.

Two years later, in 2005, shortly after Miko turned eighteen, her family moved to join Uncle Ken in Tokyo.

There were better prospects in Tokyo, her father explained.

On the long drive to Tokyo, Miko announced to her parents the type of job she wanted.

"My best option is to become a nurse. Then my job will be helping people," Miko said, from the back seat of the microcar where she was almost buried in bags of clothes and other soft items they were taking with them.

"That is an honorable intention," her mother said, over the whine of the car's little engine.

"Nursing is a proper skill. And you can look after us when we are old, instead of wheeling us into a nursing home," her father said, laughing at his joke.

"I will not put you in a nursing home. You will live with me in my house forever."

"Your husband and children might not leave room for us," her mother said.

Miko hugged the bags of clothes closer. She stared out the car's side window at the passing homes, each with a family inside.

On the doorstep of one house, a couple were maneuvering a green sofa in through their front door. High above, a long flock of birds of different shapes and sizes stretched back to the horizon. They were migrating south just like Miko and her parents. Further on, a pink van was parked selling ice creams and hot dogs.

Miko had never seen an ice cream van before. She had only heard schoolyard rumors of these rare vehicles roaming far away cities. Tofu vans were much more common.

The van's public address speaker played a song that grew louder and faded as they passed. The singing, backed by what sounded like a toy synthesizer, explained that it knew it was annoying, but asked forgiveness because the van came to deliver "a good taste".

"Please forgive me. Please give me time," sang the van.

A chatting couple held hands with their excited children as they walked towards the pink van.

Miko's eyes began to water. Seeing the couple with the sofa and the happy family going to buy ice creams made seventeen-year-old Miko realize she would be alone in the world after her parents died.

Her unfortunate face was a bad curse that would keep away a husband and meant she'd never have children to love.

Miko prayed her parents would live a long long time.

They arrived in Tokyo, the world's most populous city. It was the first time Miko had seen the vast metropolis.

Unlike the agricultural smells of the country, the city smelled of car exhaust and asphalt.

The sale of their country house, her parents' savings, help from Uncle Ken, Miko's father's construction company's monthly housing allowance, and a bank loan allowed the purchase of a two-bedroom apartment in Bunkyo Ward.

Not far from where Uncle Ken had his apartment, and in another building nearby, a small garage workshop for his taxi.

Miko's parents sold their car. Uncle Ken would drive them when needed.

Before coming, she knew Tokyo was huge, containing twenty-three wards like Bunkyo, each ward the size of a small city.

But nothing had prepared her for actually experiencing the size of Tokyo. Miko was overawed people had made such a thing.

However, their apartment was not big, especially compared to their old house. In fact, the whole apartment was only the size of their former living room.

Thankfully, it had thick walls, which was rare for a Tokyo apartment. Miko's father said that inside the other apartments he and Uncle Ken had inspected, they could hear everything the neighbors were doing. Even their conversations.

As a new Tokyo girl one of Miko's chores was collecting the mail from the apartment's letterbox in the building's foyer.

Each month, Miko found a pale blue envelope in the letterbox. The envelope contained a bank demand for the month's mortgage payment.

The day after the blue envelope arrived, Miko's parents would dress in their best clothes. Her father putting the money they had saved into his suit jacket pocket. Then her parents visited the bank to make their payment and get a red receipt stamp in their mortgage book.

One day Miko read the bank letter her father had left lying open on their low dining table.

When she saw the apartment's price, she felt guilty. Her parents had spent an enormous amount to allow her to have her own room.

Miko told her parents they should have bought a one-bedroom apartment instead, because she didn't need a room. She could roll out a futon each night on the floor.

Miko imagined sleeping in the living room on one of their quilted cotton-stuffed sleeping pads. It would have been fine. Needing only a few minutes in the morning to fold up the futon and hide it away in the closet.

"Our daughter will have her own room," Miko's father insisted.

"How could you do your drawing or study nursing without your own room?" Miko's mother asked.

Miko couldn't express how grateful she was. Despite the shame she caused them, they had taken on a great financial burden for her benefit.

Tokyo was indeed scary. Uncle Ken took Miko for a drive around the city.

Miko stared wide-eyed out the taxi's windows. She had never seen so many people.

There were places where people swarmed like ants running across a log. In other places hundreds of people slowly stampeded down the sidewalk.

But when Miko started her nursing studies, it was the trains she feared the most.

The relaxing train melodies that played when trains arrived or departed didn't project the true experience.

People were so packed in the oxygen seemed lacking, and what air was left smelled in warm weather of sweaty people, or in rainy weather of damp people—often laced with the odor of chewed food and unpredictable nose-clenching wafts of bad breath.

The train carriages droned and clacked, swaying unpredictably, making the passengers lean into each other. Often people blocked Miko's view of the outside, making her seasick and wishing to escape out the door at the next station.

She soon learned to take the women-only carriages at the front of the train because some men were disgusting and took advantage with everyone squashed together like sushi on a tray.

Moving through the crowds in Tokyo, Miko sensed a grim indifference. If she disappeared, she knew no one would notice.

Once a woman had collapsed at the train station. Her distraught daughter said her mother had been lying on the ground for many minutes, as people stepped around her. No one had helped, until Miko arrived and called an ambulance and the station master.

This attitude towards people was so alien to Miko's nature that she grew to fear the indifference. It was like the city was chanting, "You don't matter, you don't matter, you don't matter..."

Other fears also grew in her mind. Like missing her train, or being looked at disapprovingly by a stranger.

There was a man who lived near Miko's parents' apartment.

He had a white goatee beard, messy white hair, and a face full of crinkly riverbeds.

When he saw Miko coming, he would smartly look away. Hiding his face until Miko was behind him.

Each time Miko left the apartment, she hoped this man was not around. Because it was a bad feeling being rejected so openly. Miko would rush past the door to this man's home in case he came out.

Like a slow avalanche, Miko's fears compounded. Miko would worry about terrible events that might happen, and then worry some more, until the worry became an overpowering sense of impending inevitability.

Her heart racing. The tension tightening like a knot.

Soon these fears merged into a constant unease about going outside. A twisting in her stomach that spiked as the time to leave approached.

After completing school and her first year of nurse training, Miko turned twenty in December 2007.

But the next month she caught a bad flu that prevented her from attending a Coming Of Age Day ceremony.

Miko was sad, because she had looked forward to dressing up like all the other twenty-year-olds.

But, secretly, she was also relieved, since the idea of being packed in a big stadium with so many people was scary.

Miko didn't enjoy having two conflicting emotions inside her, both wanting something and not wanting something at the same time.

During 2008, her second year of nursing school, she almost made friends with a fellow student. Long-haired Akiyo who wore a silver bracelet with little colorful dangling cupcakes.

Akiyo had a salaryman† boyfriend. He sounded marvelous and Miko enjoyed hearing about their relationship.

But one day Akiyo informed Miko that her boyfriend was being posted to Germany to work in his company's European office. Akiyo was not sure her boyfriend wanted her to go with him.

"We've been boyfriend and girlfriend for three years. But I fear this posting will be the end of our relationship," Akiyo said.

Akiyo's eyes were red and her face puffy. She stared down at her textbook instead of looking at Miko. She had even forgotten to wear her cupcake bracelet.

Miko worried about Akiyo. She didn't want Akiyo's fear to come true. Each day when she went to nursing school, Miko was scared Akiyo would tell her that her boyfriend had broken up with her.

As the weeks passed, Akiyo became increasingly morose. To cheer her up, Miko let Akiyo hold Fluffy Kitty.

Fluffy Kitty complained that Akiyo tickled him, but said he liked how she hugged.

One bright April day, Akiyo surprised Miko with an orchid-pink gift box of little Japanese cheesecakes.

The cheesecakes were super creamy, and soft like cotton balls. Miko treasured the empty box, because it was the first time someone outside her family had given her a present.

The next day Akiyo arrived in the study room walking like she was running on hot coals. Her face beaming. Her hands held up to her chin as if she were about to start clapping. She rushed over to Miko, giving a little squeal on the way.

"Miko! Miko! Guess what?"

"I want to guess. But I can't guess. Oh no, suspense! I really don't like suspense. Please tell me quickly. This is an emergency situation!"

"OK, it's so exciting! Ugetsu took me to dinner last night, to the most expensive restaurant he has ever taken me. Afterwards we walked in Ueno Park. There, under a cherry blossom tree, Ugetsu proposed to me."

"He proposed!"

"We are getting married in Germany. Ugetsu is arranging it."

"Akiyo, this is wonderful! I'm filled with happiness for you. Your worrying has transformed into great joy."

Later, Miko gave Akiyo her return gift of golden Ferrero Rocher

† In Japan a "salaryman" is a white-collar worker who is, or acts as if he is, totally committed to his corporation. He joins a corporation after his education finishes and stays with that firm for life. He is known by his suit and might be called some unkind nicknames behind his back, such as "company livestock", "corporate soldier", or "dog of the company".

chocolates.

But soon Miko became sad, although she kept pretending to be happy. Because Akiyo explained she was dropping out of nursing school to prepare herself for being a homemaker. Soon she would travel to Germany with her fiancé.

The next day Akiyo stopped coming to the course.

Not seeing each other caused their almost-friendship to wither.

Akiyo was busy helping her fiancé arrange their trip. They exchanged chat messages, but less frequently as Akiyo's time to leave Japan approached.

After Akiyo left Japan, Miko lost contact with her.

While this made Miko sad, it also made her hopeful.

She had never come so close to fulfilling her dream of having a human friend.

Maybe next time I will do better. I must keep trying my best.

She resumed her childhood habit of praying for a friend. There was a railing near to her parents' apartment where she turned to go to the train station.

So each day, as she passed that railing, Miko prayed hard for a human friend.

There was another sad occurrence in 2008. Near the end of that year came the news that Uncle Ken was losing his sight.

Retinitis pigmentosa was the name of the disease. An incurable genetic disorder.

"I will miss seeing good things, but I won't miss seeing bad things. So there's a benefit," Uncle Ken said.

Uncle Ken made other jokes to Miko about his disease. But Miko could tell he was hurting inside.

She researched intensively, but apart from taking a lot of vitamin A, she couldn't find any treatment to slow down the disease's progression.

One February evening the following year, Uncle Ken arrived unexpectedly at their apartment.

"My sight has grown too narrow. Today I almost hit an old lady. I didn't see her until nearly too late."

Miko had never seen her uncle cry before. Her father comforted him with pats on his back.

"It is the end, Akio. I am finished."

So Miko and Miko's parents went with Uncle Ken as he backed his beloved taxi into its garage. For what Uncle Ken knew would be the last time.

He took the taxi's ignition key and the garage's padlock key and hung them on a gold chain around his neck.

They went together to a sake bar. Where Uncle Ken and Miko's father drank a lot of sake.

Miko and her mother drank *ramune*, a type of lemonade soda, sealed with a glass marble that drops into the bottle's neck. Normally Miko enjoyed fighting the marble with her tongue when drinking from the glass bottle, and making the marble rattle around, but it was too solemn an occasion for those sorts of games. Instead Miko quietly poured her drink into her chilled glass.

Afterwards, they guided their menfolk back to their respective apartments. Now Miko's father was the only one earning for the family.

Miko graduated in the top ten after completing her nursing exams in February 2010.

Her parents and Uncle Ken were proud when freshly minted twenty-two-year-old Miko became a registered nurse.

"Little Miko. First in the family with a real qualification," Uncle Ken said.

Fluffy Kitty was proud too. But he complained about being left on his own in her locker while Miko worked at the hospital.

"I'm sorry. It is forbidden to carry a toy cat around," Miko said.

"That doesn't seem fair," Fluffy Kitty said. "I don't like it when the locker door closes. And I'm so happy when it opens."

Now she was working, Miko enjoyed contributing to the family finances.

The nursing school had been free from the bullying Miko had experienced at school.

But at the hospital sturdily built Chief Nurse Goto and her snobbish clique of older nurses were cruel to the junior nurses.

The junior nurses called Chief Nurse Goto the "Christmas Cake Nurse" behind her back—an insult from Miko's parents' day. Because she was a mature woman without a husband. Unwanted, like an unsold Christmas cake after Christmas.

Miko refused to refer to Chief Nurse Goto that way, because it was disrespectful. And because Miko was afraid of becoming Christmas Cake herself. Miko didn't want to jinx her future by even speaking the words "Christmas Cake".

Like the school bullies, Chief Nurse Goto had her bully rules: junior nurses had to use the stairs not the elevators, they couldn't use the hospital's front entrance, and they had to spend half their lunch break washing the dishes in the staffroom. And there were many other rules like these.

Miko hated these demeaning edicts. So she broke the rules as often as possible.

Chief Nurse Goto was verbally abusive, swearing at her whenever Miko didn't guess what the Chief Nurse expected her to do. She constantly accused Miko of having no common sense. The Chief Nurse especially didn't like that Miko was from the country, and said so often.

She rostered her on the night shifts more than the other juniors, and sometimes a day shift and a night shift directly after each other.

The Chief Nurse also assigned Miko ward duties and administration duties at the same time, which was more work than Miko could do. Then she was yelled at in front of the others for falling behind.

"Why did you even bother to come here?" Chief Nurse Goto would say. "You'll never succeed. You being here is a waste of our time!"

The long hours and constant tension at work drained Miko.

When she could get a seat on the train, she slept on the way home. Sometimes when there was no seat, she put her backpack between her feet and a hand through a strap hanging from the rail above. She would fall asleep standing up.

"Here's our stop," Fluffy Kitty would say to wake Miko up when he heard the announcement.

At home she ate and slept. Lacking the energy to talk with her parents. She didn't draw anymore, and new issues of *Hidden Stealth Ninja* sat on the shelf unread. Each day, her apprehension grew a little greater.

Miko imagined how bad the coming day would be. How angry Chief Nurse Goto would get.

She hated being yelled at in front of the other nurses. The older nurses' accusing eyes scolding her, as Chief Nurse Goto stood over her spitting and gesticulating.

It was especially bad since Japanese social protocol meant Miko couldn't speak back to her *senpai*[†] to defend herself.

Instead, she had to bow at forty-five degrees to the Chief Nurse, making it seem like she was accepting the criticism as true.

Then came the most terrible day.

An elderly female patient died because of a mistake with administered drugs. The doctors were furious.

Miko was working on a different ward that day. So she was stunned when Chief Nurse Goto pointed to Miko as the nurse who had made the mistake.

She also accused Miko of destroying the related paperwork, including the bedside drug administration sheet, to cover her error.

Everything happened so suddenly. In an unexpected rush that Miko had no power to stop. She observed the events from the outside, as if watching a TV show starring someone who bore a striking resemblance to herself.

Chief Nurse Goto pulled Miko by the arm into a room filled with nurses and doctors and administration staff.

"You have brought shame on our profession, junior nurse Nishimura! A woman is dead because of your incompetence. And your inept attempts to cover your tracks make you no better than a criminal."

"But I—"

"Silence! How dare you speak back to your senpai!"

† Senpai means senior.

The unexpected event was a serious situation.

The police were involved, and it looked like Miko would be deregistered as a nurse.

Oddly, the police never interviewed Miko. It was as if they accepted the hospital's story that Miko had caused the death and destroyed the paperwork.

Miko's parents hired a lawyer. Uncle Ken contributed from his savings. Miko's father had to keep working at his construction job, so Miko's mother went with Miko to the meetings and worked with the lawyer.

Three weeks passed with proceedings down long soulless corridors in rooms with flaking paint and populated with rusty gray government issue tables and chairs.

Miko had never experienced stress like this.

Day after day, it was like iron grinding against iron, with no let up or end.

Her lawyer and Miko's mother visited the hospital and talked to the security people. They requested access to the security video for that shift. But the security administrator refused to help.

The next day, the whole thing went away.

Her lawyer visited the security administrator again. Afterwards, he told Miko's mother he was sure the security administrator had reviewed the security footage himself.

Then he suspected the administrator had confronted the hospital administration with the evidence that proved Miko was working on another ward. The security administrator had hinted that one of Chief Nurse Goto's friends had made the drug administration mistake and covered her tracks by destroying the paperwork.

The week after, her lawyer confirmed with the police the case was closed, and verified Miko would not be deregistered.

It was a better outcome than her lawyer expected.

But the damage was already done.

I am running out of dreams.

The bear attack. The years of school bullying. And now this calamitous happening.

These events accumulated like water building up against a dam until the dam could hold no more.

And so Miko lost faith in herself, and the outside world.

The world had betrayed her. It hated her. The only place she had ever been safe was in her room, with her parents out in the living room watching TV.

Her innate hope she had taken for granted as a little girl was a lie.

The truth was, bad things happened to Miko because Miko deserved them to happen. Miko was wrong. Miko was a bad person. Miko was a failure.

Her first *yakudoshi*† year had come three years late, but come it had, as Miko's shame filled the oceans and flooded the continents.

A twenty-two-year-old person only has so much fortitude.

So Miko withdrew from the world. Her fears growing and growing until even the idea of going outside made her shake.

Beyond her parents' white apartment door were only angry bears and cruel people wanting to stab her with pins.

※ ❀ ◈ ❀ ⚬← 🗵

It would take six months of self-isolation before Miko could officially be classed as *hikikomori*.

The word hikikomori means "pulling inward" or "being confined". A severe social withdrawal where the afflicted becomes a recluse, often in their family home.

Miko had not only become such a hermit, but one who also grappled with agoraphobia. The fear of entering open or crowded places.

Agoraphobia grows like a weed in the minds of hikikomori. Its tangles becoming thicker with every day of isolation.

The first month, Miko spent her time either sleeping or sitting on her bed clutching Fluffy Kitty.

Her struggle with the fiery shame of disappointing her parents and being unable to work or even go outside made her believe moving was

† Yakudoshi years are "calamitous years". Ages the Japanese believe are unlucky. For women they are 19, 33, and 37, and for men 25, 42, and 61. Although these ages do vary by region.

something she didn't deserve to do.

Her father insisted Miko come out of her room and sit at the table when they ate.

"Miko, eat more noodles. You're getting too thin," Miko's mother said.

"I am sorry," Miko said. Keeping her head bowed. "I am a burden. I will eat only the minimum."

Her father snorted.

"You're not a burden," he said. "You are our daughter."

"I am not contributing anymore. And I have brought shame on the family."

"You have not. You're innocent and everyone knows it. Right, Papa?" her mother said.

"Right, Mama," Miko's father said. "Miko, I am sure this issue you're having is temporary. You will get over it soon. But, in the meantime, I will not have you staying in your room all day. We hardly see you. At the very least, you will help Mama cook and clean."

"Yes, Father."

"And your room is messy. You will keep it tidy."

Miko nodded.

She realized her father was clever. Making her do house duties and keep her room clean forced her to move and expanded her world outward, from her bed to the entire apartment.

But going outside was something her parents were unsuccessful in making Miko do. Offers of trips to the petting zoo or clothes shopping or requests to help her mother with the food shopping failed.

Once her father tried to drag Miko towards the apartment door, but Miko cried out and pulled away, running back into her room.

Uncle Ken came over that evening. Miko pressed her ear up against her bedroom door to hear their adult talk.

"The way Miko looked at me," Miko's father said. "I am a terrible parent for doing that to her."

"She had that same expression on the day of the bear," Miko's mother said, her voice cracking.

"Akio, she was not afraid of you. You were pulling her towards the outside world," Uncle Ken said. "Your action was useful, since it tells us what we are dealing with. Chika you said it, the bear. The outside has become the bear."

"That was when all this started. I hate that bear. When the police said they couldn't find it, I hunted it in the forest with my axe," Miko's father said. "But I could not find it either."

Miko pulled away from the door. Climbing onto her bed, she cuddled Fluffy Kitty.

"How long before they don't love me anymore?"

"That won't happen," Fluffy Kitty said.

"It will. My issue will wear them down until one day they only see me as the burden I am."

After that, Miko tried to make herself as unobtrusive as possible. She did as much work as her mother would let her, and she kept her room spotless. But she started suffering a reoccurring nightmare, where her teary-eyed parents sat down on the couch for a family talk. Holding hands, they explained the time had come for Miko to leave home.

At the table, her father insisted Miko eat the food her mother served her, and so she stopped losing weight; but because she was not contributing, eating that much increased Miko's shame.

Her mother also insisted she take vitamins every day to substitute for the lack of sunlight.

The female counselor her parents hired to visit Miko in the first months was not effective. Miko was scared of this female outsider, because her face resembled the face of the school bully Moe. Also, her parents could not afford to keep the counselor coming for long.

As time went by, Miko's parents seemed to accept her condition. Their schemes to draw her out of the apartment came less and less often.

Their last big try came after she turned twenty-three. Her father encouraged her to go to a Coming of Age Day ceremony, since the flu had stopped her from attending when she was twenty.

Coming of Age Day is an important day in the life of a Japanese person. So important it is a national holiday.

Both Miko and her mother thought it would be strange to attend three years late.

"But I am not twenty anymore, Father."

"Nobody would know," Miko's father said. "You still look very young."

As he promoted his idea, Miko became worried he would really make her go.

Leaving the apartment was scary enough. But even more scary was the ceremony itself, with many people packed together in a huge auditorium.

The idea of taking part made Miko hyperventilate and her legs go weak. She put a hand on her stomach since it was becoming hard to breathe.

"I am sorry, I was too enthusiastic with my idea," Miko's father said, with a worried face. "Sit down on the couch."

Miko did.

"How are you feeling?" Miko's mother said.

Miko's surroundings didn't seem to be part of her world anymore. It was like she was viewing the apartment through a camera's viewfinder.

"Dizzy. My stomach hurts. It's hard to breathe, and I'm cold."

"Cold? How? You are sweating," her father said.

"Papa, she's shaking," her mother said. "It's another panic attack."

Miko had never had panic attacks until she became hikikomori. Even then, they were rare.

Her mother rubbed her back.

Miko didn't want to faint again. It was like being smothered. Then when she woke the rest of her day would be wrecked, because the after effects made her mind mushy.

"I have an idea," her father said. "You can celebrate with just us. You won't need to leave the apartment."

Her father quickly explained his new suggestion.

Miko was thankful. With a glass of cold water and her mother rubbing her back, the attack subsided.

So on Coming Of Age Day Miko wore a colorful rented *furisode* around their apartment, a *kimono* with long sleeves, and her parents gave her little gifts.

Miko was happy she got to dress up. But it made her sad not to have performed such an important day correctly, and to know in her heart she had disappointed her parents.

And so the sun rose in the east and set in the west, and the next day did the same.

Days passed. Turning into weeks, those weeks into months, and those months into years.

With each sun set, at the moment Miko heard Tokyo's public address system chiming the melancholy melody that reminded children to stop playing and go home, Miko felt a day of her life had been wasted.

She was ashamed of being hikikomori.

※ ✽ ✦ ✾ •⇐ ▨

To pass the time, Miko did chores, drew pictures, read manga and library books, typed essays about her many theories, and played motor racing games on her laptop.

Miko also took small joys in the minutiae of the apartment.

When washing her hands, she discovered that by filling the plughole with soap suds, she could hear each bubble when it popped. The shape of the ceramic basin amplifying the noise. Each bubble burst sounded like a tiny hammer striking the basin.

When the sun beamed through her bedroom window, it created a starfield of dust floating in the air. Clapping made the dust swirl around in energetic patterns.

Miko would toss marbles onto her bed, aiming to land them in one particular patch of the lush *sashiko* bed covering her mother had quilted.

In the expert level version of the game, she attempted to land the marbles within one of the colorful stars in the center of each patch.

Staring at the bright electric light on the ceiling and then closing her eyes made purple patterns and morphing shapes appear in the darkness. These patterns Miko imagined into adventuresome stories filled with dashing heroes and comical sidekicks.

After hanging her washing on the pull-down stainless steel clothes rack mounted high on the apartment's bathroom wall, Miko would put the stepladder away and stand under the hanging clothes.

Closing her eyes, she moved her head in gentle curves. Letting the warm water-heavy clothes lightly brush her hair and face.

Miko imagined the touch was from a handsome boyfriend who loved her. His tender hand playing with her hair and caressing her cheek.

And so in a steady retreat, the apartment became Miko's world.

A world that floated on an ocher-yellow sea of sweet smelling soft-rush *tatami* mats.

Her bed a comfortable tropical island. Her pink study desk a mountain plateau. Her cypress wood chest of drawers a tall tree. And her white bookcase an ice-shelf populated with paper penguins.

Her tropical-island bed rested under the room's aluminum framed window. Its comforting rectangular land a futon, resting on a slated base. Squishy but firm, not super-soft like the marshmallow mattresses westerners use.

Her pink mountain-plateau desk supported an ecosystem of *Happy Corgi* and *Cat in Cup* and *Gudetama Lazy Egg* stickers that student Miko had purchased from the pen shop near the train station.

A beige brushed-plastic mammoth roamed on top of the pink landscape in the form of the study laptop Uncle Ken had given Miko on her eighteenth birthday.

A pink wireless mouse lived with the mammoth in a symbiotic relationship, since the mammoth's trackpad had broken.

The pink mouse actually looked like a mouse, with big googly eyes and tiny black whiskers. Fluffy Kitty said the mouse was *shokuhin sampuru*, the fake plastic display food Japanese shops used to advertise their wares.

The mammoth had other friends too. They had migrated to the plateau as gifts from Uncle Ken on Miko's twenty-third birthday.

A chunky Logitech steering wheel with a manual gear knob, with its detached trio of foot pedals floating on the tatami sea under the plateau's overhang. These beloved plastic immigrants gave Miko a way of realistically controlling the digital cars she raced.

Miko's complete collection of *Hidden Stealth Ninja* manga penguins were stacked on top of her glossy white bookcase ice-shelf.

Their black and white spines precisely in line with each other, which was Miko's way of showing her respect for their greatness.

Akiyo's orchid-pink cheesecake gift box was the only other item allowed on the top of the bookshelf.

Miko's fiction and non-fiction library books were stacked on the shelf under Akiyo's precious gift.

Each week Miko's mother returned the books Miko had read to the library and exchanged them for a fresh pile.

Fluffy Kitty's favorite position was sitting on the desk plateau next to the laptop mammoth.

But he could be annoying by demanding to be constantly repositioned.

"I'm bored sitting here. Can I sit on the bookshelf? I want to sit by you on the bed. Miko, please put me on the windowsill so I can see if there's a tasty bird on the power line."

Drawing manga was Miko's outlet for her creativity, and reading books for her curiosity; but it was motorsport gaming that made Miko feel alive.

When Miko drove, her mind became one with her digital car.

She played the games Uncle Ken had purchased for her on their highest realism settings: Forza Motorsport, iRacing, and the Sonic and Mario Kart racing games for extra fun.

Driving was freedom. Liberating her mind from the constraints of the real world. Miko skillfully controlled her car in the relaxing digital realm where life was safe and predictable.

Little did Miko know that if she had entered an eSports motor racing competition she would have won an easy victory. The commentators waving their arms and stuttering, as they described her driving in terms normally reserved for a supernatural event.

But Miko never played online, or joined any social media, participated in forums, or read online news, because she didn't want to know anything about the scary outside. To know about the world was to invite it in.

Her parents watched TV, but Miko didn't watch with them anymore, because even the commercials were windows through which the outside could crawl.

To make double and triple sure the present-day world didn't encroach, the library books Miko asked her mother to find were exclusively about the past or fictional places or technology.

Miko was so out of touch that the entire Japanese population, except her parents and Uncle Ken, could have got tattoos, shaved their hair off, and painted themselves bright green, and Miko would not have known.

Before she became hikikomori, Miko had little interest in popular culture.

Now she was hikikomori, she made sure to know nothing.

As time passed, Miko became so withdrawn that the outside world came to her only in lingering nightmares.

A dark threat that lurked just beyond the walls of her safe apartment world.

※ ❀ ✦ ✤ ⚬⇐ 🔯

A year and a half later, two summers and a winter had passed, and a new winter had come.

But inside the apartment, Miko's little world stayed as safe as it could be.

She especially didn't miss seeing the old man who found her face so disgusting he would look away.

In December, on Miko's twenty-fourth birthday, her parents threw a party with a cake and treats and gifts wrapped in yellow. The only guest was Uncle Ken, who was now almost blind.

Family tradition meant Miko's gifts and party decorations were yellow, since Miko had been born during the early morning as a strong wind whistled around the hospital making the ginkgo trees drop their bright yellow leaves.

Uncle Ken had driven to visit newborn Miko on that day, and reported that the hills and valleys and fields were golden-yellow all the way from Sendai to Goshogawara.

For her birthday treats there were American dogs (hotdogs) on a stick, chicken skewers, corn on the cob, and sweets like *taiyaki* fish-shaped pastries and chocolate-covered bananas with yellow candy sprinkles.

"Look, Miko," her mother said. "Last night I tried this new party cupcake recipe from my magazine. Chocolate lemon fudge, iced with sweet-coconut whipped cream."

"Chocolate and lemon," Miko said. "That sounds wrong in all the right ways."

Her mother had been in full party maker mode since early morning, cooking non-stop with Miko's insistent help. The apartment smelled sweet and savory, as their house in the country had during Miko's childhood birthdays.

However, the memory-filled aromas made twenty-four-year-old Miko keenly aware she didn't possess happiness like she once had during her youthful birthday parties. Only embarrassment that she had no friends to invite.

Miko closed her eyes and fantasized that Akiyo hadn't moved to Germany. There was a knock at the door and Akiyo came in, taking her shoes off before joining them at their low *kotatsu* dining table. Tucking her legs under the table's blue blanket that trapped the warmth from the electric heater mounted on the table's underside.

Miko and Akiyo talked excitedly, trying to guess what was in the birthday gifts.

"*Moshi Moshi*. Miko? Hello, is Miko there?" Miko's father said, waving the palm of his hand in front of her.

"Sorry Father, I was daydreaming."

"Try to guess my present," Miko's father said. Handing her a long rectangular box, badly wrapped in canary-yellow paper.

Miko gave the box a gentle shake. It made no sound and was lighter than expected. She felt the colorful wrapping paper around its exterior. It had a firm cardboard base and a long top that was warmer and gave more easily to the touch.

Above the cardboard base is plastic. Maybe it is transparent plastic so you can see what is inside?

"I can't guess, Father. It is a mystery. Please help me. You know I can't stand suspense."

"I will give you a clue. I got it from a manga and anime figurine shop. Can you guess now?"

"Is it a Ren Matsuda figurine, from Hidden Stealth Ninja?" Miko said. Thinking it would be nice to own a figurine of her schoolgirl crush.

"No. But close. I will tell you," her father said. "It is a figurine of Hidden Stealth Ninja himself."

"No!" Miko said. "It simply can't be."

"It is. Open it and see."

Miko tore off the wrapping.

Her finger's detective work was proved correct. It was a clear display box with a colorful cardboard base of the type anime figurines come in. The cardboard base proudly declared:

"WORLD FIRST! HIDDEN STEALTH NINJA FIGURINE!"

But there was no figurine in the box.

The tall box was empty, except for a black plastic base. The type of base used as a stand for manga figurines.

There was a sign embossed on the baseplate:

"HIDDEN STEALTH NINJA FIGURINE".

Miko inspected the round base more closely.

Apart from the words, the base was flat, except for two footprints in its plastic, made by someone wearing double-toed *tabi* shoes. The type of shoes ninjas use.

Her father and mother were looking at her expectantly.

What a thoughtful present. My parents know what I care about.

"Thank you, Father. This is an amusing gimmick," Miko said. "I'll put the complete box next to my Hidden Stealth Ninja collection, and treasure it in the same manner."

Her father and mother shared a glance.

"You do not smile anymore, Miko," her father said. "It has been many years since I have seen you smile."

"I miss your smile too," her mother said. "When little, you were a bright and cheerful child. Papa is correct, you have not smiled for a long time."

"I apologize for not smiling. For the burden I am. And the sadness I cause you," Miko said, putting her hands together and lowering her head.

"Stop calling yourself a burden," her father said. "You are our delight."

Miko bowed to her parents.

I don't deserve such an excellent family. How long before they're fed up and treat me with the disdain I deserve? What if my nightmare comes true and they insist I can't live here anymore? Maybe Uncle Ken would let me sleep next to his taxi in his garage? There's room for a futon between the taxi and the workbench. Hopefully he would not mind.

✄ ✳ ✦ ✤ ⊷ ⌗

As you will see, to truly understand Miko's story, it is important to take a moment to admire the astounding artistic marvel that is

Hidden Stealth Ninja, Miko's favorite manga.

Every edition lovingly arranged in a splendid row on the top of her bookshelf.

Manga are graphic novels. They're tremendously popular in Japan.

Miko, along with those others in Japan who are true connoisseurs of manga, universally recognize *Hidden Stealth Ninja* as the pinnacle of the manga art form.

This premium manga features subtle and ingenious stories that rival the renowned text novels of the world.

The drawing and coloring of *Hidden Stealth Ninja* are sublime. Every page reminiscent of the fine art style of the famous Kanō art school. Especially of the works of Gahō Hashimoto.

But this manga's most awe-inspiring feature is the fact the story's hero, Hidden Stealth Ninja himself, never appears on any of the manga's pages.

Not once has Hidden Stealth Ninja been drawn. Not once has anyone heard him speak. Not once have they seen his thoughts. He is a ghost hidden just beyond the edges of the manga's bone-china white pages.

The story writer and artist, both born in Fukuoka, are so skilled that each month they create from their traditional mountainside studio a thrilling and suspenseful manga where the hero's actions are never directly seen but instead implied.

Implied in the reactions of the villains, in the glances of the minor characters, or even in the way light falls across a half-empty glass of water.

It is the paper embodiment of the Japanese communication practice of "reading the air", where people are expected to indirectly infer meaning, by reading between the lines to uncover what people are actually meaning when they speak.

Hidden Stealth Ninja is recognized worldwide as a work of unfolding genius.

In the story, Hidden Stealth Ninja's primary nemesis is Nobuhiko Nakamoto. An evil mastermind and CEO of a corporation whose name can be only imprecisely translated as "Road of Good Intentions Corp".

Nobuhiko Nakamoto's personal motto is, "I fight those who cannot fight for themselves."

Hidden Stealth Ninja himself is a mystery.

One faction of the manga's fans argues he is the most skilled ninja in history, which is why he can remain unseen.

Those in the opposite faction argue that while Hidden Stealth Ninja is obviously history's most skilled ninja, he, in addition, must also be a partly magical being. Since no ordinary human could react so fast or be invisible when needed.

An endless debate rages between the two fan factions. There are terabytes of online threads, podcasts, piles of magazine articles, even Tshirts and baseball caps arguing for each side.

The proponents of Hidden Stealth Ninja being merely a skilled human challenge the opposite side to produce evidence of his supernatural acts.

The other side admits they cannot provide direct evidence. Except to make several observations based on the manga's events and lore.

First, they point to arch-villain Nobuhiko Nakamoto's secret research department that hunts Hidden Stealth Ninja. This secret department reported an important rumor in volume forty-two of the manga.

The rumor that Hidden Stealth Ninja had lived in exile for a long time and didn't begin his good works until after stumbling across a temple filled with lights.

Chronologically, the partly-magical-being faction argue, it was after his encounter in this temple of lights that Hidden Stealth Ninja's life became charmed and showed continuous fortune.

Second, and more convincingly, they maintain that ordinary folk who leave him out a meal or make him new tabi shoes have their yearnings unexpectedly satisfied by magical means.

Or put more simply, they assert those who are kind to Hidden Stealth Ninja become lucky regarding the deeper desires of their heart.

They list many instances recorded in the manga where they claim this magic occurs.

The skilled-human faction rejects these instances as evidence, saying they're too subtle to be definite and are more likely coincidences.

The other faction points out that everything about Hidden Stealth Ninja is subtle and not easily discerned.

And so this fan debate sloshes back and forth, like a tank filled with angry crabs on the back of a truck bouncing along a rutted road. Endlessly snapping and splashing, with no discernible result.

Miko knew little of this debate, but like other sophisticated Japanese people, Hidden Stealth Ninja entranced her.

She had shared with her mother the pass phrase the manga stores required when purchasing Hidden Stealth Ninja. Each time her mother brought home the latest edition, Miko would cradle the book in her hand and run her fingers around its edges in anticipation.

She would make a pot of green tea, placing the pot and a double-walled glass on her bedside table.

Then Miko would read the manga from beginning to end in one session, with Fluffy Kitty propped up on her lap so he could read too. Fluffy Kitty couldn't read as fast as Miko, and so frustrated her by making her wait until he said it was OK to turn the page.

✖ ✻ ✦ ✸ ☙ 🎴

Two years after that birthday party it was the end of 2013 and Miko had just turned twenty-six.

Later the same month, her parents achieved their savings goal. Enough for the tickets and related expenses for their often-discussed long vacation.

Since the day they got married, they had been daydreaming together of touring the Pacific on a big cruise liner.

"You must go," Miko insisted. "It is your cherished dream."

"I will stock up the cupboards and the fridge with more than you need," Miko's mother said.

"Will you be OK?" Miko's father asked. "There will be no one to look after you."

Miko assured them many times she would be fine as long as she had what she needed in the apartment.

Father has been looking more and more worn out. Construction work is hard on the body. And Mother is feeling the stress too. A vacation is exactly what they need.

When the day came for them to leave, Miko was deeply uneasy, but she was determined to act relaxed and capable. Because if her parents left concerned she couldn't cope by herself, then that would steal the joy from their vacation.

In the week before their vacation, Miko's mother had checked the apartment's foyer letterbox each evening for the bank's mortgage demand. Thankfully, the pale blue envelope turned up the evening before they left.

Her parents visited the bank and made two mortgage payments. One to cover December's mortgage, and another to prepay the mortgage for January.

The process turned into a great hassle, like anything to do with a Japanese bank. Miko's parents reported that twelve different bank employees got involved, standing around debating, as if pre-paying a mortgage was a matter of life or death. Until finally, it was agreed that the bank manager needed to use his computer to manually calculate their January mortgage payment. This the manager did with much solemn key pressing, while the bank employees crowded around making "mmmm" and "arrr" sounds like they were observing a master brain surgeon at work.

But her parent's effort was worth it, giving them peace of mind for the month they would be away.

Arriving back late from the bank, they changed from their best clothes into their traveling clothes.

With their suitcases by the door, her parents put on their shoes.

"Mama has left that yellow and white card explaining how to contact us in the letter holder," Miko's father said. "Satellite phone calls to and from the ship are expensive. But email is a bit cheaper for us to receive. The crew will print out emails and deliver them to our cabin. So if there is something really important then email us, but if it's extremely urgent and can't wait, then it's OK to phone."

"If anything is wrong Miko, promise you will tell us. We can fly back easily," Miko's mother said.

Miko promised.

"We are sorry we will not be with you for Christmas," Miko's mother said.

"It is OK," Miko said.

It really wasn't. Christmas was when she would miss them the most.

"I promise we'll get the biggest KFC Christmas pack next year," Miko's father said.

Miko would miss their family tradition of Kentucky Fried Chicken for Christmas. Since their move to Tokyo, the family with Uncle Ken would eat far too much KFC on Christmas day. Each year that meal made Miko feel fat, even though she wasn't.

Her parents hugged Miko goodbye.

Leaving, they closed the apartment door behind them.

As the door shut, out in the eggshell-paper-colored corridor, someone else walked past.

Miko was thankful her parents didn't see her reaction to the stranger.

Moments later Miko was curled up on her bed cuddling Fluffy Kitty.

"Who did you see?" Fluffy Kitty asked.

"A man," Miko answered.

"You're shaking."

"I know. They have been gone only a minute, and already I want them back."

※ ❀ ◆ ✿ •← 🜹

With her parents gone, Miko found playing motorsport on her laptop was the only activity that shielded her mind from the intense feeling of aloneness in the empty apartment, and from the creeping sense of dread that resulted from not having her parents there to protect her.

It was the first time in Miko's life she had been apart from her parents for longer than a day.

Unknowingly, until now, she had taken their presence for granted. Their absence revealed the many ways her life was enmeshed with theirs.

She missed the clink of pots and plates in the kitchen. The warbling from the TV through her bedroom wall.

She missed the familiar music she had grown up with; primarily her father obsessively listening to his favorite band, The Beatles.

She tried playing his CDs, but discovered that knowing her father had started the music, and not the music itself, was what invoked the comfort.

When her bedroom door was open she missed the pause in her parents' slippered footfalls on the living room's tatami mats. In that pause, even without turning around, she knew they had checked in on her.

Most of all, she missed having her parents to talk to. Now, a portion of her thoughts had nowhere to go, and so bounced around inside her head becoming stale.

Whenever she went to speak, came the unsettling realization there was no one to speak to.

A yearning to be heard gnawed at her like a growing hunger which combined with the sudden drought of external acknowledgment to weaken her sense of being. These unwelcome feelings reminded Miko of the stories of forgotten spirits wandering the Earth searching for a home.

Sometimes, unthinking, she called out to her mother wondering about the current location of an item, only to be answered with a lonely silence.

Turning from the kitchen or coming out of her bedroom door revealed the disturbing absence of her father from his favorite chair.

For the first time, the items in the apartment remained static. Nothing was tidied or put away or cleaned without Miko's agency.

In the vacuum left by her parents, the outside world began seeping through the apartment walls.

This creeping threat of the outside disappeared only when she played her racing games. Miko's ability to identify with her digital race car let her dwell safely in the predictable world of the game.

Days went by. Except for cooking, eating, sleeping, and showering, Miko spent her entire time playing her racing games.

※ ✳ ◈ ✣ •⟵ 🎴

"Good morning, sleepy girl. It's Tuesday. Christmas Eve!" Fluffy Kitty said.

Miko moaned at being woken. She hid her face under her quilt.

Like a lightning bolt, Miko remembered her parents were gone. They were out of Japan. Sailing far away on the wavy watery ocean.

She scrunched her quilt up around her like a frightened mouse.

"You can't stay in bed. You will only feel worse. Remember your father said it was important to get up and move when you feel this way," Fluffy Kitty said.

Miko nodded at her toy cat's wisdom.

And stayed right where she was.

"Get up. Shower. Eat. Then you can race for the rest of the day and make these feelings go away."

After several minutes more of Fluffy Kitty's nagging, Miko applied his wisdom and got out of bed.

Quickly she showered. Miko made her usual breakfast of rice, miso soup, and Japanese pickled cucumbers with side dishes of fish, tofu, and omelet.

She placed her hands together and said "*Itadakimasu*". Which means "I humbly receive". Before eating her breakfast with a speed that would be considered discourteous if anyone else but Fluffy Kitty were present.

Finishing her meal, Miko placed her hands together and said "*Gochisosama deshita*". Which means "It was a feast".

She washed her bowls and cooking utensils and cleaned the kitchen to her mother's standard.

In her bedroom Miko pulled out her desk's rolly chair and adjusted its height so her feet rested on the floor.

She woke up her laptop from its digital sleep.

From nine until eleven that morning, Miko played iRacing. Her fears vanished from her mind as she piloted her Ferrari GT3 around the race tracks.

Miko enjoyed starting behind the field because that meant more cars to pass. Each car passed was a tasty victory.

At eleven she closed down iRacing and went to open Forza Motorsport. But her mouse pointer kept skipping, and then stopped responding completely.

Miko checked her pink wireless mouse. A tiny rectangular light between its ears was flashing red.

She turned the mouse over, switched it off, and opened its battery compartment.

Removing the two spent triple-A batteries, she said sincerely, "Thank you for your service". Before dropping the little blue and silver cylinders into her waste-paper basket.

She opened her desk drawer and took out the cardboard-backed plastic packaging that held her supply of spare mouse batteries.

"Oh no."

It felt too light. She turned it over.

Its transparent blister pack was empty!

She had no AAA batteries left, and her laptop's trackpad was broken.

"Your father keeps spare batteries in his electronics box," Fluffy Kitty said quickly.

Miko ran into the living room, slid open a cupboard in the wall, removed her father's old school yearbooks from the top of the blue plastic cube where he stored his electronics. She pulled the plasticky-smelling blue cube out of its cupboard.

She rummaged around, but found no AAA batteries amongst the obsolete digital cameras, portable Sony CD player, and collection of remote controls.

Miko checked the battery compartment of each electronic item. They were empty. Her father had been diligent in removing their batteries for storage.

Miko's forehead began to sweat. She was breathing faster.

She searched the apartment. Every cupboard, every drawer, every basket.

There were sets of AA batteries, but none of the tiny AAA batteries her mouse and heart desired.

"It can't be. It can't be. No, it can't be," Miko said.

Her eyes fell on the kitchen's wall clock.

But the kitchen clock used the fatter AA batteries. The kitchen timer used AA batteries. The remote for her parents' TV also used AA batteries. Nothing used AAA batteries.

Miko clutched at her stomach with one hand, wiping cold sweat from her forehead with the other.

The apartment's walls and furniture transformed, becoming artificial like the computer-generated scenery in her racing games.

"Miko!" Fluffy Kitty called from her bedroom. "You need to calm down or you will have one of your attacks. Quick, lie on your bed."

Miko was trembling. Her heart tap dancing. She stumbled towards her bedroom.

The dizziness came. A black ghost rushing from the window and enveloping her with a chilly hug.

Miko's body sagged in the middle and she crumpled on her bedroom floor like a dropped towel.

In the darkness, the face of the bear was watching with cruel black-button eyes.

"You utter failure. For pity's sake, angel heart, take an overdose," the bear said, its mouth not moving.

She was lying on her bedroom floor, drool from her mouth wetting the tatami mat.

"Miko! Miko!" Fluffy Kitty called. "Wake up!"

Miko moved her head and looked up at her toy cat sitting on the desk.

"Drink cold water," Fluffy Kitty instructed.

Miko forced herself to her feet. Collected Fluffy Kitty and headed to the kitchen.

Sitting on the sofa, she drank chilled water from the fridge. Its sharp coolness washed away some of the mushiness in her head.

"You collapsed; I was so afraid you wouldn't wake," Fluffy Kitty said.

In her wild search for batteries she had made a mess of the apartment.

The mess testified to her dread and goaded the panic to rise again. Her parents were not here to make life secure. She could not play her racing games. Without her games, her mind had no safe refuge to retreat to.

"Breathe. Deep slow breaths," Fluffy Kitty instructed. "Or it will happen again."

Miko followed his advice. It helped.

"I need my games. For me to cope until Mother and Father return, I must be able to race."

"You understand what that means?" Fluffy Kitty asked.

"That is not a possible solution," Miko said.

"The Lawson convenience store is only a block away. They have triple A batteries."

Miko couldn't refute Fluffy Kitty because his statement was correct.

Once before, when she ran out of mouse batteries, her mother had fortunately been here. Her mother had gone to the Lawson store. While she was away, Miko had tried to use her laptop's keyboard to operate her games, but she couldn't figure out the key combinations.

So she needed her mouse working. The only solution that made sense was to get more AAA batteries.

That meant going outside.

She debated with Fluffy Kitty a long while.

It was 2 pm when Fluffy Kitty said, "Well, why not get ready to go to the store? Then see if you can go once you are ready."

This suggestion made sense to Miko, because it was an intermediate step that was not itself scary.

Miko showered again, and this time washed her hair. She put on makeup—because wearing makeup was good manners and because it would cause anyone who saw her face less discomfort.

She dressed in loose jeans and a cyan striped long-sleeved shirt. Warm socks because it was cold outside.

She collected 6,500 yen in coins and notes from her desk drawer. These she stuffed into her jeans' front left pocket.

Her outside jacket smelled musty because she hadn't worn it for more than three years. She put on her mother's dark blue puffer jacket instead.

Miko dropped the keys for the apartment and the security key fob for the building entrance into her front right pocket.

She zipped up the puffer jacket most of the way and inserted Fluffy Kitty down her front, so his smug face could look out from below her chin between the unzipped parts.

"I'm riding kangaroo-baby-style," Fluffy Kitty said.

Miko sat on the sofa, and stared at the apartment's door.

Fluffy Kitty urged her to go. She explained she couldn't. Fluffy Kitty said he was excited to see if she would. She explained he would be disappointed. Fluffy Kitty underlined the importance of her getting batteries so she could race again and prevent panic attacks. Miko explained she was well aware of that.

It was 2:57 pm. For the following three hours they debated in spurts separated by tense silences.

Near 6 pm, Miko's fear began a sharp upward climb.

It was Christmas Eve.

She was alone on Christmas Eve for the first time since being born.

She needed to get those batteries, because her dread was becoming keen as the twilight drew darker outside the apartment's windows.

Unbidden, a traumatic memory returned of a TV documentary that had produced bitter tears as a young child. A rabbit trapped on a tiny knoll as the rushing flood rose around the frightened creature. The water rising steadily until it cascaded over its sanctuary and washed the helpless rabbit away.

I am ashamed of being so weak and messed up.

Her mind was a roller coaster, rattling along a badly lit and dodgy track. It was only a matter of time before her mind would again career off an unseen fracture and be thrown back into the airless void where the bear lived.

I will be washed away too like that poor rabbit. I have no option. I must go.

Miko stood up.

"We're on our way!" Fluffy Kitty said.

She walked slowly towards the door, like someone approaching a temperamental bomb. In front of the door, she put on her white sneakers.

She stared at the door's brushed aluminum handle.

One of her library books told the story of a Russian submarine, K-19. Where men were forced to go into a nuclear reactor. They didn't want to go, but it was the only way to save their submarine and its crew.

These men made an iron determination in their minds to go into the reactor room. Do the job required, while ignoring the danger. Then exit the reactor as soon as the job was complete.

For the next ten minutes Miko decided this would be her mindset.

"I have to do this," she said firmly.

Miko put her shaking hand on the nuclear reactor's handle. She pressed the metal lever down.

※ ❋ ✧ ✤ ☞ ◙

There was no one in the long corridor.

Miko stepped out. She made sure the door locked behind her.

The musty-dry corridor smelled of a cleaning product different from what her parents used.

"I can hear your heart pounding," Fluffy Kitty said.

"It is going to be fine. I can do this," Miko began repeating to herself.

Like a movie spaceman reluctantly exploring the inside of an alien spaceship, she walked cautiously to the elevator and pressed its cold metal call button. Then backed off to one side.

If anyone was in the elevator, she would see them first and hide.

She dreaded hearing the click of another apartment door opening behind her.

The elevator arrived. Wonderfully empty.

Miko was also relieved to find the apartment building's compact foyer devoid of persons.

Half out of habit, and more than half as a delaying tactic, Miko selected a small key attached to their apartment's door key. She used it to open their mailbox.

It had been many years since Miko had performed her old chore.

There was a single item inside the small metal box, a pale blue envelope.

Miko took the blue envelope and inserted it into her jacket's interior pocket.

Then her one excuse to delay was gone.

"I have no other option," Miko reminded herself.

She went to the apartment building's glass door and carefully pushed it open.

Outside, in the dim cold air, the narrow street was thinly lit by the sparse street lamps and a few lights on the sides of the apartment buildings.

Compared to her parents' apartment, the air was fresh and wild.

Above, rolling clouds floated by glowing softly in the vast light of Tokyo.

"Remember, you will see people," Fluffy Kitty said.

"I know. I am mentally prepared."

Miko shoved her hands into her jacket's pockets. It wasn't nearly as cold as the rural north, but gloves would have been nice.

She walked towards a small intersection, passing potted plants and an unsecured bike leaning against the pedestrian railing.

Miko saw her first person at the intersection, a woman in a white raincoat. The woman was walking down the side street that came off Kasuga Ave. It was the way Miko needed to go.

Taking long breaths, Miko focused on the ground and walked up the street on the opposite side. Then, she held her breath.

The woman's exasperated and judgmental quiddity shoved against Miko like pressure from a harsh gust. It grew, peaked, and dissipated as the woman passed.

Miko breathed again, as if coming up from a deep dive.

Soon after came two men and a young school-age boy. Their presence pressed against Miko in the same way.

After many footsteps, Miko passed a quad of whirring heat pumps padlocked away in wooden framed cages.

She emerged on Kasuga Ave.

Cars were going left and right. A motorbike droned past.

There were people up and down the street.

Close, only a few feet away, were two women and a man about Miko's age. The three were waiting together at the pedestrian crossing.

One of the women was tall wearing a tan skirt and the shorter woman wore black pants. The man wore a cheap suit and had an unusually small mouth. They stood waiting for the Green Man crossing signal.

"Steady," Fluffy Kitty said.

Miko clutched her arms around herself. Her knees were ready to give way.

"Remind me why we are walking this far. Remind me why we are late," the taller of the two women said.

"Because a certain friend of ours named Eichi," the smaller said, elbowing the male next to her. "Told us to get off at Hongo-sanchome Station when we were meant to get off at Korakuen."

"This friend keeps boasting that Eichi means wisdom and intelligence. But it seems our Eichi had parents who misnamed him."

"False marketing," the smaller said. "If we had known about this trickery, we could have put our efforts into gaining a higher quality friend."

"I blame myself," Eichi said. "For the mistake of making friends with people from Osaka. This is going on the entire night, isn't it?"

"Think weeks," the taller woman said.

The Green Man appeared, accompanied by his electronic cuckoo bird crossing sound: cuckoo, cook cook koo, cuckoo, cook cook koo...

The three walked off across the avenue's white pedestrian lines.

Miko, head down, tracked them through her hair's fringe.

On the pedestrian island halfway across the avenue, Eichi pulled a tissue out of his suit pocket.

A white rectangular strip of card dropped from his pocket onto the gritty tarmac.

Eichi didn't notice.

The lost card caught a sudden gust of wind and was blown out into the middle of the intersection.

Another gust lifted the card, and began flipping it end over end.

Flittering and fluttering across the asphalt.

Towards the side street.

Towards Miko.

The white rectangle came to rest, pressed by the wind up against Miko's sneaker.

The wind returned to a gentle breeze. Miko reached down and picked up the card.

"What is it?" Fluffy Kitty asked.

Miko studied the card. There was a hologram strip which made her realize it was valuable.

On the card in blue pen was written, "For H."

"I think it's a voucher for some aftershave," Miko said. She knew the English word 'aftershave' because it was printed on her father's brand of cologne. "Some 'Level Three' aftershave."

"Whoa! Level three. That must be the premium stuff," Fluffy Kitty said.

"Oh wow. Look at the price."

"That's a lot of money," Fluffy Kitty said. "What are you going to do? Eichi is going to miss out."

"I don't want to do this," Miko said.

The Green Man was still green, and his digital cuckoo was still singing.

Miko set off across the crossing. After the man who had lost his voucher.

She ran in little steps.

Her arms still wrapped around herself. Her hair bobbing up and down.

"You run like a girl," Fluffy Kitty said. "Is this any faster than walking?"

Miko didn't respond to her toy cat's insolence. She had to catch up with Eichi so he wouldn't miss out on his aftershave.

Also, the last thing she wanted to do was to catch up with Eichi. But she kept running.

Ahead, the three friends were fast walking. Miko didn't reach them until the Red Man forced them to stop at a small pedestrian crossing.

"Excuse me," Miko said. The three turned to her. She bowed to thirty degrees, and held out the lost voucher with two hands.

"Please look kindly upon me. You dropped your voucher."

Eichi checked his pocket. The shorter woman took the voucher from Miko.

"This is Hattori's," the shorter woman said.

"It must have fallen out of my pocket," Eichi said.

"Thank you," the shorter woman said, as they bowed back to Miko. "Our friend Eichi here is making many mistakes today. He must be in need of medical treatment."

"I am Masumi and this is Nana," Masumi said, indicating to the taller woman with her hand. "Are you going to see Aftershave too?"

"See aftershave? No. I was going to buy batteries," Miko managed. "I am Miko."

Her heart was jumping on a trampoline, with the occasional impressive double back-flip.

"What are you doing this evening?" Eichi said.

"Racing games on my laptop. Once I buy new mouse batteries."

"On Christmas Eve? Where is your family?" Nana said.

"They're away on an ocean cruise."

"You are alone on Christmas Eve?" Nana said.

Miko nodded.

"Our friend Hattori was called back to work. Can you believe it? Called back to work on Christmas Eve. He was furious. This is his," Masumi said, holding out the voucher. "It's too late for him to get a refund."

"Come see Aftershave with us," Eichi said.

"Yes. You must. You and your cute cat," Nana said.

"Miko, you're so shy," Masumi said.

Miko bowed and was about to refuse. Since she knew they weren't really inviting her, they were just making a harmonious interaction. This was part of the game. The next part was for Miko to refuse their kind offer.

"We aren't inviting you out of lip-service," Nana said. "We want you to come."

"We do, Miko. Please come with us. We are asking you for real," Masumi said.

"You've seen Aftershave before, right?" Eichi said.

"Yes," Miko said. What a strange question. She had seen her father's aftershave since childhood. It was in the bathroom cabinet, right next to her mother's perfume.

Sometimes Miko would unscrew their caps and smell the distinct scents. Her parents rarely used their fragrances though, and never if they were going outside, since they didn't want to commit "smell harassment" by allowing their scents to disturb others.

"And you like Aftershave, right?" Eichi said.

"I love aftershave," Miko said. It smelled like a pine forest. How could you not love it?

The pedestrian crossing's Red Man winked out and the Green Man appeared.

"Well, that's settled then. You have to come. Much better than being at home by yourself on Christmas Eve. And Hattori will be so happy his ticket wasn't wasted. But we must rush, because Eichi has made us late," Masumi said.

With that, Masumi linked her arm with Miko's.

Miko was so surprised at the sudden touch that she didn't resist, as Masumi set off with Eichi and Nana at a fast pace.

Normally Japanese people are not so friendly with someone they have just met, which added greatly to Miko's shock.

Is it the Christmas Eve feeling? This must be the first time this has happened in Japan.

Miko was almost running next to Masumi just to keep up.

"This is fun," Fluffy Kitty said. "I bet this shop won't only have aftershave. There will be batteries too. Our mission will be achieved."

Miko's head was filling with swirling thoughts. *How did this happen? What is happening? How do I get out of this? Do I want to get out of this? Who are they? Gosh, it's nice having someone's arm linked with mine.*

A memory flashed of a distant windy playground.

This isn't the first time this has happened!

The girl in the pink dress with the yellow ribbon, arm linked, joyfully rushing with her new friends to the jungle gym.

Miko had an idea of where they might be headed. She had seen its huge, lumpy white roof from a distance.

A big shopping mall ahead that she had avoided going anywhere near. Even before she became hikikomori. Far too many people.

Nana and Masumi talked constantly while they walked. They made fun of Eichi. Asked Miko where her family's cruise ship was taking them. Asked her the name of Fluffy Kitty. They talked about work. They lamented on how they'll have missed out on the good merchandise.

Miko was correct in her guess about the mall. After crossing a wide intersection, they turned down Hakusan Ave. Past a big Ferris wheel and a roller coaster. They turned another corner and headed towards some wide stairs.

As they rushed up the stairs, Miko was scared of tripping.

She was out of breath at the top. When she glanced up from her feet, numerous clusters of people were heading the same way.

She should not have come. Far too many people.

They crossed over a bridge of tan bricks towards the giant mall.

The mall's massive wrap-around glass awning loomed up behind short trees speckled red by tiny Christmas lights.

Ahead, bright Christmas decorations were glowing, washing the space cobbled with triangles in front of the mall with primary colors.

High up, perched on the edge of the mall's roof, a backlit cyan sign announced the mall's name,

"TOKYO DOME".

People were everywhere.

"It's going to be so good," Eichi said, skipping a few feet ahead and clapping.

"Look at him, he's like a child," Masumi said.

Then in a blur there was a whirlwind of pillars, people, roped off areas, metal barriers, bouquets of flowers against a wall, uniformed staff, yellow wristbands, red flashes from barcode readers, hands pointing in the direction they should go, and long corridors.

A bassy rumble grew louder and louder, as if they were heading towards a beach with roaring surf.

Then abruptly, they arrived.

The vast sight quenched any bravery smoldering inside Miko.

For someone who couldn't cope with being around people, Miko had walked into a nightmare.

Miko let out a yelp. But her voice was drowned out by the multitude.

She stared wildly around. This wasn't a mall. It was a vast arena. Filled with thousands and thousands of clapping and screaming people.

Ahead was a sea of people. Behind her, a giant wave of people rose up in tiered seating, threatening to crash down on Miko like a mountainous tsunami.

"We have arena tickets," Masumi said excitedly into Miko's ear. Pulling Miko deeper into the raging waters.

Being escorted to the venue by these three strangers frightened Miko. However, during her school and nursing time, she had gained experience being around small numbers of people.

But this unexpected vista went far beyond her experience, continuing on well past any imagination or even twisted dream.

Like a lurking monster seizing its chance, the panic ran towards her again, arms outstretched. Sensing her fear of the crowd and sadistically also drawn by Miko's dread of another attack.

I'm going to faint again. What will they think of me?

Miko stumbled along the green-floored aisle as white metal barriers raced past. Despite their long history of perfect synchronization, her previously reliable legs had forgotten how to cooperate.

Then, like liquid from a syringe, she was injected into the raging ocean of people.

People pressed into them as Masumi and Nana followed Eichi into the midst of the crowd.

"We've got such excellent positions," Nana said.

Ahead on a raised platform was a segment of a giant glossy white ball about twenty people high.

To each side they were surrounded by curved gray walkways ending in circular nodules, like the mouth of a shark closing around its prey.

Masumi let go of Miko's arm.

"What is this? Is that a giant eyeball? Are we at a religious gathering?" Fluffy Kitty asked.

Miko didn't reply, because she couldn't speak. The risk of drawing the crowd's attention had glued her lips shut.

Ahead, left, right, and behind, they were trapped in the middle of the arena by the crowd.

Far beyond the close-looming faces, thousands and thousands of distant people rose up to the edge of the roof.

Along with losing her power of speech, her mind was going numb. Like the tingling onset of a dentist's anesthetic. What thoughts she did have shimmied in and out of focus.

She wrapped her arms tightly around herself.

"You're squishing me," Fluffy Kitty said.

The main lights went out.

The crowd began screaming with their hands in the air as an ominous humming noise came from in front.

Then it became so dark Miko couldn't see.

The sound of wind came and the giant white sphere lit up with gray-white patterns that turned into a rotating ball.

Loud words were spoken, but Miko was approaching being catatonic.

Trembling, she couldn't understand words anymore.

Colors. Swirling. Shimmering patterns. An incomprehensible female voice. Huge translucent blue computer figurines. Girls waking up in bubbles. Computer figurines that shrunk. Words. Crowd screaming. The bassy sound of a heartbeat. Soft blue light from everywhere. Nothing but the heartbeat.

Sudden rows of intense white lights. The crowd screamed. The white sphere became an eyeball staring directly at Miko.

Then pounding music and people around her clapping with their hands in the air.

The white lights were replaced with blue lights pulsing to the music. Next, red lights grew in intensity, painting the entire arena crimson.

"It's a concert!" Fluffy Kitty said. "Miko. This is our first live show."

His words reached Miko. They gave her context for what was happening.

Three giant girls were projected onto the white sphere in metallic blue-green costumes. They began dancing.

Then, the actual girls appeared, dancing on a platform above the white sphere.

The crowd screamed and clapped and jumped.

The girl's platform sank away out of sight and their projected versions returned.

Lines of green laser light shot out from the stage ahead and swept around the arena.

The circular nodules at the end of the surrounding walkways inflated into spheres of white fabric, becoming three giant bubbles. These spheres lit up, and a girl's silhouette rose into each sphere.

The spheres collapsed and there were the same girls, dancing in high heels to the fast electropop music, one at the end of each walkway.

Fluffy Kitty was right. This was a live performance.

As the show went on Miko's trembling subsided.

The music, the infinity of pulsating lights, the girl's spirited dancing and singing drenched Miko in a soothing warmth. Even the surrounding people screaming and bouncing to the music added to the effect.

With the psychedelic shock of an epiphany, Miko realized she was standing in a massive crowd and yet was calmer than she should have been.

She had expected to be in the middle of a panic attack by now. To be lying drooling on the arena's floor. But her panic's upward trend had unquestionably ended, and instead was rapidly spiraling down.

Her mind wasn't numb anymore. Her lips had unglued. Her legs had resolved their differences and rekindled their friendship.

How can this be?

Part of it was the music. It was like liquid happiness, containing no nutrients beneficial to panic attacks.

The other obvious reason was that the crowd was utterly focused on the three dancing girls. To be judgmental of Miko, people had to be looking at her, and none of them were.

Miko even started to wonder what it would be like if she started jumping too.

It must feel nice.

But she didn't start, and instead kept her feet firmly on the ground.

"How can something so loud sound so good?" Fluffy Kitty said.

Miko nodded in agreement with her perceptive cat.

She studied each of the performers. They were about her age.

The dancing girl on the left walkway had long hair almost down to her waist.

The girl in the middle had her hair tied up in a pony tail. When she danced it flicked around frantically like the tail of a happy puppy.

The girl on the right had short hair that wrapped over her head like the salmon in salmon sushi. Unlike the other two, who were wearing dresses, she was wearing shorts.

As the song ended, the girls disappeared from the ends of the walkways. Moments later, the giant white sphere lifted like an opening pearl, and the three girls were revealed on the stage in front of Miko. Wearing new white costumes with geometric yellow, red, blue, and green slashes.

"How did they move so fast?" Fluffy Kitty said. "That's impossible."

They launched into another song.

"Their dancing is so professional," Miko said.

"It is a trick," Fluffy Kitty said. "They're robots."

Miko laughed. Then gasped, her hand flying to cover her mouth.

"Miko!" Fluffy Kitty said. "It's been many years since I've heard your laugh. What a happy moment."

The song finished and the house lights came up. The three girls stood together on stage and greeted the audience.

Miko learned their names: long hair was Kirari, puppy tail hair was Ace, and salmon sushi hair was Miyu. They began talking to the audience. The audience responding with cheers and raised hands waving back.

As they talked, Miko was surprised to discover the performers were so personable. Dashing across the stage towards their audience, waving at everyone.

Smiling and laughing, making jokes amongst themselves. Looking around, as if frustrated at not being able to speak to everyone personally.

Their actions shook Miko. She couldn't believe what she was witnessing.

These three girls were standing in front of tens of thousands of people. Thousands and thousands of people were looking directly at them.

But instead of freezing up, running away, or fainting, these girls were functioning. They were relaxed while talking to more people than Miko had ever seen in her life.

Their dancing was also a testimony to their fearlessness. Miko was keenly aware of how she stood and how she moved in public. Feet too close together or too far apart? What to do with her hands, clasp them together in front or behind her body? Put them in her pockets or not? Every movement Miko made was designed not to draw attention to herself. She even feared dropping a pencil or making noise when opening plastic wrapping.

But this girl trio were the opposite. Wonderfully free. Flourishing like peacocks with big bright tail feathers in front of a multitude and relishing the experience with joyful, confident smiles.

Miko was awestruck.

How is it possible to be so unafraid? I cannot deny what I am seeing through my own eyes.

Miko sensed her mind being stretched.

It was as if she had been living confined in a tiny room, and then the tiny room's walls had fallen to reveal a vast green field beyond.

Next came blue lights and music, and the girls were dancing again.

At one point, Kirari caught Ace's eye with a beaming smile. Ace gave her a big smile back.

Miko had another revelation. These weren't three performers. These were three friends.

An intense jealousy burned. Miko didn't mean to, but envy struck deep from within.

Miko still harbored her fantasy about being an important member of a group of close friends. Being known by her friends, and her friends being known by her, and here, right in front of her, was a striking example.

"I'm such a bad person," Miko said.

"No you're not," Fluffy Kitty said. "Why would you say that?"

"Because I have so much jealousy. And that is a bad emotion."

But soon the event's buoyant atmosphere rolled over Miko, making her forget her jealousy and self-judgment.

She was rocking on her feet in time with the music.

"Why do they keep pointing at the roof?" Fluffy Kitty said. "I can't see what they're pointing at. Is there a hole?"

Song after song came and went. The performers chatted with the audience again. There were more costume changes. Scintillating light shows. At one point, they were lifted over the audience on individual white platforms.

Miko didn't want the experience to end.

If this event had been an anime cartoon, then the air would have been full of red love hearts racing from the performers to the audience, and from the audience back to the performers.

There was a cheery joy in the air. Miko was breathing easier, as if a weight was floating off her chest. A weight that had been there her whole life.

After another chat with the audience, the trio performed an energetic song called "Extrovert World".

As the song's chorus hit, Miko couldn't help but start jumping in time with the beat. Her right hand in the air, like the others, catching the red hearts tossed from the stage.

Miko jumped and jumped and bounced and bounced. Her hair pulled straight going up. Her hair floating around her head and tickling her ears on the way down.

Chains broke apart and dropped from her body as her jumping shook loose the constrictions of other people's expectations.

Bit by bit, bounce by bounce, the thoughts of others became progressively less important.

A warm tear rolled down her left cheek.

The Miko of two hours ago would never have believed what the present Miko was doing. In public! Moving in a way that would bring attention to herself.

It was impossible.

"I'm getting the full kangaroo-baby experience," Fluffy Kitty said.

The happy songs kept coming, and with each song Miko kept jumping. There was a funny segment of audience interaction where different parts of the audience and types of people had to call out and dance. Then more songs.

For the first time, Miko felt part of something other than her family. Everyone here was in unity with Miko, and Miko with them. This is what it was like to be accepted. This is what it was like to belong.

The live show ended much sooner than she wanted. Miko would have been happy if it had continued on until sunrise.

But the final song came, then the amazing spectacle was over.

The audience clapped and cheered and lingered a long time.

After a while, Eichi led them out. He wanted to buy band merchandise before it was sold out.

Miko desired a memento for this amazing experience and used some of her battery money to buy a CD album.

Then they headed towards the exit.

The four of them, and Fluffy Kitty still riding kangaroo-baby-style, gathered in a huddle out in the Christmas-colored courtyard. Smiling fans streaming by on both sides with lambent faces alternating between red and green as they walked through the beams from the Christmas lights. Miko's ears were ringing from the music.

They compared excited thoughts; Miko found herself joining in the conversation.

"I feel so good," Nana said.

"Those three could sing a song about chainsaws, and still make me happy," Eichi said.

"Our train is due," Masumi said.

"We must go, Miko," Nana said.

"Thank you so much Eichi-san and Masumi-san and Nana-san for inviting me to join you in this wonderful experience," Miko said.

"It was our pleasure. What a lucky event Hattori's ticket found you," Nana said.

"I must repay Hattori-san for his ticket. Please tell Hattori-san I will get his money to him. But it will take me a while to save up enough," Miko said.

"Hattori would like that. You are a good person, Miko," Masumi said.

"How should I send him his money?"

"Contact me when you're ready," Eichi said, giving Miko his business card.

Miko accepted the card with both hands and inspected it carefully. She apologized for not having a business card to give back.

"I would like to also include a thank-you card," Miko said. "What is Hattori-san's first name?"

"We don't know," Masumi said.

"He hates his first name," Eichi said.

"We have been friends for years, and he's never told us," Nana said. "I suspect his parents named him after a famous ancestor with an old-fashioned name."

"Or maybe it sounds strange, or it has a weird meaning," Masumi said. "He is very embarrassed. So everyone calls him Hattori."

"I will just write Hattori then."

"We have to go, Miko," Nana said. "Our train will be arriving at Korakuen Station."

Miko bowed and waved goodbye to the three friends, and watched them walk away.

As they went, they talked amongst themselves.

Are they talking about me?

Masumi turned and called back through the passing crowd.

"Miko! We all just said exactly the same thing. About your amazing smile."

"We love your cute smile Miko!" Eichi called.

And the crowd hid the three of them from sight.

Miko's walk home in the electric night had the quality of bouncing. Knots of dispersing fans chatted and laughed in tune with the live show still ringing in her heart.

She entered the convenience store and purchased a packet of AAA batteries. The interaction with the tired shop assistant was still difficult. But not utterly terrifying, like it would have been only hours before.

Counting her coins into the shop counter's change-tray, Miko sensed the edge had gone from her fear.

If her fear of people was a sharp knife, then through some mysterious magic, the live show had blunted that knife. Miko could still feel the knife's pressure on her mind, but no longer did it cut.

Miko arrived home after the live show, swirling with sensations.

There was happiness. There was joy. There were sore jumping feet.

On entering her bedroom came the odd sensation she had left the room years ago.

Miko placed Fluffy Kitty on her desk so he could see her laptop screen. She installed the mouse batteries and accessed the Internet.

Since becoming hikikomori she had avoided going online, but Miko wanted to research the Aftershave band.

"That was fun. But don't you think Aftershave is a strange name for a girl band?" Fluffy Kitty said. "Why name themselves after fragrances for men? Wouldn't the word for feminine fragrances make more sense?"

"I wondered that too, it's a mystery," Miko said. Wiggling the mouse to make sure it was fully back to its mousy self. "Maybe it's for the gimmick value. Because that name makes people talk about them. Like we are now."

Miko reverently stuck Hattori's ticket on her wall with four tiny balls of Blu Tack adhesive putty.

Then began her research by accessing Google Search and typing,

Japanese Band Aftershave

Up came pages of videos and information about the band. She began watching and reading, fascinated.

The band's albums, music videos, their tours, and their history.

Miko loved their many costumes; each colored like a butterfly that had crashed into a kaleidoscope and fallen into a bath of glitter.

She clicked an article about Japanese idol bands.

The music journalist described the process used by corporate men to create these idol groups. Which, in essence, was selecting the prettiest girls as if picking anime figurines out of a shop display case.

Then, in another article, Miko discovered a striking fact about the Aftershave band. It made her gasp. Mouth open. Eyes wide.

"What! They did that!"

She froze. Except for her eyes. Rereading and rereading the same information.

Her hand trembled over her mouse, as this unexpected knowledge seeped into her soul. Like inspirational fuel, filling crevices and channels long dry, finding its way into machinery Miko didn't know she had. Machinery that slowly started cranking into life.

Many minutes of rereading went by before Miko put her laptop to sleep. She switched off the light and lay down on her bed.

Staring at the ceiling, tinted green by her laptop's charging light, Miko stayed awake for hours contemplating many implications.

Her mind racing, like fast marbles rolling around the interior of a glass ball.

Until tiredness came and dragged her to sleep.

Miko awoke late on Christmas Day.

"Merry Christmas, Miko!"

"Merry Christmas, Fluffy Kitty!"

Miko got up, kneeled on her bed, and rolled up her room's bamboo blind.

The world outside had lost its shadowed tinge. Sunlight soaked the apartment buildings, and high over their horizontal roofs cotton ball clouds drifted in the vivid blue sky.

After showering and breakfast and cleaning up, Miko placed Fluffy Kitty on the living room end of the empty table. Miko sat at the kitchen end.

She placed a blank drawing pad in front of her. A graphite art pencil on the pad.

Miko hid something on her lap, under the table's blanket.

"This is a conference," Miko announced.

"Fluffy Kitty is present!"

"The topic is the future of Miko Nishimura."

"That's you."

"It is."

Miko sat up straight. She drew a big letter V on the pad, with the letter's mouth facing Fluffy Kitty.

She circled the point at the bottom of the V.

"This is today."

Then she circled the left and right ends at the top of the V.

"And these are two possible futures for Miko Nishimura."

By the top left circle she drew a picture of her parents crying and a strawberry cake with arms and legs and a sad face sitting alone on a bed.

"In one future, Miko is thirty-five years old. She disappoints her parents and becomes Christmas Cake," Miko said, tapping her pencil on the left-hand circle.

"I don't like that future," Fluffy Kitty said.

"Agreed," Miko said.

By the top right circle, Miko drew her parents with cheerful faces. And a picture of herself in a long white dress holding the hand of a faceless man in a suit.

Behind them she drew a house with smoke coming from the chimney and Fluffy Kitty sitting on the roof looking smug. Coming to visit the house was a car overflowing with smiling friends.

Then from her lap Miko produced the CD she had purchased and half-slapped it down on the table, like a lawyer surprising a jury with irrefutable evidence.

Miko held her hand, palm up, in front of the CD, indicating the three dancing girls on the cover.

"The second potential future is that Miko follows the example of the esteemed members of Aftershave and becomes a successful person."

"A music career?" Fluffy Kitty said, in a surprised voice.

"Not music," Miko said. "That is not my talent. But they are successful people. If they can be successful, why can't I?"

"You could easily be a successful person, Miko," Fluffy Kitty said. "But in Japan, girl bands are manufactured. Aftershave only has the appearance of success. Girl bands, idol groups, are an illusion created by a corporation. They just spend lots of money to get unearned exposure."

"I can see you were reading from my laptop's screen last night, dear cat," Miko said. "But you got lazy and missed what I read before going to bed."

She slid the CD over the table. Until it was right in front of Fluffy Kitty.

Miko leaned towards him. She tapped the CD with her finger.

"You are wrong. Aftershave didn't have lots of money and they were not put together by grumpy men in suits."

She paused for effect.

"They made themselves."

"They did not."

"They did too. They formed Aftershave when they were schoolgirls, only twelve years old. They worked hard through many disappointments and scary choices. Year after year, they weren't successful. But they were relentless in pursuing their dream. Then one day they got their formula right and became megastars."

"They made themselves! Twelve years old!" Fluffy Kitty said. "They're prodigies."

"When I was twelve, I was scared of everything. Afraid to go into the forest. Afraid to go to school. While Aftershave was dancing in front of people and making music videos, I was hiding in the school library or eating my lunch in the bathroom. I am still afraid. At age twenty-six," Miko said, putting her elbows on the table and resting her face in her hands. "Their example fills me with regret for my lost life."

Fluffy Kitty made a soothing noise only soft-toy cat friends can make. Halfway between a purr and a burbling meow.

Miko shook her head. She pushed her *zaisu*† chair back, stood, and started pacing.

"But I will not dwell on negative emotion anymore. Negative emotions have had too much playtime inside Miko Nishimura. They fill my heart with dirt. Their time is over. Last night Aftershave filled my heart with joy. So I will take their esteemed example of success and use it to drive positive thoughts."

"This is wisdom, Miko. I am excited to hear you speak like this."

"If Kirari, Ace, and Miyu can stand in front of thousands of people and talk to them, then Miko Nishimura can talk to a few people. If they can make millions of fans happy with their songs and dancing, then Miko Nishimura can make a few people happy through the actions of Miko Nishimura. If they can be super successful persons, then Miko Nishimura can easily become a normal-level successful person. And if they can do what they have done in a wholesome manner with strong integrity, then Miko Nishimura can do the same."

"Yes Miko! Yes! I am so excited I want to jump up and down, but unfortunately I'm an inanimate object."

Miko walked over to the door and put on her mother's puffy jacket.

She inserted Fluffy Kitty down the jacket's front, kangaroo-baby-style. There was a crinkly feeling.

The envelope.

She took the blue envelope out of the jacket and placed it on the kitchen table.

She checked the apartment keys and building security tag were still in her jeans' pocket.

"Miko Nishimura is not afraid to go outside anymore," Miko said. She put on her shoes. "Fluffy Kitty. Uncle Ken is alone on Christmas day. Let's go!"

Despite her brave intentions, Miko was afraid.

But at the live show something inside her had changed, and she would not let it change back.

Miko stepped out of the apartment, closing its door firmly behind her.

---

† A zaisu is a chair with no legs for use with the low kotatsu tables.
It provides back support and often a cushion to sit on.

For the first time in three years, sunlight warmed Miko's face.

The street lamps were lollipops and the buildings fluorescent scoops of ice cream.

She moved dreamlike through the tangerine memories. Brushing her hand against the railing where she used to turn to head towards the train station.

Please may I have a human friend.

"You're doing well," Fluffy Kitty said.

"Inside I am shaking. But if I don't take action to solve my problems, who else will? I refuse to be trapped in my mental prison any longer."

Despite her brave words, Miko knew she could still regress.

She worried about the loss of the live show's emotional motivation. The point when the memory of its enabling love dried up, and her base self once again came into direct contact with the friction of the world.

The next few days will determine the rest of my life. I can already feel the happiness of the live show fading. I must lock in this change, or fall back into my habit of fearful living.

Many birds of all kinds were perched high on the surrounding apartment's balcony railings. Miko waved hello to them all.

At least now I know what is possible. At the live show I saw it with my own eyes. That can never be taken from me.

A man carrying a brown paper bag of foil-wrapped presents emerged from a side street and walked in her direction.

Miko scrunched in her shoulders. His presence passed by, like the woman in the white raincoat on the street last night, but at a diminished level. Like a hand pressing through a pillow instead of a hand pressing directly.

"I need to repay Hattori for his ticket. I don't like this feeling of owing."

"But how will you get that much money?"

"I'm not sure. Uncle Ken might have ideas. I can't be a burden anymore. I must start contributing."

Miko came to the convenience store where her father and mother brought treats for Uncle Ken. The song "Last Christmas" by Wham filtered out from behind the store's sliding doors.

She counted her remaining coins.

Several minutes later Miko exited the convenience store carrying a white cream-covered cake decorated with a circle of strawberries.

"Uncle Ken shall have strawberry cake on Christmas Day."

"I suspect Miko will soon have more cake inside her than Uncle Ken."

"Dear cat, do not question my questionable motives."

Nearing Uncle Ken's apartment, Miko walked by his taxi's garage. She stopped and took several steps backwards.

The garage workshop's matte silver metal roller door had a mountain range of moss along its bottom slat. Miko touched the scratchy metal and felt the weight of the door's rusty padlock.

She stayed standing by the door. Time passed.

"Miko. I've been staring at this door for ages. I'm bored."

"I'm thinking."

"Could you turn around so I can see something else."

"Hush cat, I am deep in thought."

An unsatisfactory amount of time later, as Fluffy Kitty pointed out several times afterwards, Miko resumed her journey towards Uncle Ken's.

The apartment building's security gate was still broken. She opened it by pulling on the exposed end of its sliding electric bolt.

Miko climbed the stairs to avoid the risk of an occupied elevator. Uncle Ken's apartment was on the third floor.

She knocked on his apartment's door.

No answer.

She knocked again.

There was a shuffling noise. Uncle Ken's voice came through the door. "Who's there?"

"Uncle Ken. It's me, Miko."

"Miko!"

A chain rattled. A latch clicked. The door was pulled open.

"Miko. Is it really you?"

"It is. And Fluffy Kitty too."

Uncle Ken reached out. He found Miko's arm and squeezed it through her puffer jacket. His pupils were wide circles that didn't focus on her.

"This is incredible. After all these years, you're out of your apartment. I knew you could do it. Your parents and I always believed your issue was only temporary. Come in. Come in, Miko."

"I have strawberry cake for our Christmas."

"Cake and my favorite niece, my day is on the up. Take a seat at the table. I just made tea," Uncle Ken said, as he switched on the lights in the kitchen, dining area, and living room.

"I am your only niece, by the way."

"Still my favorite."

Uncle Ken's apartment was a man's apartment. Faded pictures of fast cars and his taxi hung on the walls. Screwdrivers with blue transparent handles and a shabby lemon-colored battery drill lay on the kitchen counter next to unwashed dishes and an empty Sakuma's Drops can.

His prized stereo system and its tower stacks of CDs and records, including his venerated Oscar Peterson collection, dominated the wall by the door.

A white walking cane with its rolling-ball-end leaned against a pile of pizza boxes in the kitchen. The musty smell of unwashed clothes mixed with the aroma of teriyaki sauce.

"Miko is out of her apartment. What a significant day. This is the best someone-at-the-door experience I've ever had."

"Better than a pizza delivery?"

"Much better. Much better. What a Christmas present! To know you can go out again."

"I went out for the first time last night."

"Last night? Excellent. Tell me, what has changed?"

Miko placed Fluffy Kitty on the table next to her. She told her story while they consumed the tea and cake.

When she finished the story, Uncle Ken stroked his chin for a moment, before saying, "Aftershave. They're on the radio, cheering me up with their earwormy songs. I am pleased you found them. I want to thank them, so I will purchase all of their CDs."

"They have helped me, Uncle. I guess I just needed someone to show me the way."

"You say their live show ticket blew to you in the wind?"

"From where it dropped from Eichi's pocket into the middle of the intersection. Then, with another gust, towards me."

He stroked his chin some more, seeming to stare off into the distance. Time passed.

"Tell me, when you were a child. Your forest bird friends you told me about. How close did they come to you?"

"Oh, I miss my birdie birds. They ran right up to me and ate the crumbs off my shoes. When I put bread in my hand, they pecked away and looked grumpy when the crumbs were gone."

"Wild birds came right up to you? They ate out of your hand?"

"Yes, they still do. Always well behaved. Never pecking me."

Uncle Ken stroked his chin for a while more.

He nodded to himself, before feeling for the knife and carefully cutting himself another slice of cake.

"Miko. Did I tell you that when I was young, my father used to beat me with his camera?"

"No, Uncle Ken. That is terrible."

"Yes. I still get flashbacks."

Miko laughed. It was an Uncle Ken joke.

"It's been a long time since I've heard that delightful sound," Uncle Ken said. "It is good to have you back."

"I am not fully back. I am still a very afraid person. While Aftershave showed me success is possible, I know it is up to me to walk the path they have walked. But Uncle, I promise, I am going to be relentless in changing into a successful person. No more Miko hiding in a box."

"I admire your determination. I will assist in any way I can," Uncle Ken said.

"Thank you. I need to start earning to help Mother and Father, and to repay Hattori."

"Do you want a loan to repay this Hattori?"

"No. Borrowing is not what successful people do. I need to earn the money myself. I do have an idea, Uncle Ken. If I can tell it to you?"

Uncle Ken nodded.

"I love my driving games. So I think I would make a good taxi driver."

Uncle Ken smiled. Then quickly suppressed his smile.

Miko gasped.

"Uncle Ken! Is that why you gave me the racing games and steering wheel?"

"Why Miko, I would never be that sneaky."

"Yes you would!"

He laughed.

"I wanted your father to take over driving when my sight began to go. But he likes his construction work. Even when we were young, I was the one racing around on my bike while Akio was building his tree fort. Your father is happiest when he is working with his hands."

"So you thought of me?"

"There's no one else I'd trust with my taxi. But I believed my plan was unlikely to succeed. I assumed you'd go back to nursing."

Miko shivered.

"I do not have good thoughts about nursing."

"You didn't deserve what happened. What that treacherous senior nurse did to you."

"I know. But even if I wanted to nurse again, my first employment was too short. No hospital will hire me. They'll say I am impatient and lack commitment. Also, it's been three years, so my skills have turned mushy."

Uncle Ken reached up and squeezed his left shoulder, massaging out an old person ache.

"I need to reveal a secret your parents don't know. But you will need to know. If you want to drive my taxi."

"Please tell me."

"At school there was a bully. Aku Shiota. He hated me because I confessed to Suzu Mochizuki, the prettiest girl in school. Aku believed Suzu belonged to him. He became vindictive when Suzu started spending time with me."

"Is Suzu your lost love?" Miko asked. She had overheard her parents talking about Uncle Ken's lost love.

His eyes closed as he rubbed a flat palm in soothing circles over his heart.

"Is she why you never married?" Miko said.

"Suzu is a fine chocolate. Every other girl is a potato. Once you have tasted chocolate, you don't want a potato."

If Uncle Ken's heart is really this way, then he will never find love.

"What happened?"

"After school ended, she went on a trip overseas. To California. Then came the news she was married. That was a horrid day. It never even crossed my mind that could happen."

Miko considered this. She thought about Akiyo going to Germany.

"Uncle Ken, there should be rules stopping Japanese people from leaving Japan."

Uncle Ken chuckled. "A long time ago, Japan did have that rule. To be honest, we have too many rules. Rules for where to sit, where to stand, what to say, what not to say. There are enough written and unwritten rules to drown a fish."

Miko had reflected long on this subject. At school, she had even written a letter on the topic. But, she decided to respond with the standard Japanese comeback. Miko wanted to hear Uncle Ken's counter-thinking.

"But we need rules to keep society ordered."

"I'm not suggesting no rules. But many are outdated. Worse, we have rules designed to turn people into controllable sheep. Have you heard the maxim, 'When rules exist, they have to be obeyed'?"

"Yes, Uncle."

"Ever wonder who made up that rule? Why is it a rule? It insists a rule's mere existence requires it to be obeyed. Don't ask questions. Don't ask if the rule makes sense. Don't ask who created the rule or wonder at their motives. And worse, this maxim is circular. It's a rule saying we must obey rules that exist, including itself," Uncle Ken said. "Tell me, why obey every rule someone else invents?"

I didn't obey the bully rules.

"This is why I mentioned Aku Shiota. Like a lot of bully types, he became a bureaucrat. When I applied for my class two taxi license, they refused it. I couldn't understand why. Every time I tried, refused with no reason given."

Uncle Ken leaned back in his chair. Miko nibbled at her strawberry cake. Fluffy Kitty stayed still.

"It was Aku?" Miko said, after she finished her bite of delicious cake.

"Yes. That bureaucratic earthworm had burrowed his way deep into government. He has some sort of connection with the Public Safety Commission or the National Police Agency, so he can prevent me from getting my class two. One day, he phoned me to gloat. With the obscenities removed to protect your delicate ears, Aku said, 'You'll never drive a taxi as long as I am alive'."

"But Uncle, you have driven a taxi since I was little?"

"I decided to prove him wrong. So I became a renegade driver with a renegade taxi."

"A renegade taxi?"

"We are the elite of the white taxis."

"White taxis?"

"Taxis without a license. Our society operates outside the standard regulations."

"What! This is very surprising, Uncle Ken," Miko said, shifting in her seat.

"You are an adult, Miko. You have the right to know the truth. Consider our apartments. Both of them here in Bunkyo Ward, an expensive part of Tokyo. Did you ever wonder how poor country folk like us could afford to buy in such an expensive area?"

"A bank loan?"

"Of course. But the loan deposit and servicing came from my taxi business. That's why your father is working so hard to service your parents' apartment loan by himself."

"Did you pay tax?"

"I paid the same tax as a licensed freelance taxi driver. Paid indirectly, through my mechanic workshop business front. But apart from expenses like tax and our society insurance policy and running expenses, I cleared significantly more profit than a normal freelancer."

Miko's mind was scrambling up a steep cliff of understanding.

Uncle Ken has a renegade streak, but I never imagined he was a real renegade.

"Uncle Ken, you have a Western mindset. Instead of our saying 'when rules exist, they have to be obeyed' you have adopted the Western saying that 'some rules are made to be broken'."

"I have not heard that saying before. I like it. I am lucky to have such a book-loving niece full of interesting trivia."

"Will this Aku bully prevent me from getting my taxi license?" Miko said.

"Our society's spies report anyone with the family name of Nishimura, born in Aomori Prefecture, experiences a long delay before their license is granted. I suspect Aku is vetting each application. Would he punish my niece? I suspect he might. But even if you were to get a taxi license, you would need to work ten years for one of the big taxi firms before going freelance. And they wouldn't allow you to use my taxi."

"Why not? Your taxi is the same as other taxis."

Uncle Ken smiled in a conspiratorial manner.

"I built my taxi myself. The perfect taxi. But the regulator's stringent rules would never allow my taxi to be used. Fortunately, our society performs the *shaken*, the vehicle inspection, so there's no risk of an illegal vehicle red sticker. Here. You'll need to study this."

Uncle Ken stood up.

He felt around inside his kitchen cupboard over his fridge. Locating a small paperback.

Black with a horizontal red stripe on the front cover. The stripe wrapped around the spine and onto the back. There was no writing on the book's cover.

"Never show this to anyone else. This is our society's book of guidelines. Not rules, guidelines. It includes the special signs to recognize other society members. Plus, everything else you need."

"Uncle Ken, I don't know if I can be a renegade taxi driver. It sounds scary."

"Ha, no it's fun. So much fun," Uncle Ken said, fingering the two keys on his gold chain necklace. "But you don't need to decide now. First, let's see if you enjoy driving my taxi."

"I've never driven a real car. I want to! I want to!"

"Let's visit my baby. Right now. I'll teach you how to charge her battery, check the fluids, and pump up the tires. Tomorrow when her battery is charged, we'll start her up. Then you can have your first lesson."

Miko jammed the society book into her jacket's slash pocket. She reinserted Fluffy Kitty and zipped up the jacket to his chin.

Soon Miko and Uncle Ken were walking towards his garage. Uncle Ken with his white cane and Miko guiding him with her hand on his arm.

"I've wondered. Is the bonsai tree lady still up there?" Uncle Ken said.

"Yes, Uncle. Her balcony has many lovely little trees. Just as you remember."

"Thank you, Miko," Uncle Ken said. "For thinking to visit me. With your father and mother away, I have not spoken to anyone in a week."

"What about your friends?"

"I have not seen them much these past years. They have different lives now. But they're picking me up the day before New Year's Eve for our two-day long New Year's Eve sake bar crawl. I mean celebration. That is the one tradition we never break."

I am out of touch. I have never thought of Uncle Ken as a lonely person. How selfish I have been hiding away and only considering myself. This poor attitude of mine I will also change.

They arrived at the garage. Uncle Ken brushed its door with his hand.

"I have not seen my baby since that horrible day when we put her away."

He removed his key necklace, kneeled, and fumbled for the padlock.

"When I pulled this door down that evening, it was the first time I felt old," Uncle Ken said. Inserting a key into the padlock and trying to make it turn. "The world forgot me. It was like the day I finished my education. Leaving, I looked back at my familiar school, and knew in my heart I no longer belonged."

It was at that moment Miko realized her childhood was over.

An adult was speaking to her as he would another adult. The revelation about the renegade taxi, his loneliness without his friends, and now this melancholy thought of the world having no place for him. These were things once hidden from her by protective adults, but no longer.

She was being trusted.

She was one of them.

Simultaneously, Miko experienced sorrow for Uncle Ken and mournfulness at the loss of her child-self.

A new apprehension came, like being unexpectedly picked up and tossed around by a wave at the beach.

"The lock is stiff with years. I have some machine oil inside. Later, I'll get you to put a drop of oil into its tumbler."

The padlock finally clicked open.

The garage door resisted at first. Before clanking up raining specks of dirt onto Uncle Ken.

There in the gloom, his taxi sat. Its once glossy dark blue paint dulled under a layer of dust. Its tires almost flat.

Uncle Ken stroked his hand along the front of its hood, leaving trails in the dust.

"Hello, baby. I've missed you."

Miko watched the reunion from just outside the garage door.

"I will need to give her a wash," she said.

"Thank you. She deserves that," he said. His hand resting on his taxi.

"Miko. Let me give you some sage advice about men."

"Yes, Uncle."

"Never trust a man who doesn't talk to his car."

"Why, Uncle?"

"Because a man like that has no soul."

Back in her parents' apartment, the prospect of driving a car for real consumed Miko's thoughts. The clock dragged its heels. The next day the sun overslept.

That morning leaving the apartment was easier than the day before.

At the garage, it was musty inside the taxi.

Like a night's gentle snowfall, a layer of fine dust had accumulated on the top of the car's interior surfaces.

Miko sat in the driver's seat on the taxi's right hand side.

"The clutch goes in. Pull back the lever, that's first. Clutch out gradually, feel the bite. Then just pull back on the lever again. There's no need to use the clutch with gears higher than first with a sequential shifter. There, you have second gear."

Uncle Ken was in the passenger's seat. The taxi was still in the dim garage with the roller door up. The rectangle of daylight from the door not quite reaching the taxi's windshield.

Miko had inflated the tires with the garage's small compressor and the taxi's battery had been charged overnight.

She hadn't tried the engine yet. But Uncle Ken was hopeful.

They had drained out the old gasoline. Replacing it with fresh gasoline from the gas station.

People had looked at them strangely as they walked back, pulling two red plastic jerry cans in Uncle Ken's blue pull trolley. Uncle Ken pulling and Miko guiding.

Having Uncle Ken's company made people's unapproving faces easier to take, but their disfavor still made Miko uneasy.

"What does this extra lever do?" Miko asked. Wiggling the silver lever topped with a black plastic grip near the gear lever.

He chuckled. "Best to leave that until later."

"There are so many levers," Fluffy Kitty said. "Too many knobs and pedals and switches and dials and lights and buzzers. Thinking about them is making my whiskers hurt."

He was perched on the passenger side of the dashboard.

Miko smiled at her toy cat. He had never played her racing games, so he couldn't understand how familiar Uncle Ken's taxi felt.

"Please," Miko said. "My curiosity is leaping. I promise not to use the lever straight away."

"OK, but it's for experienced drivers," Uncle Ken said. "That lever controls a vector torque system of my own design. Pull the lever back and the rear wheel brakes activate and the engine's output is switched to the front wheels. Push the lever forward to apply the front brakes and the rear wheels get the power. Push the lever left, and both left side brakes activate while power is transferred to the two right side wheels. Vice versa if you push the lever right. Push hard enough in any direction and the brakes will lock up. You can control the power to the other wheels with the accelerator pedal. Diagonal pushes will apply the brakes to only that one wheel."

"How very useful," Miko said. "I wish my racing game cars had one of these levers, I could do so many more speedy maneuvers."

Uncle Ken's instructional session continued until he declared himself satisfied Miko understood his taxi.

"Uncle Ken, I read that in Japan only driving instructors are allowed to teach people to drive."

"Ha. More rules. Our society book permits me to teach you."

"I guess that makes it OK."

"It has to be me. There's no driving instructor alive who could teach you how to drive my taxi."

"When I was young," Miko said. "I always imagined you would be the one to teach me to drive."

"And I will. So let's see if my baby will fire up," Uncle Ken said. "Please fire up, baby."

"This is so exciting."

"It's not healthy for us to be inside the garage with the engine running. If she starts, give her a minute to warm up. Then drive her out of the garage, turn left, and park outside by the curb."

Miko agreed. She gripped the steering wheel tightly. Practicing in her mind the sequence of things she needed to do if the taxi started.

Her first ever drive of a real car was only moments away.

"The key," Uncle Ken said.

Miko took the key and inserted it in the steering column.

"Turning on the electrics," Miko announced. She turned the key.

Many colored lights lit across the dashboard sprinkling Miko and Uncle Ken's torsos with patches of red, blue, orange, and green. Dials jumped. A ticking noise came from the rear of the car. The duration between the ticks got longer, and then stopped.

"The fuel pump. I must have left that switch on," Uncle Ken said. "Check she is in neutral and try the starter. Keep the button down, it might take a while."

"Enabling power to the ignition," Miko said. Flicking a switch by the steering column.

She pressed the big red button.

The taxi whirred loudly, shaking from side to side. There was a loud bang. But Uncle Ken had warned that might happen.

After five seconds, the engine caught. Then died. More frantic whirring. It caught again.

The engine roared. Hurting Miko's ears in the enclosed garage.

The taxi vibrated like a big growling dog.

"There she is!" Uncle Ken said, slapping the dashboard and scaring Fluffy Kitty. "Touch the accelerator pedal a bit."

She obeyed. The engine thundered, and the vibrations grew less.

"There is a lot of smoke," Miko half yelled.

Blue-black smoke was filling up the garage.

"She's burning off years of sitting. Take her outside."

Miko pushed in the clutch. Pulled back on the gear lever to select first gear. Released the handbrake and gave the engine some revs while slowly letting the clutch up.

The taxi tensed, but didn't move.

"Sitting too long makes the brakes stick," Uncle Ken said. "Keep going. They'll unstick."

Sure enough, there was a snap from underneath. The taxi untensed and the rumbling metal beast rolled forward.

Miko backed off on the clutch to keep the roll slow. She checked right and then left for traffic, before letting the taxi roll out onto the road.

She turned left and stopped. Taking the taxi out of gear, she applied the handbrake.

"Are we next to the curb?" Uncle Ken asked.

"Yes, Uncle."

The taxi's exhaust note was hammering off the buildings.

"Switch from the straight-throughs to the stealth mufflers."

Miko twisted the handle of a push-pull rod protruding out from underneath the dash. She pushed the rod away from her. The rod disappeared under the dash with a clunk. The taxi became much quieter.

Uncle Ken clapped. "Miko, you must be the only person in the history of the world who didn't stall a manual car on their first try."

Miko laughed. Because honestly, it hadn't been that hard.

The electric system's gauges and indicators reported good electrical health. Uncle and niece waited until the water and oil temperature gauges pointed vertically.

Then Uncle Ken had Miko drive up and down the empty street. Starting from the curb, changing gears, changing back down, and then parking again. Reversing and practicing hill starts even though the road was flat.

Miko was getting bored. When she reached the end of the street, she wanted to keep going.

Uncle Ken must have sensed her eagerness. On the next run, he had her go around the block.

Soon they were driving out on the wider roads with traffic. Cars, buses, trucks going this way and that.

"Amazing. You're amazing," Uncle Ken said. "Never have I heard of a beginner doing this well. Changing gears perfectly. Knowing the road rules too. Not a single mistake. No green leaf sticker for you."

Miko was pleased her long experience playing racing games had translated into actual driving skills, meaning she could avoid the green and yellow leaf sticker beginner drivers in Japan must display on the rear of their car.

"I memorized the road rules on the Internet last night."

Miko was beginning to suspect her uncle was being funny with his praise. So far, driving was easy. Everything on the road happened so slowly it was impossible to do anything wrong. She found her mind drifting to other thoughts, but she forced her concentration back to driving.

At some point it will get difficult, and I need to be paying attention when it does.

But it never became difficult.

Near evening, after they filled up the taxi's fuel tanks and went through a car wash, Miko backed the taxi into its garage. Parking exactly where Uncle Ken wanted. She switched off the rumbling machine.

"Miko. My impressive niece," Uncle Ken said. "What do you think after your first day of driving?"

"It's relaxing, Uncle. I can see why you miss driving. Such a tranquil experience."

The next day, they drove again. This time into the heart of Tokyo. Then out on the highways.

The highways moved faster than the city streets, but not much faster.

Driving was like walking in slow motion through a herd of docile sheep. In her bones, Miko knew driving was more than this. But for now, while she was learning, she would drive as Uncle Ken suggested.

Slow traffic stopped them outside a glass-fronted shop. There was a problem evident in the window's reflection.

"Uncle Ken. The taxi is still making black smoke."

"Black smoke means a fueling problem. You'll have to help me fix it. I can't work on her by myself anymore."

Fixing a car! Miko had never heard of a girl doing that. But she would try her best.

After lunch at a noodle shop, they stopped outside Uncle Ken's garage.

"Want to go solo?"

"Can I! Can I really?"

"Go around the block."

Uncle Ken took his cane and exited out onto the sidewalk.

"Away you go," Uncle Ken said.

Miko drove off from the curb.

"Miko! You are driving Uncle Ken's taxi by yourself," Fluffy Kitty said. "How often at school did you imagine driving his taxi? I remember the many doodles you drew of this exact future now-happening event."

"I know. This must be what it feels like when a dream comes true. I'm tingling all over. I will remember this moment forever."

Miko went around the block. She couldn't help grinning the entire way.

Next, Uncle Ken instructed her to circle Tokyo Dome City before returning.

As the taxi drove by the big roller coaster and Ferris wheel, Miko was struck by the potency of the memory.

Two days ago, what a scared girl had walked towards Tokyo Dome, and what a different person had walked back.

Still afraid, but less than before. And determined.

Then Miko realized she had never felt so unafraid.

Driving. There is something about driving that fits well with me. The Aftershave girls have their dancing and singing skills, while maybe driving is my talent?

Back at the garage, Uncle Ken sent her out again, with instructions to come back in an hour.

When she returned, she found him inside his garage, dusting his tools by feel with a bright pink feather duster. He came out to the car.

"So, where did you go?"

"Around by Disneyland and down to where I could see Tokyo Bay. Next to these pink hotels. Then afterwards into the city, before circling back here."

"Did you consult the map? Your phone's navigation?"

"No," Miko said. "It's pretty easy to figure out where you are if you remember the skyline and landmarks."

"That's the first time I've heard anyone use the word 'easy' about navigating Tokyo. Back her in. We'll get dinner."

They walked around the corner. There was a rice bowl shop with a queue outside.

Like most Japanese people, Uncle Ken was very fond of queues. Miko had wondered why this was the case. Her first guess was that in Japan, following the group gave legitimacy to your actions. Joining a queue was more comfortable than risking standing out by boldly visiting a shop the group hadn't chosen.

Her second guess was that queues made people curious. People who joined lines were like gamblers taking a risk to see if what they were waiting for was good or not. It was a way of turning lunch or dinner time into a mini-adventure.

"Here's a *donburi* shop."

"Is there a queue?"

"Yes, Uncle."

"A queue. It must be good. Let's go there."

After a wait, they were seated at the counter. Miko wanted fish, and so ordered a *kaisendon* rice bowl, which is like deconstructed sushi.

Uncle Ken ordered *oyakodon*, a chicken and egg rice bowl. Translated literally, the word 'oyakodon' means "parent-and-child rice bowl".

As they ate, the woman next to her occasionally bumped Miko's arm with her elbow. Even with Uncle Ken on the other side, it was a freaky experience.

"You have to force yourself to get used to being around people," Uncle Ken said. "They say the only way to stop fearing spiders is to handle spiders."

"Yes, Uncle," Miko said. "How did you know?"

"You keep tensing up."

"Don't drop rice on my face," Fluffy Kitty said. He was riding kangaroo-baby-style, and Miko's chopsticks passed right over him.

Miko patted his head with her free hand.

"Here Miko. Take these," Uncle Ken said. He slid his hand over the countertop towards her.

He lifted his hand, revealing two keys.

"The keys to your garage and taxi. Uncle Ken, I can't."

"Yes you can. You're family. After your progress these last two days, I know I can trust you with my taxi. Drive her. Enjoy her. Even if you don't become a renegade taxi driver like I was, I want you to have use of my taxi whenever you want. Besides, it's much better than my baby sitting alone in the dark. She likes to be driven."

Miko's eyes began to water. She blinked her tears away the best she could.

Uncle Ken's taxi! What have I done to deserve such a wonderful family?

Despite the shame I have brought upon them, they're endlessly kind to me.

"Thank you, Uncle Ken. I promise to look after her and keep her clean and shiny."

"And talk to her. Don't forget to tell her she is a good girl."

Miko made that promise too.

It was late Sunday afternoon, two days later. Miko had spent the weekend driving around Tokyo.

She had used up half of the practice gasoline money Uncle Ken had given her.

"Miko. You have a serene expression when you drive," Fluffy Kitty said, from his dashboard perch.

"My face is reflecting my inner being. I recognize that driving is a religious experience."

"You are in transcendence?"

"That is how I feel. It is odd that none of the religions have recorded driving as a path to inner peace."

"You have read the major holy writings. Maybe you have discovered a higher secret that the monks and priests keep only for themselves?"

"If that's true, then it is very naughty of them to hide such a profound revelation."

Driving took no energy. Miko sensed the obviousness of the required actions flowing through her, like a cool trickling stream.

Without conscious effort, she could forecast what the other drivers were planning to do. Where their vehicles would be ten seconds from now. If they were going to hesitate, turn, stop, or speed up. The same was true for pedestrians, those riding bicycles, and the tourists bouncing along in their rickshaws.

At the controls of her taxi, the world became as predictable as counting: one, two, three, four, five, six, seven...

Above, clouds were aimlessly drifting past. Around the taxi Miko's fellow adults walked wrapped against the biting cold, as the sun journeyed down on its way to see what was happening on the other side of the Earth.

Heading home, Miko drove into Bunkyo Ward. She planned to put the taxi to bed and buy two takeout donburi bowls for dinner with Uncle Ken.

She drove by the stone edifice of the bank with its recessed windows and tall pillars, where her parents went each month to pay their mortgage.

Unannounced, the pale blue envelope fell into her mind.

Wait a minute! Mother and Father paid this month's mortgage and prepaid next month too. There shouldn't be another bank demand until February.

"What is wrong?" Fluffy Kitty said.

"I'm not sure. But the bank sent a letter when they shouldn't have."

"The blue envelope on the fridge?"

Miko nodded. The last part of her mail gathering chore was to put new letters into the blue-speckled letter holder with a duck motif that lived on top of the fridge.

"Maybe it's not from the bank?"

"It's from the bank."

"Well, why not open it and check?"

"But, is it OK to open my parents' mail?"

"Why not? You're an adult family member. Your parents are away and can't do it themselves, and it might be something they need to know."

"That makes sense, I guess," Miko said. "But I don't really want to."

She turned the taxi left, down a side street lined with five-story apartments and colorful umbrella-sized flower gardens on each corner. The only person in sight was a tiny figure walking away at the far end of a long street.

"What's this?" Miko said.

Running along the sidewalk between the yellow apartment walls and the green and white curb-rails was a little dog trailing a brown leather leash.

"Where are you heading, doggy?"

Miko drove past the running dog. She stopped next to a driveway and pressed the button to open the taxi's left rear door.

The door swung gently open.

"Are you lost?" Miko said.

The furry white-gray dog stopped. Attentively it looked up into the taxi at Miko.

It had a fuzzy beard and floppy ears that stood up straight when it heard her voice. Miko had read a book about dogs. This type was called a schnauzer. It barked once.

"Get in. We'll drive around and find your owners."

The dog barked again and jumped into the taxi's back seat.

"What is that thing!" Fluffy Kitty said. "I don't like it. Make it go away."

"Calm down, cat," Miko said, patting the dog's head. The dog licked her hand. Miko pulled the rest of its leash into the taxi and pressed the button to close the rear door.

"Bark when you see your owners."

The dog stood on its hind legs. Put its paws on the sill of the door. Its nose drew streak marks on the window glass as it looked around excitedly at the view.

"I will call this thing an anti-bird," Fluffy Kitty said.

"Why?"

"Because I really like looking at birds. And I really do not like looking at this thing. So it's an anti-bird."

"It's a dog. How do you not know what a dog is?"

Miko drove around the block. Methodically up and down each street. There was no sign of the dog's owners.

She expanded her search into the surrounding blocks.

"Where are your parents, doggy?"

Searching, Miko glanced up a side street. A middle-aged couple in brown coats stood hand in hand at an intersection. Looking up and down the streets.

Miko turned the taxi around. She drove up the side street. The couple were walking fast, heading away from her.

"What about them?"

The bearded dog made a little whine and barked.

Miko drove past the couple and stopped the taxi. She activated the taxi's door. As soon as the door was half-open, the dog jumped onto the sidewalk and tore towards the couple, yapping manically.

"Kingyo! Kingyo!" the woman called.

The dog leapt into the teacherly woman's arms and licked her face like she was an ice cream. The man vigorously rubbed the dog's back.

"Kingyo. I thought we had lost you!" the woman said. She was crying. Bearded Kingyo made quick work of licking those tears away.

Miko smiled. Because the woman was so happy, and because the dog's name was Kingyo, which means "goldfish". It was a wonderfully silly name for a dog.

The leathery-faced man approached the taxi. His wife followed, clutching her excited animal.

"Thank you," the man said. "Where did you find him?"

"He was three blocks over. Running along the sidewalk," Miko said. Indicating west with her hand.

"You're a good person," the woman said. "I was afraid we'd never see him again. How can we ever thank you?"

"Your happiness is thanks enough," Miko said.

"No, you must let us do something for you. You don't understand how much having Kingyo returned means to us," the woman said.

"I noticed your taxi produces black smoke," the man said. "I own a mechanics workshop. Please let me fix it for you. Free of charge."

"Thank you. But I expect nothing in return. I couldn't make you work for free," Miko said.

The man's eyes fixed on the silver lever next to the taxi's gear lever. Then his eyes scanned the switches half hidden by the steering column. He put his hand on the inside of the taxi's middle pillar, like he was feeling the engine's rumble.

"My name is Nagao Watanabe and this is my wife, Kayoko. Please let me fix your taxi," he said. He rubbed his finger across his left eyebrow, touched his nose with his thumb, and placed two fingers on his left shoulder.

The sign from Uncle Ken's book! Nagao must be a society mechanic.

Miko responded by rubbing her right eyebrow twice with the thumb on her left hand, then she touched her thumb to her nose and placed three fingers on her right shoulder.

Nagao nodded.

"I am Miko. My uncle owns this taxi. I will phone him and ask."

Miko made the call and explained to Uncle Ken what was happening.

"I have heard of Nagao Watanabe. He is a rank-one mechanic with a solid reputation. Please let me speak to him," Uncle Ken said.

Miko handed her phone to Nagao. He stood by her taxi and talked with Uncle Ken.

Nagao said, "A true man does not wear pink."

The secret response. Uncle Ken must have challenged him with the society's pass phrase.

Nagao handed Miko's phone back.

"This is a lucky opportunity, Miko," Uncle Ken said. "It will be much easier than the two of us trying to fix the fueling issue."

So Miko drove Nagao and Kayoko and perpetually excited Kingyo back to their apartment.

It was the first time she'd driven anyone who wasn't Uncle Ken.

Miko was both nervous and thrilled at the same time. Thrilled because she was so close to strangers and yet functioning, even though it was a bit scary. And nervous they wouldn't enjoy her driving, so she braked and turned and changed gears as smoothly as possible.

"Lately everyone is losing important things. We lost Kingyo, and poor Junpei," Kayoko said.

"He is never the happiest person, but I've not seen him this sad before," Nagao said.

"Who is Junpei?"

"My husband's apprentice mechanic. The Saturday before Christmas he had the biggest *pachinko* day of his life. While I don't approve of gambling, I admit his winnings were significant. Especially for a single day spent dropping ball bearings in those noisy flashing machines."

"A pipe had burst in the exchange point's ceiling. So it was closed when he got there," Nagao explained. "They told him to return the next day to exchange his pachinko token."

"Except he lost his token before then. Poor Junpei. My husband said when he saw him on Monday he thought Junpei's mother had died."

Miko pulled up outside their apartment.

Miko gave Kingyo a goodbye pat as she dropped off Kayoko. Nagao remained in the back seat.

"My workshop is not far. I will direct you."

The workshop's big roller door was half way up.

"Junpei is here. Drive right up to the door and he will hear us."

Miko did. A lanky black-haired teenager appeared wearing blue workshop overalls with the sleeves tied around his waist and a gray anime-character-covered T-shirt. He pressed a button next to the door. The door clanked upwards.

"Drive in Miko. Poor Junpei must have been searching the workshop again for his pachinko token."

The clean workshop was well lit, with three lift bays supporting a car each. There were many wooden benches and bits of machinery bolted to the concrete floor, and three big red rolling tool caddies, one covered in anime stickers.

Miko collected Fluffy Kitty and got out of the taxi.

"Junpei, help me get the front off," Nagao said.

"The front off?" Junpei said.

"Yes. Two hidden latches on each side behind the wheel."

They lifted the hood, grill, fenders, and front bumper off the taxi as a single piece. Carrying it aside, they placed it on a gray speckled felt mat.

The taxi looked very mechanical with its front removed. Big and small black cheese graters were bolted to the tubular frame everywhere they could fit. Two massive hairdryers on each side of the engine. There were thick and thin silver braided pipes curling around in every direction.

"What is this, Senpai? This isn't a taxi," Junpei said. "A space-framed chassis. Twin stage supercharger. Four turbos. A V12? Wait. What engine is this? I've seen nothing like this before. It's four-wheel drive too."

"Remember when I said we get in cars we can never talk about?"

"Yes, Senpai."

"This is one of those cars."

"Yes, Senpai."

Miko waved goodbye to the taxi.

Nagao used an ordinary car to drop her off at the donburi shop. Thankfully, the shop had no queue.

"I'll pick you up when she's ready," Nagao said.

"Please be careful with her. She is a family member."

"Do not worry," Nagao said. "I am honored to have in my workshop the finest renegade taxi I have ever seen."

The next morning, in an apartment far across Tokyo from where Miko lived, a salaryman lay asleep.

Like a samurai sword strike in the dark, his phone's alarm cut through his pleasant dream, leaving him bleeding cold dreariness into the cotton of his warm futon.

The salaryman vocalized the despair of his pending day as a soft groan.

He reached out to where his digital *katana* was charging on the floor next to his head and swiped away its perky tune.

A minute later, when the phone's pixels glowed Monday 6:31 am, the salaryman accepted the inevitable and got up from his futon.

Dressed in an old baseball T-shirt and his blue sleeping shorts, he zombie-staggered into his apartment's narrow bathroom.

Its cream blue-patterned floor tiles robbed the warmth from his bare feet as his breath emerged as white fog in the freezing air.

He drank a glass of water. Speed shaved with razor and foam. Washed his face and brushed his teeth. There was no time to shower in the morning, so he had showered before going to bed.

He dressed in suit pants and a vertical striped business shirt. Tightened his belt buckle's latch. Fixed his dark blue tie. Put on fresh socks and his black leather dress shoes. He draped his company ID card hanging on its yellow lanyard around his neck.

Donning his suit jacket and charcoal overcoat, he grabbed his black leather satchel and headed for the door. It was 6:45 am.

After a brisk walk through the chilly early morning light, he arrived at the factory-like Minami-Kashiwa Station, where white-gloved train pushers shoved him onto the 7:02 am train.

Five minutes later, he had two minutes to transfer trains at Matsudo Station.

At 7:47 am, his train arrived at Tokyo Station. A hectic overground and underground maze of tracks, platforms, and stairs, processing half a million passengers a day.

The salaryman and his fellow travelers burst out of their carriages like shaken soda from a can. They cantered out of the town-sized station, and towards their respective high rises.

He purchased two breakfast ham-and-cheese sandwiches, salmon onigiri, and a can of Fire Coffee from the convenience store.

He resumed his canter. The salaryman had to arrive before his boss or there would be consequences.

The red strokes of the huge glowing sign イカリ high atop his corporation's vast tri-skyscraper complex scrolled into view from behind a lesser building.

He checked his phone. The queue at the store checkout had been too long. He was three minutes behind schedule.

He upgraded his canter to a gallop.

Head down, legs reciprocating under the bottom of his coat, plastic bag of breakfast items slapping against his leather satchel.

Shortly before 11 am, the same Monday morning, Miko finished cleaning the apartment.

Housework reminded her of school cleaning time, when she had worked together with the other schoolchildren to clean their school at the end of each day.

Cleaning also made a magnificent excuse to avoid speculating about the envelope.

That envelope—that should not have come—perched pulsing blue on top of the fridge like a radioactive lighthouse.

Miko had never opened her parents' mail. Theoretically, Fluffy Kitty's advice was correct. It made sense under these circumstances. But it still didn't feel like something she should do.

Miko wanted to take the envelope to Uncle Ken's and open it there, but he was away with his friends on his two-day-long New Year's drinking party.

Her mobile phone rang.

Miko jumped, because few people called her phone. The rare calls she received were usually marketing or survey calls. It took her a moment to realize what the ringtone meant.

She walked into her room and picked up her cheap pink phone from where it was charging on her desk.

Miko breathed deep. Someone was reaching out to her while she was in the sanctuary of her parents' apartment.

"*Moshi Moshi*. I am Miko Nishimura."

"Hello Miko, Nagao here. Your uncle's taxi is ready."

Miko relaxed.

"Thank you. I was expecting it to take days. I hope you have not prioritized the taxi over your paid work?"

"No. It wasn't me. Junpei stayed up the entire night working on it. Your taxi was ninety-five percent finished when I arrived this morning. He completed our complimentary clean an hour ago, so it's ready."

"He worked all night? That was very kind of him."

"Yes. But, there's a worrying side to his kindness. I'm afraid Junpei has fallen in love with your taxi. Any moment I suspect he will kneel and propose marriage."

Miko put her hand over her mouth to hide a giggle.

"That would be a strange wedding."

"I've completed the shaken. When I asked your uncle, he said you were uncertain if you wanted to become an active society driver?"

"The answer to that question has not yet formed inside me."

"I understand. But since the taxi is here, let me produce a society license for you and manufacture the car's green plates. That way, if you decide to begin, you won't need to book an appointment. I'll also supply you with two sets of our female uniform. The waistcoats are nice. You'll like them."

"Thank you. I am impressed you make the plates too."

"The society provides a full parallel licensing system. We don't believe governments have a rightful claim to monopoly over people's right to work in their chosen profession."

"I read that in the guidebook. It is a philosophy with many interesting implications."

"I'll need the name of your taxi service. Society guidelines suggest not using the same name your uncle used."

"Like a company name?" Miko asked.

"Yes. Of course, it's not a registered company. But it's for the passengers. A name helps make our documents indistinguishable from those they have seen issued by the government."

Miko didn't know what name to choose. She searched her room for inspiration.

Her gaze came to rest on the top of her bookshelf.

With a peaceful mind-sigh, the name became obvious.

"The name is Hidden Stealth Ninja Taxi Service."

Nagao laughed. "I like it. That's the best one yet. I can pick you up, say, at 11:30 am outside the donburi shop?"

Miko agreed.

Hanging up, Miko brushed her fingers along the spines of her favorite manga, *Hidden Stealth Ninja*. Checking none of the prized volumes were protruding.

"Time to head out," Miko told Fluffy Kitty.

"So much outsideness lately. It is good for my fur."

"It's good for my chances of love and friendship too," Miko said, as she made ready. "Every day I hid in my room was a lost opportunity. It kept me safe from my fears, but it also guaranteed I wouldn't meet people. I was making my fear of being lonely come true."

"Not anymore."

"I know. Each time I go outside I feel like I'm rolling dice. Each time there is a small chance I could meet someone. And a small chance is much better than no chance at all."

"You're no longer making regrets, you're making opportunities!"

"Yes, exactly that. And I also know no one else will do it for me, I must do it myself. It has to be me."

Miko was about to put on her shoes.

And while I'm talking about being brave, maybe I will find my letter-opening courage later?

She took the pale blue envelope down from the fridge's letter holder and slid it into her jacket pocket.

Next, Miko put on her sneakers and placed a hand on the apartment's door handle.

The fear of the outside was still there, along with the taut strings of the apartment's warmth pulling her back. But what had once been overpowering was now easy to resist.

Miko opened the door and stepped out into the world.

Outside, it was cloudy and cold. A chill breeze rolled sharply down the line of the narrow street, biting Miko's nose and nibbling at her ears as she walked towards the donburi shop.

Oh no.

There ahead was the old man who didn't like her.

He had his back to her. But she recognized him easily.

I must not fear rejection. Rejection cannot be allowed to turn my world into a twisty maze.

Miko breathed deeply and kept walking.

The man was saying his goodbyes to two women his age.

The women were short and scraggly. Wrapped in long sensible dark coats. From their similar faces, Miko guessed they were the man's sisters.

The old man turned and began walking towards Miko. Tugging at his white goatee beard.

Moments later, he saw her.

First, he looked at the ground. Then as he approached her, he turned his head away, as if he had found something intensely fascinating about the glass door of the apartment building he was passing.

But this time, he was walking towards Miko Nishimura Version 2.0, who had jumped and bounced in the company of many love-soaked Aftershave fans.

Unlike before, Miko didn't need to look away to protect herself.

Miko glanced at him as they passed on the street.

In the glass door's reflection, his old-man-face was contorted in anguish.

Miko missed a step. She scrabbled for the next two footfalls to keep her footing before recovering.

My face tortures this man's soul!

Ahead, the two presumed sisters were looking at Miko too.

Miko passed the two women.

"It could be Kana," one woman whispered behind her.

"Only if she had never aged," the other whispered back. "She would look older now."

Miko stopped. She turned and faced them.

Talking to complete strangers was still a scary thing, but this time her curiosity had overpowered her fear; something her curiosity could never have done before the live show.

"Who is Kana?" Miko asked.

"Our brother's daughter," the woman said. She seemed embarrassed. "I'm sorry. But you strongly resemble Kana."

"What happened to her?"

"We don't know for sure," the other woman said. "Obito didn't like Kana's law school friends, and they had a substantial argument about the boy she was dating. Kana moved out the weekend after, and we never heard from her again. That was almost twenty years ago."

"Why doesn't your brother try to find his daughter?"

"When she went, Kana made her father promise to leave her alone. Obito doesn't break his promises."

"You young people would consider him old-fashioned in this way."

"That's such a sad story," Miko said.

"Child, the world is full of sad stories," said the one who had seemed embarrassed. "There are more sad stories than there are happy."

"I hope that isn't true," Miko said.

She farewelled the women.

"Miko! All those times before, he wasn't rejecting you. Instead, he was memory-suffering," Fluffy Kitty said.

"I know. How silly I was. I assumed my own fears were real and projected them onto his actions. How many other times have I done that with other people? When they were not even thinking the thoughts I assumed they were. I will never again presume to know what others think of me."

"I like how you're reviewing your mindset, Miko. You are growing wise."

Miko laughed at the idea of being called wise.

When Junpei was not working as a mechanic or dropping ball bearings at a pachinko parlor, he read manga and watched anime.

A lot of manga and anime. Much more than most Japanese. Even more than most other manga and anime *otaku*—the Japanese name for someone with obsessive interests.

So much so that since childhood, the tropes and themes of manga and anime had shaped many of the neural pathways in his brain.

Junpei's mind had been electrified when his senpai had arrived yesterday with this epic dark blue taxi, and by the promise of adventure personified in its girly owner. She was like an anime character, but he wasn't sure which one.

This morning he had seen the name of the world's greatest manga, *Hidden Stealth Ninja*, written on the taxi's documents in his senpai's office.

None of this was coincidence.

His bones vibrated with expectation.

Somehow Junpei knew that in the years laid out before him, before dying as an old man, he would never again be so close to what he sought in his endless hours of scanning manga pages and staring at flashing anime pixels on his phone.

He must figure out the mystery of this woman and her taxi. This would be his only chance.

Junpei observed through his senpai's office window as the woman had her picture taken. Her white toy cat sat next to the computer as she stood face on to Nagao. Nagao had his Polaroid instant camera out from the drawer below the office shrine.

The Polaroid. That confirmed it, along with the special log sheets his senpai kept separate.

Junpei had seen these strange proceedings before. Who were these people?

He continued stealing glances as he brushed the rust off the brake caliper gripped tight in the bench's vise. His wire brush grasping and swishing in his hand.

The mystery people he'd seen before were men. But this one was a woman.

She acted sweet and cute, and so shy.

But Junpei wasn't stupid. Her demeanor was obviously a trick. There was no way an inconsequential girl could control a monster machine like her taxi.

More significant was the fact that the other mystery people only ever brought in ordinary taxis for repair.

Those taxis were unmodified, standard cars from the factory. But this taxi, this wonderful machine only meters away, was a beast's beast. Designed by some mechanical genius to rip innocent roads into shrapnel.

What is she? A bank robber? A spy? An assassin?

An assassin!

It was obvious. Who else would need a race car disguised as a taxi? She could pick up her high-profile victims by pretending to be a driver for a taxi service and then outrun any police who might give chase.

With this car she could outrun the police helicopter!

Junpei stopped glancing up so often. In case the dangerous woman saw.

It was the perfect setup. Her sweet mannerisms were disarming. Her face was altered by plastic surgery to look J-Pop cute. A puffer jacket to hide her toned muscles. Everything about her was purposely designed to fool her targets into relaxing. Then BANG!

Where does she keep her silenced pistol?

In the cat, of course.

The furry toy was the perfect size to hide a small automatic gun.

"Junpei-san," the deadly assassin woman said. She was standing next to him. "Nagao-san said you worked the whole night on my taxi."

Junpei's wire brush froze. The woman's face made quick work of mesmerizing him. Like it must have done to her many victims.

His boss, Nagao, was there too.

The woman had her lethal toy cat cradled in one arm. Ready to use.

"It was so kind of you. I cannot thank you enough," the killer said.

She smiled at him.

What a smile!

Instantly Junpei's heart melted into a puddle of molten gold that fell and sloshed around inside his work boots.

The loud workshop compressor kicked in, topping up its air reservoir.

At the noise the woman startled back. Her jacket catching the end of a long 40mm wrench protruding over the edge of the workbench.

The big wrench fell, striking its head on the concrete floor.

It cartwheeled end over end across the floor, clink clink clink. Before hitting a leg on the opposite workbench's corner.

The wrench clattered to the ground and disappeared, flat-spinning wildly into the gloom under the long wooden bench.

"I'm so sorry!" the assassin said.

"Don't worry about it," Nagao said.

Junpei was impressed. She had acted genuinely startled. She was obviously a professional of the highest rank. The type of assassin only oligarchs and governments could afford.

And apprentice mechanic Junpei loved her.

She could kill him if she wanted to.

If it would make her happy.

He just wanted her to be happy.

After a few false starts, Junpei managed to say that staying up all night to work on her amazing taxi was nothing.

He wanted to say more, but his boss took the woman to her taxi and mounted something inside on its dashboard.

Junpei tried to listen to what his boss was saying. But apart from earnest thanks for finding his lost dog, he couldn't hear anything else from their conversation.

Minutes later, the taxi started. Filling the workshop with an ominous rumble.

The mystery woman put her fluffy-white-cat-encased pistol on the dashboard before reversing her taxi out on to the road.

Then she was gone.

"Junpei. Find that wrench before we forget about it," Nagao said.

"Yes, Senpai."

Junpei got on his hands and knees. It took a while before he located the end of the wrench hidden in the dark on the concrete floor behind dirty cardboard boxes under the bench's lower shelf.

Junpei had to get down on his stomach to reach. He crawled forward. Pulling the heavy boxes filled with metal spares and big greasy bolts out of the way.

He wriggled on his belly into the range of the wrench.

He reached forward and grasped the wrench.

Junpei froze.

There was a glint of gold in the gloom, only inches beyond his hand.

Something was hidden. Jammed between a workbench leg and the workshop's cinder block wall.

Junpei reached and pulled at the object. It came out easily.

A thin rectangular plastic container, etched with gold writing and covered in iridescent holograms.

Encased in the transparent middle of the container was a ten-gram gold bar.

Junpei hyperventilated. His hand shook.

Forgetting the wrench, he pushed himself out backwards from under the bench.

"Senpai! Senpai!" he called, sitting up cross-legged on the floor, cradling the small container in both hands.

Nagao came running from his office.

"What is it Junpei? Are you OK?"

"Senpai. My pachinko token. I found my pachinko token!"

He held up the glittering object for his boss to see.

On the other side of his office floor's tinted windows, high over the sparkling city, the starless night sky was inky blue.

Inside, the droning air conditioning abraded his mind like desert sand blowing across exposed skin.

The dry air. The clickety-click of fingers tapping laptop keys. The tight restriction around his throat from his cheap business shirt and the inverted hangman's noose that was his tie. Above, the over-bright glare of the cream-tiled ceiling's fluorescent tubes.

The salaryman inhaled desperation and exhaled weariness. The office's split-flap clock mounted high on a pillar clacked over to 6:56 pm.

His strict-faced boss appeared next to him.

The salaryman stood to show his respect. He nodded constantly while his boss talked, and made soft I-understand-you noises like "heee and mmmmm and oooh" with the occasional touch of "arrr".

"This evening there's a place near Ikebukuro Station I wish to try," his boss said.

"Heee. Oh, sounds good," the salaryman said, and nodded more vigorously.

"We'll catch the train together."

"Mmmmm, yes, of course," the salaryman said, nodding like his boss's words were a stunning revelation. Then realizing his boss had finished, the salaryman transformed his nodding into bowing.

His boss strode off to inform the next team member about where they'd drink tonight.

Ikebukuro Station? That's Toshima Ward. Why so far?

Five years ago, when recruited by Pēpāwāku Masutā Corporation straight from university, he had stood tall in this same office.

His recruit-suit pressed. His eager mind soaking in young pride and relief at having been selected.

During his first three years of working, the salaryman discovered deliberately oversleeping on the weekends was enough to refresh him for the next week's work.

But in the two following years, his weekend sleep strategy reduced in effectiveness.

Until he bottomed out.

During this past year, he had been as hollow each Monday morning as on the preceding Friday night.

This depleting trend can't be good. I am walking a path I have not chosen, towards a destination I don't want to go.

It disturbed him that he couldn't remember the last time he had been happy. Like a deceased man's electrocardiogram, the salaryman's life-joy graph was a flat line from one side of the screen to the other.

He daydreamed, as he often did, about visiting his sisters. It was guaranteed they'd cheer him up. But visiting them had proved impossible. It had been over two years since he had last seen them in person.

At 7:08 pm, the office workers quivered in unison as Ken'Ichi Yoshimoto got up from his window seat and started his rounds of the bosses' desks.

Ken'Ichi's evening task was to report when Chairman Tarō Ikari walked down the office complex's wide marble stairs towards his waiting limousine.

Chairman Ikari was the big boss of Ikari Conglomerate. The conglomeration that owned Pēpāwāku Masutā Corporation. He also was the leading member of Japan's most powerful keiretsu.

This made Chairman Ikari one of Japan's most important men.

The entire office waited for the Chairman to leave, because in Japanese business tradition it is rude to leave before your boss.

Leaving earlier threatens your career prospects. To enforce this Japanese workers are expected to call out loudly when they arrive at work and again when they leave, preventing them sneaking off home without being noticed.

While most Japanese companies do not make their workers wait for their executive leader to finish, Ikari Conglomerate had taken the wait-for-your-boss practice to the next level.

Now Chairman Ikari had left, the lesser bosses could go. After the lesser bosses, their team members could leave too.

Such was the long tradition practiced at the Tokyo headquarters of Ikari Conglomerate.

With the Chairman gone, the salaryman and his teammates kept working diligently, or more accurately, expertly mimicking diligent work.

They kept a furtive eye on their boss's separated desk, which crossed the T at the end of their team's twin rows of long communal desks.

When their boss started packing items into his briefcase, that would be the signal to begin cleaning their own desk areas. In strict compliance with the company's "5S" methodology: Sort, Set in order, Shine, Standardize, and Self-discipline.

To prepare for his next day's work, the salaryman would clean his desk and ensure his stapler and ruler and pencils were in the exact location the company had determined maximized workplace organization and productivity.

Afterwards would come their train journey to Toshima Ward for tonight's boozy *nomination*† drinking party.

At eight that Monday evening, Miko's taxi was parked on a side street in Bunkyo Ward.

Miko had been having fun driving fast. The taxi felt more alive after being fixed. The engine had been sluggish before, but now it revved eagerly up to the 11,000 RPM red line on the dashboard's tachometer.

Miko was reading by the light of the taxi's ceiling-mounted courtesy light. Inspecting the synopses of her fresh batch of books from the library.

When the librarians saw Miko's library card, they were pleased to meet her at last. They asked about her mother, admired Fluffy Kitty, and made comical comments about being overly jealous of her parents' ocean cruise.

Republic by Plato was a thick book Miko had read before, but that was several years ago and this was a new translation with a revised commentary.

Meditations by Marcus Aurelius looked intriguing, and the man on the cover had an impressive beard.

One Hundred Years of Solitude by Gabriel García Márquez had been on Miko's reading list for a long time. So it had excited her to discover the library had a copy.

The *Makioka Sisters* by Tanizaki Jun'ichirō was like a Jane Austen novel. Miko enjoyed Jane Austen's novels and had read each Japanese translation.

"So, what have you decided to do with the envelope?" Fluffy Kitty said.

"Oh that," Miko said.

She fished the envelope out of her jacket.

"I can't email Mother and Father and ask their permission, because just knowing about the letter's existence will make them worry. I don't want to spoil their vacation."

"Be brave. It's OK to make big decisions when you're an adult."

Miko sighed. "I guess you are right."

She turned the envelope over and took several minutes carefully prising the flap open. She didn't tear a single part.

There was a thick folded cream sheet of bank letterhead inside.

Typed below the bank's name was a terse letter signed by the bank manager.

Oh no.

"Miko. What is it?"

"It's really bad."

"What?"

---

† The Japanese word "nomination" is a combination of the Japanese word "nomi" which means drink, and the English word "communication". It refers to the art of communicating while drinking alcohol. Another Japanese word "nomikai" means a drinking meeting or party, where colleagues and clients can get to know each other better.

"Mother and Father owe a lot of money. And the bank is demanding payment before the end of January."

"How? Your parents paid this month and prepaid next month. They won't owe anything more until the end of February."

"Wait, I want to understand it," Miko said. She forced herself to read the letter again. Calmly.

"OK. So it's saying when the bank did the manual transaction to pay January 2014 in advance, they discovered my parent's loan had been set up incorrectly in their system eight years ago. The wrong algorithm had been selected to calculate the loan's interest rate."

"That isn't your parents' fault."

"I know. And the manager says that too and apologizes. But he also says Mother and Father are 'contractually obligated' to make up the extra accumulated interest. From the tone of this letter, I don't believe they're going to back down."

"How much?"

Miko showed Fluffy Kitty the figure.

"That's a lot!"

"It's over two mortgage payments. Mother and Father have calculated their vacation budget down to the last yen. They don't have the money."

"You have to tell your parents."

"No. Not yet. It will wreck their vacation. Father will be filled up with anxiety. They'll end their trip and fly home. I can't let their cherished dream turn into a nightmare."

Miko rubbed her face, hoping the letter on her lap would vanish. But when she opened her eyes, it was unfortunately still there.

"Uncle Ken will not be thinking clearly at the moment. So I will keep it a secret until New Year's Day. Then Uncle Ken will know what to do. Maybe we can borrow the money from him and pay off the bank. Spreading out the repayments over time so Mother and Father can afford it."

"That's a good idea. Then you wouldn't have to tell your parents until they return. You will have saved their vacation."

"Yes," Miko said. "That would be an effective solution."

Movement in Miko's peripheral vision made her glance up.

An old lady with a walking cane and two plastic shopping bags stood on the sidewalk, gently waving to get Miko's attention. Miko lowered the front passenger window.

A boy of about eight or nine ran along the path and stood next to her. He wore a black and blue checkered coat and blue jeans.

"Hello. My grandson and I would like to go to my apartment. It is by the corner of Kasuga Ave and Denzuinmae Street."

The past five days, when she wasn't driving, Miko had been memorizing maps of Tokyo.

"That's about two kilometers away. Were you going to walk home with those bags?"

"Yes. It seemed like a good plan at the time. Oh, you're not in uniform. I don't mean to impose on your night off."

I can't not help her. And then I will know if I enjoy being a taxi driver.

"Don't worry. I can still take you to your home."

Miko pressed the button to open the taxi's rear passenger door. She started the engine and the taxi's meter.

The old lady chatted as Miko drove.

"What a clever driver you are. Not using a map or phone to navigate."

"Thank you."

"Oh look, I do enjoy seeing the city birds. There are so many new varieties in Tokyo, for the longest time we would only see crows, pigeons, and sparrows."

"I've always seen lots of types here. They're so pretty, and friendly too," Miko said. Slowing at an intersection.

"I can tell from your accent you're not from Tokyo."

"I migrated from Aomori Prefecture eight years ago."

"Well, that makes sense, because migratory birds don't use maps either. They follow their heart and end up exactly where they are meant to go."

The nice thought made Miko smile.

"Grandma! Look," the boy said, pointing at the taxi's license mounted on the dashboard. "Hidden Stealth Ninja Taxi Service!"

The boy jiggled excitedly in the rear vision mirror, like he was first in line to ride Splash Mountain at Tokyo Disneyland.

"Don't yell," the old lady said. "You'll hurt the nice driver's ears."

"My friends won't believe me. Hidden Stealth Ninja Taxi Service!"

"You're yelling again. I'm sorry, it's his favorite manga."

"Grandma, can I talk to the driver?"

"Only if you do it in a normal voice."

"Driver. Driver," the boy said, in an almost-whisper.

"Hello," Miko said.

"Do you know the answer to the great debate?"

"The great debate? Sorry, I don't think I do."

"Can I tell you my idea? Can I tell her Grandma?"

Miko chuckled at his enthusiasm.

"Of course you can tell me."

"So, I agree with the side that says Hidden Stealth Ninja is both a human and a partly magical being."

"I guess he could be," Miko said.

"But," the boy said. "And this is my idea. I don't think Hidden Stealth Ninja knows he is magical. I bet he thinks he is ordinary. No different from ordinary humans like us."

"How could he not know?" the old lady said.

"Because he's so used to his powers they seem normal to him. So he doesn't notice. Like when I eat rice, I taste rice, but how do I know other people taste rice the same as I do? Maybe they taste something different. Maybe they don't taste anything. How could I tell? Maybe Hidden Stealth Ninja can't tell either? I bet he assumes everyone experiences life the same way he does."

"I'm sorry," the old lady said. "He has so many ideas. He drives his parents crazy."

"It's fine," Miko said. "I had many ideas when I was young too. I like his idea."

The trip took a few minutes. Traffic was light.

"Thank you. I adore your cute cat," the old lady said, as Miko stood by the door to help them out of the taxi.

The old lady paid Miko in coins.

Miko stood next to her taxi, appreciating the shiny coins in her hand. *My first fare. It felt nice making their lives better.*

It was 11:34 pm. The salaryman, his boss, and eight other colleagues were on their third nominication bar of the night.

The heavy drinking meant he was thoroughly sloshed.

There had been karaoke singing; but the salaryman wasn't sure when or where.

His brain was operating like a fat man running across melting ice. It took a long time for his mind to slide to a stop, to focus on anything, and often the thing that came into focus was not the object he had intended.

He had even started forgetting to show proper respect by keeping his glass lower than his seniors when clinking with an enthusiastic *kanpai!*

Ponytailed Marisa was about to cry. She wanted to be at home with her husband. But Marisa also wanted her job, so here she was. It was expected.

The salaryman felt sorry for her in a vague sort of way. Then that feeling morphed into concern about the lights hanging above their table, which had begun moving in ways they shouldn't in the copious amounts of wafting cigarette smoke.

The salaryman didn't smoke, but his colleagues were volcanoes.

At 12:04 am his boss thanked everyone for coming in a slurring speech that lasted a triple age of the Earth.

By 12:12 am the salaryman was outside in the cool air.

Lovingly bidding his colleagues a safe night and good journey, somewhere, wherever they were going. His use of *keigo* respectful language failed several times with his seniors, but they didn't seem to notice in their similar drunk state.

It was too late for the trains. And even if it wasn't, he couldn't be bothered figuring out which trains to catch. And anyway, he couldn't remember the way back to Ikebukuro Station.

He walked the streets of Toshima Ward. His surroundings distorting like he was a fish viewing the world through its watery bowl. Seeking a taxi to take him home.

He staggered up to the first parked taxi.

A green and red taxi from Chakapoco Taxi Service.

The driver saw him, but oddly didn't open the taxi's rear door.

The salaryman tapped on the taxi's rear window. The driver powered it down.

"Where are you going?" the heavily mustached driver asked.

The salaryman gave him his address.

"Sorry. Can't help you. Kashiwa City is east of here," the driver said.

"What? I don't understand."

The driver's mustache twitched. He pointed at his taxi's roof.

"Are you stupid? Finding it hard to read in your inebriated state?" the driver said.

"What?" the salaryman managed again.

"Read the sign," the driver said.

"Um, Chak-a-po-co Taxi Service."

"Exactly. We don't head east. We don't head west. We don't head south. Chakapoco Taxi Service only goes north."

"What?" the salaryman said.

The taxi driver rudely powered up his rear window. Leaving the salaryman staring at his own confused reflection in the raised glass.

He staggered on. When he asked, the next taxi had no problem with traveling towards any point on the compass.

Soon the salaryman was sitting in the taxi's rear seat. His forehead pressed against cold glass, staring out at scrolling electrically lit streets.

At 12:55 am, he arrived at his apartment.

At 1:11 am, after a quick shower and vigorous teeth brushing, he changed into his shorts and fell into bed.

In five hours and nineteen minutes his alarm would wake him. Then his day would repeat. The same loop, over and over.

He groaned, and sank into a nightmareless slumber.

Tuesday morning, Miko parked her taxi in a narrow private car park in Arakawa Ward. She paid for an hour and placed the meter's ticket inside on her taxi's dashboard.

"Are you really going to do this?" Fluffy Kitty asked.

"I want to be happy. Also, I know other people want to be happy. So how can Miko Nishimura desire joy for herself, while not wanting the same for others? She cannot be a selfish person. So I have decided that when I find an opportunity to make someone happy, then I will do my best to help them."

"But shouldn't you put your own happiness first? Why take risks for others?"

"Because I cannot bear seeing other people unhappy."

"You can't fix the world, Miko."

"Maybe I can. Maybe I can't. But that doesn't stop me from wanting to."

And the truth is, I might never have happiness in my life. In reality, I will probably always be alone because of my troublesome face. But even if that sad result happens, I will still help others. They can be happy instead, and I will find my joy through their smiles.

Walking a block east, Miko stopped in front of a squat two-story office building. Mink gray and well maintained.

The name of a law firm in shiny brass above its twin mirrored glass doors.

Miko stared at her reflection, split down the middle by the gap between the glass doors. She breathed deeply, went to move, but remained still.

Her heartbeat increasing. Her stomach twisting. A minute passed. She lifted her heel to take a step, but faltered.

A flash of memory. The three Aftershave girls resplendent in their costumes, talking to thousands of people.

If they can do that big thing. Then I can do this little thing.

Miko stepped forward. The twin doors slid aside.

Inside was the office's reception area.

Glossy magazines on a coffee table. Glass-walled meeting rooms to one side. Designer chairs that were stylish, but looked uncomfortable.

The receptionist was applying Stay On Balm Rouge lipstick. The older lady inspected Miko, and Fluffy Kitty's face poking out from Miko's jacket.

"Cute cat," the receptionist said with a smile.

Miko lightened at the friendly welcome.

"How can I help?" the receptionist asked.

"My name is Miko Nishimura. I'd like to talk to one of your lawyers. Kana Narita. I apologize, but I don't have an appointment."

"I knew it would be Kana. I'll see if she is free. Can I tell her what it is about?"

"Her father."

Miko waited. Sitting in a surprisingly comfortable, uncomfortable chair.

Several minutes passed before three people emerged from a door next to the reception desk.

One was Kana in a dark gray business skirt and jacket. The other two were suited men. One Kana's age with small ears, the other much older with tight gray curly hair.

The three of them stared at Miko.

"Kana. Miko could be your daughter," the receptionist said.

"An amazing resemblance," the younger man said.

It is a good sign the receptionist feels able to talk freely to her seniors. However, it is disconcerting to meet someone with my face. Is this how I will look when I am old?

"Let's use the Amanokaze Room," the younger man said.

Inside the glass-walled meeting room, the older man took the seat farthest from the door. Kana sat next to him, and the younger man sat across the table next to Miko. Miko was closest to the door.

The receptionist brought in bottled water, four glasses, and paper coasters embossed with the firm's name.

The younger man's name was Noboru Iwai, and Miko could tell the stern old man was Kana's senpai.

Miko explained why she had come to see Kana.

"How did you find me?" Kana asked, after taking time to digest Miko's explanation.

"I searched online for lawyers in Tokyo with your first name. An article came up you wrote about property liens, and your picture looked like me. And Arakawa is close to Bunkyo too. But I didn't know for sure it was you. Until now."

"My father didn't send you?"

"No. I've never spoken to him. Just your two aunties."

"You chose to come here by yourself?" Noboru said.

"Yes. Kana's father and her aunties have no idea I'm here."

"Your visit disturbs many old ghosts," Kana said. "In twenty-one years, he has not chosen to contact me."

"Your aunties said when you left, you made your father promise to never contact you again. They also said he doesn't break his promises."

Kana looked up at the ceiling, her mouth slightly open. A long moment passed.

"Did your father make that promise?" Noboru asked.

"He might have. In the heat of the moment, I may have demanded it. I can't recall."

Kana closed her eyes and pursed her lips.

Minutes passed in silence before she opened her eyes again.

"Miko. It has been many years. I feel it has been too long."

"Kana-san. I cannot tell you what to do," Miko said. "But for me, I don't know how I'd be without my parents. There would be a deep hole in my world. As you said, your father is the only immediate family you have left. It is true you fought with him. However, most families fight occasionally. I am wondering why your father doesn't deserve a second chance? Don't we all deserve a second chance?"

"I hate to say it, but I don't need him anymore. I'm sorry to be honest with you," Kana said.

"Family are not paper cups we throw away once the drink has gone," Miko said. Tapping firmly on the table. "Unending grief transforms love into never-ending pain. I saw the evidence of your father's anguish in that door's reflection. Maybe you don't need your father, Kana. But I am telling you that your father needs you."

For an instant the glass meeting room rang like a bell.

The air smelled alive, as if there had been a thunderstorm.

Kana shrank in her chair like a scolded child, clasping her hands, chin lowered, looking up at Miko with wide eyes.

Kana's senpai made an almost imperceptible grunt.

Noboru studied Miko afresh, like a man suddenly discovering he was sitting next to someone famous.

"I'm not sure what you want me to do," Kana said.

"I drive a taxi. I will drive you to your father's home. Knock on his door. I'll drive you straight back if it doesn't work out."

"You mean now?"

"This moment," Miko said. "Or I fear you never will. Today is New Year's Eve. It is the perfect time."

The lawyer looked at her senpai. The only sign Miko detected was a momentary dropping of her senpai's face. A sort of half nod.

"I will come with you," Kana said.

Half an hour later Kana was sitting in the back of Miko's moving taxi.

"I have not been down these streets for a long time."

"Nice memories?" Miko asked.

"Bittersweet. Walking to school with my friends. Falling off my bike on that driveway when I was seven. There used to be a *wagashi*† shop over there. Its owner was an artisan chef who made these *imagawayaki* that resembled an orange. Their sponge interior was segmented like an orange. The bean paste was orange-colored too. There was no taste of beans or orange skin when you took a bite. Instead the whole imagawayaki had the juicy fresh taste of a peeled orange. Mouthwatering."

"Mmmm, so yummy sounding," Miko said. "I very much wish I had a time warp machine so I could travel back in time and try one."

Kana went quiet as the taxi turned down the street to her father's home.

Miko pulled over two doors down. She switched off the rumbling engine.

"I have discovered everything good is hard," Miko said. She activated the taxi's rear door.

Kana gave Miko a half-smile and stepped out of the taxi.

Miko watched from inside the taxi as Kana crossed the road to her father's door.

"Miko. You were forceful in the meeting. I have never seen you like that before," Fluffy Kitty said.

"I was angry. And what Uncle Ken said about there being too many rules is growing into a strong tree inside me. So I have decided that, when needed, I will speak my mind even if I am of lower position or it risks upsetting group harmony."

"Those seniors paid attention to you. They did what you instructed. It was like you were the senpai and they the *kōhai*."‡

"That is because what I said made sense."

---

† Wagashi are traditional Japanese confections made of rice cake, bean paste, and fruit.
‡ Kōhai means junior person.

"You're so brave, Miko. I wonder what is about to happen with Kana and her father?"

"Dear cat, my books have taught me that some cultures view time as a continuous thread. Others see time as a series of important moments. Like pearls on a necklace. For Kana and her father, this next moment will become a pearl. But a white pearl or a black pearl? I can't tell."

Kana took a long time to work up her courage.

Finally, with a straight back, she stepped forward and knocked.

Nothing happened. The door remained closed. Miko worried that Kana's father wasn't home.

But then the door opened a hand's width. It closed. Before opening fully.

The old man stood in the doorway with his white hair and white goatee. Hooking a dangling security chain into its holder on the door's jamb.

Next, he faced his visitor.

At first, his face was frozen. Then came a strong inhale, like he had been dropped into an icy river.

He shook, clasped his hands together and dropped to his knees, bowing his head before his daughter.

In Japan, bowing while on your knees is how you say sorry for the worst of failings.

Her father was either sobbing or repeating a phrase. From the taxi Miko couldn't make out which.

Kana took half a step back.

With his head still bowed, her father reached his clasped hands out towards her.

Miko suspected her father had rehearsed this meeting many times in his mind.

Will it end like Obito-san imagined?

Kana's stiff-backed business-person stance thawed. She stepped forward and clasped her father's hands.

At the touch, the old man began clearly sobbing and bowed lower.

Kana rested her right hand on her father's head. His sobbing subsided. She was saying something to him.

Whatever she said made her white-haired father look up at her. His teary eyes shining.

Kana took her father's arm and helped him to his feet. She walked him indoors, closing the door behind them.

Three minutes later, Miko's phone beeped with a message.

Miko. You don't need to wait. I will be here the rest of the afternoon. Thank you.

Miko showed the text to Fluffy Kitty.

"That is a good sign."

"It is. But the next time Obito-san sees me on the street, that's when we'll know for sure. Will he look away, or will he be happy to see my face?"

Miko started the engine and drove her taxi off from the curb.

It wasn't until New Year's Day that Miko could see Uncle Ken again.

The first day of 2014 was sunny and windy, and significantly warmer than the last days of the past year.

Miko decided not to tell Uncle Ken about the bank letter until after they had celebrated.

"Happy New Year, Uncle Ken!"

"Happy New Year, Niece Miko!"

They toasted each other with hot green tea and exchanged New Year postcards. They had agreed to hand deliver their postcards since it seemed silly to post them. Uncle Ken's green-pen writing was wobbly but still readable.

On the dining table sat *osechi-ryōri*† in two sets of three-tiered wooden *jūbako* boxes.

In the box's compartments there were simmered shrimp, broiled fish cake called *kamaboko*, black soybeans called *kuro-mame*, *datemaki* sweet rolled omelets, pickled vegetables, *tazukuri* dried sardines, and many other tasty things, including a grilled lobster each.

There were compartments filled with appetizers and sweets too. Next to the boxes, Uncle Ken had also placed bitter oranges.

"This truly is a feast, Uncle Ken. I believe you want your niece to be fat like Pusheen."

"Hey, no rival cats allowed," Fluffy Kitty said.

"We are celebrating your emergence from hiding, Miko. And your uncle's happiness at not being alone on New Year's Day."

"To new beginnings," Miko said.

"New beginnings."

They clinked their cups together.

Once they had enjoyed their New Year's Day feast and cleaned up, Miko sat Uncle Ken down at his kitchen table.

"I have a very serious issue I need to discuss with you," Miko said.

"Go ahead," Uncle Ken said.

She explained about her parents paying their January mortgage in advance.

Then she read the bank's letter to Uncle Ken.

Uncle Ken proceeded to say some extremely rude things about the bank manager. Then apologized to Miko's burning ears.

"It is good you found the letter. Otherwise, the payment would be overdue by the time your parents returned. But I can't afford that much,"

† Osechi-ryōri are traditional Japanese New Year foods. Often served in compartmentalized jūbako boxes.

Uncle Ken said. "My savings are gone. I only have my disability payment, which barely covers my weekly expenses. So I will phone the bank when they open on Monday and try to sort out a payment plan. My name is on the loan documents as guarantor, so there's a chance they'll talk with me. Otherwise, I could remortgage this apartment."

Miko was ashamed. Uncle Ken had used some of his savings to fight Nurse Goto's false accusations. Every year he had bought Miko expensive birthday presents.

"No, Uncle Ken. I will take on the responsibility to pay the bank," Miko said. "Before Mother and Father return. So they don't need to worry for a single second."

"How? You have no money."

"I will earn money by becoming a taxi driver."

"Are you sure?"

"I've already had my first fare."

Miko explained how she had enjoyed helping the old lady get home.

It is exciting to have a solution.

"And I love driving. So I can have fun while solving Mother and Father's bank problem. And I can earn enough to repay Hattori too," Miko said. Placing the coins from her first fare on the table.

"It could work," Uncle Ken said. "Let me give you some basic taxi driver advice."

He suggested forming a habit of immediately putting away a portion of each fare, so Miko could pay tax while also affording maintenance, tolls, and fuel.

With his guidance, Miko worked out on paper how much she needed to set aside each week to make the loan payment.

"And what about your share?" Miko asked.

"After the bank is paid, not before. Give me what you feel is fair for using the taxi. Not too much though, because you're doing the bulk of the work. In the end, what you earn is your money to do with as you please."

"I was thinking half."

"Too much. No, much less. Besides, afterwards you'll continue to help your parents too?"

"Of course. For twenty-six years they have carried me. I owe them a great debt. I am full of gratitudes towards Father and Mother."

"Good. And don't worry. Realize you're already making a payment to me. Sometimes I hear you driving my taxi. I can recognize the sound she makes a mile away. It makes me happy to hear my baby having fun."

Early afternoon the next day Miko was crouching down by the taxi in Uncle Ken's chilly garage. Her charcoal pencil marking the outline of her new company name on the taxi's front passenger side door.

The charcoal pencil wasn't the best tool for the job, but Miko only needed faint markings to guide her when she applied the acrylic lacquer.

Miko had calculated how much she needed to earn for each of the remaining twenty-nine days of January. To meet the bank's demand, repay Hattori, and have enough left over for living, tax, and fueling the taxi.

She would drive every day. No weekends off, until she achieved her goal. If she had a good day, then she would save the extra money to offset lean days.

I can't let my parents down. I can't let Hattori down.

She had drawn a bar chart in her notebook with twenty-nine hollow bars. Days of the month along the X-axis, and yen up the Y-axis. Each bar matching the height of her daily goal. At the end of each day, she would color in the day's bar with the amount she earned.

"Don't let that gunk near my fur. It'll never come off," Fluffy Kitty said, when Miko opened her pot of yellow paint.

"That's why you're on the workbench. Far away from danger."

Miko painted the characters for *Hidden Stealth Ninja Taxi Service* onto the taxi's front doors. The yellow looked striking against the taxi's glossy dark blue paint.

隠されたステルス忍者タクシーサービス

Miko liked that two of her favorite katakana characters were in the name: girl with long hair running ス, and the comical smiley face シ. Her other favorite characters were the enthusiastic smiley face ツ, and the winking smiley face ン, and the embarrassed smiley face ジ.

Afterwards, Miko masked off the doors with newspaper and tape.

A few hours later she returned and sprayed on a clear coat to protect the painted symbols.

"Let's get dinner. Tonight we will seek customers."

Miko ate alone at the *yakitori* shop. A deliberate strategy to help speed up the reduction of her fear of strangers.

The live show had taken the bulk of the fear away. But there was still residual unease she needed to work through.

Tonight, she would begin regularly carrying passengers in her taxi. She had to be able to interact with them professionally and proactively. She must not seem timid.

I'm handling spiders.

It was unsettling. To her left was a ruffled salaryman wolfing down his food. On her right a woman courier driver who ate with one hand while scrolling through fashion photos with her other. Miko felt the warmth of their presence. She could hear them breathing and chewing.

But Miko ate unhurriedly, refusing to give into the stirring panic.

Finished, Miko arranged her used stainless steel skewers neatly and picked her plate up with two hands from her segment of the long table and placed it in front of her on the high counter. To make it easier for one of the kitchen staff to collect. She exited the yakitori shop in a relaxed manner.

"Impressive, Miko," Fluffy Kitty said. "Could you have imagined doing that ten days ago?"

"I couldn't even leave the apartment ten days ago."

That evening, Miko took the taxi out.

Her first time as a taxi driver was a surreal experience. There was trepidation while hunting for fares. Surprised delight when people actually wanted her to drive them, and uneasiness when these strangers got into the taxi. Worry they might guess she was new on the job—making Miko concentrate hard on doing everything perfectly. And finally, happy relief when she arrived at the correct address, and her passengers paid their fare and thanked her for the trip.

"I can't believe it's working!" Miko said, after dropping off her first passengers.

"See, I knew you could do it," Fluffy Kitty said. "To be honest, sometimes I impress myself with how often I am right about things."

"You are so humble."

"I am very proud of how humble I am. It is one of my forty or fifty best characteristics."

Miko had three fares that evening. Two people who hailed her while she drove by, and a couple who walked up while she was parked.

The walk-up couple went from Kabukichō to their apartment near Fukaya Station. It was a long way, and so a big fare.

Miko wasn't sure why the couple didn't take the train, and felt lucky they had chosen her taxi.

By midnight, the amount of cash in her hand made the taxi business seem most promising. It wasn't enough to meet her goal for the day, but that was because she had only worked in the evening.

Miko had decided to work two shifts every day. One in the morning, and one in the evening. She was sure she could meet her daily goals that way, and her earnings would increase as she improved her customer-finding skills.

On the way back home from Fukaya, Miko tested how fast she could make the taxi go.

The answer was very very fast indeed. Uncle Ken's taxi was extremely powerful, and her racing game skills had translated directly into her ability to drive an actual car.

In a straight line, Fukaya was about seventy kilometers across Tokyo from Miko's home ward of Bunkyo.

At this time of night, Google Maps had estimated an hour to drive through Tokyo from Fukaya to the outskirts of Bunkyo Ward.

But Miko had driven the distance in under twenty minutes.

"Why do the other cars drive much slower than us?" Fluffy Kitty asked.

"They're driving at the speed limits set by the government."

"But why are those limits set to such slow speeds?"

"I have wondered that," Miko said. "I suspect they chose the speed limits to suit the lowest common denominators."

"The what?"

"The people least able to drive and the worst cars. In Japan there are many people over a hundred. So I theorize the government found some hundred-and-ten-year-old people, gave them micro-cars from the 1960s, and told them to drive around Tokyo. The government would have recorded what speed those old people were comfortable driving at. That's how they must have set the speed limits. Because I can't imagine another reason for setting the limits so far below a sensible driving speed."

"Like the speed we are driving?"

"Yes, exactly. It's a wonder people put up with driving so slow, they must feel frustrated every time they get in their cars."

Sporting a big smile, Miko arrived back at Uncle Ken's garage.

She reversed the taxi in. As she walked past the driver-side front wheel, she felt an intense heat baking through her jeans. The heat was radiating from the wheel's disk brake. Miko checked; both front brake disks were scorching hot, smoking a little, and even the taxi's tires were hot to the touch.

Driving. What a joyful experience.

"Dear cat. Be informed. Without doubt, Miko Nishimura has found her vocation."

The next day, in a ward close to where Miko lived in Bunkyo, a lanky middle-aged man was fast-walking.

Arato Asada stalked savagely, slicing through a group of young friends standing together in the chill evening air.

His gray synthetic fabric convenience store uniform rustling under his coat.

His well-worn army boots thumping the sidewalk with midfoot strikes, following how the authorities wisely instructed Japanese people to walk. Arato was aware governments in other countries didn't instruct their citizens in such matters. He couldn't imagine living with such uncertainty.

Arato snarled at the emasculated young men with their effeminate styles and demented thoughts about treating their women as equals. He glared at the young women out wandering the streets at night when they should be homemaking.

With wanting eyes, he noted the passing of each taxi. He had been a white-gloved taxi driver once. Until epilepsy brought on by the stress of his wife taking his son had invalidated his driving license.

He yearned to drive taxis again. But the doctors would not clear him until he had no epileptic episodes for five contiguous years.

"Curse you, witch, for what you did to me," Arato muttered.

He hadn't given her permission to leave, but the wench had gone anyway, taking his only son with her.

She had made many false accusations about him. Including that he had struck both of them with the back of his hand.

Remembering these claims made Arato thump the ground even harder. He had never hit his wife or their son. She had lied through her wizened lips to the police and the courts.

The avalanche of shame Arato endured, due to his wife's false words and the loss of his taxi job, had forced him to move from their apartment of many years to a part of Tokyo where no one knew him.

The judge had awarded his wife full custody of Nobuhiro.

Sixteen years had passed since Arato last saw his son. And more distressing than the lost time was the knowing, deep in his heart, that he would never see his son again.

A reunion was a hopeless dream for two reasons: first, because the courts forbade Arato from ever contacting Nobuhiro; and second, because Arato could imagine the malicious lies his ex-wife had invented to poison his son's mind against him.

Nobuhiro will be twenty-six this year. I had so much to teach him.

"Hey!" a young guy said as Arato barged past.

"Get a haircut. You look like a girl," Arato replied, without breaking stride.

He turned around a corner. A dark blue taxi was heading towards him.

He couldn't stand seeing women drive taxis. Their fragile temperament was not up to the task.

And this girl had a ridiculous white toy cat sitting on the dashboard.

How unprofessional! I shall report this infraction to her company office.

"Hidden Stealth Ninja Taxi Service?" Arato said. "What sort of name is that?"

Arato's mind clicked, almost audibly.

Could this be a renegade taxi?

His heart pounded.

Those scoundrels, stealing fares from licensed taxi drivers. They deserved to be thrown in prison.

The girl was too young. Most taxi drivers were in their forties.

In uniform, but no white gloves!

Not only was that unprofessional, but another clue pointing to an illegitimate taxi.

And the engine sound. What taxi sounds rough like that?

The taxi turned the corner and disappeared.

Tomorrow he would call his friend at his old taxi company and get him to check the registry for a Hidden Stealth Ninja Taxi Service.

If the company wasn't in the registry, he would know for certain he had detected a renegade taxi.

His next call would be to the local police.

Then Arato remembered tomorrow was Saturday.

He cursed under his breath. His taxi company friend didn't work on the weekends, and the police would not listen unless he had confirmed his suspicion.

He would have to wait until Monday to make his phone call.

His frustration was compounded by an urgent sense pushing at the back of his head. A sense that resonated with his anger. There was almost a voice riding on the harmonics: *This woman must be stopped. She is a threat to all legitimate taxi drivers.*

Now, somehow, Arato knew beyond doubt that he had discovered a renegade taxi. Which made his frustration even greater, because he would still have to wait until Monday to confirm that fact.

Only then could he call the police.

On Monday morning the 6th of January Miko finished cleaning up her breakfast. Her mother had put a glass jar of pickled eggs in the fridge. They had been tasty.

Her mother's flock of blue-yellow duck fridge magnets slid downwards when she closed the fridge door. Miko returned the lazy ducks to their assigned altitudes in their white metal sky.

Her phone played a tune. It was Uncle Ken.

"I phoned the bank. As I suspected, they cited the privacy laws and refused to discuss anything with me. It didn't matter that I am guarantor."

"But you are family. What if I called them?"

"I asked. They don't care that you are your parents' daughter. They'll only discuss the matter with the mortgagees named on the mortgage agreement."

It was disappointing news. However, the vanishing of that small hope and the realization there was now no other way forward, except to earn the required money, made Miko's determination set like molten sugar into hard candy.

She contemplated everything that had changed. Her first taxi weekend had exceeded her goals. At this rate she would soon have enough to repay Hattori and the extra mortgage interest her parents owed. She just had to keep the pace up.

After the phone call, Miko picked up Fluffy Kitty.

"I feel like a different person. The whole world is opening like a flower," Miko said. She placed a moleskin notebook her parents had given her for her birthday and Fluffy Kitty on the dining table.

"You aren't afraid anymore?" Fluffy Kitty said.

"Still afraid. But not super scared like I was before the live show. However, I am struggling with anxiety. Driving the taxi makes it go away. But otherwise, I am an anxious person."

"This makes me worry about you."

"Don't be. I have been considering this problem. My conclusion?

Anxiety is a good thing."

"Good? How can it be good?"

"Because I have trained my mind to step outside of myself when anxious, and be objective. I ask myself, 'why is Miko anxious?' I conclude it is because Miko fears something bad will happen in the future. Like freezing up when talking to people. Or becoming Christmas Cake. But conversely, I have also noticed there are many things Miko is not anxious about. Like not knowing how to play pachinko."

"But you have never been interested in pachinko."

"Exactly. I don't care about pachinko, or water skiing, or collecting stamps. So I have no anxiety about those things."

"Are you saying you need to learn to stop caring about the things that make you anxious?"

"No, dear cat. The opposite. What I am anxious about are the things I must care about more. My anxiety tells me what truly matters to me. I am anxious about talking to people, because I want to talk with people. I am anxious about spending my life alone, so I know I want a boyfriend. I am anxious about my parents deciding I am a burden, so I know I want to become a benefit to them instead. I am anxious about owing Hattori money, which tells me I must repay him."

"Miko! You have turned a bad thing into map directions for your life."

"Now you understand. Anxiety shows me what I desire. Therefore, I must press into those areas. I will learn to talk to people like the brave Aftershave girls. I will try to find someone to love. And I will help my parents with money to make their life easier. And, I am going to quickly repay Hattori."

"But I have seen the pain that anxiety causes you. I don't like seeing you in pain."

"Faithful cat, I have come to accept some bad news. That sometimes there is no way around painful feelings. Instead, I must push through the pain. So I have determined not to let my anxious feelings stop me anymore. They will not prevent Miko Nishimura from going forward into her dreams. Instead, I have decided to learn how to function despite my anxiety."

"Can you really do that?"

Miko carried Fluffy Kitty into her room so they could jointly appreciate the poster she had purchased of the Aftershave band. It was mounted with Blu Tack adhesive putty on the wall above her desk, next to Hattori's ticket.

"Our Aftershave girls must have been anxious about many things as they pursued their dream. I bet sometimes it was tough and depressing. But their success proves they pushed through their anxiety. And so, like them, I must do the same. There is no other way. Unless I am to shrink from what deep down I want to become and end up as a nothing person. But since I do not want to reach the end of my life hating myself, I will press forward."

"I desire to see my friend become stronger. I pledge my support to Miko the relentless."

"You are a good cat."

"And cheaper than most to feed."

Miko chuckled.

She admired the poster girls' cheerful yellow and orange clothes.

The photo had Kirari with her long black hair in the front, face on to the camera. Miyu and Ace stood back-to-back behind her.

Miko had selected this poster from the many of Aftershave, because each girl's hair seemed to merge into one. Flowing down like a waterfall to the bottom of the photo. This, Miko decided, symbolized the unity of their friendship.

I am also anxious that I have no friends. So, one day, hopefully, I will have friends too. Just like the lucky Aftershave girls.

Miko went into the living room, slid open the door to her father's plasticky smelling electronics cupboard, and rummaged around. She pulled out her father's old school yearbooks and placed them on the table.

"What are we doing?" Fluffy Kitty asked.

"Detective work. Let's see what we can find out about Uncle Ken's lost love, Suzu Mochizuki."

Miko poured through her father's yearbooks, searching for Suzu's name. It didn't take long to find her.

"Suzu was in the same year as Father and Uncle Ken," Miko said. "She is pretty."

The black and white photos showed Suzu with long straight hair and a quirky mischievous smile.

Miko searched through the photos around the articles and sports teams.

"Look. Suzu with two others," Miko said, indicating a photo of three girls posing with victory fingers.

Miko searched the yearbook portraits again. Until she found the other two.

"Yuko Takahashi and Sachiko Moriyama," Miko said, writing their names down in her notebook.

As she continued scanning the pages, Miko wondered if Yuko Takahashi was related to Mr. Takahashi the fish seller who had saved her from the bear.

"See. In this assembly photo. Yuko and Sachiko and Suzu are sitting together. That confirms their friendship."

Miko took copies of the photos with her phone's camera. Then transferred them to her laptop and printed them out on her parents' printer.

She stuck the photos onto the pad next to her detective notes.

Then she made ready to start her first taxi run of the day.

Police Superintendent Ritsu Shoji savored his second coffee of the morning.

He traced his finger down the line of a scar across his left cheek. The reminder of a knife fight he resolved when he was a junior police officer.

When angry, the scar bent into an inverted V. His underlings called this the "Twisted Warning", and knew then to be extra careful.

Superintendent Shoji's station ran like well-oiled clockwork. Everything that could be thought about had been thought about, and then doubly thought about just to make sure.

Each police officer and civilian who worked for him adhered to the discipline of *kodawari*, the relentless pursuit of perfection. His police station had the highest standards in Tokyo, and Superintendent Ritsu Shoji meant to keep it that way.

He placed his big coffee mug down on a polished silver coaster.

His desk phone rang. He punched a flashing line button.

"Superintendent Shoji."

"Superintendent. I have civilian Arato Asada on the line. He insists on talking to you about a renegade taxi operating in our area."

"Put him through."

Superintendent Shoji listened to Arato's story.

"And you are certain this company is not in the registry?"

Superintendent Shoji listened some more. He asked more questions. He chastised the man for not taking a photo of the taxi in question.

After thanking the concerned citizen, he hung up.

Superintendent Shoji could feel the tension in his cheek as his scar bent into the twisted warning.

In Japan, multiple policemen will chase on foot after a car that made an illegal U-turn. Bicycles are registered, and woe betide anyone caught riding a bicycle not registered to them. They shouldn't be surprised if they end up surrounded by police and spending a night being interrogated.

The Superintendent punched in a three-digit extension.

"Get in here."

Moments later, Police Chief Inspector Fuminori Kumazaki stood straight as a samurai spear in front of his boss's big government-issue desk. Notebook and pencil in hand.

Superintendent Shoji slid a sheet of paper across his desk to the Chief Inspector.

"We have a renegade taxi operating in our area. Do you think that is acceptable?"

"No, Superintendent."

"I want this woman apprehended immediately. And her taxi impounded."

"Sir. Within an hour, every officer will be searching for—" Chief Inspector Kumazaki said, picking up the piece of paper. "For a dark blue Toyota Crown Comfort Taxi with the company name 'Hidden Stealth Ninja Taxi Service'. I'll also have my team go over the surveillance camera recordings from that area when the taxi was reported."

"I believe you meant to say within half an hour, Chief Inspector. I will not suffer this sort of vehicular anarchy in my precinct."

"Yes sir. I will get the order out immediately."

At 2 pm that same Monday, a woman in a blue coat vigorously hailed Miko's taxi from outside a Hamster and Mouse clothing store.

"Hamster and Mouse" wasn't the store's real name of course, it was the nickname Miko had given the chain store because their shop logo only displayed the chain's initials. Obviously they wanted you to guess their full name, and that's what Miko had done. It made her happy to put some of the few English words she remembered from school to good use.

One of the other English words Miko remembered was the word "middle". At school she had noted the word middle started with the letter M, and amazingly, the letter M was in the middle of the alphabet. Her English teacher hadn't found this startling fact as interesting as Miko had, but then Miko was rather fond of the letter M.

The woman's tall male companion wore a tan coat. He slumped his shoulders and looked away as Miko pulled the taxi up next to them. She opened the rear door.

"Get in," the woman ordered.

Miko stiffened. Uncle Ken had warned her that some fares were not pleasant experiences.

The man pulled his coat up and slid into the taxi's back seat. His head hung low. He took a strong interest in his hands.

The woman got in beside him. She gave Miko their destination. Her eyes were bloodshot.

Miko closed the rear door and started the meter. She drove away from the glass-fronted clothing store.

"We don't have to do this," the man said.

"Ha! I'm not staying in this sham of a marriage a day longer," the woman said.

"But I do love you. Look, I'm saying it plainly, nothing more about the moon."

"More meaningless words. When's the last time you hugged or kissed me, without prompting?"

"Yesterday."

"I stood in the doorway blocking your way in, refusing to move until you greeted me. That's prompting."

"I'm just not wired to show affection. My family never showed affection. I still love you."

"I'm sick of talking in circles with you. Years pass and nothing changes," the woman said. "Driver."

"Yes," Miko said.

"We're going to the lawyers to stamp our divorce papers."

"Don't tell the driver," the man said. His voice drenched in shame.

"That is sad news," Miko said.

"Not as sad as spending all my time stuck in a relationship with someone who never shows the love he so earnestly claims to have. I've lost so many years. I want to be free. I want to find someone who truly loves me."

"I do love you," the man said.

The woman half laughed. Half snorted.

Miko was not enjoying this experience. She couldn't think of anything to say to make things better for the couple.

"Driver," the woman said.

"Yes."

"Please get us there as fast as you can. I want to get the paperwork over and done with. So I can start my new life."

Miko looked over her shoulder at the woman.

"As fast as I can? Are you sure?"

"Yes," the woman said. "As fast as you can."

"OK."

Miko pulled out the push-pull rod, switching the taxi over to its straight-through mufflers. Then punched the gear lever forward twice, chunk chunk, dropping down a couple of gears.

She planted her sneaker on the accelerator pedal.

The taxi leapt towards the horizon in a cacophonous roar of engine and squealing tires.

The tire smoke and thunderous noise filling the artificial canyon created by the buildings.

Like a missile riding the smoky plume of its rocket exhaust the dark blue taxi approached the T-junction at the end of the street, where the taxi needed to make a ninety degree turn to the left.

Miko flicked the wheel to the left and back again to send the taxi into a four-wheel drift, just like in her racing games. She increased the engine power to keep the four wheels over-spinning, to ride sideways on the lack of traction between the wheels and road.

Effortlessly she tracked the taxi's constantly shifting balance point, taking into account the weight of her passengers and the shifting mass of the sloshing fuel in the tank, the pulsing air resistance, the slight undulating twisting of the space framed chassis, and the varying friction of each tire as it flexed, bent, and heated under the strain.

Exactly when needed Miko made micro-adjustments to the steering wheel and accelerator to compensate for where she predicted, always correctly, the taxi's balance point was moving.

Squeals of delight came from the taxi's back seat.

Miko smiled with fellow-feeling. That's how driving joy affected her too.

She admired her taxi's reflection in the shop window straight ahead. The taxi was face on, with smoke billowing leftward from its tires. The taxi's paint glistening in the early afternoon sunlight.

A woman with long flowing pink hair, a pink coat, and a pastel green skirt stood by the shop window. Her mouth was open wide as she appreciated the sight of Miko's taxi sliding by.

Miko admired her costume. A blue, white, and pink muffin-sized cupcake was stuck to the side of the woman's hair band.

Her wrists were covered in cyan and pink bracelets. Her hair was full of clip-on bows and little cupcakes and ice creams. Under her left eye was a row of sparkly stick-on diamantés. On her right cheek were tiny red and purple musical notes. Finishing the cute look was an extra fluffy pastel blue handbag.

Miko was thankful for Harajuku fashion women like her, who put in the effort to brighten Tokyo's dull winter days. It was such a pleasant surprise to see these fun-costumed people.

Turning her attention to the shop, Miko admired the colorful coats on the mannequins behind the glass. One coat had bold yellow, navy blue, and red vertical stripes. Another coat was black with white accents around its seams.

Once she had repaid the bank and Hattori, she planned to save up for a better coat. Her mother's puffer jacket was fine, but her mother would want that back. A nicer coat would help Miko look more presentable and increase her chances of finding love.

In reality, it would take more than a nice coat to achieve her goal of finding a good man to spend her life with.

Miko hadn't decided to do it yet, but she was contemplating saving up for plastic surgery.

She had read about the doctors who can fix an ugly face, so a consultation seemed a sensible first step to discover how they could help her.

She would seek out the most experienced doctors, because they would have dealt with difficult cases before.

The taxi was almost entering the T-junction. Miko backed off the power to stop the wheels over-spinning and used the extra grip to slow her sideways drift.

She applied the power again, at exactly the right moment, to transition the taxi smoothly from its sideways slide into forward motion.

The taxi entered the new street, precisely in the center of the correct lane.

Chopping up the gears, the taxi accelerated along the street. The G-force from the acceleration pressing Miko firmly into the back of her seat.

Miko planned the optimal route to the couple's destination, while weaving between the slower cars.

A rail bridge swept overhead as if the bridge was falling past a window.

Again, she imagined how frustrated the other drivers were.

They must be itching to drive at a more sensible speed like me, but can't bring themselves to break the rules.

Miko glanced in the rear vision mirror and smiled. Her passengers were cuddling.

The tall man had his arms wrapped around his wife. She was snuggling her face into her husband's chest with her arms wrapped around his torso.

He had his face pressed into his wife's hair, giving her a big kiss with his wide open mouth.

They hadn't stopped squealing with delight.

But now Miko couldn't tell if this was still because of the fun of driving, or because at the precipice of divorce they had rediscovered their love for each other.

Driving fast, predicting where every moving or potentially moving object ahead would be when her taxi arrived, required little mental effort.

So Miko enjoyed the sights. The construction men waving their flags, the Tokyo birds swirling in the distance, a traffic cop looking the other way at a kingfisher hovering in front of him, the tempting honey toast shops.

I looooove honey toast!

After a few minutes, they arrived. Miko spun her taxi a hundred and eighty degrees around from one side of the street to the other. Coming to a perfect stop, with the taxi aligned neatly next to the curb outside their lawyer's office.

With a haze of tire smoke drifting around the car, Miko announced their arrival. She opened the rear door. Smoke wafted through the opening.

The man paid the fare with a shaking hand.

As Miko drove away, she glanced at the couple in the mirror.

Standing on the curb, the woman was embracing her husband. Her face still buried in his chest.

The husband had his arms wrapped around his wife, pulling her close. A hand stroking the back of her head.

"Look. They're both trembling," Fluffy Kitty said.

"I know. I have heard that love can be overwhelming," Miko said. "I hope one day to experience it myself."

Tuesday evening, Police Superintendent Ritsu Shoji sat in his dining room cross-legged on his brick-red *zabuton* cushion. His cherished wife Saya opposite him, and his young teenage sons Satoshi and Takato to either side.

Their dinner spread on the low-legged kotatsu table.

They sat with their legs covered by the table's thick brown blanket. Recessed in the floor under the center of the table, protected by a grate, charcoal embers warmed the trapped air.

Miso soup and a deceptively simple bluefin tuna and rice dish his wife had prepared were on the table. The fish recipe had been passed down from mother to daughter. Its secret was in the herbs and the staggered heating and cooling of the fish.

One of Superintendent Shoji's favorite things was returning home and being greeted by the fragrance of his wife's cooking.

But tonight it was not enough to cheer him up.

His *minka* home had been his parents', passed down over eight generations. A traditional Japanese home of wood accents, paper lattice sliding doors, landscape decorated panels, tatami mats, and rafters reminiscent of the beams inside a wooden ship's hull.

Superintendent Shoji's home had a sense of permanence that grounded his spirit, by connecting him to his ancestors. His friends joked he was house-proud, and Superintendent Shoji freely admitted the truth of their assertion.

But tonight his house was not enough to cheer him up.

His wife Saya wore a traditional kimono to dinner each evening. Saya had noted that her husband's late mother had worn a kimono in the evening. She had told her husband when he had inherited the house that her wearing a kimono would deliver him peaceful happiness.

She also said he would enjoy seeing their sons having the same experience he once had in the house where he grew up.

Saya had been correct. Superintendent Shoji considered himself lucky to have a wife so wise in the soft ways of people. He himself knew only the mind of the criminal. He was lost in dealing with honest folk.

But tonight his good fortune in a marriage partner was not enough to cheer him up either.

The mood around the table reflected his own. His sons were solemn. Saya had sensed his disharmony. It was impossible to hide such things from her.

Together they humbly received the food and began their meal.

Saya didn't begin to eat. She was considering him, and was about to speak.

"There's a renegade taxi operating in my area," Superintendent Shoji said. "It's been two days. I was sure we would have made an arrest by now."

"You are frustrated. I can tell," Saya said.

"I put my best man on the case. He has every officer on alert. We have a team reviewing video from surveillance cameras around the city. The traffic management department are keeping an eye out with their real-time cameras. So far nothing. Not even video evidence of this taxi driving past."

"Chief Inspector Kumazaki? If anyone can find it, he will," Saya said.

"Tell us about this taxi, Father. We will keep a lookout on the way to school," fourteen-year-old Takato said.

Thirteen-year-old Satoshi concurred enthusiastically with his older brother.

"A woman driver. It's dark blue. A Toyota Crown Comfort. Claiming to be operating for a company called 'Hidden Stealth Ninja Taxi Service'".

Takato and Satoshi burst out laughing.

Superintendent Shoji was shocked. This was most unlike his sons.

"We are sorry, Father," Takato said, after a glance at his father's face. "But someone is playing a practical joke."

"What do you mean?"

"Father. Ninjas are very hard to see," Satoshi said.

"Yes."

"And a stealth ninja is even harder to see," Takato said.

Superintendent Shoji made a worried grunt.

"And a hidden stealth ninja is impossible to see," Satoshi said.

"Father, permission to leave the table to get an exhibit to build our case," Takato said.

Superintendent Shoji nodded. Takato disappeared towards his room. Soon returning with a manga book in his hand. He passed the book to his father.

"This is Hidden Stealth Ninja. Its hero Hidden Stealth Ninja has never been seen in any of the pages. Not in any edition of the series," Satoshi said.

"Never, Father. Not once," Takato said. "That is the amazing thing about Hidden Stealth Ninja. Some readers even believe Hidden Stealth Ninja doesn't exist, and the events recorded in this manga are an incredible sequence of coincidences the characters attribute to an entity because they can't conceive that the events are coincidences."

"That is a silly theory," Satoshi said. "One or two or even three events could be coincidences. But not hundreds and hundreds. Hidden Stealth Ninja is real, but so good at his job no one has ever seen him."

Superintendent Shoji's blood began boiling as he thumbed through the comic book.

"It is like someone asking you to hunt for a fairytale character, like Hoteiosho or Totoro," Satoshi said.

"Also," Takato said. "If you go against Hidden Stealth Ninja, you will have bad luck."

"Yes, that's right," Satoshi said. "It's much better to be kind to him, because then you'll have good luck. Often, when someone wants something deeply and is kind to Hidden Stealth Ninja, they end up getting what they want without needing to do anything."

Saya gave him the we-need-to-talk look.

"Carry on eating. I must speak with your mother."

Saya and her Superintendent husband met in his study.

"Someone is trying to make a fool of you," Saya said.

"Reiji or Gando. It must be them. They have never been able to match the efficiency of my station."

"This is not of humorous intent," Saya said, her brow furrowed. "What if it reaches the press that you ordered your department to arrest a fairytale character?"

"Or TV or social media," Superintendent Shoji said. "I will deal with this."

Saya returned to the dining room.

Superintendent Shoji dialed his father's old rotary phone.

Chief Inspector Kumazaki's daughter answered. Swiftly Kumazaki himself was on the line.

"Yes sir?"

"The Hidden Stealth Ninja Taxi Service complaint is a hoax. Someone is trying to make us look bad."

"No wonder we've found nothing, sir."

"Call it off, Chief Inspector. Right this moment. For the rest of my life, I don't want to hear another thing about Hidden Stealth Ninja Taxi Service."

"Straight away, sir."

Superintendent Shoji slammed the phone down. He took several minutes to calm himself. He dropped his son's manga book into his work satchel and returned to his family dinner.

"Today is Exciting Goal Achievement Day Number One," Miko said, as she drove her taxi through the dawdling early morning Tokyo traffic. She slid her phone back into her jacket pocket.

"What did the message say?" Fluffy Kitty asked. Looking on smugly from his dashboard perch.

"Eichi says Hattori sends his apologies because he is too busy with his job to meet. But I can drop Hattori's ticket money off to Masumi. She will come down from her office and meet me on the street at exactly 10:30 am."

Owing Hattori his ticket money had been nibbling at Miko's mind ever since the live show. She hoped Hattori would forgive her for taking two weeks to pay him back. Because it wasn't like she had borrowed a little money from a friend for purchasing something insignificant, like tea from a dumpling shop. Instead it was a sizeable amount, owed to someone Miko didn't know, for something he had really wanted for himself.

On the way to the live show, Masumi said Hattori had been enthusing for months about seeing Aftershave. Miko could imagine his intense disappointment at missing out on his long dreamed of experience.

Since repaying Hattori was the smaller of Miko's two financial goals, it was the one she reached first. Using the excess income she had been earning over her daily goals, it had taken her only six days of double shifts to save up enough.

Miko's priority was her parents' mortgage, but she was well on track to save up that big amount.

After today, she would redirect the sum she had been putting aside each day for Hattori towards their mortgage.

"Miko," Fluffy Kitty said. "I am enjoying your progress in a secondhand manner."

"The word you're looking for is 'vicarious'."

"I don't know that word. But considering how you must suffer reading your piles of boring books, I don't think those sorts of words are worth the effort to know."

"Remember how I read the dictionary when I was fifteen?"

"Yes. It reminded me of that TV movie where the monk whips his back."

"Funny ha ha cat. And the word you were looking for there was 'flagellate'," Miko said. "Dictionaries are amazing things. They contain every idea important enough to become a word. By reading the dictionary, I quickly learned the broad scope of mankind's thoughts."

"If I did that, the boredom would make my fur drop off."

Miko didn't reply to her uneducated feline. Because she was driving past a school.

Her eyes were drawn to a schoolgirl, about ten years old. Her long black hair tied in a ponytail and wearing a bright pink backpack.

The girl was walking next to the school's red brick wall. Her head bowed lower and her steps became shorter as she approached the school gate.

Miko started breathing shallowly. She gripped the taxi's steering wheel.

The girl put her head down further, like she was watching her feet.

She turned from the sidewalk into the gate.

Then she started rushing, across the school's crowded courtyard, towards the school building's arched entrance.

"Why are there no teachers on duty?"

From the crowd of children, two larger girls emerged. One with two sullen friends in tow, the other with three.

The seven bigger girls blocked the smaller girl's way. Surrounding her like a hungry mouth wrapping around food. Until the girl with the pink backpack was hidden from Miko's view.

"No you don't," Miko said.

She switched the taxi over to its straight-through mufflers. She depressed the clutch with her left foot, and with her other foot gave the accelerator a solid punch.

Free of road resistance, the V12 shot up the rev range. Its supercharger whining, the turbos howling, the engine thundering, and the exhaust gasses breaking the sound barrier as they raced out the taxi's tailpipes.

The engine's sudden shrieking, and the exhaust's sonic boom, roared and cracked throughout the school yard.

In unison, every schoolchild jumped on the spot.

To Miko's delight, the schoolgirl with the pink backpack took advantage of the distraction.

Having slipped through a gap between the bigger girls, she appeared and darted towards the school's entrance. Her pink backpack jiggling back and forth as she ran.

Miko stopped the taxi outside Masumi's office block in Sumida City at 10:27 am. There wasn't a good place to park.

Cars rushed by. Some pulling out from behind her in a frustrated fashion.

Thankfully, Masumi was there waiting.

Miko powered down the passenger window and Masumi leaned in.

"Miko. You're a taxi driver."

"It's good to see you, Masumi. I'm sorry I can't talk long, I'm holding up traffic," Miko said. Handing Masumi a homemade pink envelope containing a thank-you card and exactly the right amount.

"I'll try and get it to Hattori soon. He is very busy. I'll text you when it is delivered. He was so pleased his ticket got used."

"Thank you again for taking me to see Aftershave. I can't explain how much it meant to me."

"The rumor is they're performing at the NHK Hall in March. You should come with us. Eichi will buy the tickets the moment they're available. Should he get a ticket for you?"

"Yes please. I super really want to go. I can get you the money."

"When they announce, I'll message you with the details."

"Thank you," Miko said. "I'm sorry. I have to go."

Masumi glanced at the traffic.

"I understand. See you in March," Masumi said. "Bye-bye, Fluffy Kitty." She reached in the passenger window and patted Fluffy Kitty on the head. Then she stepped back and began waving.

Miko drove off from the curb, waving back.

I can't believe I'm going to get to see Aftershave again. With my Aftershave fan friends!

Miko had never been invited to anything before, not even a birthday party.

Masumi's unexpected invitation made warm feelings swirl inside Miko.

Maybe if we go to enough live shows together, then Masumi, Nana, Eichi, and Hattori will let me become their full-time friend?

The possibility zinged within her like a pending miracle.

"I like Masumi," Fluffy Kitty said.

Miko agreed wholeheartedly.

At noon Miko went home for lunch. After eating, she planned to nap, refreshing herself for an afternoon and evening of fun driving.

That was if she could calm down. The prospect of going to the live show with the four friends was buzzing in her mind.

Miko added water to a chicken rice set and started the rice cooker. She grated some carrots and chopped spring onions she had purchased from her first visit to the supermarket in three years.

While her lunch was cooking, she found her notebook and sat at the dining room table.

Neatly written at the top of a blank page was a phone number of Sei Ibusuki. A mutual school friend of her father and Uncle Ken.

Miko had found the number in her father's address book. She hoped Sei Ibusuki was still in Goshogawara, living in the same yellow and brown house she had visited twice with her parents when young. Miko also hoped Sei would not recognize her voice.

It took a touch of brave thinking before Miko dialed the number.

In the electronic tones that indicated the phone at the other end was ringing came haunting echoes of her old Aomori Prefecture life.

A man answered.

"This is Ibusuki."

"Hello, sir. I am a researcher trying to locate three friends from your school. Sachiko Moriyama, Suzu Mochizuki, and Yuko Takahashi. Would you be able to help?"

There was a pause. Miko had a vision of a man searching in the dark recesses of his mind's library, then cracking open a dusty book.

"I remember them. What's this for?"

"It's preliminary research. Partly regarding the longevity of school friendships. We have a copy of a school yearbook, and from the pictures we've deduced they were friends."

Please don't ask for more details. I can't reveal I am researching my uncle's lost love.

"Yes, they were. Always hanging out together under the same tree on the sports field. Suzu? I recall years ago, she went overseas and got married. That is the last I heard of her."

"What about Sachiko Moriyama or Yuko Takahashi?"

"Yuko went away around the same time. I have not heard of her for a long while. But Sachiko is here in Goshogawara. She married the mailman after he delivered her a glove catalog. That's how they met. Ha! Whoever thought a glove catalog could be a romantic token?"

Miko chuckled along with Sei.

"Do you have Sachiko-san's phone number?"

"Well. You know the privacy rules," Sei Ibusuki said. "But you have a trustful voice. Do you have a pen and paper?"

Miko did. She copied down Sachiko's number.

She thanked Sei for helping with her research. After a few pleasantries and extended goodbyes, she waited for Sei to hang up, since it would be rude if she hung up first.

Miko made notes in her notebook. Then placed a call to Sachiko Moriyama.

An old lady answered. She informed Miko that Sachiko would not be home until the evening.

Miko promised to phone back then.

Closing her notebook, Miko went to finish preparing lunch.

She sprinkled a packet of egg rice seasoning onto the cooked rice to add extra flavor.

"I humbly receive. And thank you Kuribayashi-san for growing my carrots and Oshitani-san for growing my spring onions. Your hard work has allowed me to make this delicious meal."

Printed on the vegetable's price ticket were the names of the farmers who had grown the vegetables. At the supermarket Miko had memorized their names so she could thank them later.

She sat cross-legged at the table eating while flicking through a glossy catalog of women's coats.

But it was hard to pay attention to the coats, because Masumi's thrilling invite to Aftershave's March live show kept leaping in front of her thoughts and doing an impressive look-at-me dance.

After cleaning up, she went into her bedroom and curled up on her bed.

She cuddled Fluffy Kitty, who began purring. Despite the excitement about going to the live show, Fluffy Kitty's soothing noise helped Miko fall asleep.

Sandwiched between the Imperial Palace and Tokyo Station is the half square kilometer that contains the Tokyo's business district.

At 2 pm that same Wednesday, deep in the business district, the salaryman was swaying gently at his long communal desk.

His earnest colleagues on either side of him playing an endless game of Bop-A-Mole with the keys on their laptops, while the office's corrosive environment was steadily dissolving him like a boiled sweet in the mouth of a geriatric senior.

His Microsoft Excel spreadsheet on his laptop screen was blurring. Not visually, but as if viewed through a fuzzy field of disinterest.

The salaryman was able to focus his eyes on the financial model. But on detecting the grid of dull numbers in their jail bar columns of gray and light blue, his mind rejected the vision outright like a lactose-intolerant man dry-retching at the odor of milk.

He stretched. It didn't help.

He stood up and walked to the water cooler.

A motivational poster above the cooler showed a determined man with ice picks and rope climbing a snowy mountain. The text read, "Please Continue Trying To Do Your Best".

There, he filled a plastic cup with chilled water. The glug glug as the water drained from the big inverted plastic bottle flashed into a vision of drowning.

A weight around his legs dragging him down into the depths. The surface of the water high above. The shimmering light getting dimmer. Fading to pure black.

He drank half of the water. Keenly aware his boss had noticed he was away from his desk. But the salaryman needed to get his edge back if he was to complete his work.

He went to the bathroom. He poured some of the chilly water on his hand and rubbed it into his face.

Drinking the rest, he screwed the cup up, dropping it in the recycling bin on the way back to his desk.

He carried on with his work. But only for a few minutes.

His eyes were hurting from lack of sleep. He wanted to sleep badly. Just to collapse onto his futon and not get up for a week.

An email notification slid in from the bottom right of his screen.

He checked his email client.

His boss had assigned him another report. It had been a mistake to get up from his desk. His boss had taken it to mean the salaryman didn't have enough work.

The salaryman fantasized about picking up his chair, storming over to his boss's desk, and smashing his boss's brains in.

The salaryman was shocked he had thought of that. It was not like him. It was most disturbing.

He forced himself to get on with his job.

Like wringing more juice out of an already squeezed lemon, he compelled his mind to concentrate on his task.

He knew the effort would give him another terrible headache. But he hoped the alcohol from this evening's drinking with his boss would help dull the pain.

At 3:15 pm that same day, Miko was parked along the street from the school.

Soon coated and scarfed wrapped schoolchildren streamed out on their way home.

The two bigger girls Miko had seen this morning emerged with their friends in tow. They rushed along the sidewalk, turning left at the corner, and disappeared behind the corner shop.

Miko kept a careful eye on the corner where the bully girls had disappeared.

Sure enough, one of the big girls poked her head out, scanning back towards the school gate. Before hiding behind the shop again.

Time passed, measured by the slow metronome of the bully's head appearing and disappearing.

"I'm still sleepy," Fluffy Kitty said.

"When I woke, you were talking in your sleep again. You said, 'Miko! Miko! Be careful when it snows. The penguins come out, and they're small and easy to trip over'. So, you know, thank you for the advice. But after that you kept asking 'what do you call it when an octagon and a hexagon waves at you, or a parrot is playing the drums?'. Is that a riddle, or maybe one of your jokes? Tell me, what is the answer?"

"How would I know? I was asleep. And I'd still be asleep if you hadn't woken me."

Miko refused to respond. Because this topic was a trap. Given a chance, Fluffy Kitty would go on for hours moaning about humans not sleeping enough.

After ten minutes, the flow of children became a trickle. Five minutes later, there were hardly any children walking past.

"Wait here," Miko said.

She opened her taxi's door.

She walked along next to the school's red brick wall. Towards its open iron gate.

At the gate, she took a step into the school's courtyard.

"Hello," Miko said.

"Hello," said the girl with the pink backpack. She was standing a meter in from the gate's post, behind the brick wall.

"You know they are waiting around the corner. By the bakery."

"I know."

"How long has it been going on for?"

The girl didn't answer. Her head lowered, but her eyes stayed on Miko's face.

"A long time?"

The girl nodded.

"My name is Miko Nishimura. I was bullied at school too. I am a taxi driver now."

"I can tell your job from your uniform. I want my job to be games programming."

"That sounds like one of the few office jobs that would be exciting," Miko said. "Are you going to the train station?"

The girl nodded.

"Are you safe from bullies at the train station?"

"I stand by adults. So the bullies leave me alone."

"A good strategy. I will drive you to the station."

"I don't have any money. One of the bullies takes the money Mother gives me."

"That's an awful thing to happen. But today your trip will be free. You see, my taxi belongs to my uncle. When I was your age I dreamed about my uncle and his taxi coming to drive me past the waiting bullies. Now my uncle's taxi will do that for you. With me driving instead."

"Free?"

"Zero yen. I promise," Miko said.

The girl pursed her lips.

"My parents say not to talk to strangers," the girl said. "But you're not a stranger. I've known you a long time. You have a white cat."

"I do. A soft-toy cat," Miko said. Thinking that was odd. She knew for certain she had never met this girl before.

"I am Hanaka Hiyakawa," the schoolgirl said.

"Hanaka Hiyakawa. Such a rhythmic name. Follow me Hanaka."

Hanaka walked behind Miko. Keeping Miko between her and the street corner.

Miko opened the taxi's rear door. She stood by while Hanaka climbed in, before going around and getting in the driver's seat.

"What is your cat's name?"

"That's Fluffy Kitty. He's been my friend since I was ten years old."

Miko drove off from the curb. Hanaka shrunk down as they turned the corner.

The bullies knew what was happening. Their unblinking eyes tracked Hanaka in the back of the taxi. Miko could sense their anger at being outsmarted. As if somehow Hanaka had done them an injustice by not letting them beat her up.

"Hanaka, one thing I've discovered recently is that life gets better as you grow up."

"I'm scared at school, Miko-san. I can't concentrate. When I am older and start sitting exams, I don't want to become a *rōnin*."[†]

"I'll make sure you don't. I will pick you up outside your school again tomorrow and take you to the train station," Miko said. "And I'll keep picking you up until I can think of a solution to your bully problem."

"Why would you do that for me, Miko-san?"

"Because when I was your age, I dreamed of someone doing it for me."

Hanaka nodded and remained silent as she watched the houses, apartments, shops, and the occasional temple stairs with their red goalpost-like *torii* gates pass by the taxi window.

A luxury Star Train emerged next to them from under a bridge that ran over the road, decelerating as it disappeared on rails that curved behind a supermarket.

As the train station came into view, they caught up to the throng of children.

Near the station, a tough-looking schoolboy walked with his two friends. Hanaka shrunk down.

† Japan has a set of standard exams that act as gateways into higher levels of schooling. Students who fail the exam become "rōnin", meaning they have to spend the next year studying to retake the exam. Historically a rōnin was a masterless samurai whose lord had died and who had chosen not to commit ritual suicide. This type of samurai was forced to wander since he did not belong to any lord. A failed student is called rōnin because he does not belong to any school.

"Is he going to be a problem?" Miko asked.

"Jun is one of the leaders. He twists my hair until I give him my lunch money. Playing rugby must make you mean. I think that's why he is a bully."

Miko pulled up to the station and opened the passenger door.

"I'll watch you until you are safe. I'll see you tomorrow afternoon, Hanaka."

"Thank you, Miko-san," Hanaka said. She scrambled out of the taxi.

"Look at Hanaka," the boy Jun said. "She's getting out of her limousine. She's a movie star."

"Hanaka, can I have your autograph?" one of Jun's friends said, laughing.

"No. We are not worthy to even speak to a celebrity of such high status. Her bodyguards will throw us to the ground," Jun said.

Hanaka made herself small, hiding her face from the boys. Putting her hands into her backpack's straps, she jumped to seat the bag on her back, then hurried off towards the train station's entrance.

The schoolboy Jun bid farewell to his friends, who disappeared into the train station. After that Jun kept walking.

Miko drove and parked further up the road.

In the taxi's mirror, she watched Jun. He turned left down a side street.

Miko started the engine, turned around and parked in the entrance to that side street. The street was long and straight.

Jun kept walking. Six minutes later he turned left into a distant street and disappeared.

Miko slapped the ball of her fist into the palm of her hand, which is the kind of thing Japanese people do when a thought has popped into their head.

"This is boring," Fluffy Kitty said.

"I'm having an idea," Miko said.

"Well, maybe that's exciting for you. But it's boring for me."

Miko started the taxi. She drove east for about ten minutes until she found a building she had noticed on Tuesday while driving two salarymen back to their office.

"Miko. Why are we outside an acting school?" Fluffy Kitty asked. "You haven't decided to change career again?"

"You're coming with me," Miko said. Plucking her toy cat from his perch.

She stood outside the cheaply constructed brown building. Fluffy Kitty tucked under her arm.

Miko had codified the example of the Aftershave girl's fearlessness into a simple Miko-rule, which went like this: Miko Nishimura is not allowed to be afraid of speaking to new people unless they number over fifty thousand persons.

Miko guessed the acting school building couldn't hold more than a few hundred people.

The rule's criterion was met. So Miko marched towards the school's entrance.

Not long after 7 pm that Wednesday, Miko parked her taxi in a Tokyo side street.

There was a quiver of bikes neatly locked up in a row outside the rear of a warehouse. A soggy sparrow was hopping back and forth along the bike seats, like it was playing hopscotch.

Plinking on the taxi's metal roof were falling drops of water from the sky, pitter-pattering together in a comforting fashion.

The rain-slicked road glistened with the neon-blue from a building's tall sign. A long puddle rippled with expanding rings from the impacting drops, and wobbly reflections of people walking past hiding under transparent rain-mushrooms—which is what five-year-old Miko had named, and present-day Miko still called, umbrellas.

A plastic bag full of Miko's winter-treat loot rested on the passenger seat.

The best snacks came out in winter as limited editions. Miko had bought packets of winter potato chips with "twinkle snow" cheese, sweet milk puddings, and Earl Grey milk-tea chocolate-covered cookies that resembled tiny snow-covered mountains. There were also Lotte Ghana white truffle chocolates, and Lotte single wrap powdery snow Choco Pies with a strawberry hidden in the middle.

Miko phoned Suzu's friend Sachiko Moriyama and explained she was trying to locate Suzu Mochizuki.

"Suzu went overseas many years ago. She worked at a coffee shop in California and then married the owner. I've had no contact with her since."

"Do you think your friend Yuko Takahashi might know more about Suzu?"

"Yuko moved to Osaka soon after Suzu went overseas. Unfortunately, I haven't heard from her either. I would have liked to stay in touch."

"I am sorry."

"When you're young, you believe your life will be perfect. But it isn't. Friends drift apart. You miss them, but you can't expect them to stay around just so you can be happy."

She described to Miko how she, Suzu, and Yuko spent school lunchtimes sitting under a tree listening to music on Yuko's little radio. It was obviously a favorite memory. Miko wished she had school memories like Sachiko's.

It's a dead end. I can't think of another way of finding out about Suzu.

"I would like to know if Yuko became a minister," Sachiko said. "I wanted to be a *mangaka*. But instead of a manga artist, I've become a clerk in an agricultural machine shop. Suzu wanted to be a model, instead she became a shop assistant selling coffee. It would be nice if one of us became what we dreamed."

"A minister?"

"Yuko's parents were novel because they were Christians. We didn't know of any others in Goshogawara. Yuko wanted to become a minister ever since eighth grade, when she went with a traveling Christian group visiting the hospitals in Goshogawara. She helped with encouraging the patients. Yuko believed there were so many lonely people that it had to be someone's job to visit them. If you find Yuko, please let me know if she achieved her dream."

"I promise I will," Miko said.

After the call ended, Miko sat contemplating the shadowed glistening neon-blue street.

Yuko could be the next link in the chain to Suzu. It might be impossible to find an ordinary person in a big city like Osaka. But finding a minister in Osaka. There might be a chance of that.

The next day after school, Jun Kida farewelled his friends at the train station.

Because the new school term had begun only three days ago, there was no rugby practice yet. But it wouldn't be long before Jun and his teammates would stay behind after school to practice their passing and kicking and scrumming.

He turned the corner down the long street. There, in the far distance, was the intersection to his home. He wished he had a bicycle. He could be home much faster, but his parents insisted walking was safer.

A dark blue taxi rumbled past him and stopped ahead by the curb. The same taxi he'd seen yesterday.

Today he had pulled Hanaka's hair extra hard, because she had held back the money her parents must have given her for that taxi ride. He had explained to appease him, he wanted all her money. Not just her lunch money.

Hanaka had insisted the taxi was free, and for that lie he had twisted her ear until tears flowed like twin rivers.

The taxi switched off its engine.

Both passenger side doors opened. Two men got out. One tall. The other short and stocky. They were wearing matching dark suits and black sunglasses.

Even though the dark glasses hid their eyes, Jun could tell they were looking at him. They didn't seem happy.

"Jun," the nearest man said, pointing towards the taxi's open door. "The boss wants a word."

They know my name?

Jun froze. The man's arm was heavily tattooed.

As the man had stretched out his arm to point at the open door, tattoos were revealed between his white cuffed shirt sleeve and his wrist.

They are Yakuza!

Japanese gangsters have many tattoos. Especially on their arms.

What do the Yakuza want with me? What have I done? Are they betting on school rugby games? Do they want our team to lose on purpose?

"Don't look so worried, Jun. Step into the boss's office. He has a little job for you."

The other man stepped forward.

"I'll hold your bag," the stocky gangster said. He held out his hand.

Jun didn't see what choice he had. He couldn't outrun these adults, and had no idea what they would do to him if he refused.

He glanced inside the taxi. An older man in a black long-coat occupied the back seat. His mustache and goatee were gray. On his head, he wore a black felt train driver's cap. The boss didn't seem particularly concerned about his men's ongoing operation to get Jun into the taxi.

Jun slipped his schoolbag off his shoulders and handed it to the stocky gangster.

The gangster nodded towards the taxi.

Jun got in. He sat looking straight ahead at the rear of the passenger's seat. He clutched his hands together.

A woman was in the driver's seat. Her head covered in a baseball cap and eyes hidden in the taxi's mirror by pink-rimmed sunglasses.

"How is school, Jun?" the old man said. In a deep raspy voice.

"Good sir," Jun said. In a small schoolboy voice.

"As I am sure you are aware, Jun. I have many business interests of a lucrative nature."

"Yes," Jun said, bowing his head. Still not looking at the man.

"During these business interactions, I end up owing favors to certain people."

"Yes," Jun said, bowing his head.

Jun had decided that quickly saying yes and bowing his head would be his primary strategy for this meeting.

"During a drinking night, one of my business associates overheard the father of Hanaka Hiyakawa say his daughter was being bullied at school. So my associate called in his favor. He has asked me to see this bullying stopped."

"Yes."

"I thought a rugby player would be the ideal candidate to stop a few bullies. That is why you are sitting here, Jun."

"Yes."

"I will pay you a token one-time fee. Ten thousand yen. In exchange, you will ensure Hanaka Hiyakawa is never bullied again."

"Yes."

"Good. To be clear. You will stop little Hanaka from being bullied for the rest of her school years. Your job is vital, Jun. These cruel bullies, as delinquent as they are, are still children. I will be very disappointed with you if I am forced to have my men deal with these bullies directly. Understand, I have never enjoyed doing unpleasant things to children. It's the screaming, it spoils my whole day and gives me earache. So you will make sure I am not forced to commit such a distasteful action."

"Yes," Jun said, bowing his head with more vigor.

"And bullying includes Hanaka getting the silent treatment, or people pretending she doesn't exist, or her being excluded from groups or not being selected for teams. It includes mean words, stealing from her, and playing unkind tricks. Anything like that stops too."

"Yes."

"Then we understand each other. My men will pay you," the old man said. He dismissed Jun with a flick of his hand.

Jun got out of the taxi. Standing, his legs almost gave way.

The stocky gangster returned his schoolbag.

The tall gangster showed Jun a crisp ten thousand yen note. With one hand, he placed the note in Jun's jacket pocket. With the other hand, he pressed down firmly on Jun's shoulder.

"Jun. I wouldn't recommend you disappoint the boss. Not now. Not three years from now. He does not forget, and we'll be watching."

With that, the two men got into the taxi. The taxi's engine barked into life.

It roared off from the curb. Accelerating away faster than any car Jun had ever seen.

Leaving Jun Kida alone on the sidewalk, standing in a cloud of blue tire smoke with his knees knocking together.

It was cloudy and cold. As he marched along the sidewalk, children flowed around Arato Asada like a frightened school of fish.

He didn't enjoy seeing schoolchildren. With their backpacks and wide-eyed franticness the boys reminded him of his son, Nobuhiro.

Once at the park, a swan had bitten Nobuhiro's finger. So Arato had joked with Nobuhiro, "Clean your room, or in the night the swan will get your finger" or "Do your homework or the swan will bite your nose."

Arato shook his head, forcefully shaking these cherished memories out of his mind. Since these reminders of his son were an accelerant, inflaming the smoldering shame that for years had been cooking his skin.

As he approached the street corner, there was a roar. Then a dark blue flash.

Arato pivoted around.

"I don't believe it!"

It was that same taxi. Full of thugs. Driven by a girl. The same girl.

Her baseball cap and pink sunglasses didn't fool him.

Arato was on the phone to the police faster than a dwarf onto a pub wall.

"Hello. I am Arato Asada. I phoned last Friday about a renegade taxi. It just went past—"

"Is this the Hidden Stealth Ninja Taxi Service?" the police officer asked.

"Yes. I—"

"Stop it with your hoax complaints. Or I will arrest you for wasting police time. You should be ashamed."

"But I just—"

"Hidden Stealth Ninja Taxi Service! Do you think we are stupid? You will be up on serious charges if you try this again."

Then, the police officer hung up.

Arato Asada stood still in the flow of schoolchildren with his mouth open wide.

The hand holding his phone slowly dropping from his ear.

On the outside, Arato was tranquil. Like a tree on a quiet day. Or a monk meditating next to a trickling stream in a Japanese zen garden.

Then his eyes bulged. His ears turned red. His nose flared like a flying squirrel landing on a tree.

Inside the nuclear reactor of his mind, the fuel channel caps began rattling as the cooling water ceased to flow. In unison, the thin black needles of Arato's control room dials swung over into the bad-place with the speed of pine trees caught in a megaton blast.

The occupants of his mind took notice. The rats began scurrying down the anchor chain. The birds squawked, flapping into the sky. The hedgehogs curled up into balls. The octopuses squirted ink.

He began yelling.

Words came out schoolchildren ought not hear. The passing children scattered away from the screaming man.

His arms pumping up and down. His army boots stomping on the sidewalk.

Arato the perpetually mad couldn't accept this scorching insult.

It had happened again. It was exactly the same as the police and courts not believing him when he denied hurting his wife and son. He knew he had never done those things. And likewise, he knew this renegade taxi existed.

He had just seen it!

Yet the police claimed he was hoaxing.

Arato had believed the police officers respected him for reporting the renegade.

Before this phone call, he had daydreamed about being congratulated when the renegade driver was arrested.

But then he discovered the police didn't trust him. It was a shameful reversal that tore at his self-esteem.

"I will prove it by videoing her taxi," Arato said. "With my irrefutable video proof, I will force them to arrest that driver and apologize for this insult."

He stomped off along the sidewalk. A vast smoking entity crackling and sparking with white-hot determination.

"Miko. Your taxi is a rocket ship," gangster boss Takuji Yoda said.

Miko, brimming with driving joy, pulled up outside the acting school.

"My elder brother Ittetsu," Takuji continued. "Is schedule manager for Jekyll. Ittetsu often needs to get places fast. Can I give him your number?"

"Yes, Takuji-san. I would be happy to drive your brother."

Miko didn't know what a schedule manager was, or anyone called Jekyll, but phone bookings were always nice.

Miko, with Fluffy Kitty and the three student actors, found Chihiro Ueno in the school's messy dressing room. Memorizing lines while eating a boiled egg from a microwaved cup of *oden*.

Gangster thugs Jirō Murata and Toshiaki Sakurano took off their dark overcoats and rolled up their sleeves. Exposing the three-inch-long tattoos Chihiro had painted above their wrists.

"How did it go?" Chihiro asked. She opened a bottle of rubbing alcohol.

"It was a masterful performance," Takuji said.

"I felt bad," Miko said. "Jun's face. I didn't expect him to get that scared."

"Don't worry. He'll live," Takuji said, peeling off his fake goatee. "It was for a good cause. For Jun's bullying to stop and him become protective, and for it to last, he had to be afraid."

"Takuji. When you're famous, reporters will ask you about your first paid acting job," Jirō said. Chihiro was using an alcohol-soaked cotton ball to remove his fake tattoo. "And you'll have to be honest that you were employed to frighten a child."

"Ah. Such synergy when a job and natural talents align," Toshiaki said.

"Behold! I am having a vision. A vision of the future," Takuji said, waving his hands at his two friends. "I see you both standing outside, lonely in the rain. Due to not being invited to my Academy Film Prize after-party."

Miko paid the acting students and the makeup artist their agreed amount.

She had used some of the money saved for her parents' mortgage to help little Hanaka, but she still had twenty-two days left before the end of January. Miko was confident she could make up the amount.

Miko had thought often about emailing her parents, to let them know she was able to go outside again.

But it wasn't an emergency, and her parents would have to pay a fee to have her email delivered to their cabin. Miko knew how carefully they had budgeted for their trip.

Also, she knew they would be so excited that they would phone her, and their satellite call would cost them even more. And then, if they did phone, her mother would ask if there had been any mail, and so Miko would have to tell them about the bank letter.

Knowing about the letter will make Father panic and fly home. So I must keep my happy secret to myself until they return, otherwise my burning desire to share my good news will spoil their trip.

After Jun's and the actor's payments, Miko only had enough paper yen in her pocket for dinner for her and a gasoline dinner for the taxi.

But more fares were waiting out there in the city. She had determined that once she had paid her parents' mortgage she would begin saving for her March Aftershave ticket.

Friday morning the salaryman arrived home. He fumbled for his keys before stumbling into his chilly unlit apartment. There was the damp smell of unprocessed laundry.

The kitchen wall was tinted blue, from his microwave's glowing clock. Its digits read 2:09 am.

Like a lead weight settling deep in his stomach, he realized he had only four hours' sleep before his work cycle started again.

He massaged his head with the tips of his fingers. The Wednesday afternoon headache was still there, flashing inside his skull like a police strobe.

His previous work headaches had never lasted more than a day. Normally, alcohol and sleep banished them.

But he wasn't concerned.

He wasn't concerned because he didn't care. He didn't have the mental energy to stir up concern about his headache's unexpected longevity.

The salaryman also knew his inability to become concerned about himself was another bad sign. But only abstractly, since he couldn't bring himself to care about that either.

He needed a way out.

However, oddly, the idea of quitting his job had never put its hand up in his mind. And even if it had, the salaryman would not have allowed it to speak.

He had a reoccurring nightmare. He was jobless, floating inside a sphere of a thousand narrowed eyes. His ears whipped with endless sighs, tongue clicks, and teeth hissing.

But far worse than the social shame of being jobless, was the shame when his parents found out.

"Don't embarrass me in public!" his mother had said many times when he was a boy.

His military father had been exceedingly direct regarding his disgust at the ignoble failure of unemployment.

Quitting his job would show a complete lack of common sense. And scorched deep in his psyche were the burn marks from his father's emphatic speeches on the necessity for common sense.

For his soft little-boy mind, now wrapped in the firmer ways of a man, unemployment was an unbearable thought.

The salaryman could never quit his job. In the same way he could never bring himself to walk around Tokyo naked.

But still, he didn't want the responsibility of work anymore. Instead, he fantasized about a long sleep in a warm bed. Of waking when his body decided to wake instead of being woken by his alarm.

His fantasy involved checking himself into a five star hotel for a two-week stay. Doing nothing but sleeping and eating.

No emergency phone calls summoning him back to work. No laptops. No photocopying. No morning *chorei* meeting and speeches. No morning radio exercises. No *hanko* stamps. No nomination. No meeting prep. No long meetings. No work colleagues. And no boss.

Just a blissful long sleep in crisp sheets under a heavy duvet.

But it was only a fantasy. Impossible, like the pretty girls who passed him at the train station that he knew he'd never see again.

He sighed.

I have buried my bones in the company.

He brought his toothbrush up to his mouth.

In the harsh light of the mirror's fluorescent tube, his hand was trembling.

He stared at the shaking toothbrush's reflection.

The thought came to him, and it wasn't for the first time.

There is a way out.

At 11:40 am Friday Miko returned after a five-fare morning, backing the taxi into its cozy garage.

Today she was having lunch with Uncle Ken. She hoped they wouldn't need to walk too far to satisfy his incessant quest to find a shop with a queue.

But first Miko needed to make a phone call.

The taxi's garage had good phone reception, as long as the metal door was rolled up. So Miko sat in the taxi while she phoned.

The garage plus the taxi made a comfy office.

Outside, a pink mini-mobile cafe covered in adorable anime characters rolled past. A tiny truck with a flat-nosed cabin and golden angel-wing flaps hinged down over its coffee serving area.

In her notebook, Miko had written the phone number of every big-sounding Christian organization in Osaka. At least the ones her Internet search found.

She had Googled for the name Yuko Takahashi first, but there had been no useful results.

On her fourth phone call, a vicar said the name Yuko Takahashi sounded familiar. He suggested calling a Christian organization near Sakai City Medical Center. The organization managed a visiting ministry for the city's patients.

Miko was grateful for his advice, because that organization was not on her list.

"Mearī speaking."

"Hello Mearī-san. I am trying to locate Yuko Takahashi from Goshogawara."

"That is my old name."

"It is? You have changed your name?"

"Most keep their baptismal names. I chose to follow the tradition of taking a new name for a new life."

Miko found this idea intriguing.

"Like the idols?" Miko said. "They have a stage name, and also their real name."

Mearī, formerly Yuko Takahashi, found this comparison hilarious.

Please let Yuko, who is now Mearī, know something about Suzu!

Miko explained her quest for information about Suzu Mochizuki.

"I exchanged a few letters with Suzu. But she must have moved and forgot to tell me. My last letter was returned."

"Do you know which part of California she's in?"

"No, these letters were when she was in Kōfu City."

"Kōfu City? How long ago was this?" Miko said, sitting up straight in the driver's seat.

"Five or six years ago. Roughly."

"She and her husband moved to Kōfu City?"

"No. Unfortunately, her marriage wasn't good. She arrived back in Japan almost destitute."

Miko gave Fluffy Kitty a wide-eyed look.

"Mearī-san. Do you know how I can find her?"

"Suzu moved to Kōfu City for an English teaching position. But her sideline specialty is English CV doctoring."

Miko explained she was unsure what that meant.

"If you need to submit a curriculum vitae in English overseas or in Japan, Suzu will help make your resume more acceptable to foreign companies."

Miko asked more questions. But Mearī couldn't provide any more clues.

"Thank you for your help," Miko said. "One suggestion. When I spoke with your old school friend Sachiko Moriyama, I thought that she would enjoy hearing from you again. She will be very pleased to know you have become a minister."

"I would like that too. I will call her," Mearī said.

Miko gave her Sachiko's number, and they said their goodbyes.

"What is it?" Fluffy Kitty said.

"I don't want to count my *tanuki* furs before they've been caught. But Suzu is back in Japan. And we simply have to find her."

At 3:20 pm that same Friday afternoon, little Hanaka Hiyakawa climbed into the back seat of Miko's taxi.

"Miko-san, what have you done? I have not been bullied today. Not when I arrived, or during class or lunch or sports. I can't remember a day like this."

"This is how your school days should be, Hanaka. If you're ever bullied again, then I want you to send me a message the instant it happens."

"Thank you, Miko-san," Hanaka said. "I made you a gift."

She pulled out a picture from her schoolbag and gave it to Miko.

Hanaka had used colored pencils on a plain A3 sheet.

"Thank you. This is pretty. You are a skilled artist."

It was a picture of a woman standing in a forest. The woman had her back to the viewer with her head turned slightly to the right. Her bob-cut hair hid most of her face.

She wore a kimono and in her right hand carried a lantern. Sitting next to her under the lantern, also with its back to the viewer, was a white cat wearing a little kimono made from the same patterned material as the woman's.

Gathering around them were birds in the trees and rabbits, foxes, and other animals.

Crossing the left corner of Hanaka's drawing, a little stream ran under a wooden bridge. A fish was jumping out of the water. With its attention, like the other animals, focused on the woman.

"It's a picture of the dream I've been having, ever since I started school," Hanaka said. "I could never see the woman's face. But I knew you were coming to rescue me."

Miko didn't know what to say. She didn't want to spoil Hanaka's dream by saying it can't have been a dream about her.

Obviously, Hanaka's dream must reflect a child's conviction that everything will work out in the end.

Miko had once felt life was like that, before Nurse Goto's lie.

She decided to dodge the implied question with a promise.

"I will treasure your drawing, Hanaka. I will keep it until I am a little old lady."

Hanaka smiled at Miko's promise.

Miko started the taxi, and drove Hanaka to the train station.

"They aren't there," Hanaka said, as they turned the corner by the bakery.

"Yes. It's the first time I've not seen them waiting," Miko said.

The absence of the hiding bullies had been Miko's first sign that her strategy had worked.

At the train station, Miko opened the taxi's rear door.

"I won't be driving you to the station anymore. The danger is over," Miko said.

"I understand. Like in manga stories, the hero never can stay around.

You have other important jobs to do. Thank you. I will never forget you, Miko-san."

Hanaka bowed low to Miko for a long moment. When Hanaka looked up, her schoolgirl eyes were teary.

Miko reached out.

They clasped hands through the gap in the seats. Hanaka bowed low again.

"I wish you a happy life," Miko said. "Now, you don't want to miss your train."

Hanaka nodded. She twisted around on the seat so her legs were out of the taxi's door, and jumped out.

Giving a wave goodbye, she disappeared into the crowd, her pink backpack jiggling as she ran to catch her train.

It was at that moment Miko knew for certain she wanted to have children.

Miko wanted little people she could love, and who loved her back.

It didn't matter that many other Japanese her age were deciding not to have children; instantly she rejected the strong societal pull to copy what those others were doing.

Additionally Miko knew this goal was not something she would have to reassure herself she wanted. Unlike some of the achievements modern society promotes, such as building a career or being famous, she simply desired this with no mental effort. It was like a light switching on. The type of light that can never be switched off.

At 11 pm that Friday night Miko was driving, searching for fares in Chuo City while munching on a bag of Lemon Tea Popcorn hidden in her door's map pocket.

Her phone rang.

"Hello. Is this Miko? I am Ittetsu Yoda. Older brother of Takuji Yoda."

"Yes, I am Miko."

"My brother said to call you if I needed a taxi to pick me up and take me somewhere fast. I lost track of time and so my meeting went on too long. I need to get to Narita International. But I'm very late. Can you help?"

"I can. Where should I pick you up?"

Thankfully, Ittetsu was in central Tokyo, not far away.

Two minutes later Miko slid her taxi to a halt outside a Tokyo office block.

A confident-suited man with messy hair and a small metallic blue rolly suitcase rushed up to the taxi.

He threw the case into the back seat and climbed in after it.

"Miko? I'm Ittetsu."

"Good to meet you. Narita International, Ittetsu-san?" Miko said. She pushed the button to close the taxi's door.

"Yes, Narita. I can't miss my Seoul flight. My schedule is totally packed.

I will lose my job. Please go fast, Miko."

"Seatbelt on please," Miko said.

As soon as his seatbelt clicked, Miko accelerated the taxi at the limit of its tires' adhesion.

Ittetsu was thrown back in his seat.

Miko glanced at her new passenger in the taxi's vibrating mirror.

He had an odd expression.

As if someone had unexpectedly splashed a bucket of ice water on his face, and then he had seen a ghost, and after that ten Samurai running at him with razor-sharp swords.

She had been experimenting with using the silver lever. With her hand on its black grip, she applied the brakes on the taxi's left or right side to make her taxi drift in a wavy line through the traffic, like a downhill slalom skier weaving between flags. Her taxi pivoting precisely around the central axis of the other cars.

There was a symmetrical beauty to this style of driving, which Miko found relaxing.

Coming to the freeway on-ramp, Miko chopped up through the gears as she accelerated the taxi up the ramp.

She loved the music of the four turbos and the whine of the supercharger. The way the sound reverberated off the freeway's barriers and crescendoed in a growl each time she went under a bridge.

"Who are you?" Ittetsu yelled over the noise. "Are you a Formula One driver? Am I on a hidden camera show?"

Miko shook her head at Ittetsu's funny thoughts.

Other cars were shooting by like their owners were driving in reverse.

Then drifting around a bend, Miko came across three cars going a lot faster than the others. They were across the freeway, door handle to door handle, taking up a lane each.

The car in the middle was squat, covered in reflecting silver foil with bright neon blue lighting up the road underneath. The rear of that car was labeled Lamborghini.

An electric blue car with fat tires and a silly dinner-table-sized rear spoiler was to its left. It was labeled Supra.

The third car was a glossy yellow that glowed like fresh custard. It had even fatter tires and flames flashing out its exhaust below its four dinner-plate round taillights. It was labeled Skyline.

Miko appreciated the three drivers' effort to travel at a more realistic speed than the dribbly-crawl of the other freeway cars.

But why be so half-hearted about it? Why aren't they going as fast as they can?

The cars were blocking the three lanes. And she needed to get Ittetsu to the airport.

Miko honked her taxi's air horns. She didn't like using the horn because it wasn't polite, but she felt she needed to in this situation.

The three cars ahead shimmied at the sound. The Lamborghini and Supra moved to opposite edges of their lanes.

They are very kind.

Miko dropped a gear and depressed the taxi's accelerator.

Her taxi passed through the opening, drifting slightly sideways trailing tire smoke. As Miko again hovered her accelerating taxi at the limit of its tires' grip, expertly balancing the tires' traction with the engine's increasing torque.

She glanced at the rapidly receding cars in the mirror and flashed her hazard lights twice to say thank you.

The three male drivers of the shiny colorful cars were in their twenties. The two outer drivers had manga-hero hairstyles, while the driver of the inside car wore a white baseball cap.

But it was the fact their facial expressions were the same that amused Miko.

Each had his head thrust forward. Big wide eyes. Mouth open, forming an almost perfect letter O. Their tongue poking out, like a doctor had made them say "ahh".

As Miko accelerated her taxi back up to a more sensible speed, they vanished behind her.

She checked the mirror, to make sure her passenger wasn't looking. He wasn't, so Miko sneaked a piece of Lemon Tea Popcorn.

Nearing the airport, there was slow traffic ahead. Backing up as the cars funneled through a single lane in the distance. The other two lanes were taken up by bulky yellow roadwork machines doing whatever it was those machines do.

Thankfully, the road workers had removed a section of the barrier between the opposite side of the freeway, not far before the traffic jam started.

And there was another gap in the barrier too, after the roadworks ended.

Miko checked. There were no cars coming towards her on the other side of the freeway.

With a touch of front brakes, she unsettled the taxi enough to drift the car sideways through the first gap onto the other side of the freeway.

The taxi zipped across the distance to the next gap in less time than it took for her father to suck up a noodle.

Near the second gap Miko unsettled the taxi again, taking into account that where the barrier had been was dirt instead of asphalt. She drifted the taxi through the opening, back onto the correct side of the freeway.

Dirt sprayed out into the trees, and Miko was back on track to the airport without needing to drop out of top gear. The entire episode took only a few seconds.

"Miko-san. I take back asking who you are. Instead, what are you?" Ittetsu yelled over the engine's roar and white noise of the air rushing over the taxi's bodywork. "That maneuver was incredible. If I hadn't seen it with my own eyes, I never would have believed it. How can you react so fast? You drive like a *shodō* master painting with his brush on the roadway."[†]

Miko smiled.

"At first I was afraid," Ittetsu yelled. "But, even though we are traveling much faster than a bullet train, I am at peace. I trust in your skills completely. How is it possible I am this calm?"

Not long afterwards, they arrived at the airport.

Ittetsu checked his watch.

"Miko. I have plenty of time to catch my plane. I can't thank you enough," Ittetsu said. He handed Miko cash for the fare.

"I hope you have an enjoyable flight. And your meetings go well," Miko said.

"Please. Take my card. If you ever want to meet Jekyll, I will arrange it. Tickets, party invites, autographs, merch, selfies, backstage. Whatever you want."

With two hands Miko respectfully took Ittetsu's card.

"I will. Thank you," Miko said. She didn't have the heart to tell Ittetsu that she still didn't know who Jekyll was. His brother had mentioned Jekyll too. So she made a mental note to look him up before Ittetsu needed another ride.

"Thank you. I will use your taxi again, Miko-san."

With that, Ittetsu climbed out, extended the handle on his rolly suitcase, and dashed off towards the check-in counters.

Miko closed her eyes and breathed. Savoring the satisfying smell of hot engine, warm tires, and toasty brakes. Before putting her taxi in gear and driving off from the terminal.

"You have a lot of happy customers," Fluffy Kitty said.

"I enjoy having a job that makes people's lives better," Miko said. "They worry about being somewhere. And I make their worry go away."

Two hours later, it was 1 am. A chilly Saturday morning.

As the salaryman walked, the world crunched under his feet like discarded insect skins.

His Wednesday headache still pulsed pump-like in his head and, for the third time in a row, the evening's sloshy alcohol-fueled nomination had failed to dull the obstinate skull pounding.

At least he had three days of sleep ahead. Saturday, Sunday, and Monday. It was a bonus day on Monday because of Coming of Age Day, a national holiday.

He wouldn't have the energy to shower when he got home. Instead, he would flop onto his futon and wake up when his body wanted. In anticipation, he had already disabled his phone's alarm. He was certain

† Shodō is Japanese calligraphy.

three days' sleep would cure his headache.

Actually, he wasn't that certain. He had never had such a long-lived headache.

What's more, his motivation at work had dropped to zero. The world fading to grayness, buzzing like electrical equipment after a heavy rain.

He walked. Hunting for a taxi home. Lifting each foot as if breaking free from magnets hidden in the sidewalk.

A dark blue taxi approached from behind along the quiet road. Its availability light on its dashboard red, meaning it was vacant.

"Taxi," the salaryman said. Waving his hand.

The taxi's indicator came on and it rumbled to a stop next to him. The taxi turned on its hazard lights. He slid into its back seat.

"Where can I take you?" the pretty female driver asked.

The salaryman gave his address and followed her instructions to do up his seatbelt.

As the taxi pulled away from the curb, he pressed his temple against the door's cold glass, to short-circuit his headache. But quickly withdrew because the glass was vibrating.

He glanced around the taxi. Its dashboard had more lights and dials than any other taxi he'd ever seen.

On top of the dashboard was a stuffed toy cat. The salaryman's old-self would have smiled seeing this fluffy white soft-toy, with its smug face and big fluffy tail. But his current-self felt nothing.

"Nothing," he decided, was the best description of him. Apart from the smothering responsibility of his job, he was a void.

I'm not even a ghost inside a shell, I'm just a shell.

Everything that had defined him: hopes, dreams, hobbies, music, had been sucked dry, reduced to abstract concepts devoid of any concrete form in his life.

His phone chirped. A message from his boss. He held his breath:

Esteemed Team. Unfortunately, we are behind with the Project Cherry Blossom 48 reports. Our executive team needs these reports by Tuesday morning. So I'll see you this morning at the usual time. If we can't get the reports finished, we'll work Sunday too. Let's do our best.

The salaryman's mouth dried up.

A tear rolled down his cheek. He brushed it away with a trembling hand, like an old man removing his monocle.

This sudden unexpected idea of going back to work later this morning loomed like a sheer rock face with no handholds.

He closed his eyes for a long while.

"Driver," he said.

"Yes sir?"

"I need to change my destination. Please take me to Meiwabashi Street."

"The intersection end or the bridge end?"

"The bridge."

When Miko drove, she regularly checked her taxi's rear vision mirror. To stay aware of what was happening on the road behind and to monitor her passengers.

When the salaryman's message came, he had shed a single tear.

Has his girlfriend rejected him? Has one of his family died? Is he in terrible financial debt?

Miko drove over the blue arched Meiwa Bridge and stopped at the start of Meiwabashi Street.

"Thank you," the salaryman said. He paid.

The salaryman shouldered his satchel's strap and walked back towards the bridge.

"I could have dropped him off on the other side," Miko said.

"Maybe he enjoys walking over the water," Fluffy Kitty said.

"He's not a happy person," Miko said. "Maybe he works for a black company?"†

"Maybe. Few of your salarymen passengers have been happy. Are we going home now?"

Miko nodded. She was pleased she didn't have an office job like that poor man.

"What's he doing?" Miko said.

The salaryman had stopped outside a small mechanic's shop. He stood staring at the shop's teardrop flag sign.

After a minute of good solid staring, he walked up to the sign. The bottom half of the sign was hidden behind a parked car. The man bent over and disappeared.

The teardrop sign began wiggling like an epileptic belly-dancer. Before toppling over behind the row of parked cars.

"I don't believe it," Miko said. "He is stealing that business's sign."

But the salaryman emerged clutching something else. She couldn't see what it was. But it definitely wasn't the sign.

"Maybe the business owner wronged him?" Miko said. "Or does it have something to do with the sad message he received?"

The man continued towards the bridge.

"Uncle Ken said to expect odd behaviors when driving people," Fluffy Kitty said. "I believe this is our first strange story."

After the man walked out of the taxi mirror's view, Miko totaled up her night's fares. The amount was pleasing. She turned the taxi around and drove back towards the bridge.

† In Japan an exploitative business that requires long work hours and pays little is called a "black company".

Ahead in the middle if its span, illuminated beneath the bridge's floodlights and broken security camera, stood the salaryman.

He had stopped in the sidewalk rest area under the bridge's single iron arch. His dark leather satchel on the ground beside him.

He was fiddling with something on one of the small brick viewing seats.

Miko slowed the taxi to a crawl.

"What's he doing?" Fluffy Kitty said.

"He's making a little building out of his train and credit cards."

Miko stopped her taxi across the road, just past the matte blue pillars supporting the bridge's iron arches.

Oddly, the man seemed oblivious to the rumbling taxi only fifteen meters behind him.

The salaryman stood. Looked down at his card house for a long serious minute.

He took a deep breath. Then loosened his tie, unfurling it from his collar. He knotted one end to the front of his suit pants' belt. He crouched down, working on the tie's other end with something hidden behind the satchel.

"I've got a bad feeling," Miko said.

The man picked up a heavy white plastic pyramid and clutched it to his chest.

It was the weighted base of a teardrop sign.

Moving to the bridge's low railing, he stood at attention. Staring north out over the clean water of the Shinnaka River.

Miko pulled on the handbrake and unclipped her seatbelt.

The man took a step forward. The movement revealed exactly what Miko had feared; that the other end of his tie was knotted to the pyramid.

"Oh no!"

Miko flung her driver's door open and leapt out, sprinting across the road.

She jumped the short pedestrian barrier, landing in the sidewalk rest area without breaking stride.

The railing was too high for the salaryman to step over. So he leaned down, put his left shoulder on the railing, while clutching the weight to his chest. He hooked his right leg over until he was almost lying along the railing.

"Stop!"

The man let the weight go. It fell towards the river.

Miko leapt at him. She gripped his right shoulder and hooked her hand around his belt. She dropped to the sidewalk, using her weight to pull the man down from the railing.

The salaryman fell half on top of Miko. With his hips pulled upwards by his tie that curved over the railing and down to the weight dangling on the other side.

His legs scrambling to hook over the railing so he could finish the job.

"Let me go!"

"No!"

The tie was pulling the man's belt up in a vee from his waist.

Miko recognized the type of belt buckle. A ratchet style like her father used. She let go of the belt and activated the buckle's tiny release lever.

The belt split in two.

The tie's knot binding against the belt buckle. The falling weight pulled the belt upwards. The belt's free end snaked around the man's hips, zipping through his belt loops.

The man's whole body fell to the pavement, on top of Miko's legs.

The buckle clanged loudly against the railing. The falling weight whipping the belt over the railing with a snap.

Seconds later, a hefty splosh came from below.

Moving like lightning, Miko readjusted her grip. From behind, she wrapped both her arms around the man's neck.

He stunk of alcohol.

"Let me go," the man gargled. He struggled, trying to get up.

"No. Because you'll die."

His struggling allowed Miko to move her legs. She locked them around the railing's vertical bars for more leverage.

"I can't take it anymore. I want to be free."

"Dying isn't free. It's just being dead."

"I'm dead already. A living death. Working, working, working. No sleep. I want to sleep."

"Then try sleeping in your bed instead of a river."

He might try a really big squirm.

Miko gripped her opposite elbows tightly, to lock in her hold around the salaryman's neck.

"Driver, you don't understand. It will never end. I can't do this anymore. Up at six, work, drinking, hardly any sleep. My boss piles work on me. Hattori do this. Hattori, we need you back here now. Hattori, this file—"

"Hattori? Your name is Hattori?"

"Yes."

"The Hattori who couldn't make the Christmas Eve live show with Masumi, Nana, and Eichi?"

The salaryman froze.

"How could you possibly know that?"

"You got called away by your work. Your friends let me use your ticket. I am Miko."

"No way. You are Miko?" Hattori said. "But that's impossible, I chose your taxi at random."

"Well, it's me, and here I am."

It was several seconds before Hattori spoke again.

"Miko, can I ask you a favor?"

"Maybe."

"Please stop strangling me."

"Only if you promise not to jump."

"I promise."

"On your honor?"

"Yes."

"Don't disappoint me. Sit up against the railing."

Miko let go. They sat next to each other on the sidewalk, their backs against the cold railing.

"If you move, I will grab you," Miko warned. She scrutinized him intently for any sign of pending action.

"I understand," Hattori said. He massaged his forehead.

"I must thank you, Hattori. It was my first ever live show. A magical treat. I can't describe how wonderful it was."

Tears began streaming down Hattori's cheeks. He wiped them away with his hand, but they kept coming.

"What is it?"

"I wanted to see them. I haven't seen them for two years. Work keeps getting in the way," Hattori said. He breathed in deep. "I grew up with Aftershave."

"You know them?"

"No, not like that. I grew up with them on TV. On the radio. I'd hear them in the malls. When I felt sad, I'd play their music and be happy again. Going to their live shows was my biggest boost."

Miko considered this.

"Are you in love with one of them?" she said. "You must be. Which one?"

"All three, sort of. But not how you mean. I'm not going to say how. It will sound silly."

"As silly as jumping off a bridge? Come on, tell me your secret."

"But I've never told anyone."

"Maybe you've never had the right moment? Maybe you've never had the right person to tell?"

Hattori wiped away fresh tears. He glanced at Miko. Then focused above, looking up at the bridge's iron arch.

He explained he was an only child, and he and his parents had never got on, and that he had lived alone since the age of seventeen in a small apartment that wouldn't let him keep pets. And because of work he hardly ever saw his friends.

"So, with Aftershave. This is going to sound dumb," he said. "You promise not to tell anyone?"

Miko promised.

"They are my imaginary sisters."

"Imaginary sisters?"

"I've always wanted a proper family. My whole life I've been jealous of others who had siblings. So, I sort of adopted them in my mind. I was young. I didn't even mean to do it, but it just happened that I started thinking of them that way. Go on. Laugh at me if you want."

"No. I think it's kind of sweet."

"Not weird?"

"It's not weird to dream about having good things."

"Thank you. That's validating."

"A good choice," Miko said. "Not like what you just tried to do. I want you to promise me you'll never try that again."

Hattori closed his eyes and massaged his forehead with his fingertips, like a spider doing press-ups.

"Miko. Somehow, I know you're someone I must be honest with. I don't know if I can make that promise."

"Then baby steps. Promise me you won't try again for one week. Just one week."

"I have to get up in five hours and go to work. I don't have any energy. I can't face it, Miko. This is the end of me."

"Then call in sick."

"I would need a doctor's certificate."

Miko smiled. "Have you ever got a Train Delay Certificate?"†

Hattori nodded.

"Well, I have something better than that," she said. "You will come with me now."

She stood and pulled Hattori up by his arm. He didn't resist.

Obeying Miko's orders, he gathered up his card house and slid the cards back into his wallet. He picked up his satchel.

She marched him, her hand gripping his arm, to the rear door of her still running taxi.

"Promise me you will not jump out of my taxi?"

"I promise."

Miko drove him through Tokyo to the nearest hospital, and parked in a visitor spot.

"I am going inside to get what you need. Promise you will stay in the taxi until I get back."

Hattori nodded.

"If you are gone when I return," Miko said. "I will immediately call Masumi and Eichi, and we will spend the rest of the night searching for you."

"Please don't tell my friends," Hattori said. "Please don't tell anyone."

"I won't have to tell if you are still here when I return. I need one of your business cards."

Miko examined his card. Unusually, there was no first name. She confirmed with Hattori the fax number went directly to his team.

With her pen she recorded the other details she would need on a sheet of pink Sumikko Gurashi notepaper. She asked for his date of birth, his

† Train Delay Certificates are certificates that Japanese train companies issue to passengers if a train is more than five minutes late. To help employees avoid trouble for arriving late to work.

home address, his blood type, and other medical information.

She put on her mother's puffer jacket to hide her driver's uniform. Then left Hattori in the taxi and went hunting for the hospital's entrance.

Miko hadn't been inside a hospital since those horrid meetings triggered by Nurse Goto's accusations.

The utilitarian sheet-vinyl flooring, the wooden handrails running along the side of the extra-wide corridors, calming pot plants on the window sills, and the pervasive tang of quaternary ammonium cleaner and hydrogen peroxide conspired to resurrect unwanted memories.

Ahead, a white-uniformed nurse swiped a card.

Miko followed her through the secure door.

The nurse stopped to speak to an orderly wearing blue cotton scrubs just beyond the door. About moving a bed with a faulty wheel.

Miko stood behind the nurse as the doors closed and locked with a click. Thankfully, the orderly ignored her. The last thing Miko needed was someone asking why she was here.

Please don't ask to help me. I don't need any help.

As quietly as she could, she stepped past them.

She followed the ceiling signs and soon found an empty nurse admin station.

The yellow multi-page forms she required were stacked in a file organizer shelf under the counter. She took one, and filled it in with the details copied from Hattori's business card and her cute-character-covered notepaper.

The stamps needed were in a drawer, and so was the password for the computer. The English word 'PENCIL' written on a paper strip taped to the inside of the drawer.

As Miko two-finger typed on one of the computers, a nurse appeared at the end of the short corridor.

This nurse had permed hair—radical for a hospital—tied back in a ponytail.

The nurse approached.

Walking down the corridor towards Miko.

Miko froze. There was nowhere to hide.

The nurse arrived at the admin station and came in behind the counter, standing next to Miko, only about a meter away.

Ignore me. I am not here.

Miko breathed in noiseless shallow breaths.

The nurse reached far under the counter, fiddled for a moment, before extracting a chocolate and almond SOYJOY muesli bar.

She tore one end of the packet open, and mouse-like nibbled away, while glancing up and down the corridor.

After eating half of the chocolate-coated bar, she folded the crinkly wrapper over the remaining half.

With another glance in both directions, she inserted the bar back somewhere far under the counter.

Then, assuming a straight-backed purposeful disposition, the nurse exited the admin station and went on her way.

Miko breathed fully again, and typed faster.

The laser printer clicked and whirred, making faint white ozone smelling smoke.

After a brief fight with the fax machine, Miko tore off the form's front sheet and folded it, putting it in her jacket pocket. Before filing the form's remaining pages into the bottom of the correct pile.

Thankfully, no one bothered her on her way back to the taxi.

Hattori was still there. Curled up on the back seat in the fetal position. Snoozing with his head on his satchel.

Miko didn't wake him. She drove smoothly back to Uncle Ken's garage and backed the taxi in.

"Did you forget to drop off your passenger?" Fluffy Kitty said.

"Until I get assurances he won't try that again, I'm not letting him out of my sight," Miko said.

Miko switched on the taxi's courtesy light and tried to wake Hattori with words. But in the end she had to tickle his ear with Fluffy Kitty's feet.

"Where are we?" Hattori groaned.

"You are staying at my parents' tonight," Miko announced. "Don't worry. My parents are away."

"What about work?"

"See this," Miko said. She gave Hattori the yellow sheet of paper. "This is like a train delay certificate for medical emergencies. I've faxed a copy to your work. It says you were in a taxi incident on the way home. You were not seriously injured, but the doctor has ordered you to take the next seven days off work."

Hattori took the paper.

"You mean I don't have to work? For a week?"

"It's a legitimate certificate. I recorded your emergency consultation in the hospital's computer," Miko said. "You can sleep for the entire week if you want."

"I, it's. I don't, I don't know what to say. It's the most wonderful thing I've ever seen," Hattori said, staring at the certificate. "I'm sorry. I am crying again. I don't usually do this."

"It's fine," Miko said. "I was a nurse. What you have is burnout. Crying is normal."

"Burnout?"

She nodded. "It's very common in Japan. Let's get you to bed. We'll talk about this more when you wake up tomorrow."

Miko guided Hattori to her parents' apartment.

She put fresh sheets on her bed. And informed Hattori she would be sleeping out in the living room if he needed anything.

"You're very trusting of me," Hattori said.

"I cannot believe Masumi, Nana, and Eichi would have a bad person as a friend," Miko said. "Turn off your phone. Sleep in tomorrow as long as you want."

With that, Miko exited, closing the door to her room behind her.

She gathered a spare duvet and pillows and a musty guest futon.

She unfolded the futon out in front of the apartment's *genkan.*[†]

Not satisfied that Hattori couldn't sneak out without waking her, she hunted through the kitchen drawer and found her father's small padlock. She locked the apartment's door chain. Preventing the door being opened from the inside. The key went into her jean's pocket.

Brushing her teeth, Miko slept in her clothes.

She had a single dream that night.

She dreamed of a tradition, where on the last evening of each month lonely people would place a blue light in their window.

In her dream she was a schoolgirl again, but living alone in a high Tokyo apartment. Sadly she taped a string of blue lights to the inside of her window. Finished, she focused out beyond the glass. The whole city shimmered blue.

Shortly after 11 am the next morning, Miko walked to get an early lunch. Fluffy Kitty was riding kangaroo-baby-style.

Hattori followed behind. His head hung low. He had emerged from Miko's room at 11 am. Seeming less wraith-like than on the bridge.

On this wintry Saturday morning, a few clouds were drifting high across the ribbon of pale-blue sky between the buildings above.

The day's chill air gnawed at Miko's cheeks.

"They do many breakfast options. Bacon and egg rice bowls, miso soup, eggs with *furikake*," Miko said. "They even do pancakes with maple syrup."

"Those all sound good. Except pancakes are too heavy in the morning."

"Have you turned your phone on?"

"No."

"Don't. Not until after breakfast."

"What should I say?"

"I suggest not answering calls from work. Friends only. Let work go to voicemail."

"OK."

Around the corner up ahead appeared Kana Narita, walking next to her father Obito.

This time, the old man didn't look away. Instead, he smiled. His face crinkling warmly.

"Hello, Miko," Kana said.

"Hello, Kana-san. What a nice surprise to see you and your father. This

---

[†] A genkan is a shoe pit inside a Japanese home's front door. This is where you remove your shoes before entering the home.

is Hattori."

The four of them bowed and exchanged greetings.

"Kana. I thought you were Miko's mother or older sister when I saw you," Hattori said.

"A most fortuitous resemblance," Obito said.

He stroked his white goatee. "A resemblance that led to an extraordinary act of kindness. One that if I lived another sixty years, I could not repay."

He bowed low and long to Miko. Miko returned the bow.

"I apologize for how my past reactions towards you made you feel. Please forgive an old man."

"There's nothing to forgive," Miko said. "I completely understand."

They talked for a while more before parting. The old man and Kana securing a promise that Miko and her family would eat with them once her parents returned.

"May I ask? What was that about?" Hattori said.

"Just a successful suggestion I made to Kana."

They carried on to brunch.

But now Hattori walked beside Miko. Occasionally glancing at her.

Miko worried she had something stuck in her hair or on her face. When Hattori wasn't looking, she tried to brush whatever it was away.

Miko was pleased. Unlike Uncle Ken, Hattori didn't insist on walking around forever until he found a shop with a queue.

The donburi shop didn't have a queue. It was nice to walk straight in.

They both enjoyed a bacon and egg rice bowl. Hattori insisted on paying. He also bought Miko a bottle of her favorite lemon tea, and a pot of hot jasmine tea for himself.

They sat opposite each other at a small round mustard yellow table amidst the bustle and chatter of the cheap restaurant. Fluffy Kitty sat on Miko's lap because there wasn't room on the table.

They were close to the kitchen. The grill sizzled, and a wok went thunk thunk as the chef tossed its contents and stirred the falling rice with his metal spatula.

'Buoyancy', 'bounce', and 'vitality' were not words Miko would have used to describe her brunch companion.

Hattori's angular fringe hairstyle badly needed a comb. His coffee eyes were bloodshot. His face was youthful but worn.

Is this the first time I've eaten alone with a man my own age?

She couldn't recall another instance.

How my life has changed since the live show.

Her priority for this meeting was to win a promise from Hattori never to attempt to end his life again.

But Miko sensed Hattori didn't want to address that subject.

However Miko tried to direct the conversation, it skirted around the edges of that particular swamp. Never heading into its unpleasant interior.

"Do you feel dry inside?" Miko said. Pouring more jasmine tea into Hattori's freshly empty cup. "Lacking energy? Have you lost interest in work? Have you lost interest in your hobbies? Is life like chewing on bubblegum with no flavor?"

"You describe it exactly. So it is true, I have burnout."

"You're a plane that has run out of fuel. You need to land and refuel. Can you take a long vacation?"

Hattori shook his head. Miko expected that. In Japan you must consider your coworkers when taking vacations since they'll be burdened with the work you're not doing. Taking a long vacation is considered selfish and could make Hattori's coworkers hostile.

"Then quit your job. Rest until you have recovered and afterwards go freelance like me, so you can control your hours."

Hattori recoiled back into his chair, waving his hand in front of his face and shaking his head. It was not a small reaction.

I felt such shame when I stopped being a nurse. How much worse it must be for a man.

"Then reduce the hours you work," Miko said. "You can't carry on like this."

"But I can't be irresponsible if the other team members are still working."

Miko sighed. "Our work culture is like an oven with no exits. No wonder there is so much *karōshi*."

Karōshi is a Japanese word meaning death from overwork.

"I am envious of Europeans," Hattori said. "I read they work about forty hours a week. Working in Europe must be like taking a vacation. I can't even imagine only working nine to five. The article said Americans work more, but not by much. They can still do their own stuff in the evenings. Why are they like that and we are like this?"

"Oh boy. It is one of my favorite things to wonder about such questions," Miko said, leaning forward. "I love reading about history and religions and concepts. A long sequence of past ideas and events has defined how we think now. Our present is the sum of the past. It is fascinating. I wrote a letter about this very subject at school, but my English teacher said it was too long to translate. My letter was about Japan's economic boom, Bushido and the Edo period, and our base belief systems, and how they underpin our work culture. And also how our current societal rules echo the coping strategies invented during the Edo period to avoid that time's social repression."

Hattori tilted his head and studied Miko. "You have a cute personality, Miko. And you're smart. I've met a lot of girls who act dumb even when they're not."

"I don't think it's honest to act dumb," Miko said. She twiddled with her bamboo chopsticks.

Is there something in my hair again?

"I agree. It isn't honest," Hattori said. "I want to read your letter. I want to know what made our work culture this way."

This request surprised Miko. Her parents and Uncle Ken and Fluffy Kitty got bored with Miko's ideas. They kept changing the subject. Except for Fluffy Kitty, who had no manners. He would simply state he was bored over and over until Miko gave up.

"Are you sure?"

"Yes please. It is a relevant subject for me. Can you send it to me? I'll send you a chat invite."

Miko replied to his message with her letter. To her amazement, Hattori opened the document straight away and began reading.

If my theories were alive, then this would make them very happy.

"So you were writing to Emma Rose?" Hattori said, looking up from his phone.

"Yes. We were each given a question from a different Canadian student to answer. The exercise was to write our answer in Japanese, then translate our words into a correctly formatted letter in English."

"You don't mind me reading it now?"

"No it's fine. Please continue."

Miko watched his eyes. They really were moving up and down, following the lines. He was actually reading what she had written. She couldn't help smiling as she refilled his empty cup.

Occasionally he nodded, or said 'ha hmmm', or 'oh, that makes sense', or 'of course'. He pursed his lips. Other times his lips seemed to be mouthing the words.

"I should have paid more attention in history class," Hattori said at one point. But not to Miko, to himself.

The best moments were when Hattori chuckled briefly and smiled.

"What's wrong with him?" Fluffy Kitty whispered. "He's reading one of your theories. How is the boredom not making his head melt?"

"This part about being like atoms doing things to other atoms, or rocks banging together," Hattori said. "I've thought about that too. It's so bleak."

"When I drive in the city, I sense a terrible bleakness. As if seeking comfort, we go within ourselves, only to find a cold empty space with no way out."

"Hopelessness," Hattori said. "Hopeless despair."

"Yes, exactly. I sense there's much suffering under the surface. So many wearing the approved mask of society to hide their true state. I fear behind these masks there are many faces screwed up in pain."

Hattori nodded.

"And I feel it's getting worse. I believe that's why we have so many escapisms. Computer games, manga, anime, pachinko—"

"Drinking," Hattori said.

"Yes. Because our reality is too unpleasant. Surely there should be joy in reality too? Escapisms are fun, but their universal existence and potency are a testimony against us. It is as if our individuality is so undernourished it seeks imaginary places where the self can be honored rather than diminished. Like anime girls having pink, yellow, and blue hair, an obvious reaction to our schools forbidding any hair color other than black."

Hattori closed his eyes and leaned back. He breathed deep.

"Your letter is enlightening. Now I get the reasons for our work culture. But I don't see a way out," he said. His eyes still closed. He rubbed his face with his hands.

"Not seeing a way is not the same as there being no way," Miko said. "I am worried you will try again what you tried at the bridge."

Hattori opened his eyes. He glanced at Miko, and then fixed his gaze on his empty rice bowl.

"I don't know why it is, but I can't make myself lie to you. I want to say I will be fine. Lie, like I lie to everyone about how I am inside. But misleading you feels wrong. Sort of pointless, like lying to someone who already knows the real answer. The truth is this wonderful week you've got me will soon be over. Then I'll return to work, and this dryness will build up again," Hattori said. "Miko, I can't fight it any longer. I don't know when. But I know for certain I will be standing on another bridge."

Miko knew Hattori had expressed his *honne*. The Japanese word honne means a person's true feelings and desires.

It contrasts with the word *tatemae,* which is a false front or façade. Tatemae means expressing what you are expected to express by Japanese society, according to your position in society and your circumstances. Tatemae is a kind of ritualized lying designed to reduce social discord and maintain group harmony.

Miko considered tatemae as another way the group suppresses the individual. Her whole life she had felt uneasy when expressing tatemae.

"Give me a month," Miko said. "One month to find a way out for you. Please."

Hattori looked up. He held Miko's gaze. He nodded.

"Say it, Hattori. Make your promise."

"I promise. One month from today."

After brunch, Miko drove Hattori to his apartment.

"Call me if it becomes too much," Miko said.

Hattori nodded.

Miko opened the taxi's rear door. Hattori took his satchel, but he hesitated halfway out the door.

"Will I see you again?" Hattori said.

"I will be checking on you each day."

"Each day. That sounds good. Perhaps I can buy you lunch tomorrow?"

"I agree. I'll pick you up here at quarter to twelve. Keep resting."

"I will. That is the easiest promise to make," Hattori said. "Goodbye, Miko. Goodbye, Fluffy Kitty. Goodbye, taxi."

He stood by the curb and waved as Miko drove off.

Miko couldn't help but note that Hattori had spoken to her car.

In Japan, customer service is highly regarded. Receiving more attention than it does anywhere else in the world.

Which is why the short dumpy man buying a box of limited edition Coconut & Brown Sugar Pocky acted so surprised when, halfway through the transaction, temporary convenience store clerk Arato Asada pointed his finger at the store's window, and screamed "aaaaaarrrr!".

Then ran from behind his counter, and straight out the store's door.

Video security footage, that Arato Asada later deleted, showed his customer standing confused. Had he purchased the Pocky sticks or not?

The Hidden Stealth Ninja taxi had driven past.

Since the police had rebuffed him on Thursday, Arato had spent every spare moment hunting that taxi. Staking out significant intersections in the areas where he had seen it before. Clutching his phone, ready to record the evidence needed to prove his veracity to the local police.

Burning hundred-and-fifty-octane shame-fuel, Arato pounded after the enemy taxi.

Ahead, he made out its shiny dark blue roof and lit vacancy sign amongst the tops of the other cars at the intersection.

Pedestrians gave him disapproving looks. Chastising him for running. But for once, Arato didn't care. They couldn't know he was acting to protect society.

The traffic lights changed and the taxi moved away. Too far off to video.

He continued his pursuit.

His arms pumping up and down. Chest out. Head back. Mouth open to suck in air. The shock of each footfall pulsing up his body. His store clerk name badge fluttering behind his neck on its black lanyard decorated with an array of tiny fried eggs.

But ahead was a crossing. The Red Man glowing.

What should he do? He had never jaywalked in his life.

However, this was a special occasion. He was on the trail of a dangerous criminal.

But when he reached the crossing, he skidded to a halt.

The Red Man was red!

Arato couldn't bring himself to break the rule.

Ahead, his blue-roofed nemesis moved off, on towards another intersection.

Like a starting gun, the Green Man appeared, accompanied by the very-unlike-a-starting-gun sound of an electronic chirping chick.

Arato leapt back into the pursuit.

But the same thing happened at the next street. And the next. The taxi would stop several intersections ahead. The Red Man would stop Arato. The taxi would escape. The Green Man would appear. Rinse and repeat. Arato wasn't getting close enough to video the renegade taxi.

The taxi took a left turn.

The mall!

"Mid foot strike!" yelled an old angry faced man, his arms rammed down straight at his sides like a gymnast supporting himself on rings.

"Sorry," Arato said. He corrected his running style.

He skidded sideways on marble tiles as he turned, barreling into the mall's gaping mouth.

"No running!" the mall's security guard ordered.

"Sorry," Arato said. He reduced his pace to a fast walk.

The street the renegade taxi had turned into wrapped around the rear of the mall.

This was his chance.

He knew at the end of the mall's food court, on the opposite side of the building, an expansive glass window overlooked the street the taxi had taken.

He mounted the escalator and steamed up its right side, passing the people correctly standing to the left.

He zigzagged through the food court tables towards the huge window.

Arriving, he leaned against the stainless steel tube railing built to prevent people and machines bumping into the tall sheets of glass.

I got you!

Below, right in front of him, was the Hidden Stealth Ninja taxi.

He whipped out his phone. His phone was old and took many seconds to start recording. So he selected its still camera mode.

He aimed his phone down and started repeatably pressing its photo button.

But he was startled when two seagulls fluttered crazily against the other side of the window. Their wings making a thrumming sound on the glass.

A moment before, out of the corner of his eye, he had detected the birds flying towards him.

If I hadn't been here for them to see, the dumb birds would have whacked straight into the glass.

The taxi had gone.

Arato reviewed his photos. He had taken nine shots of the taxi.

In the first photo, the seagulls had got in the way. He swiped to the second. Again, the seagulls hid the taxi. The third was the same.

"You stupid birds!" Arato said when he reached the last photo.

The people eating stopped and looked at him. In Japan it was rare for a grown man to yell "you stupid birds" in a food court.

"Sorry, forgive me," Arato said.

He turned his back, gripping the metal railing as if wringing out a towel. The seagulls had wrecked every photo.

The running caught up with him. Panting. His mouth as dry as burned toast, his legs tenderized by a thousand chefs with little metal hammers.

"Nothing will stop me," he said to himself. "I'll get you in the end."

He exploded into a coughing fit.

Pounding his chest with his fist to make it stop.

He tried to say "I'll get you" again. But he only produced a series of dry croaks.

A middle-aged server with her hair in a bun arrived from the nearby ramen shop. A paper cup of water on a black plastic platter.

He attempted to say thank you, but it came out as croaks.

Arato took the cup and drank.

With his throat eased, he could finally thank the thoughtful woman with non-croaking words and a grateful bow.

Then, dejected, Arato trudged back to his convenience store.

The next day, Miko picked up Hattori for lunch.

Miko was impressed with how he looked. Dark turtle neck shirt and dark gray dress jeans. His coat was fashionable.

In comparison Miko was underdressed with her puffer jacket and bright white T-shirt with a cartoon mouse and a speech bubble that said, "Squeak!".

It was worse when they arrived at the restaurant. It wasn't a cheap restaurant. There was even a man who took their coats.

The walls and benches and tables were constructed of light-colored cypress wood. The restaurant smelled sweet, like the chest of drawers in her bedroom. Her father had made her drawers out of the same wood.

Fusuma panels depicted fishing scenes, and red *chochin* lanterns made with silk over bamboo frames hung from the wood ceiling.

They sat at a wooden counter and watched a sushi chef prepare their meal in front of them. The white-hatted chef didn't seem to mind Fluffy Kitty sitting on the counter staring at him with his cat-seen-fish attitude.

"This is too expensive," Miko whispered.

"Actually, it isn't expensive enough," Hattori said.

Miko glanced at Hattori.

What a strange response.

Hattori explained it was respectful to put your phone on mute and to avoid taking calls, since the sushi chef would want their full attention focused on the experience.

"It's OK for us to talk, but talking on a phone is rude," Hattori said. "First admire the sushi. Each piece is an artful endeavor by the Chef. But eat it quickly, because the flavor degrades from the moment it is made and the warmth from the Chef's hands is lost. Try to eat each piece as a whole, since it is not good to damage its form. And, if you would like, use your hands to eat so you can feel the sushi. I have found touching it adds to the experience."

After slicing wizardry with his super sharp knife, the Chef served them their first two sushi pieces on a bamboo *geta* plate, complete with wasabi he ground in front of them from the underground stem of a *japonica* plant.[†]

"I've never had real fresh wasabi," Miko whispered. "I've only had western wasabi."[‡]

Miko tried her first piece of sushi. Simple tuna on rice. It melted in her mouth.

"My taste buds are dancing!" Miko said. "I am surprised that food like this exists."

"Fine food is one of my guilty pleasures. I read magazine and online reviews to find out about the best places. Then I save up enough to treat myself. I don't eat much during the day I've booked, so I'm becoming hungry when I arrive. In that state, I can truly enjoy the experience."

"What an interesting hobby. It's as if a whole new world has opened up. One where magic spells are cast in my mouth."

"The worst is the following day. Having to eat normal-people-food again," Hattori said.

"But without normal-people-food, how could this be a delight? Without the ordinary to contrast with, we can't have treats. It is the distance between them that makes the best special."

Hattori smiled. "I hadn't thought of that. I will now feel better after my food experiences."

"Do you feel better?"

Hattori breathed in. "A bit. Sleep helps. It's nice sharing this time with you."

"Your eyes aren't as bloodshot. I believe you have combed your hair."

"I had a long shower too," Hattori said. He turned to Miko. "Say, do you want to fan talk?"

"Fan talk?"

Miko didn't miss Hattori's sudden changing of the subject.

"About Aftershave. Nana and Masumi and Eichi and I spend hours fan talking."

"I've never done that. How does it work?"

"We just tell each other our thoughts. Then we discuss. You start."

She shrugged. "OK. So, I've written an essay about Aftershave. If you'd like to read it?" Miko said.

She needed to figure out another way of uncovering how Hattori was doing.

He must have intense shame about what he tried. That's why he changed the subject.

---

† Japanese horseradish.
‡ Most wasabi in inexpensive restaurants is simulated; made with common western horseradish, sweetener, and food coloring.

Hattori chuckled. "Of course I would. You should start a blog."

Miko placed her chopsticks on her little ceramic *hashioki* rest, and used her phone to attach a copy of her essay to a chat message.

Hattori explained to the Chef that he was not doing social media, but was reading something Miko had authored. The Chef seemed to appreciate being told.

Once again, Miko enjoyed watching Hattori. It was fun seeing someone else react to her ideas.

"It's so true these things you've written. It is like our trio naturally belong together. And they don't feel manufactured," Hattori said. "And I also agree they aren't an idol group. Instead they are, like you say, their own unique thing."

He kept thumbing his phone's screen upwards.

"'Aftershave is like the Japanese Beatles'?" Hattori quoted. "That's the band old people like. 'Because the whole is greater than the sum of its parts'?"

"After The Beatles broke up, their individual members produced good music. But never super amazing like when they were together. The Aftershave members are each very talented, but working together they have created something far beyond the total of their individual abilities."

"Like in anime when the team members are losing, and so they join together to form a giant robot to defeat their enemy?"

"Exactly," Miko said laughing. "Any two Aftershave members together is a one plus one equals two situation. But the three members together, that's when their talents magically mix to make one plus one plus one equal ten."

Hattori nodded and kept reading. His mouth parting slightly in the last paragraphs before he finished Miko's essay.

He put his phone away in his pocket.

"Your essay ends with this 'Magic of Love' section with these four Greek words for love. Your conclusion is so obvious, once someone points it out. I didn't know the Greeks classify friendship as a type of love. I knew there was something more to Aftershave than their music and dance."

"The Greek word *Ludus*, their dancing together is joyful, like children playing. *Pragma*, they have a mature friendship—"

"Mature friendship?"

"They know each other well, including each other's faults, and despite those faults, they are committed to their friendship. And *Agape*, exampled in their universal love and appreciation of their fans. And *Philia*, their actual strong bonds of friendship," Miko said, sipping her green tea.

"Like you say, it explains their magic," Hattori said. "And you also say this magic is why they have so many international fans? We've often wondered how, especially since those fans don't know Japanese. How can they understand their songs?"

"They don't need to, because at its core Aftershave is a representation of love. That's a language every human understands. Everyone yearns for love. And so as Aftershave demonstrates love in their music and dance and interviews, people are drawn to them."

Hattori went to say something. Then paused. Before finally speaking.

"Miko," Hattori said, quietly.

"Yes?"

"You're the most interesting person I have ever met."

"Ha, that can't be true."

"It is. I don't know how many hours of fan talk I've been involved in. But I've never heard anything so insightful."

"Did I get fan talk wrong? It was my first time. Tell me what you talk about."

"No. I can't. After that, I am too embarrassed to say."

"Be fair. I want to know."

"Alright, but don't laugh at us," Hattori said.

"I won't. I am looking forward to hearing these examples."

"OK. One example, we wonder about Kirari. Who do you think she shares her deepest secrets with? Her friends or her cat?"

"What an interesting question. Cats are easier to talk to than people, and they're better at keeping a secret secret. So I vote for her cat."

"You agree with us then."

"What do you wonder about Ace?"

"She is such an extrovert. So we wonder if Ace was at dinner with lots of interesting people, and she was challenged not to talk. Could she do it? Or would she find it impossible to remain silent?"

"She would find that super difficult. When people focus their attention on Ace, it's like lighting a sparkler."

"Again, you agree with us. And Miyu," Hattori continued. "She dislikes skirts and dresses, and prefers shorts instead. Right?"

"True."

"So we wonder, if she gets married one day, will Miyu wear shorts to her wedding?"

"She might! She does have a quirky sense of humor," Miko said. "I would never have thought of these questions."

"It is the job of fans to think of these things," Hattori said.

"I can see it is important work. I must try harder."

"Do your best."

They both laughed. Miko with her hand over her mouth like she always did.

The excellent sushi kept coming. She found it easy to talk with Hattori.

Miko gently worked in questions about Hattori's work.

She learned about the endless nominications, the reports and paperwork, and waiting for the famous chairman to leave before the lesser staff could stop working.

She discovered Hattori's boss scanned the floor, looking for anyone up from their desk. And that his boss yelled at his workers in front of the others, like Nurse Goto used to yell at her.

Bully rules. Bullying bullies everywhere.

"I'm worried," Hattori said. "At work, there's this new recruit. When I give her instructions, she nods her head each time she says *hai*. And boy, she says hai a lot. More frequently than anyone else."

"What worries you about that?"

"I worry that if I talk too fast, her head will fall off."

Miko laughed.

It is a good sign he can make jokes.

After lunch finished and she had dropped Hattori outside his apartment building, Miko drove away with her taxi's availability light green—meaning the taxi was unavailable.

"Where are we going?" Fluffy Kitty said.

"The library."

"Oh no. Not the boring library. Please no, not there. I've just been tortured for hours with delicious-smelling fish being waved in front of my nose. Now you want to take me into that book-infested pit of gloom. What have I done to deserve such maltreatment?"

"I see you're in a complaining mood."

"I only have one mood. By the way, Hattori seems nice."

"Yes he is."

"I knew it," Fluffy Kitty said. "You like him."

"Don't be silly."

"You like him! You like him! You like him!"

"Even if I did. He wouldn't like me back with my problem. So the discussion is moot."

"Have you ever considered that the school bullies were lying to you about your looks?"

"Don't tease me," Miko said. "No one would lie about that aspect of a person."

"You have too much faith in humans. One day, you will learn it's better to listen to your cat."

Before becoming hikikomori, Miko had frequented bookstores and libraries.

Being inside Tokyo Metropolitan Central Library was like swimming in a massive vat of interesting toffee. Thousands and thousands of sweet books, waiting to cure the curious of their curiousness.

Miko liked to imagine that an author's mind became pregnant with an idea. Then, after exceptional pain and struggle, their mind gave birth to a baby. Their mind-baby.

Bookstores and libraries were giant nurseries where thousands of mind-babies cried out for attention.

Miko placed her backpack, Fluffy Kitty, and a yellow legal pad on one of the russet-grained study desks.

There were two rows of these desks arranged two abreast next to the windows. Unoccupied, except for a male student reading manga at the room's far end. He was using a mauve reusable book cover to hide his manga's title.

"Behave," Miko whispered. "I need to concentrate without constant interruptions. Like when I was studying."

"At least tell me why I am in agony? Trapped in this book-ridden prison of endless boredom. This bubbling stew of mindless tedium. This—"

"Yes, I get it. I get it. We're here because I know Hattori was honest with me yesterday. He will die if his work conditions don't change. I must save him. Before he heads back to that bridge."

"How will us being in this festering zone of dullness achieve that? Are you going to tie books around Hattori so he'll float?"

"This is serious. I have to invent a strategy. So no interruptions."

Soon Miko had business magazines and books piled on the wooden desk. She hunted through the history of Hattori's Pēpāwāku Masutā Corporation and of Ikari Conglomerate, scribbling pages and pages of notes on her yellow pad.

Chairman Tarō Ikari became Miko's primary focus.

She had known since her school days he was head of Ikari Conglomerate, and head of the country's most powerful keiretsu. She remembered watching the Chairman's speech on her bedroom TV the evening of the bridge incident, when she was fifteen.

Thankfully, the articles about the Chairman were as plentiful as leaves in a forest.

A particular event stood out, involving a two hundred billion yen failure of a significant computer game release.

Ikari Conglomerate blamed a single man, one of their directors, Daisuke Kuroda.

Daisuke was a close associate of Chairman Tarō Ikari. They had been school friends.

Yet, Daisuke had taken the fall for the expensive mistake.

Something is not right here.

Miko delved deep into the event's history. Until the library closed.

"Finally," Fluffy Kitty said, as Miko packed up. "So did my long hours of suffering bear fruit?"

"I have a strategy to save Hattori," Miko said.

"Does it involve any more libraries?"

"It involves a two-way attack. The first through public opinion. The second through the ego of Hattori's chairman."

"Sounds good. Don't know how it will work, or what it means. But it sounds good."

"Try to understand. Hattori is trapped in his deeply ingrained mindset.

A mindset constructed over his lifetime to cope with our work culture. He sees no way out."

"So, you're going to make a way out?"

"Exactly. In a way, Hattori's mindset is rational, given the nature of his trap. So I must change that trap."

"Our country's work culture? How can a twenty-six-year-old taxi driver hope to change that?"

"Because, while it is true I am an insignificant twenty-six-year-old person, the difference now is I have hope. I like to imagine how the Aftershave girls felt, starting their group when they were only twelve. I bet all they had was a hopeful dream too. And look at what happened."

Outside, it was already dark. Miko strode towards her taxi. Tumbling in her mind were the many obstacles that could derail her strategy, and ideas for ways to counter them.

In the dim lighting, in the shadow of the trees that surrounded the car park, Miko saw someone. The person-shape quick walked deeper into the trees and disappeared. For a moment Miko swore that shape had moved like Senior Nurse Goto.

Stop being paranoid, and concentrate on the mission. This will be the most important thing I've ever done. To save Hattori, I must be a brave person. Braver than Miko Nishimura has ever been.

It was dark at 7 pm when Miko backed her rumbling taxi into its garage.

Hanging tools, the garage door, and other metal items rattled in sympathetic resonance with the taxi's rumble. Becoming suddenly still when Miko switched off the engine.

Tonight Miko needed to collect a takeout from their favorite yakitori shop for a late dinner at Uncle Ken's.

But first, she located a business card stuffed in the center console and dialed its number. A recorded woman's voice informed her the call was being redirected internationally.

"Hello. Ittetsu Yoda? This is Miko, the taxi driver."

"Miko! My heroine! I caught my plane. Thanks to your amazing driving skills I'm here in Seoul, organizing this tour. Instead of sleeping in a cardboard box under the Shinjuku rail bridge, as an out-of-work manager."

"I'm happy you made your flight. About what you offered, I've decided I'd really like to meet Jekyll."

Miko had researched Jekyll. He was one of Japan's biggest rock stars.

"That I can do for you. In fact, for saving my career, I'll arrange for you to marry him."

"That won't be necessary," Miko laughed. "Could I just drive him someplace in my taxi? I'd prefer it if he didn't know it was an arranged meeting. To make it more natural."

"You're in luck. Last Wednesday a trainee manager selected reverse by accident, and backed our main van straight into our secondary. He banged up both vans beautifully. So Jekyll is using taxis and rental limos for the next few weeks. How about this Tuesday evening?"

"Tuesday is perfect. I hope your trainee is OK?"

"Our staff manager popped a pressure valve. But Jekyll defended the trainee, so he's still with us," Ittetsu said. "Right, so on Tuesday, I'll call you with the details."

"Thank you for arranging this. I will look forward to your call. Please have an enjoyable evening in Seoul."

Miko waited, letting Ittetsu hang up first.

"You don't even like rock music," Fluffy Kitty said. "You say it sounds too angry."

"Only modern rock. But Jekyll is number one so often, which means he has genuine talent and an enormous fan base. So, I plan on putting both those things to good use."

Monday was the 13th of January, Coming of Age Day 2014.

At 11 am Miko was sitting in a cozy Starbucks across from Chihiro Ueno, the trainee makeup artist who had helped protect little Hanaka from the bullies.

Rushing past the cafe's window were lots of twenty-year-olds wearing colorful furisodes.

Miko sipped her tasty hot chocolate. Listening while Chihiro continued her phone call with Suzu Mochizuki.

Miko liked how Chihiro's fingers danced side to side on the table when she was talking, and how her fingers jumped on the spot when she was listening.

"My English is passable. But not good enough to sound natural to a native speaker," Chihiro said. Her metallic-red mobile phone up to her ear—the phone was rimmed with fluffy pink fur and covered in Little Bird Shopping Street coffee shop stickers.

Suzu Mochizuki had been easy to find. There was exactly one English CV doctor in Kōfu City.

Suzu even had a website with her picture. Her face was older, but it was the same face from the school yearbook; the face Uncle Ken had fallen in love with so many years ago.

"I agree. Much better in person. If I paid for the tickets, could you take the train and meet me in Tokyo?"

Miko leaned forward.

"I know a quiet cafe. Perfect for talking," Chihiro said. She looked at Miko and held her eye. "Your husband won't mind you being away for the day?"

Chihiro listened to Suzu's reply. She shook her head at Miko.

"Well, maybe you could bring your boyfriend? You both could explore Tokyo afterwards."

Miko squeezed her Starbucks cardboard cup. Then put the cup down, afraid she might squeeze too hard and create a hot chocolate disaster.

"Oh, well, looking around by yourself would be fun too," Chihiro said. "So I'll have a good think about this. I'll call you back with my decision."

After a few more pleasantries, Chihiro rang off.

"So," Chihiro said. "No husband and no boyfriend."

Miko clapped her hands several times. Held them together in the prayer position and thank-you bowed to Chihiro.

"Sorry to have made you do this. But thank you. You have been super helpful," Miko said.

She placed some paper yen on the table to pay Chihiro for her good work.

The next evening, mega-rock-star Jekyll tossed his yellow plastic bag of swag into the back of Miko's taxi and followed it in.

The light from a nearby street lamp projected through the transparent bag, casting a long yellow triangle on the taxi's beige vinyl seat. Inside the bag were expensive items the fashion show's sponsors hoped Jekyll would be seen wearing.

Most of the items he would give away. Except the gray wool Prada scarf. Fender would enjoy sleeping on that.

He fixed his seemingly messy, but actually carefully designed, rock-star hair in the car's mirror.

As the taxi's door closed, his twelfth sense—a sense peculiar to celebrities—detected fans converging on the taxi.

"Hi," he said to the driver.

His fans began to congregate respectfully outside the taxi's door.

He missed his luxury vans, both now wrecked. The staff managers who drove him knew not to talk. These taxi drivers didn't.

Not that he didn't enjoy conversation, but he liked to daydream as he traveled. There was something about moving that stimulated his creativity.

He had been more creative when younger. So, as he approached the grand age of fifty, he clung to every trick that helped him commune with his waning creative fire.

"Hello," the taxi driver said. "Nice to meet you."

It was a girl.

"I like your cat."

"That's Fluffy Kitty. He rides with me."

She's pretty. What a soothing voice, such cadence.

The taxi rumbled into life.

As they drove off, Jekyll waved at his throng of smiling fans.

Was my wave too flippant?

He chastised himself. He didn't want a viral video of him waving dismissively at his fans.

Over the years past, the young musician's novelty of having devoted fans had worn off. During his early rock days in Tochigi Prefecture, where he was born, he had cherished each new fan and treated them with deep respect.

I must not let my weariness show.

He would soon forget them. *So many faces.* But they'd live with the memory of meeting their musical hero Jekyll for the rest of their lives.

I mustn't crush their hearts by treating them unworthily.

I am a professional. I will be professional. As penance, I will interact with this driver. She will feel privileged to have my attention.

"What did the staff tell you?"

"Never to reveal your home address. I promise, your secret is safe with me."

"It's not much of a secret anymore," Jekyll said. "What's your name?"

"Miko."

"You a fan?"

"Not really. Sorry. But not because of you. I'm just not into rock or metal. But I have heard your songs before."

"You are honest."

"I have seen a video clip from one of your live shows. I must tell you, there's one instrument you play masterfully."

"I've been playing guitar since I was eight years old."

"No. Not the guitar. The crowd."

Jekyll chuckled. "The crowd will turn on you in an instant. You must grab them by the throat from the moment you walk on stage and never let go."

"Sounds scary," Miko said. "And you have a new album coming out?"

Jekyll exhaled. "In a couple of weeks. The product of two years of sweat."

"What have the people who've heard it said?"

"That they love it."

"But, isn't that what people always say to famous people?"

"I know," Jekyll said.

"Don't worry. If it's bad, people will still buy it."

"Thanks."

"They just won't buy your next album."

Jekyll sank back into the taxi's seat. "You really know how to push an entertainer's buttons."

"I wouldn't worry," Miko said. "Unless your new album is a rehash of your old ones."

"There are some fresh themes."

"Are you sure? Let me guess. Boy meets girl. Young rebelling against their parents. Life styles. Lost love. Found love. Self-motivational stuff. Death. Bad relationships. Drinking. Drugs. The devil. It's lonely being famous. Rejection. Individuality. Hypocrisy. Depression. Partying.

Money. Lack of money. Wanting money. Needing money. Possessing too much money. The wrong people having money. How am I doing?"

Jekyll tilted his head back against the headrest and rubbed his eyebrows with firm strokes.

"Don't be sad," Miko said. "Most artists stick to familiar topics. They avoid subjects that matter."

"Those subjects matter."

"They're the safe subjects. They won't get you in trouble. It's what people expect rock musicians to sing about. If only there were an artist brave enough to use their platform to confront the genuine issues of our society."

"Like what?"

"Well," Miko said. "How about companies exploiting their workers? That's a genuine issue. A few days ago, I pulled a salaryman off a bridge. He had tied a heavy weight to himself. He chose to drown rather than face another day at work."

"Oh wow. That's horrible."

"To be honest with you, sir, the pattern of our work culture makes me angry. Every night I see salarymen and women who are like zombies..."

Jekyll listened to the driver talk as the taxi rumbled on through Tokyo.

She detailed their long hours, unpaid overtime, compulsory drinking parties, being too tired for relationships, the terrible consequences of burnout, and cruel bosses who treated people like expendable cogs in their corporate machine, encroaching into their workers' personal lives and interfering in their workers' personal decisions, and most of all, stealing their workers' time.

This was nothing that Jekyll hadn't heard before.

But the girl's concern. Her passion. And her voice. There was something about her voice. Hammered her ideas into his mind like silver nails through his skull. Yet, her words were as soft as a feather pillow.

"... many thousands of your fans are suffering like this. I'm sure you realize you'd just be another wannabe musician without your fans, right? So in return for your fans' help, the least you could do is express their pain through your music?"

Jekyll grunted in agreement. The taxi girl continued.

"Perhaps write a song that does more than express their pain. You could use your platform to help push society to reject these terrible practices."

Jekyll breathed sharply at the implications.

The driver spoke of challenging the core of Japanese work culture. If he did that, there would be no rewinding that tape. His business contacts would feel slighted.

"Maybe I could write a song like that," he said.

"But you won't."

"I won't?"

"No. Because despite any enthusiasm, the pushback from business would be enormous. You will surrender. You'll let the suits prevent the song being released."

"I do have a backbone."

"I'm sure. But how long could your backbone cope with pressure from the top?" Miko said. "You have to admit it would be hard."

"Of course it would be difficult."

"To succeed, you'd have to write and produce the song fast. Get it released before word got around. Circumvent the official release procedure. That's what I suggest."

"Fast," Jekyll said under his breath.

The taxi pulled up in front of his apartment complex.

"Here you are," Miko said. "Your staff prepaid."

"Thank you. Maybe keep your ear on the radio."

"I will. And since I know the pressures you will face, I'll be super impressed if you make that song."

They said their farewells.

Jekyll got out. Almost forgetting his swag bag.

Standing out on the sidewalk he felt refreshed, like he did after a vacation-sleep. He stretched in the crisp clean air like a waking baby.

Kasei, the luxury apartment's bald doorman, opened the wide polished copper doors for him.

"Kasei, has there been a storm?"

"No, sir."

"Odd," Jekyll said. "I could swear—"

He looked around. The sidewalk and road were unexpectedly dry.

Entering the building's plush foyer he took his private elevator up to his penthouse suite.

Once there, Jekyll stood still in his tennis-court-sized living room, staring out his floor-to-ceiling windows at the expanse of electrically lit Tokyo. A glass of whiskey in hand.

His ginger cat Fender resting on the sofa, ignoring him.

He stood unmoving, like a statue. Frozen still because the taxi driver's concern for Japan's suffering workers was gripping his mind. He could spare none of his brain's processing power for minor concerns, such as moving his limbs.

Like a miniature tornado, the driver's words were streaking around him.

His body tingled nose to toe. The rush had started as she spoke, but here in front of his windows it was crescendoing like a rolling timpani destined to end with a final smash of a gong.

After dwelling long on her concerns, he decided to think specifically about the song.

If he wrote it, what would the song be like? How should it sound? What mood should it set? The lyrics, the chorus, the hooks, the refrain?

At the moment he considered each question, the answers came to him. Like bolts of lightning arcing across the inside of his skull.

Even when young, Jekyll had sensed his creativity only as a far light he strained to see. Like a man in a dark forest, unsure that he saw through the web of swaying branches the faint light of a distant window.

Now, for the first time in his life, he stood inside that far off room. Basking in its creative glow.

"Meow," Fender said.

Fender had jumped up on the onyx side table in front of his matching bookshelf.

His cat pawed the spine of an old red notebook jammed between the travel guides he used to learn about the countries he was touring.

The tatty fabric covered book was his first composition notebook. Purchased back in his Utsunomiya days with his teenage pocket money.

"Of course," Jekyll said. "It still has some blank pages."

After patting his cat, he pulled the hallowed hardback out of the bookshelf and opened it on his smoked glass dining table.

Turning to the first blank page, near the back, he wrote,

My Time, Your Time

and underlined it twice.

He dialed his schedule manager.

"Ittetsu. It's me. Cancel everything for tomorrow and Thursday."

"No. No. I don't care. Tell them I'm sorry. I promise to come on next week."

"Sure. I can do fifteen minutes instead. And get the band in to the studio first thing tomorrow morning."

"Then get him on a flight back. Tonight."

Jekyll dialed his producer.

"Keiichi. I'm pulling 'Mechanical Love'."

"Because it's B-side filler. We're producing a new track tomorrow."

"Yes, I know the CD press schedule. We've still got until Friday. And I want that session guy, tall with the rings. Forgotten his name."

"No. Bongos. He's a bongo god. Rings in his nose."

"Yeah. Him. Get him there on Thursday morning with his full kit."

Jekyll made several other phone calls that resulted in many panicking.

Next, he placed his worn acoustic guitar on his lap and started strumming. Soon he was recording sensational new riffs and lyrics in his red notebook.

As he worked, in the far back corner of his mind, right next to the part where he wondered about the mysterious origin of the white fluff he discovered in his belly button each morning, Jekyll puzzled on why the hundreds of song suggestions from other people had never gripped him, and yet, in an instant, this young taxi driver's idea had set his heart ablaze.

Wednesday evening Miko scouted Hattori's work.

The complex stretched for several blocks. Three fat towering skyscrapers linked by squat buildings, crescented around an ornamental park.

A one-way serpentiform street bounded the western end of the park. Opposite that park, executive cafes and restaurants lined the street's western side.

This was the central office complex of Japan's powerful Ikari Conglomerate.

Miko scrunched in her shoulders and tucked in her chin as she stared up at the mirrored glass monsters looming above her. Faceless and sheer in the night. Each skyscraper reflecting the bright moon, like an accusing eye of a giant cyclops.

"What are we doing in this place?" Fluffy Kitty said.

"Reconnoitering."

"Another boring dictionary word. Let's go see if there are any birds in that park."

"Later. First we must explore the beginning of this road."

Miko took the sidewalk to the complex's entrance.

The main road joined the complex's one-way street through a turnoff flanked by two imposing gray tiered stone pillars. Solid, lean, and tall, like emaciated ziggurats.

Miko examined the stainless steel eyelets set into the side of each pillar.

Behind the eastern pillar was an inset loading zone, four car lengths long. Designed to feed the barn-sized service doors set in the slab gray side of the nearby building.

Miko didn't notice a security camera high on the top of the gray building, aimed down at the complex's entrance.

She checked the time. It was almost 7 pm.

"Now we'll go to the park."

At the park, Miko sat on the bench seat farthest from the wide marble stairs that ran down the center of the park. Under a cherry blossom tree to hide her from the offices above. The tree didn't have its flowers yet, it wasn't cherry blossom season.

"You and Hattori had a long lunch today," Fluffy Kitty said.

"It was a nice lunch."

With each passing day off work, Hattori's eyes were less bloodshot. Today he had made several funny jokes.

He had impressed Miko, by posting an envelope to the business whose teardrop sign's base he had taken. Apologizing anonymously and paying with cash for the damage and inconvenience he had caused.

"Your lunch with him on Monday was long too. And yesterday's lunch went till after 3 pm."

"Because I need to check up on him."

"You mean because you need to cross out Ren Matsuda inside your pencil case, and write 'Hattori' there instead."

"Very funny."

A white robin with a splodge of red feathers on its chest landed on the other end of the bench.

It made little jumps towards Miko, then stopped halfway, eying Fluffy Kitty.

"It's OK," Miko said.

The robin came closer. It hopped up onto Miko's right knee.

"How has your day been flying around in the sky?" Miko asked.

"Cheep cheep cheep", stated the robin.

"Why, that sounds like you have been very busy."

Miko ruffled the feathers on the back of the robin's neck with the tip of a finger. Then she smoothed the feathers down, before ruffling them up again. She repeated the process, since birds seemed to like the feeling.

"Yum yum yum!" Fluffy Kitty said.

"Stop it. You always do that," Miko said.

"Yum yum yum!"

"Stop it."

"I'm trying to, but, but, yum yum. Yum yum yum!"

"Hush cat. Here is the limousine."

A short black limousine threaded its way along the street, wafting to a stop in the reserved space at the bottom of the stairs.

Miko noted the time: 7:05 pm.

Five minutes later Chairman Tarō Ikari emerged from the center skyscraper's revolving glass entrance.

Dark suit, carrying a black briefcase. Head high, shoulders back, the great man paused to survey his realm.

Unrushed, he walked down the middle of the marble stairs like a lion striding through his pride.

Glancing up from under her blossom tree, Miko spotted an office worker staring down from each floor. Exactly as Hattori described.

The driver stood holding the rear door as the Chairman climbed in.

Less than a minute later the limousine drove off.

Miko glanced upwards again. The floor watchers were gone.

Four days later it was a dark Saturday evening, and Arato Asada was on patrol.

He midfoot stepped along the sidewalk in marshal rhythm. Muttering to himself.

People sensed him coming, keeping out of his way like runners before a charging bull.

Then it happened.

The Hidden Stealth Ninja taxi crossed the intersection ahead, driving left to right.

Arato broke into a run.

Arriving at the intersection he turned right. About fifty meters ahead, the street lamps reflected off the shiny dark blue taxi as it indicated right and turned down a side street.

"Yes!"

Arato knew a shortcut to an overbridge that spanned the road the taxi had taken.

He launched himself into the narrow alleyway that zigzagged through splotches of light emitted from the grungy rear windows of the ground floor apartments. Dodging the bicycles and lumpy air conditioning units that populated the alleyway.

A cat darted out of his way.

Arato reached the overbridge. The road dipped down under the bridge from the left, and rose again on the right. However, the streetlights on both sides revealed an empty road in each direction. Not a single car. Not a single person.

Arato cursed. How could he have missed that infernal taxi again!

"Thank you," a male voice said from below.

Arato ran over to the bridge's left side and leaned over the metal railing.

There, below, lit by the streetlight, was his enemy.

A man in a white karate *gi* tied with an orange belt was walking away from the renegade taxi.

Arato pulled out his phone and fumbled to unlock its security screen.

The departing passenger opened a door in an apartment building and disappeared inside.

After unlocking his phone, Arato touched the screen to bring up his camera application.

Below, the girl was talking to someone in the taxi. It might have been her silly toy cat.

He tapped the record icon on his screen. It took several long seconds for his old phone to start recording.

There! He had it. He was videoing the girl and her taxi. The very things the police claimed he had invented. On his screen her face was clear and identifiable.

He kept the phone's camera fixed on the taxi as he walked across to the other end of the bridge, so he could video the company name on the side of the taxi's door.

Hidden Stealth Ninja Taxi Service. In yellow paint on dark blue, as clear as a lightning flash across a night sky.

He sensed the evidential video rushing into his phone, pulsing almost like a vacuum cleaner sucking up lumps. Guzzling the life force out of the girl with her illegal taxi and her stupid fluffy toy.

The taxi started its engine and pulled away from the curb.

But it was too late. There was no escape now for Hidden Stealth Ninja Taxi Service.

He climbed up on the railing and leaned out to video her departure, tracking her taxi as it drove under the bridge.

The righteousness of his actions overwhelmed him.

"The nail that stands out," Arato said gleefully. "Gets hammered down!"

He tossed his head back and started laughing.

The police would thank him. This rule-breaking renegade girl was doomed.

His glee grew into a mighty belly laugh. But his vibrating body made him overbalance.

Before he knew it, Arato's hands were scrabbling at the wrong side of the railing.

He was falling.

He struck the concrete lip of the bridge.

It threw his twisting body out into space.

Then his body wrapped around a nearby lamppost. Sliding down its thick metal stem.

He gripped the post, slowing down his fall. But not by much.

As he fell, he didn't notice a protruding metal strip nick his neck.

The offending hose clamp secured a round speed limit sign to the lamppost. But the sharp end of its metal strip hadn't been trimmed.

Arato landed on the sidewalk mostly on his left leg. His legs collapsed under him from the force of the impact, twisting him around so he sat on his backside, leaning awkwardly half against the lamppost.

His phone bounced on his lap and clattered onto the concrete.

The fall had occurred so quickly.

Arato couldn't believe it had happened. To other people maybe, but not to him.

A wave of cold washed through him.

His phone seemed unharmed. He picked it up. It was still recording. It didn't have any new chips or scratches.

Something red squirted over his phone's screen.

Someone is behind me squirting ketchup on my phone?

The bizarre thought seemed the only explanation.

He turned to see who had the ketchup bottle. There was a sharp pain in his neck.

Instinctively, he reached up. But before his hand arrived, something warm squirted against the palm.

He looked at his palm.

Blood?

It's blood.

My blood!

Arato pressed his hand against his neck. A pulse of warm wetness squirted out between his fingers and then trickled down his arm. A coin-sized chunk of his neck was missing, slippery with blood.

Oh no.

To his right and left, the street was empty.

"Help me," he said. Then louder, "Help me! Help me!"

Yelling hurt. It made more blood come out.

But worse than that, Arato was sure no one would hear.

And even if they did hear, he knew they wouldn't come, because no one wanted to risk getting mixed up in someone else's problem.

More blood was running down his arm. Then its horrifying warmth was seeping under his collar and down the front of his chest.

I'm bleeding out.

Expanding outwards from the inner core of his body came an eerie weakness, seeping like chill water.

It was at that moment that Arato Asada. Former taxi driver and temporary convenience store clerk. Realized he was going to die.

He looked around at the world. The empty sterile street. The yellow rectangular lights sprinkled across the high gray slabs of the apartment buildings receding above, each window burning bright with unreachable hope.

It was unfair. Wasn't he worthy of more? More time? More love?

Was he a wicked man instead?

Did he deserve to die like this? Alone and forgotten in his moment of passing.

As his body grew colder, how Arato yearned for someone to embrace him. Like his mother did when he was a boy.

Even for the look of a concerned stranger. Anything, instead of this bitter loneliness.

He forced himself to focus on his phone. With one hand he stopped it recording and tapped to bring up the phone's keypad.

Arato tried to dial 119 for help, but his finger kept slipping on the blood covered screen.

He couldn't make the screen's 1 button register a tap.

His body was becoming weaker.

He tried to wipe the blood away. The effort made him feel faint.

There was a mighty roar and screeching of tires.

Blue smoke filled the air, swirling around the rear of a dark blue taxi.

The renegade girl appeared running out of the tire smoke, carrying a green first aid kit.

"I thought I saw someone fall in my mirror. Let me look. What's your name?"

"Arato. I don't want to die. Please help me."

The girl ripped open a big packet. A large cotton gauze pad.

"Arato. I'm going to pull your hand away."

She did. Then she pressed the pad up hard against Arato's neck.

"Put your hand back and press firmly."

He obeyed. Pushing the pad tightly against his neck.

"Arato, your artery can't be cut too deep. Otherwise, there would be much more blood. Can you stand? I'm going to drive you to the hospital."

The girl helped him stagger into the back of her taxi. His body hurt in several places from the fall, but not sharply enough to be a broken bone or to override his fear of his squirting neck.

The driver dropped his phone on his lap and fastened a seatbelt around him.

She asked him about his medical conditions and any drugs he was taking. She inquired if he was allergic to anything, and asked specifically about penicillin and if he had ever had any reaction to anesthetics.

"I need you to stay upright. Keep your head above your heart. Keep the pressure on. What's your blood type, Arato?"

"Type A," he managed.

It is reassuring how she keeps saying my name. Is she a professional paramedic?

"That's the most common. You're going to be fine, Arato."

It's so far to the hospital.

The girl closed the door and ran around to her driver's seat.

"It's so far," he managed.

"Not really."

There came a shrieking roar and Arato's world exploded.

Pushed back so hard into the taxi's seat he missed a breath.

The end of the street zoomed up. Then was gone. He was flung to one side as a different street appeared. Then another.

The taxi's cabin howled. The girl's hands danced in a blur over the controls. The city lights streamed by like tracer rounds in a war movie.

It wasn't possible to go this fast.

Am I dead already? Is this the journey to the afterlife?

Two days later, on Monday morning, the hardware store's blue-tinted glass doors parted for Miko.

As the doors opened Miko thought she saw flashes of lightning reflected in the blue glass, followed by a sudden intense glare. As if a giant camera flash had gone off in the city behind her.

Followed a second later by a rumbling thunder that was silent in her ears but shook her bones.

But on looking over her shoulder, the city was its normal tranquil self. The sky blue with a few clouds and a thick flock of birds spiraling around what must have been a good thermal.

Inside the store, the other customers were all male, wandering the aisles searching for vacuum-packed magic items and squeeze tube potions crafted for them by DIY wizards.

It was Miko's second visit to the store. She had spent yesterday scrubbing, with the chemicals she had purchased during her first visit, to remove Arato's blood from the taxi's rear seat.

"I'm enjoying exploring shops again, like we used to," Fluffy Kitty said, from his perch on the metal shopping cart. "You know Miko, it's been only a month. I'm proud of the progress you've made."

"Thank you. The fact is, before the live show I didn't believe I could be this confident. But here I am. In fact, I'm freer now than I've ever been," Miko said, brushing some of her disobedient hair back into place. "For the longest time I believed there was an unclimbable mountain towering over me. But when I saw those three girls standing at the top of that mountain, suddenly I knew there must be a way up. So I've started climbing. I have a long way to go. But I'm so pleased when I look back and see how far up I have come."

"Climbing?"

"Overcoming my fears and changing my troublesome long-ingrained thinking patterns. It is such a laborious task, because a marble in a bathtub will always roll into the plug hole. And that's what our minds are like. It's very hard to change the shape of your bathtub."

Miko scanned down an aisle filled with spades, other digging tools, and mini-sized wheelbarrows with shiny red or canary yellow paint. She was searching for the home security section.

"What's been the hardest?"

"Breaking free from the prison of other people's thoughts. My entire life I have cared too much about what other people think of me. I've made progress adjusting my thinking patterns over the past month. But even with the help of the live show, it's still a struggle."

"Is it possible to entirely escape that pressure?"

"Only by abandoning society. Which I will not do again. Instead, I am learning to reduce the influence of other's opinions and increase the importance I place on my own desires," Miko said, picking out two large padlocks and placing them in the shopping cart.

"You will always place your desires first?"

"No dear cat. That would make me a selfish person. Instead, I will decide whether to place myself or the group first in each instance. This balanced approach seems healthiest. And so deleted in my head is the rule that the group automatically overrules what Miko wants. From now on, I will be defined by what I choose, not by the group's choices."

"But people will say you lack common sense and are stupid for not knowing how society works. You're brave to be a nonconformist."

"People can think whatever they want. But nonconformity is not my goal. If I base my life on rejecting the ways of the group, then that means my life is still being directed, in an inverted fashion, by the group. It isn't conforming or not conforming that matters to me. Instead, I am pursuing my heart's leading with no reference to the group. I want to become the authentic Miko. No longer do I want to live inside someone else's idea of how Miko should be."

She picked out a large rectangular corrugated-plastic sign that read, "Boots, Vests, and Hardhats Mandatory".

Yesterday at lunch, Hattori was apprehensive about his return to work today. He asked for a lunch promise on the weekend, since he wouldn't have time during the week.

"You're biting your lip. Are you worried about Hattori?"

Miko nodded.

"Hattori promised you a month," Fluffy Kitty said. "He doesn't seem the sort of person who breaks promises."

"I know. But last Wednesday I felt an oppressive force from those offices. And we didn't even go inside. It was like I could sense those office workers being drained. Hattori already has burnout. So I am afraid he won't be able to hold on that long. This makes me determined to carry out part two of my strategy soon. But the newspapers say Chairman Ikari is overseas, and not back until Sunday. By the time the Chairman returns, there will be only two weeks of Hattori's promise left."

For Miko, Hattori's first week back at work passed too slowly.

There were only a couple of moments when Hattori had time to chat with her via the messaging app.

Saturday came.

Hattori had spent the morning sleeping, so they met for lunch at 1 pm. Sitting next to a big double-glazed window in a small cafe.

The coffee grinder was grinding. The frothing-wand hissed, before gurgling angrily as its nozzle was drowned in milk.

Hattori's eyes were more bloodshot than a week ago. His skin careworn.

There were long silences between them. Miko would ask a question, but each time the conversation petered out.

Miko stared out the window at the people walking past while thinking up what to say next.

After they finished their toasted sandwiches, Hattori ordered another cup of coffee.

While the coffee was being made, he sat back down. He placed his elbows on the table and thumbs on his cheeks, and massaged his forehead with his fingers.

"I'm sorry, Miko," Hattori said, from behind his hands. "I've looked forward this whole week to seeing you again. But I don't have the energy. It's hard to put one thought after the other."

"Don't worry," Miko said. Breathing easier. The unexpected long silences had made her insides squirmy.

Discovering that Hattori had been looking forward to seeing her was a happy relief.

"Just relax and be yourself. You're not a performing seal. I don't expect to be entertained."

"I hope I'm entertaining. Sometimes."

"You are. But you're under work pressure again. Muddled thinking is a symptom of burnout."

Hattori nodded and kept massaging his forehead.

"I was so scared I'd be called into work today," he said. "Tonight I'll have another good sleep. So tomorrow I'll be more fun to be around. I promise. I mean, if you're able to have lunch with me tomorrow?"

"I am planning to. I need to keep an eye on you."

"Cool," Hattori said. He stopped rubbing his forehead, opened his massaging hands like window shutters, and studied her from between them. "Miko. If I wasn't like this, burned out, I mean. And if you didn't think I needed watching. Would you still want to meet?"

"Of course," Miko said. "We've had some good conversations."

"We have, haven't we," Hattori said.

There was a glimmer of a smile.

The shutters closed as he returned to massaging his forehead.

Imagine how happy he will be if my plan succeeds and he isn't overworked anymore.

Hattori's coffee arrived.

"Miko?"

"Yes."

"I will trust you with another of my secrets," Hattori said. He took out his phone and tapped on its screen.

He turned his phone so Miko could see.

There was one word on the screen.

"That isn't? That can't be," Miko said.

"It is."

"Oh. I see."

"Never tell anyone."

"I won't. I promise," Miko said. "But why? Why did your parents?"

"I suspect my father was drunk when he filled out the birth registration application. But he claimed later it was to make me tough. With a name like this, he said, I'd have to either sink or swim."

"Sinking isn't something you are allowed to do."

Hattori grunted.

He drank his new coffee like medicine.

There was another period of silence, but Miko didn't mind now she knew the reason.

Outside the window, a couple were holding hands. The woman wore a blue coat, and the tall man's coat was tan. They waited at the crossing next to the cafe's door for the Green Man's permission to cross.

The girl rested her head against the man's shoulder and was rewarded by a quick kiss on her hair.

"Do you know them?" Hattori said.

"I can see her ring, but not his," Miko said, craning her neck. "Can you see if the man is wearing his wedding ring?"

"He is."

Miko concurred. She had seen the glint of gold too.

"Who are they?"

"One of my first ever fares. They were on their way to get divorced."

"Well," Hattori said. "They don't look very divorced to me."

Monday, 27th January, had been sunny and clear except for a few lonely clouds that had swum leisurely across the Tokyo sky.

By evening, the scraggly tops of the commercial district's trees were swaying in a crisp breeze.

At five to seven, Miko parked her taxi in the loading zone behind one of the tall pillars that guarded the entrance to the expansive Ikari complex.

Above the gray loading doors, the complex's three skyscrapers loomed high against the city's hazy glow. A night sky scattered with only a few of the brightest stars.

A speckled pattern of lit skyscraper windows glared down suspiciously at Miko.

She switched off her rumbling taxi.

Sitting in the driver's seat, she struggled into the fluorescent orange high-visibility vest she had purchased at the hardware store. Its color didn't suit her.

"This is it?" Fluffy Kitty said.

"It is."

"Do your best."

At precisely 7 pm, Miko stepped out of the taxi and put on a yellow hardhat.

Her heart was playing an impressive drum solo, with lots of crashes and rolling snares.

She pulled out her other hardware store purchases from the taxi's trunk.

The heavy metal chain was the most difficult. She lifted half the chain out. Dropped it on the asphalt. And dumped the other half on top.

Miko waited until the traffic lights upstream turned red and the feeder road down to the complex had emptied itself of cars.

By the light of a street lamp, she padlocked one end of the hefty chain to the stainless steel eyelet in the left-hand-side pillar.

She dragged the chain across the entrance to the other pillar. Feeding the chain through the eyelet, Miko heaved on the chain, ratcheting it up higher with each pull.

Once the chain hung in a shallow arc between the pillars, she padlocked it in place.

She lay out a line of six hip-high orange traffic cones and attached the big plastic sign she had purchased to the middle of the chain. Miko had painted the sign over with white paint, and added new bold lettering.

The sign now read:

ROAD CLOSED

She finished her amateur traffic management by linking the cones with reflectorized extension bars and fitting two orange strobes. One each onto the top of the cones that flanked the sign.

In the flashing orange light Miko removed her vest and hardhat and tossed the strobing items into the taxi's trunk.

She double-checked her work. In the moderate gusts, the plastic sign was tap-tapping against the cones.

"Time to be super brave," Miko said, firmly closing the taxi's trunk. "Braver than ever before."

She drove her taxi at a stately pace along the complex's twisty street.

Easing to a stop in the waiting zone at the bottom of the park's wide marble stairs. She switched the engine off and opened the rear passenger door.

Miko preened her taxi driver's uniform. Then stepped out of the taxi and stood next to its open rear door.

Over the park the faintest fog lingered in the chill air, sheltered from the wind in the lee of the towering buildings.

She placed a gray wool driving cap on her head to hide her face in case Hattori looked down from his office.

Hattori's presence, he was up there not far away, quickened her resolve and quietened her nerves.

The empty park was tranquil. The fog pierced from above by sharp cones of yellow from the ornate lamps.

The pairs of light cones that illuminated the stairs shrank away from Miko, as the park rose from the street towards the skyscraper's ground floor. Converging like ethereal pillars drawing the eye to the center skyscraper's tall rotating-glass door.

A background hum of low white noise from the powerful air conditioning plants on the tower's roofs was punctuated by the ticking beat of the taxi's cooling engine. A distant siren started far away and grew fainter.

Miko completed her transformation by slipping on white gloves.

In each of the floors above a face was pressed close to the glass. Waiting for the same event as her.

Time passed. Miko had arrived at precisely five past seven, and now she had been waiting for six minutes.

Has the limousine made a phone call? Is he coming out another way? If so, why are his workers still watching?

Each second passed, with the tremendous speed of a sloth riding a turtle that was sleeping on a glacier.

Miko shifted her feet. She made sure to keep her back straight.

Has my strategy failed?

At the top of the stairs, a figure of a man churned around inside the revolving glass.

He emerged, dark suit and black briefcase, and hesitated.

Then he began down the steps. Slower than Miko had observed ten days ago.

A minute later, powerful renowned Chairman Tarō Ikari, head of the mighty Ikari Conglomerate, stood in front of Miko Nishimura (formerly a schoolgirl from the countryside near Goshogawara in Aomori Prefecture).

"Deepest apologies, sir," Miko said. She bowed. "Your usual car experienced, um, physical difficulties at the last moment. It is hoped my humble taxi will be able to serve you this evening. Tomorrow your normal car will return."

"Physical difficulties?" the Chairman said. His voice baritone gravel.

"It is most embarrassing, sir," Miko said. Bowing again, lower.

"I am not unaccustomed to taxis. My home."

"Yes sir."

The Chairman climbed into the taxi. Miko closed the door behind him. Resisting the urge to slam it.

Being angry was not an emotion Miko often experienced. When she had spoken with Jekyll, it had been the harsh work culture that had made her angry, not the rock star himself.

But here was the man who was personally responsible for Hattori's unholy dilemma of grinding work or death.

Miko reminded herself about the importance of self-control. While she didn't plan to treat this man kindly, she needed to resist letting her emotions sabotage the goal of her mission.

She walked around and climbed into her driver's seat.

The Chairman had his arms folded and nose upturned, staring at Fluffy Kitty.

"Driver. Do you believe your mascot projects the image of a professional service?"

Miko started the taxi.

"Sir. I believe he projects the image of a cat."

The Chairman hissed in air through his teeth.

Miko drove out of the waiting zone.

"Driver. Back here. There's a chemical smell."

"That will be from the cleaning products I used a week ago to clean up the blood."

"The blood?"

"Yes. A man fell off a bridge and cut himself severely. I took him to hospital."

"How did he fall?"

"I'm not sure, sir. But I don't think it was deliberate. It was not a high bridge," Miko said. "However, sir, I have been having trouble with bridges lately."

Miko turned south towards Azabu-Jūban. The area where the business magazines said Chairman Ikari had purchased a multi-floor penthouse.

"My civil engineering firms manufacture fine bridges," the Chairman said.

"Sir, it is not the quality of the bridges that have been the issue. This month, I pulled one of your employees off a bridge. He had tied a weight around himself and was proceeding to jump into Shinnaka river."

There was a long pause.

"That is most concerning. I will have his name."

"No sir, you will not."

"He is my employee!" the Chairman said, slapping his hand on the back seat.

Miko didn't jump at the Chairman's raised voice or the bang on the seat. She had read about this man's temper and so had already steeled her mind to resist his forcefulness.

This was difficult, because in Japan to maintain harmony you are expected never to answer when yelled at, and instead give in without a fight.

I knew he was a bully. But I will not obey bully rules.

"Sir, I cannot give you his name. For his own protection."

"His own protection?"

"From you."

"From me! Driver, I dislike what you are insinuating!"

"I'm insinuating that you don't care about your workers. That you treat them like slaves. That you are a bad person. So sir, I'm not surprised you don't like what I am insinuating."

He thumped the seat again.

"How dare you speak to me in this manner!"

"Sir, I will speak to you in any way I see fit. And given that this honest, hard-working man was driven to end his life because of your policies and your management, I believe I am speaking to you exactly the way you deserve."

"It is not your place to answer to your senior in this manner," the Chairman said. His voice quieter, but soaked in imperious righteousness.

"Bully rules."

"What?"

"That's a rule made up by bullies like you. I ignore those rules. I will say what I want to say. And I will speak to whom I want to speak."

"You are promoting societal disharmony."

"Disharmony for you, maybe. Not for me. In fact, it would create disharmony inside me not to express my thoughts."

"That is not the Japanese way."

"Just who gets to define what is the Japanese way? And don't you go talking about Japan, sir. Your policies show you don't care about Japan one bit."

"I love my country."

"What is Japan? The land or the people?"

"It is both, and our traditions."

"Which of those is more important," Miko said.

There was a pause.

"People," the Chairman finally said.

"You don't really believe that."

"I do."

"No you don't. Because your actions betray you. Your companies make people work long hours. Consistently calling people in on the weekends. Your managers insist on after-work drinking even when people don't want to go. If people fail to meet these harsh conditions, then their jobs are threatened."

"Our work hours are consistent with other Japanese companies."

"Suppose I told you I beat my slaves the same amount as the other slave owners. And expected that to be a justification for my actions," Miko said. "You steal unpaid hours from people through fear of losing their jobs. You reward your managers with mandatory friendship through the drinking culture. You don't care that your employees don't have time for their families, or even time to find someone to make a family with. You, sir, are an exploiter."

"Driver, you are ignorant of Japanese work culture. Painting our traditions with the twisted strokes of a slacker. Japan's business success has been born from our trusted procedures. And you insult my motives. The truth is I seek to invoke the sacred traditions of the samurai."

"But sir, wouldn't a businessman be the same as a merchant? Didn't the samurai hold merchants in disdain?"

"It is not that simple. I focus on the traditions."

"No you don't, because traditionally samurai had honor, and you do not."

"How dare you—"

"Daisuke Kuroda," Miko said. She turned and held his gaze. "Daisuke Kuroda and the Divine Code Computer Games fiasco."

Miko turned back to the road.

The rumble of the engine and the occasional tick-tock of the taxi's indicators filled the long silence that followed.

"I know what you did," she said, quietly. "On the same day the decisions were made that doomed the project, Daisuke Kuroda was interviewed in a business travel magazine in Hawaii. He wasn't even in Tokyo. It was you. You were in charge. You made those mistakes. And you let your school friend take the fall." Miko turned and looked at the Chairman again. "I know Kuroda-san must have offered to take the blame. But you chose to accept his offer. You let your friend's reputation be destroyed. And that means you have no honor. Because an honorable man would never have done that."

The Chairman's face grew hollow. Miko returned her attention to the road.

"What is this?" he demanded. "Blackmail?"

"The better question to ask, is this. Are you a bad man, or a good man following bad rules?"

"I don't understand."

"If you're a bad man, then there's only one way for me to get what I want. But I prefer to hope that inside you are a good person."

"So not blackmail?"

"I guess that depends on your true character. I want you to reevaluate certain traditions. I believe traditions should serve the people, not the other way around. Once, traditions were new ideas. Useful in their day. But as time passes some traditions sour. You obviously believe this too, since your significant Divine Code failure didn't result in you committing *seppuku*."

"Seppuku!"

"If you believe you are following samurai traditions, then after such a monumental failure, an honorable death was your only path to protect your reputation and attenuate your shame. But obviously, you're selective about which traditions to follow and which to give up. So if you can give up seppuku, I suggest you give up some other traditions too."

"Wait. Where are you taking me? This is not the route to my home!"

"I'm taking you to the train station. There you will sit and watch your employees. You will reflect on the misery in their faces, and so let their suffering touch your heart."

"I demand to be taken home. This is kidnapping!"

Miko's foot tapped the throttle. The taxi roared forward. The Chairman was thrown back into the seat. Miko chopped down a gear to engine-brake the taxi. It popped and hissed as it slowed, until it again matched the speed of the other traffic.

"How does it feel not to be in control of your life?" Miko said. "Like your workers held prisoner to your policies. So you will go and watch their faces."

The Chairman was silent. He was struggling to put on his seatbelt.

"You claim to love Japan. But Japan is dying. Our country's population is aging because we are not having enough babies. Without more children, Japan will shrink until our old people can't be supported, and then Japan will end. Surely the survival of our nation is more important than hanging on to outdated business traditions? Especially when those traditions are destroying our country's future."

"How is that my fault?"

"Your policies and those of business tyrants like you are preventing relationships. Our country needs time for romance, not more work," Miko said. She turned into the road to the train station. "The young heart of Japan is vanishing. And these odious business traditions are the dagger being pushed through its heart. The time to act is now."

"There are many causes—"

"The impossibility of relationships is the largest cause. And don't make the mistake of believing the young will obey your bully rules forever. The young will either rebel or withdraw from this game that's rigged against them. Either way, the young will abandon the elderly. Then our society will disintegrate. Surely that's not an outcome you desire?"

"No one wants that," the Chairman said. "Driver, wait, there's another smell back here. I think your taxi must have an electrical fire. The smell is getting strong. Your car's wires must be arcing."

Miko checked the electrical system's gauges as she pulled up outside the train station. The readings were fine, and none of the dashboard's warning indicators were lit.

He is trying to distract me.

She stopped the taxi at one of the entrances to Tokyo Station. Miko liked this entrance because there were metal cones on the sidewalk that resembled the tips of giant crayons. Each time she dropped people off here she wished some artistic person would paint the cones in fluorescent crayon colors.

Now to give him his final directions.

"Soon your workers will arrive at the station. Go, and watch their faces. Do not go home until you perceive their hearts. And you will share in their pain without constraint."

Miko turned to the Chairman.

"Also, ask yourself, sir. What will be the legacy of Chairman Tarō Ikari? Do you want to be remembered as one of the old tyrants, hated and despised? Or do you want to be revered as the legend who brought about needed change? Chairman Tarō Ikari, 'Savior of Japan'. So, as you watch your employees, also think carefully about your legacy."

"You expect that your little speech will influence me?"

"It depends on that question I asked. Are you a bad man? Or a good man mistakenly employing bad rules?"

Miko pressed the button and the taxi's rear door opened.

The mighty Chairman said nothing more. He staggered out onto the sidewalk.

Miko drove off, heading west.

There was a road she needed to reopen.

Chairman Tarō Ikari watched the infuriating taxi depart. He memorized the taxi company's name.

How dare a child speak to her senior like that.

Without his approval, she had delivered him to a place he didn't choose to go.

It's kidnapping. I am sure of it. And her taxi is a fire hazard.

The sweet electrical odor hung in the air. Like the after-effects of lightning, but more potent.

It was the clean chlorine tang of ozone. He knew it well from visiting his factories that used arc welders.

The Chairman pulled out his black titanium Gresso Regal mobile phone and dialed the number for the police.

He knew the Commissioner General. The police would jump to the instant remediation of this insult he had suffered.

Soon, insolent girl, you will be under arrest and your faulty taxi impounded.

He stood righteously tall in the chill air. Winding his way through the police phone system until he had an actual police officer on the line.

"This is Chairman Tarō Ikari of Ikari Conglomerate. Just this moment, I have been abused and kidnapped by a taxi driver."

"Sir. We will come immediately. Where do they have you captive?"

"No, one person. The driver let me go. At Tokyo Station."

"He let you go?"

"Yes. She, it was a woman."

"You were kidnapped by a woman?"

"She took me to the wrong destination against my will."

"I see. What was the name of this taxi company? Do you have the taxi's plate number?"

"I didn't get the number. But the company was Hidden Stealth Ninja Taxi Service."

Laugher burst from the Chairman's expensive phone.

The call was muffled, likely the policeman had put his hand over the phone's microphone, but the Chairman could still hear faint voices.

"What is it?" someone said.

"Hidden Stealth Ninja Taxi Service," another voice said.

"Again!"

There was more muffled laughing, along with a single pained groan.

The policeman's voice returned to its normal volume.

"Listen carefully. Call us about this again and you'll be spending the night in a cell. Now you must excuse me, oh great Chairman Ikari. Because I have the Emperor on the other line. He's just been kidnapped by the Peach Boy."

Multiple people burst out laughing.

Then the line went dead.

Chairman Ikari stood rigid, holding his phone in front of him. Staring at the offending device with the angry bulging eyes and furious frown of a bewildered samurai.

What is happening?

Rapidly he glanced around. The buildings, the train station, the cars, the people. The world seemed normal.

I will take a taxi home.

But the Chairman didn't move.

As he thought about how to locate a taxi, he found he couldn't put the needed sequence of taxi-finding actions into any sensible order. The more he increased his concentration, the more vigorously his mind splashed aimlessly around in a turbulent sea of discombobulation.

It's the voice of that child.

Her glittering words were spinning around and around him, like fiery comets orbiting his soul.

He was embarrassed that the strong man he thought he was had been so unnerved by the speech of an audacious girl almost a third his age.

However he tried, her words were impossible to ignore. Sweet, softly spoken even in anger, but slipping between the joints of his armor like the tip of a dagger.

Why did I keep talking to her?

Normally he gave impertinent people the silent treatment. But she had been too goading. She had forced him to react.

I will not stay here. I will go home.

That determined thought produced a tightness in his chest. And a churning in his stomach, that rapidly escalated into a quivering inside his entire torso.

It was like an extreme version of the unease he experienced when he angered his wife and couldn't tell what he had done wrong.

With one hand, the Chairman rubbed his stomach and with the other he squeezed the back of his neck.

But if I did stay?

I could prove her wrong. It won't take much time. A few smiling workers and I can leave. Besides, I am thirsty.

The Chairman began walking. Into the station entrance, across the north walkway, and up towards the entrance closest to his office complex.

On the way, his mind became clearer and the disturbing quivering diminished.

There, by the entrance, he found a narrow cafe. Empty, with a few seats and a counter dominated by a silver coffee machine that hissed and steamed like an impatient locomotive.

"Are you the owner?"

"I am," the white-aproned man behind the counter said. He bowed.

"I want you to close for an hour," the Chairman said. He took out his wallet and dropped a pile of ten thousand yen notes onto the cash tray.

"Certainly, sir."

The owner came out from behind the counter and closed the shop's glass door. He reversed the door sign.

"Lock the door and turn off the lights," the Chairman said. He took a seat at a small round marble-topped table by the window. Placing his briefcase next to his chair.

The cafe went dark. The door's latch clicked.

"Americano with whiskey."

"Sir, the rules don't allow—"

In the dim light the Chairman held up five more ten thousand yen notes.

"Of course, sir."

Soon they came. It was easy to identify his employees by their yellow lanyards. Deliberately chosen in that garish color to make it easier for security to spot intruders. His company's standardized blue and white ID cards dangled under their chests.

The truth was the Chairman had long witnessed his employee's after-work demeanor. He had seen their obvious depletion as a pleasing sign they had given their whole effort to his company.

Business is war. Employees are dutiful soldiers obligated to sacrifice their essence for their lord.

But like butter on the sun, the girl's incandescent words had melted that particular dogma.

A sensation came of his first day at school—he had felt so frightened and out of place.

The Chairman took a sip from his spiked coffee. He watched the endless faces. He hadn't expected every employee to be unhappy.

His hand began trembling.

What has that girl done to me? Have I lost my edge? Am I no longer fit to be a businessman?

Now he perceived their gaunt faces dotted with hollow eyes, as if their bodies were oversaturated by a powerful spotlight.

They trudged by in droves. Empty and hopeless. Moving because they must.

Their dry-pain sucked the moisture from his heart. There was no joy. Not even a single forced smile.

He sensed the cavernous despair of a people trapped in a journey to death, marching under the searing heat of their unreachable wants and grinding their feet on the sands of their crushed dreams.

In the dark cafe, the Chairman's whole body began to tremble.

His coffee cup rattled on its saucer.

What is wrong with me? That electrical smell.

The scent filled his nostrils.

Maybe it was a vapor? Did she drug me!

Without warning, the Chairman's long-nurtured defensive barrier that protected him from the risk of empathy shattered with the impossible horror of cracking bone.

Now his worker's spirits reached out unfettered, plucking freely on the strings of his saddest memories.

Then the deluge of his worker's massed horror flowed into the Chairman's being.

The force of this unexpected torrent pinned his soul to the ground.

A cacophony of a thousand overlapping experiences flashing and fading like falling tinsel: the bright hum of the supermarket, the long drone of packed trains, vampiric leaving and arriving in the sunless dark, desperation wrapped in drunkenness, a dog whining through a door for its master, the night after a traumatic breakup walking home and seeing the apartment's window unlit, a tasteless ready-made meal, yelling at a tired spouse, hands shaking on Sunday evening, waiting in rain under a broken umbrella, lonesome weeping in the dark.

As the waves of long quiescent misery struck, the Chairman moaned loudly in nightmarish unformed words.

His arms half raised, he spasmed in his chair like a ghoul under trial of exorcism. Eyes bulging to the ceiling, face pulled back in undiluted anguish.

Like a heavily struck tuning fork the glass in the cafe's window, door, and food cabinet rang in unison.

The cafe's owner retreated behind his shop counter. Crouching down in the corner, knees to his chin, hands over his ears, his forehead turned and pressed against the wall.

Tuesday, Arato Asada lay sitting half up in his bendy hospital bed. His neck wrapped in bandages.

The way his neck moved when he swallowed hurt. Twisting his neck also hurt. Talking wasn't so bad, but still managed to hurt.

He didn't want any more of the painkillers. They made him feel weird.

His hospital room had four beds, but the other three were empty. He assumed the room's white and pale-green decor was meant to be soothing, but instead it projected the ambiance of a damp garden.

Today Arato had a visitor.

The renegade taxi driver sat in a chair next to his bed. Her smug toy cat on her lap.

The driver's name was Miko, and this was the second time she had visited.

Ten days ago, when he fell from the bridge, Arato suspected his fall had made him delirious. Because he remembered being driven at incredible speed through the streets of Tokyo.

Faster than was humanly possible, especially given the incongruity of that aggressive speed compared to the sweet shy nature of Miko.

He recalled walking towards a street corner, and seeing her taxi race by full of thugs. But he couldn't equate the speed he had witnessed that day to the unearthly velocity his mind obstinately claimed it remembered.

No, the fall or drugs or the transfusion, or something, must have befuddled his mind, creating a false memory of that drive to the emergency room.

Miko had brought him more flowers. They sat in a chipped porcelain vase on the small bedside table that held the TV.

Arato liked the flowers. Not because they were pretty, but because they gave the nurses the impression family had visited him.

The truth was that apart from Miko, no one else had visited.

Arato's injury had forcefully stopped his daily routine. A rhythm he had used to mask the reality of his life.

Giving him a week of unwanted time to reflect while lying still and staring at the cucumber shaped stain on the ceiling.

He was forty-nine years old. His prime time for making a girlfriend had passed.

The future stretched out before him like a railroad track. The tracks squeezing towards a distant vanishing point. The point where he would die. Alone.

No one would shed a tear at his passing.

He had read about old people dying in their apartments and not being found for many months. These *kodokushi* (lonely death) events were increasingly common in Japan.

He conducted a thought experiment where he imagined filling his apartment with food. Then remaining in the apartment, never going out, never phoning or messaging anyone.

Who would become concerned enough to come look for him? Who would make the effort to force his apartment door to find him?

No one. No one would come.

Arato didn't want to spend his life separated from people. His fall had taught him that. He didn't want to be alone with no one to hold his hand when he passed.

But trapped in this bed, he couldn't help but stare into his obvious future. An arid vista that kneaded dread into his bones.

The girl was talking. She had a soothing feminine voice.

Miko had a lot of theories about everything. Some of her theories should have made Arato mad, but her innocent fascination with her own ideas somehow didn't trigger his anger.

This surprised Arato.

Because lying here he had realized the one thing Arato Asada was good at was getting angry, at everything.

The rhythm of Miko's speaking helped too. A poetic iambic dimeter of stressed and unstressed syllables that lulled Arato's mind into a gentle rocking.

"...*onsens* and onsen eggs and manga and safety and bullet trains and cherry blossoms and sushi and shopping and parks and *onigiri* and vending machines—"

"Vending machines," Arato said, laughing. Laughing made his throat hurt.

He had asked Miko to list what she liked about Japan, since she had talked so much about the rest of the world.

"Every country has good and bad points," Miko said. "Japan has the best vending machines."

"How can you know that? You have never been out of Japan."

"I read a book about vending machines."

"A book about vending machines? Who would write such a thing?" Arato said. "So, you believe Japan has bad points too."

"Yes. Every country has. We can't ignore our bad issues. If we do not face them, then we will never solve them."

"I have come to understand that truth," Arato said.

Being stuck in this hospital bed, and being forced to reflect made Arato admit he had some bad points himself.

He had reviewed the video he took of Miko's taxi. But he couldn't watch past when he had laughed.

The sound chilled him, and it was he, Arato Asada, making that evil sound.

What is wrong with me? How did I become this spiteful?

"So tell me, what is Japan's most significant issue?" Arato said.

"We are driven by shame."

Arato swallowed.

It made his throat hurt.

Without warning her soft words had thrust deep into his mind, effortlessly piercing his many strong walls and firmly shut doors, and consoling with warm rapport the bruised inner him that those age-hardened defenses were built to protect.

"Shame," Miko continued. "Means we fear making mistakes. Especially in public. Which is why we have created so many social rules and rituals to codify order. As a framework to help us avoid making those mistakes. While our rigid social rules might help us avoid our fear of shame, they also kill spontaneity and honest expression. I don't believe it is healthy for a nation to be driven by such a negative emotion."

"So, what's the solution?" Arato said. He was sweating.

"During my surprise live show, I learned I can operate without worrying about other people's thoughts," Miko said. "And then I read *Meditations* by Marcus Aurelius."

Arato gave her an inquiring look.

"An old Roman Emperor with an impressive beard. He said, 'Nothing that goes on in anyone else's mind can hurt you'. So I have determined my mind will induce the only shame I will feel. I will not feel shame based on what I imagine other people are thinking of me. Or even what they tell me they're thinking of me."

"That sounds difficult."

"It is," Miko said.

There was a knock on the door.

In came two policemen.

One in his fifties, stiff with the rigid air of a bureaucrat. Dressed in a pristine uniform with a silver and gold insignia—three gold bars on either side of a golden *asahikage* sun.

He had a scar across his left cheek.

Why has such a senior police official come to see me?

The other policeman was baby-faced, barely out of school.

Miko didn't seem concerned.

"Hello," she said.

"Sorry for interrupting. We've come to follow up Mr. Asada's accident," the younger policeman said.

Miko excused herself. Promising to visit again the next time a fare brought her close during visiting hours.

She stopped at the room's door and gave Arato a cheery goodbye wave.

Arato was annoyed. Miko would have stayed longer if it wasn't for the police deciding that now, of all times, was the moment to make their visit.

Their interview was tedious and involved the younger policemen asking the same questions over and over in different ways. As if they expected him to change his story.

He wished Miko was back. It was refreshing talking with someone like her. Miko seemed interested in his life, without wanting anything in return.

The senior policeman remained silent during the interview. But his lip began curling, causing the scar on his cheek to transform into an inverted V. He glared down at Arato with undisguised disgust.

Arato explained several times he hadn't been trying to kill himself and no, he didn't need counseling. The younger policeman made notes and filled out a form he didn't show Arato.

Finished with their paperwork, Arato hoped they'd go away.

Miko's visits were heartening, like hot chocolate on a wintry day. Whereas the two policemen made dreary company.

But instead of leaving, they stood over him, close to the bed.

"Now, Asada. I am Superintendent Shoji. I am here to deliver you a serious warning," the older policeman said. "Your Hidden Stealth Ninja Taxi hoax caused much wasted police time. If you make up anything like that again, you will spend time in police custody. Along with your comedian friend who called my station yesterday evening."

Arato couldn't believe this sudden ambush. An unexpected dressing down, right in front of this child policeman. Arato gripped the bedsheets. His cheeks burning.

The senior policeman went on. His voice getting louder. He pointed his finger in Arato's face—a rude thing in Japan.

"You should be ashamed of yourself. We have serious work to do and are not to be used as targets for your frivolous, time-wasting amusement."

It was like being in court long ago. With the disbelieving judge taking away his son.

How Arato had wished back then he could have produced irrefutable evidence to prove his innocence. Evidence the judge couldn't ignore. Evidence that would see him redeemed in the eyes of the people present.

The senior policeman's scorching words heated Arato's entire face. Tears welled up. His lips and mouth desert dry. The familiar fury at injustice rising within him.

I'll show you.

Arato reached onto the bedside table and picked up his phone.

The policeman still yelling in his face.

"I forbid you to record this interview," the senior policeman said.

"I will not record anything," Arato said. "I have evidence."

"What evidence?"

"I will show you."

Arato unlocked his phone. He selected his video of Miko's taxi.

The phone displayed the first frame of the video.

Arato's finger hovered over the triangular play icon.

By pressing the icon, he could end this embarrassing ambush.

Miko would go to prison.

But in return, Arato Asada would be exonerated, and he would force this rude policeman to apologize.

But Miko had saved his life. And she couldn't visit him anymore if she was in prison.

But he was innocent. Hidden Stealth Ninja Taxi Service was real!

The two policemen glared down accusingly.

Arato's finger moved towards the play icon.

"We are driven by shame."

His finger froze.

His breathing became shallow.

After a long moment, he moved his finger down to the lower right corner of his phone's screen.

Hovering over a different icon, one shaped like a trash can.

If soft adorable Miko can make herself not care what people think. Then shouldn't I, a grown man, be able to do the same? Why do I care so much about what these men think? Does their view of me matter? What difference does it make? The time has come for me to take action to conquer my fear. Or I will be like this for the rest of my life.

He touched the icon.

A message appeared in a dialog box on the screen:

ARE YOU SURE YOU WANT TO DELETE THIS VIDEO?

Arato Asada breathed deep and long.

He touched the YES button.

An empty horizontal bar appeared.

From left to right, the bar slowly filled with green.

Until it reached the end.

A new message appeared over a single silver OK button:

VIDEO DELETED

There was a soft knock on the hospital room's door.

Soft but startling.

Arato and the two policemen turned.

The handle moved. The door was hesitantly pushed open.

Tentatively, a man in his mid-twenties entered.

Clean cut. His business shirt open at the collar. His face strikingly familiar.

"Hello. Please forgive my intrusion. I am very sorry to bother you," he said, bowing. "I was going past when I noticed the name on the door. My father's name was Arato Asada. My mother said he passed away while he was away on vacation. But just in case, I thought—"

"Nobuhiro?" Arato said.

"Yes, that is my name. Nobuhiro Asada."

Arato gasped. The face. It was his son's face!

"Did the swan bite your finger again?" Arato managed.

"Father. It is you!"

The young man rushed to Arato's bed. Staring down in amazement at his find.

The two policemen stepped well back. Watching the unfolding event open-mouthed.

"I don't believe it, Father. We have a mirror on our *tamaya* altar for you. Mother said you were dead."

"Well I'm not. Not yet."

"If I'd known you were alive, I would have searched for you. I, I, Father, this is incredible!"

A young woman's pretty face peeked around the room's open door.

"I never went on vacation," Arato said. "I wanted to see you, but I was prevented legally. Your mother took me to court, and the judge made it so I could never approach or even contact you. Then your mother moved. Taking you with her. I didn't know where you had gone."

"But why?"

"She told the judge I was physically abusing you."

"That's ridiculous," Nobuhiro said. "You did nothing like that."

"I know. But the judge didn't believe me."

"Nobuhiro?" the woman at the door said.

"It is my father," Nobuhiro said. Beckoning the woman in. "It's his face, but older."

"That's because I am older," Arato said.

He wanted to laugh, but he was afraid if he did the amazing event would vanish, like a rainbowed soap bubble popped in the air.

Nobuhiro looked like his son, but mature. It was a bizarre feeling seeing his son's head on an adult body.

The pretty woman in a cream designer coat entered and approached the bed. Carrying two small coats. A boy of about five in a white shirt and brown shorts ran after her. A little girl of about three in a brown patterned dress followed.

The two uncomfortable-looking policemen used the opportunity of the now unguarded door to quietly exit the situation.

"This is my wife, Katsura, and this is our son, Satoshi, and our daughter, Miki."

Arato looked from his son to Katsura to Satoshi and back again. Miki had disappeared, hidden by the tall bed.

He was breathing too fast. A tear rolled down his cheek. With a shaky hand, he wiped it away.

"I'm sorry," he said.

"It's OK," Nobuhiro and Katsura said.

His son sat down in the chair where Miko had been. He squeezed Arato's arm.

"You saw my name on the door? It's too incredible. After so many years," Arato said.

"They transferred our appointment to this hospital. We were coming back from getting Satoshi's tonsils checked. When Miki ran down your corridor," Katsura said.

"I was chasing the bird," little Miki said. Appearing from next to the bed. She climbed up onto her father's lap.

"There was no bird," Satoshi said.

"Was too," Miki said. Glaring at her big brother.

"There are thirteen million people in Tokyo. How could you have found me? This is a miracle," Arato said. "But, but, I am not a good man, Nobuhiro. I do not deserve a miracle."

Tears flowed. His son squeezed his arm more.

The little girl transferred herself to Arato's bed. The mattress compressed with the weight of her presence. She kneeled next to his knees, her dress resting on the bed's blanket like a bell.

"I went after Miki," Nobuhiro said. "When I picked her up, I saw my father's name on the door. Of all the names on these many doors, yours is the only one I noticed. It's such good luck, Father."

Little Miki was staring at Arato. Two bright curious brown dots, fixed on him like he was the most interesting thing she had ever seen.

"This is your grandfather," Katsura said.

Miki looked at her mother for confirmation and received a nod.

"I can have two? Two whole grandfathers?" Miki said. "For real?"

"Yes. Lots of children have two. And now you and Satoshi do too."

"Nice."

She shuffled forward to assist her father. Wrapping her warm little hand around Arato's index finger.

"It's my birthday soon, Grandfather. I will be four. I want unicorn sparkle pens, and you're invited to my party. I'm going to have a chocolate birthday cake. And if you're good, I will let you have a big slice…"

Two hours later, Miko was searching for a fare. Her taxi rumbled to a stop at an intersection.

The radio DJ introduced Aftershave's bouncy song "Chocolate Boogie". Miko turned up the volume.

"Their three voices together have such concinnity."

"If I ever wrote a book," Fluffy Kitty said. "Its title would be, 'A Hundred And One Ways A Cat Suffers When His Best Friend Talks Like An Alien'. Then, finally, I would get the sympathy I deserve."

"You're too lazy to write a book."

"True, but while asleep, I could use a ghost cat to write the book for me."

Ahead, in the cyclical war that rages eternally between the crossing men, the Red Man suffered a setback as the Green Man overpowered him.

Pedestrians began walking in front of Miko's taxi. Every person stepping in perfect time with the music.

The unexpected synchronization was mesmerizing.

"This is weirdly funny," Fluffy Kitty said.

"I bet you only see something like this once in your lifetime," Miko said.

When the traffic lights turned blue she pushed in the clutch and selected first gear. She drove off, keeping a careful eye out for customers signaling from the sidewalk.

"In entertainment news," the radio DJ said. "Jekyll's eighth album, *Zombie Duck,* was released yesterday evening. And is creating controversy with the track 'My Time, Your Time'. Business leaders are denouncing the song as inappropriate interference by the artist. While social media is exploding with supportive comments from corporate workers across the country. Official figures aren't in yet, but my contacts tell me 'My Time, Your Time' has already shot to number one across the charts. Here's Jekyll's latest hit."

The song played. Raw and driving. The verses alternated between mocking managers and encouraging workers to rebel by going home at 5 pm. The chorus with its wild guitars and pounding bongos invoked the screams of workers trapped in an endless comedic hell.

"Wow," Fluffy Kitty said.

"I know," Miko said. "It's perfect. One down, one to go."

That evening, Chairman Tarō Ikari flew in one of his Airbus Super Pumas from the grounds of his country estate into Tokyo. His uniformed pilots landing the long red and white helicopter on top of a skyscraper in the Tokyo Commercial district.

The modern mirrored glass tower that housed his keiretsu's private bar.

He didn't often travel into the city by helicopter. Flying the noisy machines in the city was considered bad manners. But the duration of his cross-legged contemplations in his tranquil *tsukiyama* garden had necessitated using the fastest method of travel to return.

His Gresso Regal mobile phone rang. He sat in the leather comfort of the spooling down helicopter for the conversation.

"Yes?" he said. "Correct. Your forensics team. My private PA will arrange the briefing."

He hung up and slid his expensive phone back into his suit pocket.

His keiretsu's private bar took up the top floor of the building.

It was the ultimate attic bar. Dark brown leather seats and dark wood walls. The room glowing in the amber radiance of a thousand backlit whiskey bottles.

A chest-high stone fireplace crackled at the western end of a cluster of leather sofas and armchairs, with their side tables each sprouting a miniature table lamp.

This was the meeting area for their eighteen strong keiretsu.

From these seats, the keiretsu discussed their joint business policies, and so wielded tremendous power over Japan's business world.

The other seventeen chairmen, also heads of vast business empires, sat amidst wisps of cigar smoke. Drinking whiskey or warm sake.

Expensive tailored suits and bespoke indoor shoes adorned the heavyset men. Most were in their late fifties or early sixties.

Chairman Ikari passed the bar's small karaoke stage.

The men acknowledged Chairman Ikari's arrival with nods and lifted beverage glasses.

"Scaring the city's cats, Ikari?" Tadahisa Yoshimura said.

Chairman of the Senshi No Doryoku Conglomerate Yoshimura was, after Ikari, the second most powerful man in the room. In a dark suit and silver tie, his arms spread easily on his leather armchair's rests, a square-cut glass of whiskey in one hand and a smoldering cigar in the other.

Ikari smiled at being chided about his manner of transport.

After greeting his fellow keiretsu members, he took his customary leather armchair opposite the fire, at the head of the group.

He ordered a glass of Yamazaki 35 single malt whiskey and a thick La Aroma de Cuba Churchill cigar.

Like a good minion, the chief waiter somehow was present while at the same time not existing. He vanished back towards the bar, trailing a mist of unimportance.

This was a crucial meeting. At the end of the evening, Ikari would make an announcement that would shock the keiretsu.

I must lay the mental groundwork masterfully or face a strong rejection.

"Have you heard Kimoto's pampered pet's latest hit?" Yoshimura said.

Junji Kimoto was Chairman of the Nanamoto No Ki Conglomerate.

Grey and balding, he wore a dark blue suit and blue tie with a gold tie clip. One of the companies owned by his conglomerate was the music entertainment group that had signed Jekyll.

"Track selection is an operational matter," Kimoto said. "When I conveyed my displeasure, I was informed the artist had exchanged that song for another at the last moment. He used the time pressure of the fixed CD replication schedule as an excuse to avoid seeking appropriate permissions."

"Feast your ears on this, Ikari," Yoshimura said. He waved his hand. Another minion who had been waiting for this moment pressed play on the karaoke system's CD player. The song started instantly.

The incongruity of a heavy rock song playing in the bar's plush settings struck first, but then came the lyrics.

The icy gasoline of destiny poured into Ikari's soul.

How can this be a coincidence? I could not ask for a better beginning to my thesis.

Jekyll's destiny-gasoline continued gushing out of the karaoke speakers, soaking the embers of the insolent taxi driver's words and reigniting those flames in Ikari's heart.

Over the past evening and day, Ikari had thrown himself into frantic research and deep meditations. The driver's ideas growing inside his mind like spreading branches of a tree, branches that had budded and sprouted into many related thoughts.

These expanding ideas had become Ikari's heart's urgent campaign. Driven by the shattering misery he had experienced at the train station in his unprecedented fit of raw empathy.

These new heart-intentions were already emerging as concrete actions and orders that had kept his corporation's policy makers, lawyers, and human resource staff frantically drafting and redrafting new procedures and policies.

His event coordinators were melting their phones to meet his two-day deadline for Thursday evening.

The old version of Tarō Ikari watched on in amazement, in a disembodied sense. Never in his wild speculations had he expected to become a compassionate person.

His cigar and whiskey arrived. The few drams of whiskey in his glass worth over five hundred thousand yen.

Kimoto sank a little into his seat as the song ended.

"This will stoke disharmony," one of the other chairmen said.

"Kimoto. You must chastise your artist most severely," another said.

"No," Ikari said, as he cut and lit his Churchill.

Everyone watched him. Ikari turned and puffed his cigar in the ornate lighter's hissing flame to get it smoldering as he liked.

"Gentlemen. I believe a strong wind is coming. A tempest that will blow through business and our society. This song is the first gust."

"What do you mean?" Yoshimura said.

"Japan has two possible futures. Our country will either grow and flourish, or wither and die. Our population has stopped increasing and instead has entered a decline. The trend has become dangerous. I've had my quantitatives build a model, and their forecast trend is disturbingly forceful towards the negative."

Ikari took a sip of his whiskey. He was not worried about anyone interjecting during the pause since he was the senior.

"Please indulge me. I have written a short memo to set the foundation for my proposal."

At a slight upward movement of his cigar, one of Ikari's personal minions appeared. With a quick bow, his assistant handed each big-man a black wooden folder containing two sheets of typed paper.

"Reading is too much like work," Yoshimura said.

But Yoshimura read the memo along with the others.

Ikari waited until the last chairman closed his folder.

"As you see, I have concluded our employee management policies have contributed to our country's decline. By actioning policies that have squeezed every possible hour out of my workers, I have been stealing their time and making it my own, like Jekyll's song said. Long working hours and ostensibly voluntary after hours drinking sessions mean my workers have no time for a private life. No time to meet someone to marry. And no time to have a family, even if they do. The thunderous realization hit me yesterday evening as I surreptitiously watched my workers at Tokyo Station. The realization that I, like some odious vampire, have been sucking the life out of my country and converting it for my own benefit and that of my shareholders."

"That is a harsh assessment," Yoshimura said.

"Nonetheless, regretfully true."

"But these are also our shared practices and traditions," Kimoto said. "Surely Japan's success was built upon these foundations."

"As my memo details. We must face the obvious truth that relentlessly working our employees is no longer producing the good results of the past. We are breaking our own bones for no gain."

"I find it unsettling to question our procedures," Yoshimura said.

"Yes. Disturbing. Unsettling. Unpleasant even," Ikari said. "However, I still want us to spend this evening exploring exactly that question."

The other chairmen nodded, and so the debate began.

Ikari studied their body language and listened carefully to gauge their mindset, attempting to discern the motivations driving their words.

The men filled the next two hours with serious discussion, serious cigar smoking, and serious drinking.

His suggestion of restricting nominications to once a week caused a strong reaction.

"Without the lubrication of alcohol, how can we overcome this fear of expressing ourselves honestly? We have ingrained this fear since childhood."

"We need to learn how. It can't be impossible."

"But, as Ikari's memo points out, without nominications uncharismatic managers will not have a social life. It would mean removing a significant perk of management."

Ikari guided the debate subtly. His hints and brief statements directed the discussion, flowing their thoughts over the arguments necessary to underpin his pending announcement.

He was perplexed by how effortlessly his fellow chairmen were echoing his ideas. He had expected strong resistance. It was common for a splinter faction to form to oppose any proposal, but none did.

Instead, there was a sense of ease. Like walking downhill.

It was as if their conversation was water flowing along an unseen riverbed. A riverbed that had been purposely constructed to guide them towards a single conclusion.

Has Jekyll's song softened their hearts, as the taxi driver's words softened mine? It is striking the driver's words and Jekyll's song both have the same flavor.

"Already many young are giving up on society. When we are old, we will need them, but they'll no longer need us. If we continue to disrespect the young, they could turn on us."

"That could never happen."

"It is already happening. Many young are opting out of society. Throwing themselves into escapisms."

"Escapisms we provide for considerable profit."

Some of the chairmen chuckled.

"The risk is that we lose the young. If we continue to treat them harshly, then they'll stop respecting their seniors and refuse to help us when we are old."

"Respect goes up, not down. The young must learn to obey. They must occupy their place."

"The old ways aren't working. No longer can we be harsh with them. We must care about their dreams and their happiness."

As the evening drew late, Chairman Ikari concluded that his memo, Jekyll's song, and the hours of debate, had loosened the ground enough to allow him to dig in his own spade.

"Esteemed colleagues," Ikari said. "Do not doubt that this typhoon is rising in intensity. We believe we are a sturdy tree. But our roots are rotten. We must bend with the wind or we will be broken."

"How could our position be threatened?" Kimoto said. "We are unassailable."

"Do not be so sure. World history has often recorded a change in public attitude sweeping all before it. I acknowledge it would require more social pressure to occur in Japan, but there is no guarantee public opinion will not reach that dangerous tipping point," Ikari said. He took a slow sip from his glass. "But our personal preservation is not my motive. I would rather see my house fall and lose everything, including my life, instead of witnessing my beloved country die."

"More dire sentiments," Yoshimura said.

"What we do in the present must keep in mind the generations to come. It is selfish to only consider ourselves. We have the foresight to see the future and the capacity to act. So, listen carefully, this is the policy I will announce this Thursday evening."

Chairman Ikari detailed his plans. To a room of frozen figures. Shocked eyes and mouths opening wider with every sentence.

There was silence for more than a minute when he finished, before Yoshimura spoke.

"This will apply to your entire group?"

"Every entity."

"The consequences will be far-reaching. This will flow through our own businesses and every industry. We will be forced to match your policy to retain our talent," Yoshimura said.

Kimoto downed the amber contents of his whiskey glass in one gulp.

"I apologize for the disturbance this will cause," Ikari said. "But I'd rather we face short-term pain than the diminishment of Japan. In choosing between sacrificing our work culture and our country, I am choosing to place our work culture upon the altar."

"Is this really necessary? Many other factors contribute to Japan's troubles," Kimoto said.

"True. Many factors. But our workplace practices make up an extremely significant portion of those factors. And they are under our control. I feel duty-bound to do what is in my power."

"But there must be a loss in productivity," Kimoto said. "The extra hours aren't all wasted."

"We could save much work effort by downgrading our customer service expectations from the level of absolute perfection to just very good," Chairman Yoshimura said.

"Sacrilege!"

There was laughter.

"Next, he'll suggest we base promotions on merit instead of seniority or stop expecting our workers to be so submissive."

"Maybe we should? Maybe it would encourage initiative and so reduce the burden of management. And it would allow younger managers, who would be more in tune with current social trends and technology."

"More sacrilege!"

"Yoshimura is right to raise these questions. We must not be afraid of considering every possibility," Chairman Ikari said. "And Kimoto is correct, too. There will be a loss in productivity. I plan to counter that reduction with a well-rested workforce and by embracing modern technology and business practices. In fact, long-term I predict my group's productivity will increase."

"What do you mean?" Kimoto said. His brow furrowed.

"It's 2014. Yet in Japan we still use fax machines en masse. Faxes are fifty-year-old technology. And mountains of paper forms for everything. Hanko stamps and photocopying and folders filled with paper. Physical receipts. Face-to-face meetings involving time-wasting travel," Ikari said. He scanned the faces of his fellow chairmen. "We are stuck in the 1980s, and suffering a strong case of Galápagos syndrome. The world has moved on from these tired ways. Japan is not an isolated country anymore. We must match the innovations the rest of the world have adopted, or risk becoming uncompetitive."

"What replacement procedures are you proposing?" Kimoto said.

"Electronic forms and electronic signatures. More reliance on email. Video meetings when physical meetings are unnecessary. The automation of office procedure with minimal human intervention, including far fewer sign offs. Fast and efficient computerized processes that do not involve handling paper."

Grunts of both approval and worry came from the other chairmen. These new ways would mean much work for them.

It was already late, but the keiretsu's chairmen stayed with Chairman Ikari, discussing the implications of his plan well into the early morning.

"Ha. Suddenly, they didn't care about privacy laws when it came to taking money," Uncle Ken said. He was sitting in the taxi's passenger seat while Miko drove.

Miko chuckled. Uncle Ken had come with her to the bank to make sure everything went well when Miko paid off her parents' mortgage demand.

She had a receipt, and a special note and a red stamp in her parents' mortgage book to prove the payment was completed.

"You are a good daughter, Miko. I know my brother. He would have been distraught returning and finding that unexpected letter. And you were right, if we had told him he would have cut their trip short and flown straight home. Today, I am a very proud uncle."

"Thank you," Miko said. She had felt the pressure lift off when the bank manager stamped the documents. "I like being useful and making progress in life. It's so much better than being stuck in my room."

"Let me share with you a secret. In movies, music and books, being bad is admired. But the truth is any idiot can be bad. Instead, it's hard to be good."

"It is hard," Miko said.

"Remember when you were little. When we folded paper planes together out on your parents' deck. You spent ages coloring in your paper with bright patterns and colors. Ignoring your uncle's warnings so much crayon wax would make the paper too heavy to fly."

"But it didn't."

"No, it didn't. My paper planes crashed into the ground, or got stuck in a tree. While your colorful planes flew perfectly. Down the hill along the treeline. Then, when they were high enough, they went out over the treetops. Flying straight until they were just a faraway speck. Or," Uncle Ken said. Pointing at the taxi's roof and twirling his finger upwards. "Your planes swirled around and around over the forest, climbing higher and higher until they disappeared into the clouds."

"I haven't made a paper plane for ages."

"I was a jealous uncle, you know. I carefully copied how you folded your paper. This time, I told myself, my plane will fly like Miko's. But no. My plane failed each time, while yours flew away into infinity."

"We used to sit there with our legs dangling over the deck. Drinking apple juice with ice and watching until we couldn't see my plane anymore."

"Good memories," Uncle Ken said. "You've had a hiccup, Miko, because of that cantankerous nurse. But you're back on track. Each time watching from your parents' deck, I thought my niece's life would be like her paper planes. Climbing higher and higher. And so your life will be, Miko. You'll see."

"I hope so."

The taxi turned a corner and purred as it gained speed.

"I got you a treat," Miko said. Putting a small plastic soda bottle into Uncle Ken's hand.

"Thank you."

Uncle Ken twisted the cap open with a phhssssss, and took a sip.

"Mmmm, Fanta Muscat, its fizzy green-grape taste warms my heart. And being driven around in my taxi also warms my heart. My heart is so very warm at the moment," Uncle Ken said. "Tell me, where is this place we are going to celebrate?"

"It's where you promised to take me once. But never did," Miko said.

The first half of the surprise was going to be fun. But Miko expected the second half to be nerve-racking.

"I'm sorry I forgot my promise."

"Well, that's where we are going."

"A mystery destination. And why did I have to dress up in my best?"

"It wasn't for the bank. Scruffy uncles are not allowed in this place."

"Ah. Intriguing."

It was a sunny Wednesday morning. As Miko drove, Tokyo bustled around them. The last two days had been pleasantly cozy compared to the chill on Monday.

"Where are we now?"

"Somewhere," Miko said.

"Can you be more precise?"

"Say planet Earth," Fluffy Kitty said.

"Planet Earth."

"I see. I am being punished for forgetting."

Miko parked the taxi. She walked Uncle Ken along Nanaibashi Street.

There was no sidewalk, but that didn't matter since there were no cars either. The street was only for walking. They passed pink vending machines selling drinks and a shop displaying blue-white *sometsuke* porcelain bowls and cups.

"There are some nice cafes here, Uncle."

"Is our destination close?"

"Yes. Maybe when we finish, we should come back here for lunch?"

"That is good news. It means my favorite niece expects me to survive wherever she is taking me."

Miko led Uncle Ken down the wide stairs.

"A park or a garden," Uncle Ken announced. "Rustling trees, and I smell water nearby."

"One point," Miko said. "See if you can earn more points before reaching our final destination."

Inokashira Park in western Tokyo is a tranquil wishbone-shaped pond surrounded by cherry blossom trees.

Miko guided Uncle Ken with a hand on his arm as they walked towards Nanai Bridge.

Many adults were strolling or sitting on the benches. There was only one child. He ran around in circles, running faster and faster in decreasing spirals until he fell over. Then he got up and did it again.

His mother sat on a brown ceramic seat that encircled a tree, watching with delight while videoing his antics.

They crossed Nanai Bridge. The longest bridge over the pond.

Not far out on the water, a couple were laughing and bickering over the controls of their swan boat. Their boat had an elegant neck with big eyes and a black beak.

Hattori's messages were coming less frequently now. He admitted he was tired, but promised he was looking forward to having lunch again on Saturday. Miko wished Saturday would hurry up.

"Inokashira Park," Uncle Ken said. "Swan boats."

"One more point. Clever Uncle."

"Are we hiring a boat?"

"Yes. You must complete your promise. You can pedal and I will steer."

"Not fair. You can pedal too, since you are young."

They turned left to the concourse outside the boat house. Inside, a man in a blue shirt and cap took their money and produced a ticket from a vending machine.

"I will come and help," he said.

Another blue-shirted man at the end of the dock prepared the swan boat. Its roof hinged back to allow entry.

Miko and the two men took great care getting Uncle Ken safely into the boat. They promised to look after his white cane during the half hour rental.

Soon niece and uncle were pedaling around on the pond. The boat rocked. The hidden paddles splishing and splashing as they churned under their seat.

The three-spoked steering wheel seemed reluctant to do its job, but by turning it to full lock the boat would eventually change direction.

Miko navigated the boat down to the far reaches of the pond. Past the cherry blossom trees, minus their blossoms since it wasn't the season.

She turned the boat around and headed back towards Nanai Bridge.

"There are ducks," Miko said.

"I am lazy. Let's go into the middle and drift."

They talked taxi business as they rested. The boat's hull occasionally slapping gently in the wake from a passing swan boat. Miko sent a quick message on her phone.

"We are over the time on our ticket," Miko said. "Are you hungry? Let's get an early lunch."

They pedaled back to the dock.

Walking back over the bridge, they climbed the stairs to Nanaibashi Street.

"Where shall we eat?" Miko said. "There's a chicken wing place, a yakitori skewer place, and many cafes."

"What is the time?"

"Eleven thirty."

"Are there any queues?"

"Only at one. A small cafe up ahead on the left."

"A queue. At eleven-thirty in the morning!" Uncle Ken said. "Let's go there. It must be good."

So Miko and Uncle Ken added themselves to the four-man queue.

The small cafe had only a few outdoor and indoor seats. Every table occupied. Behind the counter and the coffee machine were shelves of alcohol. It was likely the cafe converted into a small bar at night.

The queue started to move faster as the men ahead brought takeout coffee and left one by one.

"We are first in line," Miko said.

Inside the cafe, a man with a dark green cap got up from his table. He dropped his cup and plate off to the counter.

"There's a free table," Miko said.

"Let's go," Uncle Ken said.

Two women were sitting at the table to the right of the free table.

The woman facing the entrance was Miko's parents' age. While her blonde-haired companion, sitting with her back to the door, seemed about twenty.

Paperwork and notepads rested on the table between them.

When Miko entered with Uncle Ken, the older woman glanced up at the new arrivals and returned to her notes.

But then she looked up again. Her eyes following them as they collected menus and walked to their table.

Miko sat Uncle Ken in the chair next to the older woman and propped his white cane up against the wall. The older woman ignored Miko. She stared at Uncle Ken.

Miko sat down on the other side of the table and began reading the menu.

"Excuse me," the older woman said. Leaning towards Uncle Ken. "Ken? Ken Nishimura?"

Uncle Ken sat bolt upright. Breathing in sharply.

"Suzu?" he said. "Suzu Mochizuki?"

Uncle Ken had enunciated the six syllables as a sequence of rising and falling notes. Miko understood. Over the years, the name of Uncle Ken's lost love had been so honored in his mind that her name had become a melody.

"Yes. Yes Ken, it is me. What a wonderful surprise to meet you here."

Uncle Ken turned towards her and reached out, finding Suzu's arm. Suzu didn't seem to mind.

Her eyes flicked back and forth, scanning his face like a newly discovered masterpiece.

Then Uncle Ken bowed his head.

His chin quivered.

"I am sorry, Suzu. But I have become blind."

Miko tensed.

"It is OK, Ken."

"It is?"

"These things happen. I'm so very pleased to meet you again."

"As I am you."

The two school friends talked rapidly for several minutes, before Uncle Ken began explaining how he was in the area today. Then he remembered his manners.

"This is my niece, Miko. Akio and Chika's daughter."

"Hello, Miko. Nice to meet you. I knew your parents. We were in the same year together at school."

"Nice to meet you too," Miko said. She gave the best sitting-down bow she could.

"And this is my client, Kaori. I'm sorry Kaori, I've been very rude, it's just—"

"I completely understand," the blonde Japanese woman said. "It's a rare surprise to meet an old friend. You must take full advantage of this lucky event."

"You don't mind?" Suzu said.

"You have already spent more time with me than I paid for. And your advice has been extremely useful. I need to leave anyway, I have another appointment. Thank you so much," Kaori said.

Suzu stood to farewell her client.

"Would you like another coffee?" Miko said.

"I don't want to interrupt your day out with your uncle."

"You are not. Kaori was right to point out that you two must take advantage of this time," Miko said. "Tell me what sort of coffee you like."

Miko took orders.

She went to the counter. When Miko looked back, Uncle Ken and Suzu were deep in conversation. She ordered coffees and a ham cheese onion toasted sandwich for Uncle Ken.

Now the cafe had more tables free. Most of the other patrons had left.

"Uncle Ken, I'm going to go for another walk in the park. I'll come back in about an hour."

"Oh no. I have spoilt your trip," Suzu said.

"You really haven't," Miko said. "This is a special moment for Uncle Ken. And I get to see him whenever, anyway. You two must catch up."

As Miko left the cafe, she glanced back. Suzu was moving her things over to Uncle Ken's table.

"Let's go to the pond and investigate those ducks more," Fluffy Kitty said.

"Always thinking of yourself."

"I am a cat."

"Later. First, we have a job to do."

Miko walked back down the steps into the park and turned right.

Under the leafless trees were a group of young men and women standing around blonde Kaori. Suzu's client leaned back on a rustic wooden log fence bordering the pond.

Miko approached.

"Hello," Miko said. She bowed in greeting.

"I was just telling the guys what happened," Kaori said. "How is it going with your uncle and Suzu?"

"Very well so far," Miko said. "I have your payments."

First, Miko paid the four men who had formed the queue outside the cafe.

Second, she paid the men and women who had taken up the other tables to make the cafe full.

Third, she paid the man with the dark green cap who had reserved the table next to Suzu and Kaori.

But when she came to pay Kaori, Kaori refused.

"You already paid for Suzu's train trip and consulting fee. Her advice was so useful, Miko. Not only for my English CV, but also for my main CV," Kaori said. "So I believe I've received more than enough payment."

"Are you sure?" Miko said.

"Totally," Kaori said, pulling off her blonde wig and becoming Chihiro from the acting school. She pulled out hairpins and shook out her black hair. "But tell me. Why did you insist on me using a disguise and a false name?"

"Because while I know you're studying makeup, I was afraid you would become an actress too," Miko said. "Then Suzu might see you on TV, or in a movie, and become suspicious."

"Chihiro is good at acting. It could happen," one of the queue men said.

"Please understand, everyone. This is a forever-secret," Miko said. "You must promise to never tell anyone. Even if you do become super famous in the future, and a handsome or pretty reporter asks you about your past work."

The acting students agreed. Making a solemn promise to keep Miko's plan a secret forever.

They talked for a while. Before the students went to catch their train.

Miko killed time by walking in the park. Listening to Fluffy Kitty complain about the injustice of wanting to eat birds but not having an actual mouth to do the eating with.

Miko worried having Fluffy Kitty riding everywhere kangaroo-baby-style might have stretched her mother's puffer jacket.

I will buy Mother a new jacket and keep this one.

After an hour, she returned to the cafe. And was relieved to find Suzu was still there with Uncle Ken.

They were so engrossed in conversation Miko was reluctant to interrupt. So she returned to the park. There was a petting zoo that would be fun, and an aquatic park.

An hour later she had seen the squirrels and rabbits and the Tsushima leopard cat and the penguins and mandarin ducks (not allowed to be eaten, a fact that disappointed Fluffy Kitty) and peacocks and swans and foxes and deer and grebes (also not allowed to be eaten) and goats and monkeys and raccoons and fish.

She had also made sure a good number of the guinea pigs were cuddled and petted and a fingertip rubbed in little circles on top of each of their tiny heads.

Full of cute animal happiness, Miko returned to the cafe. Apart from fresh coffees on the table, nothing had changed.

Uncle Ken and Suzu were both sitting forward in their seats, chatting. Suzu occasionally tapping Uncle Ken's hand to emphasize a point.

Uncle Ken's hand. The one receiving these occasional finger taps. Rested further forward on the table than was required for him to pick up his coffee.

Miko approached.

"You were quick. Bored of the park?" Suzu said.

"I thought you'd be away an hour," Uncle Ken said.

"It's been two hours."

"It has not," Uncle Ken said.

"My goodness. It's one thirty," Suzu said.

"The park is so pretty. Why don't you two go for a walk?"

Suzu and Uncle Ken liked that idea.

Miko waited until they finished their coffees.

She followed them around the park. Back far enough, so she couldn't hear what they were talking about.

Suzu guided Uncle Ken once around the pond and through the various forested areas. Then around the pond again.

They rented a swan boat. Miko watched from the bridge as their swan disappeared towards the end of the pond. It came back into sight and drifted next to the biggest grove of blossom trees.

Their time ran out. So Miko purchased them another ticket. This kept happening. Their swan drifted around the pond with only the occasional stirring of the waters behind, propelling their giant bird away from the shore.

Miko became bored. So, when she purchased their next time extension, she asked the attendant for one of their A4-sized flyers.

She sat on a bench and carefully folded the flyer into a paper plane.

Glancing around, she made sure no one was watching. She didn't want people worrying she was littering.

Miko launched the paper plane lightly along the path, next to where she had rendezvoused with her acting school team.

The plane flew straight, swooping down the path between the trees to where the path curved right. There a gust of wind caught the plane and blew it leftwards up over the tree tops and out across the pond.

Miko returned to the bench. Sitting, she cuddled Fluffy Kitty in both arms, resting her chin between his ears and watching the progress.

Her paper plane drifted around the pond in lazy circles, gradually gaining height.

"I should have bought a bottle of Aomori apple juice," Miko said.

After the plane had climbed higher than the height of her apartment building, it stopped circling and drifted south in the wind.

Soon it started climbing again in slow circles that spiraled south. Miko couldn't see what was under her paper plane because the park's trees blocked the view, but it must have been well out over the city.

After twenty or so minutes, her plane became a dot high against the clear blue sky. Then, just like when she was little, Miko suddenly couldn't see it anymore.

"I better get them another ticket," Miko said.

She paid the attendant. Then walked out into the middle of the bridge and watched the forgetful swan boat bobbing in the water.

"Didn't you say this pond is cursed?" Fluffy Kitty said.

"Only for couples. They're not a couple yet, so they can't break up."

"Maybe it works in reverse for not-couples?"

"I hope so."

Miko purchased more time extensions. Until their forgetfulness became silly. She rented a regular paddle boat with a blue canopy and went in pursuit.

"Ahoy," Miko said. She pedaled backwards to prevent a collision.

"Are we over time?" Suzu said.

"A bit."

"I thought the sun was low."

"Boat rentals are closing soon. Let's go and get an early dinner," Miko said.

"That's a good idea," Uncle Ken said.

"I want to. But the train back to Kōfu City, I'll have to check when the last one leaves."

"Do you need to be back for work tomorrow?" Miko said.

"No. I don't have any appointments."

"Well, I hope my forgetful uncle told you my parents are away. So you are welcome to stay with me. I would like the company."

"And my niece has another good idea," Uncle Ken said. "I know an excellent place we could meet for breakfast tomorrow."

"Is that really OK, Miko? Could we go to Ginza tomorrow, Ken? I've never been."

"I'll drive you both there, and pick you up after you are finished," Miko said.

The three of them went to dinner. Later, while Suzu was in the convenience store buying a toothbrush, Miko advised Uncle Ken to air out his apartment in case Suzu came to visit.

"My apartment smells?" Uncle Ken said.

"Like old socks."

Last night when his boss had ended the evening's nomination, Hattori had resisted the urge to phone Miko to taxi him home.

He resisted because he didn't want her ever seeing him drunk again. Especially not staggering around with his tie wrapped around his head like a *hachimaki*.[†] Instead, he hailed a taxi from the street.

He had plugged his ear buds into his phone and listened to Aftershave songs to cheer himself up on the way home.

That night he had dreamed Aftershave was actually a big corporation occupying a massive skyscraper in Tokyo, and he was one of their many employees.

The department he worked for took up an entire floor and had one job, finding homes for lost kittens.

Kittens were everywhere. Jumping on the desks. Chasing things on the floor. Skittering across their laptop keyboards and hanging around, staring with expectant eyes demanding pats.

Meanwhile, everyone, including him, was furiously working on their computers and phones finding homes for the playful baby cats.

The office walls around him were full of color. Which, combined with the kittens, filled him with dream-joy.

By his desk hung three radiant posters drawn in flamboyant 8-bit graphic style. One poster of frightened pixelated people running, hands in the air, from a long-haired 8-bit girl chasing them with an 8-bit snake. The other posters were of a broken 8-bit snow-globe snapped at the base, and a girl's leg kicking an 8-bit shoe into a multicolored sea of audience pixels.

Then his phone's spiteful alarm abducted him out of his happy slumber.

Opening his sleep-sand eyes Hattori had winced in disappointment at the smack-in-the-face memory of where he really worked.

Later that day, the large floor chronograph at his actual job clacked over to three-dreary-o'clock in the afternoon. He reluctantly exited his dream-reminisce and returned to the dull reality of his drab office.

The abrasive drone of the air conditioning and heatless glare from the ceiling's tubular suns had finished their daily task of drying out Hattori's soul.

† A hachimaki is a Japanese headband, often with a rising sun motif and kanji characters on the front. It is worn as a symbol of courage, or more mundanely to keep the sweat from dripping onto the wearer's face.

His eyes, when left unattended, were closing by themselves. His laptop's screen would blur and then his head nod forward.

"Attention everyone."

His boss was standing amidst their work benches.

"The compulsory meeting has been moved to Tokyo Dome. The employees of every company owned by Ikari Conglomerate are expected to attend. Even though Tokyo Dome is the biggest enclosed venue in Tokyo, most other employees will be forced to watch over a video link. We are fortunate to have been allocated seats."

Everyone nodded their heads.

"Bring your coats and bags. I suspect this significant meeting will go long into the evening. Our floor has been assigned buses. We will stay together as a team and follow the directions of the yellow-vested transport coordinators. One last item: I have been instructed to reassure everyone this meeting is not about restructuring or redundancies."

Hattori's work colleagues nodded in unified satisfaction. Hattori matched their nod, but a little late.

At least this will get me out of the office.

The bus ride was stuffy, but pleasantly kinetic.

As the crowd of fellow employees walked from the parked buses to Tokyo Dome, the cool air and being outside during actual daylight was for Hattori like a drop of water to a man dying of thirst.

Hattori had no illusions about his future. The burnout had consumed the wooden structure of his soul. Now only smoldering embers remained.

He alternated between craving the relief of ending his life, and annoyance that in his last days he had met Miko.

It was as if the universe had waited for Hattori to begin sliding down the chute of doom, and at the last minute, before flinging him out into the black void, it had sadistically waved in front of him the very joy he had sought ever since his young teenage self had become aware of girls.

At their last meeting, Miko had worn a fluffy white sweater.

Could she be any sweeter? Was she deliberately torturing me?

The truth was he wasn't still alive because of his promise, but because this weekend he would see her again.

Don't be stupid. Why would someone like Miko ever want me? I'm a loser. First impressions are important, and her first was watching me trying to throw myself off a bridge. You couldn't make a worse first impression.

His heart sank further at the impossibility of a relationship.

Even if I had the time to court her, she would choose someone else. Maybe she already has a boyfriend?

That was the one question Hattori had been afraid to ask her. He couldn't stand the idea that Miko was taken.

The massive stadium's gates and corridors came and went. He entered the arena through Gate 41, into the rumble of ten thousand conversations.

Then he was crabbing sideways into a blue D seat, high in Tokyo Dome's stands.

To his left and right, the stands were packed. Below, like a forest of dark-suited people-trees gently swaying and twisting, stood the masses of employees upon the flatland of the dome's baseball field.

In the center of the baseball diamond surrounded by the human forest was a rectangular stage with a plain, and from this distance tiny, podium.

Behind the stage was a row of terraced seating made of steel scaffolding and wooden benches.

"Hattori. What do you think?" Kaji Itō said. The Assistant Project Manager leaned forward from his seat behind, twisting and untwisting his fingers in his yellow lanyard.

"No idea," Hattori said. "But it seems rushed. Obviously, it was considered important to get everyone together fast. Imagine the expense and wasted productivity."

The big men emerged, walking down a fenced-off aisle and found positions on the seating behind the podium.

Even at this distance, their bearing and the deference they received and their dark suits marked them as very important people. Likely some chairmen and chief executive officers who ran companies in the conglomerate.

Hattori's boss shuffled crablike across and sat down in the row in front. Two seats to Hattori's left. He clasped his hand together and moved his head in jerks as if he were searching the dome's vast space for predators.

Hattori assumed he regretted not being seated before the big men came out. His tardiness might be conceived as hubris.

There was a dark irony to being in Tokyo Dome with his boss.

His boss had called Hattori back on Christmas Eve to finish an inventory report that could have waited until the end of the month. Because of him Hattori had missed his much dreamed of live show.

Did he know how much it meant to me? Did he recall me out of spite?

The incendiary thought sizzled in his mind. But there was nothing left to burn. No energy remained for hatred or revenge. Instead, the watery indifference saturating his will extinguished the white-hot thought. Nothing mattered anymore to Hattori.

Except Miko Nishimura. She was the only thing that pulled him. The only source of motivation. The one assurance Hattori was still a living being.

She is the home I've always wanted.

And she was completely out of reach.

If only I could spend regular time with Miko, then she might grow to like me.

Maybe, given time, he could overcome her first impression. But it was impossible. Even if he carried on living, he would not have enough time to spend with her. He needed his weekends to sleep.

If only Miko could see him at his best, rested and fun, then maybe her heart would turn to him.

Miko had suggested he quit his job. But his social anxiety was an immovable barrier. He could never be an unemployed man.

He couldn't lose his place in society.

His often absent father, a military man, had impressed most sternly on Hattori that an ignoble failure like being unemployed would not only bring shame on Hattori himself, but also on his family, his friends, his neighbors, and the Emperor and the people of Japan.

Hattori had learned little from his father, but the one certitude his father had planted deep in Hattori's being was the simple maxim that 'shame is worse than death'.

This is why Hattori had gone to the bridge. It was the better of the two options.

His father would regret his passing, but he would understand Hattori's choice.

Maybe I should leave a letter for my parents this time? So they know I was thinking of their honor too. To leave them no doubt, and let them know that at my last I considered them. I believe Father will take pride in his son having the strength of character to avoid shame in the way of our ancestors.

It was not solely the risk of shame. Piled on top of the shame was another reason that made quitting his job impossible. The fact that Miko wouldn't be interested in an unemployed man.

Miko would be kind towards him, but he knew women only desire productive men who can both provide for a family and demonstrate the social validation of employment. If Miko didn't desire him, then any chance of a relationship would be gone.

But even if he didn't quit, his burnout would soon make his work performance substandard. Which would cause him to be fired.

So, if he didn't take action soon, then, no matter what, the horror of unemployment was inevitable.

What did Miko say?

"Shame is worse than stubbing your toe. It's worse than really wanting chocolate and not having any. But shame isn't worse than death."

Hattori chuckled to himself, imagining his father overhearing Miko, he would have turned red while ejecting steam out his ears.

The stadium's big screens came to life. Filled with a live feed of the empty podium.

The Herculean sound system hissed and popped. Fifty thousand heads turned towards the screen. The noise level dropped as conversations paused.

The big screens reminded Hattori of the online footage he'd seen of the Christmas Eve live show.

He groaned.

Why did I tell Miko that? Was she only pretending to be OK with it?

Hattori had sworn to himself to keep his imaginary-sisters fantasy a secret.

Likely Miko didn't want to say what she really thought, due to my mental instability at the time.

His ears and cheeks burned. He covered his face with his hands.

She must think I'm insane.

Inspirational music boomed out across the stadium, stoking emotions alien to the tedious images accompanying the music.

A montage of waving employees, enormous machines, aircraft, ships, bridges, buildings, missiles, oil refineries, software companies, robots, banks, chip fabs, entertainment, mining, satellites, farming, manufacturing, computer games, medical equipment, and pharmaceuticals.

There were other images Hattori couldn't categorize, including horses running and a forest of pine trees and a series of blue laser flashes in a stainless steel laboratory.

As the music faded, a big man climbed onto the stage. His dark suit was likely worth more than Hattori's annual salary.

"Welcome everyone to the magnificent Tokyo Dome. Welcome to those physically present and our group's employees watching on video link around the country. I am Mitsuharu Igarashi. I am one of the directors of Ikari Conglomerate. It is my humble task to set up parameters for our meeting. Before passing this podium over to the Chairman of the Board of Directors of Ikari Conglomerate, I must underline..."

The important man droned for twenty minutes.

Hattori feigned the expected rapt attention, matching the artifice of everyone else seated in the volcanic-crater-sized amphitheater. He risked glancing left and right.

We're all lying. Is this who we are? A nation afraid of showing our inner selves? How can we be close to anyone if we can't be honest?

Were those his thoughts or Miko's?

It was hard to tell. He loved listening to her talk. Her sweet voice enthusing over her ideas.

It was like tuning into a radio program he listened to when he was a teenager. That show had a knack for interviewing passionate science professors and researchers.

"... and now I invite to the podium Chairman Ikari. Chairman of the Board of Directors of Ikari Conglomerate."

The big man of big men walked out onto the field. Surrounded by an entourage of five. Three men carrying satchels and two burly men bulging in their suits and strutting like gorillas.

The clapping lasted until the Chairman mounted the stage and halted the noise with a brief imperial palm.

He greeted everyone in the stadium and those across the country watching via video link.

"Japan's business methodologies are not based on rigid formula but on a philosophy," the Chairman said. "A philosophy that served our country well up to the turn of the millennium. However, in this new millennium, I believe certain aspects of our business philosophy have been holding back the advancement of Japanese business. And worse, have been detrimental to the fabric of our society."

Nice of you to notice.

"Our business philosophy is born from our cherished traditions. From those illustrious few who first drew the outlines of our traditions on the soil of Japan, and from the generations of our ancestors who dug those lines forever deeper," the Chairman said. He took a sip of water from a bottle. "But, even as eminent as our ancestors were, they could not have foreseen the advent of disruptive technologies and the needs of modern business and society. Indeed, these traditions are so entrenched on our collective minds that we modern Japanese can barely perceive another way of acting. But I propose we must perceive new ways in some areas at least. While I cannot speak for Japan, I can speak for the businesses I oversee. So I am mandating changes to our bedrock philosophy. Changes which I have named 'Productivity and People'. To increase business productivity while also improving the lives of our employees. I do not believe these are mutually exclusive goals."

Hattori sat back, cupped his elbow in his hand and rested his chin on his thumb.

"How many times have we invoked the spirit of *ganbaru*? 'Do your best' we say. We pledge unyielding commitment until we complete our set task. This tenacity, this uncompromising persistence through hardship, is one of our strong characteristics as a people. A wonderful tradition. But also a tradition open to abuse. There are times when we need ganbaru, in times of natural disaster, war, or vital business actions. But it has become our default attitude towards work. When instead it should only be reserved for moments of utmost importance. Getting in your car do you push the accelerator pedal to the floor and keep it there for the complete trip? Will not the car's engine explode? Do you run everywhere you go? Do you yell every time you speak?"

The Chairman paused and examined the vast crowd.

"No. Of course not. So why do we act this way towards work? Hard work is expected; however, a constant striving at the limits of our endurance cannot be justified. While our businesses may seem to benefit in the short term, we are in fact harming the long-term prospects of our employees and our country."

Hattori was no longer feigning interest. It was like listening to Miko.

"To this end, I have convened this group-wide meeting of more than four hundred thousand employees to emphasize the importance I am

The Hikikomori

placing on our new Productivity and People initiative. Those who manage people make no mistake. There will be serious consequences if you do not implement these new policies."

Hattori's boss shivered.

"We will roll Productivity and People out over the coming months. We are producing training courses and videos and booklets that will be mandatory. But there are certain parts of our group's new business philosophy that I now will detail. These parts are effective as of this moment."

On the word 'moment', the Chairman thumped the podium. The amplified thud echoed around the stadium.

He took a sheet of paper from a folder and placed it in front of him.

"First. Employees will work no more than eight hours a day. These eight hours exclude breaks. So, for example, if you start work at eight in the morning and take an hour for lunch, then you must finish work at five in the evening. We expect you will leave your office or factory after that time. You may work an extra half an hour at your discretion if you believe it is necessary. But this must not happen regularly. Your manager must approve any overtime beyond this half hour limit. And you will need to justify why overtime is required. Your manager will report it. A special team will consult anyone working too much, to discover how your overtime can be reduced. And be warned, don't try cooking the books. These teams are experts in detecting discrepancies."

Hattori was sitting forward. His trembling hand covered his open mouth.

Had he really heard what he thought he had heard?

As if reading his mind, Chairman Tarō Ikari repeated the same information using different words. Ending with another veiled threat to managers who thought under-reporting overtime would be a worthwhile strategy.

"Second. Employees are to work no more than five days a week. While there are exceptions for certain job types, the bulk of our employees will not work over five days. The same overtime reporting structure will be in place for those rare instances when working more than five days is required."

My Saturdays are guaranteed!

The palm of Hattori's hand was hot from quick breathing. Around him people were leaning forward, open-mouthed, some clutching their knees.

"Third. Allotted annual leave will not be increased, but we will expect employees to take at a minimum eighty percent of their annual leave each year. Not taking leave will no longer be seen as a virtue. And, unless it's an emergency, employees are not to be contacted regarding work-related matters while on their vacation."

The Chairman paused, as if waiting for people to catch up.

"Fourth. After work, nominication is now strictly voluntary. While this has always been the case in theory, the unwritten rule is that employees must attend. This unwritten rule is now revoked most forcefully. Also, since I realize this will be difficult to police, from this moment on it is group policy that nominications may only occur once a week. To repeat. Managers may only invite their team out for dinner and drinks once a week. Compliance will be strictly monitored. So even if an employee feels obligated to attend, they will only lose one night a week."

And there it was. A mere eight hours of work a day. At least four week nights to himself. His weekends free.

Hattori clutched both trembling hands over his mouth, catching several involuntary sobs.

I can easily cope with this new schedule.

This means I don't have to die.

Around him people were exchanging startled glances. Others sat like statues. Some were reacting like him. An older woman Hattori had seen around the office was openly wiping away tears.

The Chairman must have sensed the reaction. He started from the beginning and summarized the four new rules.

Hattori was grateful to hear them again. The first time had the quality of a dream. The second time couldn't be a mistake.

He fought to control his trembling. The Chairman went on.

"We are shifting our focus to rewarding productivity and not time spent at work. Being present in the workplace beyond eight hours is now considered a negative indicator. These concepts are now central to our group's modified fifty-year plan."

"Hattori. Can you believe it?" Kaji whispered from behind.

"I'm struggling, it seems too wonderful," Hattori whispered back.

"Appeals to group ethic and group needs are no longer to be used to shame people into working longer. I want you to have hobbies. I want you to have real friends. Real relationships. I want you to see your husbands and wives and children. And I want you to sleep well."

Like a dam breaking there was spontaneous applause. Which in the stands turned into a standing ovation.

When the thunderous noise died down, Chairman Ikari continued.

"It is six in the evening. Unless you have vital work that must be completed before tomorrow morning, you are to collect your things and go home. Or go wherever you would like to go. I humbly thank you for attending this meeting."

Like heavy rain came more applause as the Chairman bowed to his employees. As one the entire venue bowed back.

Soon after, clutching his satchel to his chest, Hattori stumbled through the stadium's crowded corridors and found himself ejected into Tokyo Dome's swirling courtyard.

He roamed back and forth among the crowd for a few minutes,

bewildered, like a zoo animal unexpectedly released into the wild.

Then he stood still. Staring up at the white dome outlined in the evening sky.

Miko lives near here.

He pulled out his phone and dialed her number.

❀ ❁ ❀ ❁

Miko was driving Uncle Ken and Suzu. Uncle Ken wanted Suzu to experience one of his favorite *shabu-shabu* restaurants.

With Miko's encouragement, Suzu had moved her Friday appointment to Monday. So she could stay again at Miko's tonight and the weekend too.

Uncle Ken approved of this arrangement.

Miko's phone rang.

"*Moshi Moshi.* I am Miko."

"Miko. It's Hattori. You won't believe what's just happened. Are you busy? Can we meet? I'm at Tokyo Dome City."

"I think I can. Wait, I will check."

Miko asked Uncle Ken and Suzu if they'd mind having dinner alone.

They said this was something they were able to do. Suzu promised to cook so Uncle Ken wouldn't burn himself on their table's pot of boiling broth.

"Hattori. I can. Shall I pick you up at Korakuen Station?"

"No. There are massive crowds and buses are everywhere. Tell me where to meet away from the dome and I will walk there."

They agreed on a cafe near Uncle Ken's apartment.

"Who is Hattori?" Suzu said.

"Just someone I know," Miko said. She wanted to say her friend, but Hattori wasn't really a friend.

Maybe one day he will be. If I can solve his work problem, then maybe he will become my first ever friend.

"A boy? The one who lost the ticket?" Uncle Ken said. "When do we meet him?"

"Don't tease me," Miko said. She kept facing forward, so Suzu wouldn't notice she was blushing.

After dropping Uncle Ken and Suzu off, Miko raced back to Bunkyo Ward.

Parking in the garage, Miko sent the smoke rising from the taxi's disk brakes swirling as she rushed past. She pulled the roller door down and fast walked to the cafe.

The cafe was glass-sided with wickerwork chairs and round wooden tables. A wide photo of a sunlit tropical beach extended across the rear wall.

Miko located Hattori at the back of the cafe, under the photo's palm tree, sipping a coffee. Looking businessman-like in his suit and tie. His face was pale and his eyes bloodshot, but his face lit up when he saw

Miko.

He is a handsome man. I've never seen him smile like that. It is a good sign.

"Miko. You won't believe what happened. Sit down, do you want coffee? Food? They have sweet donuts. I'll get a menu."

"No, I can't stand being inflated with suspense. Please tell me your news before I burst."

Miko listened to Hattori's amazing tale.

After he had revealed Chairman Tarō Ikari's four points, Miko forced her face to stay still. No smiling allowed.

My plan was a success! This is such an excellent result.

"How do you feel?" Miko said.

"Like a prisoner who hasn't seen the sun for ten years and without warning is set free," Hattori said. "I can't thank you enough, Miko. If I had known what the Chairman was planning, then I never would have, you know. How we met."

"It's our forever-secret," Miko said.

"You're such a good person," Hattori said. "Without you, I... Oh, Miko."

Hattori's face contorted. He planted his elbows on the table and hid his face behind his hands. "Without you, I'd be dead." He shook with several mini-earthquakes that rattled the table.

"It's OK. It's all better now," Miko said, reaching and squeezing his arm.

"I'm sorry. What a mess! What a mess!"

"Breathe. Deep breaths. It's going to be fine. You still have burnout, but the difference now is you have hope."

Hattori nodded.

Miko coached him on breathing, and he calmed.

After some minutes, his face emerged from behind his hands. He stared down at the table.

"I'm sorry. I can't imagine what you think of me," he said. "You've seen me at my worst. I'm better than this you know."

"I do know. I can tell you're a good person."

"Really?"

"Yes. You're like someone who has been suffering in an abusive relationship. But I believe fundamentally you are of good character."

"You're so kind, Miko. You're the kindest person I've ever met," Hattori said. He paused and then said, "How lucky your boyfriend is to have you."

"What?"

"Your boyfriend. He's lucky."

What is he talking about?

"I don't have a boyfriend."

"Oh," Hattori said. He sat up in his chair. And stretched for a moment. "Sorry. I find that surprising."

"Not really," Miko said. She stared down at her hands. "When a girl has a face like mine, her prospects are limited. I am considering plastic surgery to fix things once I can afford it."

Miko didn't want to talk about her problem. It made her sad.

She glanced up.

Hattori was staring at her. His mouth half open, his brow furrowed.

"Sorry. I don't understand?" he said.

Miko crossed her arms and legs and looked away.

"I was born ugly. I can't help how I look."

She didn't want to cry.

Please change the subject.

"Are you kidding me?" Hattori said. "You're so pretty my eyes hurt when I look away."

"Don't be cruel," Miko said, and burst into tears.

She couldn't help it. She'd thought Hattori was a nice man, but now he was making fun of her.

She clutched at Fluffy Kitty and made herself as small as she could.

Hattori was next to her.

One arm around her shoulder, squeezing her arm with his other hand.

"Miko," he whispered. "You're not ugly. Who on earth told you that?"

"Everyone," she whispered back.

"Your family can't have."

"No. They're very kind. So they never said anything about my looks."

"Then who told you?"

The warmth of his unexpected cuddle and the concern in his voice made her melt.

So she whispered to him what they had said. She remembered every single word, spoken to her by cruel lips. Every word since she was a little girl.

"Stop," Hattori said. "I can't stand hearing this. Give me their names again, and I will hunt them down. I will punch each of them so hard their face will bleed. I will take a baseball bat to this Nurse Goto."

"You can't do that."

"I can. They're bullies. I hate bullies."

"I hate what they do, not them. They must be unhappy inside. I think they just need help to become happy. Then they'll stop being mean."

"You're such a better person than me," Hattori said. "But you need to realize they were lying to you, Miko. You have to understand that."

"No," Miko said. "No one would lie about that part of someone. Even bullies."

Hattori chuckled. "Everything about you is sweet. You see the entire world through your own kind eyes. But you need to grasp that other people are not like you. Especially bullies. They would totally lie about your looks. In fact, it's the first thing they'll do."

"Truly?"

"Truly. Think back, and give me your honest opinion about these bullies. I want you to rate their attractiveness. Ugly, average, or pretty? Were any of them pretty?"

"No."

"I thought so," Hattori said. "I can tell you exactly why they lied to you. They were jealous of your looks. They were insecure. So to make themselves feel better, they were trying to pull you down to their level. Because your beauty was a testament against them."

This made sense to Miko. It sounded like one of her theories.

"So you weren't. You weren't being mean?"

"Of course I wasn't. I love your little button nose, and your bright eyes, and your adorable mouth, and the shape of your hair, and your perfect cheeks. I love the way you smile, it's like an explosion of happiness. The whole world glows when Miko smiles. And your mischievous look when scheming. And the way you put your hand over your mouth when you giggle. And you bounce when you're excited. I bet you didn't know you bounce, but you do."

"Maybe I do, a bit," Miko said. "It's so hard to believe. No one's ever spoken to me like this."

"Who are you going to believe? Me, or Nurse Goto and that idiot Moe, or any of those other fist-targets," Hattori said. "You must have been extremely isolated, Miko, if no one has ever complimented you on your prettiness. It's almost like you've never told anyone else what those bullies said? Anyone would have told you they were lying. Didn't you tell anyone?"

"I had no one to tell. Except for Fluffy Kitty."

"Well, you've got me now."

Miko really liked the sound of that.

"Like a friend?" Miko said.

"Yes, a friend."

I have a friend!

Miko wanted to jump up onto the chair. At twenty-six years of age, Miko Nishimura had her first friend!

"But—" Hattori said.

"But?" Miko said. "That 'but' sounds scary."

"Not scary. I'm your friend. Absolutely. But, I was also thinking of being more than a friend. If possible?"

"Like a good friend?"

"Yes. But more than that."

"A best friend?"

"Yes. But, well, more than that."

"A lifelong best friend?"

"Yes," Hattori said. "Yes, could be. Lifelong. If things work out."

"That sounds nice."

"It does, doesn't it." Hattori got up, fetched his chair, and pulled it around. He sat next to Miko, putting his hand back on her arm.

"Listen, you were right when you said that now I have hope. It's true I'm still exhausted, but after the Chairman's speech so many repressed possibilities flourished in my mind. I realized that after work I can spend time with friends, I could have a hobby. I could even have a girlfriend."

Miko looked away. She didn't know how she felt about Hattori having a girlfriend.

"My father never spoke to me much when I was young. And he was often harsh when he did," Hattori said. "But sometimes he was caring. Once, while we were in the car waiting to drive onto a coastal ferry, he turned to me and gave me this advice. He said, 'In life, good things come along rarely. So if you find something good, grab it fast before it disappears.'"

Miko heard Hattori speaking, but his girlfriend idea had blindsided her. She hadn't considered the possibility.

Girlfriends get very jealous. She won't let me and Hattori stay friends.

"And so I believe I've found someone good," Hattori said.

"Oh," she said. "I understand."

"You do? I hoped you would. The entire time walking here from the dome, I was thinking about how to tell you."

"You don't need to tell me. It's your own life. I'm just happy you're free."

"I don't need to tell you?" Hattori said. He withdrew his hand from her arm. "I'm sorry. I thought. I mean, I had hoped..." His voice tailed off.

There was silence between them for a while, before Hattori spoke again.

"Is it because of how we met?"

"What is?"

"Your reaction."

Miko glanced at him. He wasn't making a lot of sense.

She recalled her nursing training.

Irrational thoughts and mood changes are common with burned-out people. I shall encourage my new friend and give him good advice.

"Don't be sad," Miko said.

"It's hard not to be."

"I suggest for the next few weekends you rest. Go straight home after work on the weekdays too and get long sleeps. You'll start feeling better."

Hattori sighed, leaned forward and stared down at his feet. He nodded slowly.

"I'm so dumb," he said. In a small voice, almost like he was speaking to himself.

"No you're not," Miko said. "Why do you think that?"

"Because I have these feelings. I thought they meant something." He took a deep breath. "But having feelings inside you doesn't mean the other person has feelings too. It's deceptive how your heart tricks you. It's like being lifted up high by someone you trust. Then they drop you onto rocks."

"I am confused. Are you talking about this girlfriend? She doesn't like you?"

"Evidently not."

What good news!

"What bad news. I'm so sorry," Miko said. Resisting signs of glee.

I am such a duplicitous person.

"You don't need to be sorry, you can't help not having—" Hattori said. He sat up and looked straight at Miko.

"Wait a minute. Who do you think I was talking about?"

"This girl you like."

"And who is she?"

"I don't know. Nana or Masumi. Or maybe someone at your work?"

"No, Miko. No," Hattori said. He put his hand back on her arm. "I was talking about you."

"Me?"

"Yes, Miko. I am confessing to you."

I'm being confessed to?

I'm being confessed to!

The most impossible of impossible things to happen had just happened.

"Oh," Miko managed.

It was like a pillow, for years twisted hard in her stomach, was suddenly let go, uncrumpling, becoming soft. The world around her was transforming into a warmer place with crisp edges and brighter colors.

"I'm sorry. I am so bad at confessing. I wanted this to go well. I should have planned what to say better," Hattori said. He squeezed her arm. "Please think about it. At least spend time with me and find out what I'm truly like. Even if you haven't got feelings for me yet, then given time maybe—"

"Stop talking," Miko whispered.

"Sorry."

Hattori froze. Like a man balancing on a knife's edge. Watching Miko as a captive man watches a judge about to pronounce his verdict.

Miko searched his coffee eyes.

She saw love and fear. Joy and misery. Pleading prayer. The horror of despair. Wild hope.

"Hattori."

"Yes, Miko."

"I accept."

❀ ❀ ❀ ❀

A week later, on Saturday 8th February 2014, Miko and Hattori and Nana and Masumi were sitting cross-legged around the dining table in Miko's apartment. The table's blanket covering their laps and the table's underside heater on full.

Outside, the temperature had plummeted since yesterday. Snow was falling past the apartment's living room window. Sometimes the white specks drifted downwards, but mostly they scattered, blown about in the chill northwesterly.

Nearby on the floor, Eichi sprawled on the heated rug like a cat on a warm car hood.

Fluffy Kitty, afraid of getting glue in his fur, lounged on the couch's armrest, his fluffy white tail drooping lazily over the couch's side.

"Watching this hard work is making me sleepy," Fluffy Kitty said. "Cats were clever enough to avoid inventing scissors and glue. Meaning we don't need to waste good sleeping time using them."

Miko smiled, as she drew the outline of another blue-foil star.

The five humans were folding and cutting and sticking. Surrounded with multicolored paper and tinsel and sheets of shiny metal foil. Paper cuttings littered the tabletop and were speckled across the blanket and rug.

Each time he cut paper, Eichi pursed his lips like he was trying to thread a needle.

The apartment smelled of paper glue mixed with the plastic aroma of freshly pulled sticky tape.

A squadron of helium-filled balloons imprinted with the words "Welcome Back" floated up against the ceiling in the corner of the living room over the TV. Their jellyfish-like string tentacles dangling from their bulbous foil bodies.

Strung from the kitchen across to the opposite corner of the room, a large multicolored banner displayed the same message.

Miko's parents were returning the next day, and Hattori and his friends had come to help Miko decorate the apartment for her parents' welcome back party.

Except, now Nana and Masumi and Eichi were not only Hattori's friends, but also Miko's friends.

They had loudly declared their friendship when Hattori had surprised them with his new, and first-ever, girlfriend.

Hattori had instructed them to wait at their favorite cafe to meet his mystery girlfriend.

When Hattori arrived with Miko, the three friends were delighted with their surprise.

They assumed Miko and Hattori had met because of Hattori's live show ticket. This was an assumption Miko and Hattori were happy to let them continue with.

I have four human friends. And one is a boyfriend. Zero to four in one week. Life goal achieved.

"If you had to fight a celebrity, who would you fight?" Hattori said.

"What is it with you and fighting celebrities?" Nana said.

"Stephen Hawking," Eichi said.

"Who?" Nana said.

"He's a famous English physicist."

"A scientist can't be a celebrity?"

"Can be. And he is."

"Well, I wouldn't fight any celebrity," Masumi said.

"Don't anyone dare suggest fighting our Aftershave girls," Nana said.

"I'd never suggest that," Eichi said.

"We've watched their 'Extrovert World' dance, and seen how they punch," Hattori said. "The three of them could punch you all day long and it wouldn't hurt."

"It would hurt emotionally," Eichi said.

"Fair point," Hattori said. "Who has the double-sided tape?"

"Remember not to lose the tickets this time," Nana said. Digging the tape out from under some foil sheets and passing the roll to Hattori.

"Stop it with that," Eichi said. "Two things. First, if I hadn't lost Hattori's ticket, then Miko and Hattori would both still be single. Second, I am not our friendship group's comic relief."

"We humbly thank you," Hattori said. "For your deliberate mistake."

Hattori and Miko fake-bowed to Eichi.

"You two have only been together a week and already you're anticipating each other's actions," Masumi said.

Miko laughed. She liked what Masumi had noticed.

"It must be going well," Masumi said.

"It is," Miko said. "But there's one thing I'm afraid of."

"What's that?" Hattori said, turning to her.

"The reversal. In the love stories I've read, the couple get together, and then there's some terrible complication or misunderstanding and the romance falls apart. Like in *Pride and Prejudice* Elizabeth mistakes why Mr. Darcy separated Bingley and Jane. Or Edward's engagement to Lucy in *Sense and Sensibility*."

"A reversal? I don't like the sound of that," Hattori said. "Let's not have one of those."

"Agreed."

"You've read so many books, Miko," Nana said. "More than all of us put—"

There was a rattle from the apartment door. Voices outside. A series of thumps and the door shook.

"Who's that?" Masumi said.

"I don't know," Miko said.

There was a rapid clicking of metal being pushed into the door's lock.

No one else, not even Uncle Ken, had keys to the apartment.

Oh no, the reversal. This is where everything falls apart.

Miko took Hattori's hand and squeezed.

Had someone complained to the police about her closing the road to Hattori's work complex? Or had they reported her renegade taxi?

The lock clicked and turned.

The handle rotated downwards.

The door was nudged. Gently, it swung open.

There was no one out in the corridor.

Just the blank eggshell colored wall on the opposite side of the corridor.

A man's foot pushed a brown cardboard box in through the door. The top of the box was spotted with melted snow.

"Oh," Miko said in her quietest voice. She squeezed Hattori's hand tighter as a sink for her fright.

A woman appeared walking backwards. Pulling a black rolly case on its little wheels into the apartment's genkan.

"Okaachan!" Miko cried out.

Miko leapt up and ran to the woman. Embracing her mother in a most un-Japanese display of affection.

"Miko," her mother said. Turning around. "Let me get in the, the—"

Her mother froze. Staring into the apartment.

Miko followed her gaze. Miko's four friends were standing out of respect for Miko's mother.

"Your poor mother arrives home and gets rugby tackled," Miko's father said. Lugging a suitcase in from the corridor. "Our daughter should join the All Blacks. We got to meet three of their players, um, in—"

Her father was now also frozen. Staring into the apartment.

"We didn't expect you back until tomorrow?" Miko said. "Not that I'm complaining. But your welcome back party decorations are only half done. So sorry."

"We had to, um, the ship's desalination plant got, contaminated, somehow," Miko's father said, speaking like a robot that needed its batteries charged. "So, we had to come back a day early. Who—"

"My friends were helping me decorate," Miko said.

"Your friends?" Miko's mother said.

"Yes, come and meet them," Miko said. She gently pulled her mother inwards.

Without taking her eyes off Miko's friends, her mother removed her shoes and put on her slippers. But unlike normal, she didn't point her shoe's toes towards the door. It was the first time Miko had seen her mother forget her strong habit.

Abandoning the suitcase in the doorway, her father followed.

"This is Nana and Masumi and Eichi."

Each bowed to Miko's parents as they were introduced.

"And this is Hattori. My boyfriend."

"Your boyfriend!" Miko's mother said. She gaped at Hattori.

Hattori bowed low. "It is my pleasure to meet you both."

Then, Miko's mother did something that would become a family legend.

She took several steps forward and poked Hattori in the shoulder. She gasped. Then speedily retreated and linked arms with her husband. They exchanged wide-eyed looks.

"Let me help you with your cases," Hattori said. Taking the unexpected shoulder jab in his stride.

Miko's parents' tracked Hattori as he moved past. With Eichi's help, he brought in the other suitcases from the corridor.

Miko's father managed to speak once the door was closed and the suitcases and the box lined neatly against the wall.

"Thank you," he said.

Hattori and Eichi bowed.

This time Miko's parents remembered to bow back.

"We should let you and Miko have time together," Hattori said.

"We were planning to get lunch at a cafe anyway," Masumi said.

"Were you going to the cafe too?" Miko's father said to Miko.

"We were all going."

"You'd go outside?" Miko's mother said.

Miko nodded.

"How did you meet your friends?"

"On the way to a live show."

"You went to a live show?" Miko's father said.

"Yes, Father."

"But the crowds?"

"About fifty thousand people. At Tokyo Dome."

"You went to Tokyo Dome! Fifty thousand!"

"My apologies, Mother and Father. While you were away, I have become the world's worst hikikomori."

"In life, some things are good to fail at," Miko's mother said.

"We will celebrate your failure," Miko's father said.

Miko laughed with her hand hiding her mouth, before smiling at her parents.

"Oh," Miko's mother said, turning to her husband. "I remember that sound."

"Mama, look," Miko's father said. "Her smile, it's back."

In unspoken unison, her parents stepped forward and embraced their daughter.

"It's been so long," her mother said.

"We missed you," her father whispered.

After the embrace, her parents smiled too.

"The decorations are nice," Miko's mother said.

"Nana and Masumi made the banner, and Hattori and Eichi put it up..."

Miko explained the decorations. Enthusing over how the apartment would have sparkled if they had finished.

Miko gave each of her parents a floating Welcome Back balloon. Her mother and father held them, pinching the string of their balloon between their thumbs and index fingers.

Her parents asked many questions about the decorations and thanked the person responsible as Miko gave credit.

Still clutching each other, their silver balloons hovering above their heads, her parents moved over to the couch and inspected the little paper hanging-lanterns.

"Masumi made those," Miko said.

"Thank you, Masumi," Miko's mother said.

Miko was pleased. Her parents were using the decorations as a starting point for interacting with her friends.

"How did you cut the diamond shape?" Miko's mother asked.

"I'll show you," Masumi said. She took a sheet of paper and scissors from the table. "You crease it in half, and then in half—"

There was a knock on the apartment door.

Miko's parents swiveled towards the door like frightened prey.

Miko skipped over and opened the door.

"Uncle Ken. Guess what. Mother and Father are home early."

"They're here?" Uncle Ken said. He stepped in and let Miko take his white cane. "What good news."

"Hello, Ken," Miko's mother said. "Thank you for checking up on—"

A woman stepped in too. She quickly took off her shoes and linked arms with Uncle Ken.

Miko's parents stared at this apparition.

Both of their Welcome Back balloons floated up and bounced lightly on the ceiling, going dunk dunk dunk.

Then they spoke in unison.

"Suzu?"

"Hello, Akio. Hello, Chika. Yes, it's me. How many years has it been?"

"So many," Miko's mother said.

"Miko has kindly let me be a guest in your apartment while visiting Ken. I hope that's OK?"

"Suzu has been such good company," Miko said.

"Yes. Of course it's OK," Miko's mother said.

"It is most fortuitous you two have returned at this moment," Uncle Ken said. "We were coming around to surprise Miko and her friends."

"Then help Miko prepare for your welcome home party after the surprise," Suzu said.

"What do you mean surprise us?" Miko said.

Uncle Ken stood up tall. He took Suzu's hand.

"I am pleased to announce that Suzu and I have decided to correct the mistakes of the past," Uncle Ken said.

Suzu held out her other hand. Palm down.

There, sparkling on her ring finger, was a small diamond set in sliver cherry blossoms mounted on a thin platinum ring.

"Uncle Ken is getting married!" Miko said, jumping and clapping. "This is such an exciting moment."

"Ken. I never thought I'd see the day," Miko's father said. "Congratulations, big brother. But such a fast engagement?"

Uncle Ken was born only minutes before his twin brother, which made Uncle Ken the senior.

"We saw no sense in waiting," Uncle Ken said.

"We had an honest discussion about the past," Suzu said. "And discovered we have both been dating each other in our minds for years. Daydreaming about what it would be like if we were together."

Uncle Ken nodded.

"The truth is, I should have sought Ken years ago when I returned from California. But I was ashamed of my failure. And I believed Ken would have forgotten about me."

"Never. Not for a single moment," Uncle Ken said.

Miko's mother started fanning her face rapidly with her hand. She sank against her husband.

"Mama?" Miko's father said. As he guided his wife to the couch and sat beside her.

"I'm sorry. It's too much," Miko's mother said. "I feel like the whole world has changed."

"Miko. A glass of chilled water," Miko's father said.

Miko raced to fulfill the request.

"Don't worry, Chika," Uncle Ken said. "You can't die from an overdose of good news."

"I'm sorry, Ken. Suzu. I'm very happy for you both. Just give me a moment."

Miko's mother sipped the water. Miko scooped up Fluffy Kitty so he wouldn't be knocked off the armrest.

"How did you two get back in touch?" Miko's mother managed.

"I was in Tokyo. My client chose to meet in a cafe by Inokashira Park," Suzu said. "And amazingly, because it had a queue, Ken chose to take lunch at the same cafe."

"It's true. A one in a million chance," Uncle Ken said.

"What if you had chosen a different cafe?" Suzu said. "We might never have met again."

"I don't believe in fate," Uncle Ken said. "But us meeting again, it was fate. It would have happened no matter what."

"Miko, why don't you go to lunch with your friends," Miko's father said. "Let Mama rest. We'll catch up with Uncle Ken and Suzu. Then we can have a family dinner tonight."

Miko understood.

"Let's get lunch," Miko said.

"And Hattori," Miko's father said. "Please join us for dinner tomorrow evening. We will be more ourselves then."

"I would be honored," Hattori said.

After the farewell salutations and bowing were completed, Miko and Hattori and Nana and Masumi and Eichi and Fluffy Kitty headed out the door.

Before the elevators. At the bend at the end of the corridor. Miko glanced back.

Her father and mother were standing outside the apartment door, watching. Smiling and embracing.

Miko waved goodbye and skipped over to her friends.

While they waited for the elevator, Hattori put his arm around her. Miko rested her head on his cozy shoulder.

Eight happy months passed as winter warmed to spring, and spring to summer, and summer cooled slightly to indicate the start of autumn.

Outside the apartment it was a toasty September day.

Hattori was waiting out in the living room, talking with Miko's father and Uncle Ken and their new friend Obito Narita, while Miko got ready for tonight's Aftershave live show.

Miko had bought a dress for the occasion. Masumi and Nana, her fashion consultants, had gone shopping with her. Miko hoped Hattori would like it.

"You look very pretty, Miko," Fluffy Kitty said. He was resting on the dresser next to her wall mirror.

"Thank you."

"Oh, you agree. So now you're happy to listen to your cat."

Fluffy Kitty was still miffed Miko had believed Hattori straight away when he explained the bullies were lying to her, and not when Fluffy Kitty had told her the same thing.

"I said I'm sorry. Your statements laid the groundwork Hattori built on."

"So at last the cat gets some credit," Fluffy Kitty said. "Miko. We have been friends for a long time. I hope I have helped make your life better."

"You have. So much. You are my most faithful friend."

"That makes me feel happy," Fluffy Kitty said. "You know, girls sure take a long time to get ready. Hattori will have a white beard like Mr. Narita's when you're finished."

"Makeup is art. It takes time to get it right."

"I have been wondering. Why does Uncle Ken's wife still wear makeup? Uncle Ken can't see her face."

"Because he keeps telling everyone how beautiful his wife is. So Auntie Suzu feels she must present well to honor her husband," Miko said. Snapping her foundation clam shell closed and locating her eyeliner. "But I do worry that it stresses Auntie Suzu a bit. You wouldn't understand, but when a woman gets older, she knows her looks have faded."

"So why doesn't Uncle Ken tell the truth about her looks?"

"Don't be mean. Auntie Suzu is still attractive for her age. Remember, Uncle Ken went blind before they met again, so he still sees Auntie Suzu as the beauty she was at school. That is his picture of her. So even when she is eighty, he'll still be raving about his wife."

Fluffy Kitty was silent for a while.

Miko applied her eye glitter.

"Miko."

"Yes, dear cat."

"About the live show tonight."

"Yes."

"I am thinking maybe I shouldn't go."

"What!" Miko said. She stopped and stared at Fluffy Kitty. "You've gone everywhere with me since I was ten. Everywhere."

"I know. And I love being with you. But you're a big girl now. And I've noticed other grown-up girls don't carry their soft-toys around."

"I don't know how to feel about this idea."

"Well, maybe you should try listening to your cat the first time for once. I think you should try going outside without me. You'll have Hattori with you. And Masumi and Nana and Eichi too."

"It will feel strange."

"I know. But you have a happy life now. So I think the time has come. Be brave."

Miko breathed deep, and exhaled slowly.

"OK. I will try. Just this once, though."

"Good," Fluffy Kitty said. "It will take time, but I know you'll be fine, Miko. I wouldn't suggest this if I weren't sure you were ready."

Miko nodded, and they chatted some more as Miko finished her preparations.

As Miko was about to head out into the living room, she shouldered her tiny blue diamanté encrusted handbag and automatically went to pick up Fluffy Kitty.

"Oh," Miko said, checking herself and leaving Fluffy Kitty sitting where he was.

Instead, she patted him on his head.

"Have a fun live show, Miko."

"We will. I'll see you soon."

As Miko opened her bedroom door, she stopped and turned.

She smiled at Fluffy Kitty.

"I love you, Fluffy Kitty!"

"I love you too, Miko, always," said Fluffy Kitty.

At that moment Miko had no way of knowing, but those were the last words she would hear Fluffy Kitty say.

When she returned from the live show, Fluffy Kitty would be just an ordinary soft-toy, the kind that doesn't speak back.

In the years to come, Miko would often reflect on this moment. She came to understand that Fluffy Kitty knew this would be the last time he would speak. But he couldn't say so directly, since he was afraid Miko would cling to him and refuse to go to the live show with Hattori.

Miko's sadness was deep. As grief tends to be. But Hattori was diligent in comforting her, and her friends rallied around.

Only Hattori knew the truth about Fluffy Kitty.

Miko was not embarrassed about having had a talking soft-toy friend, but Hattori recommended it was best to keep the details to themselves.

Miko could never describe how in words, but her sadness was also tempered by the sense that Fluffy Kitty had never truly gone away. He was in some way inside her, still complaining and making jokes.

But, Miko missed her talkative cat friend. So, secretly hoping that one day he would speak again, she kept Fluffy Kitty the silent soft-toy close to her for the rest of her life.

🌸 🌸 🌸 🌸

Hattori sat in the living room talking with Miko's father, Uncle Ken, and their new, but old, white-goatee-bearded friend Obito Narita.

Obito and his daughter Kana were still grateful for Miko's intervention, and had kept their promise of inviting Miko and her family to dinner.

Obito was older than Miko's father and Uncle Ken, but in the months following their first dinner Obito had become firm friends with the twin brothers, and the three men often went drinking together.

This evening they were excited because Miko's father's construction company had over-ordered *Jichin-sai* packets for their ground-breaking ceremonies, and had given two of the elegantly presented surplus boxes to Miko's father.

The reason for their excitement: each packet contained a 1800 ml bottle of premium quality sake. The packets also contained rice and salt, but the three men weren't so interested in those other ceremonial components.

Hattori sat, waiting for Miko. Glancing at her bedroom door.

Auntie Suzu and Miko's mother chatted in the kitchen space as they cooked.

"Your chairman's policies were speedily adopted by the members of his keiretsu," Obito said. "And in only a few months, the other keiretsu have been following too. The trend he began is cascading rapidly throughout the country."

Hattori nodded. "I feel privileged to have been present at his famous speech. I must confess at the start I expected another boring corporate talk. But his speech soon revealed its true significance. No one in the dome was faking their attention. We were spellbound."

The door to Miko's bedroom opened, and a moment later Miko came out.

Her radiance made Hattori stand up. A sweet sleeveless summer dress of white with patterns of light blue leaves. Her hair as soft as ever and her face glowing with youthful beauty.

I am such an impostor. When will she realize she could have anyone she wants?

Miko smiled back at his unconcealed adoration, and Hattori's heart melted, as it did whenever she smiled.

"I'm going to be the envy of the whole live show," Hattori said.

"I can't get over the resemblance," Obito said. "Every time I see Miko I go back to when my daughter was young."

"How is Kana?" Miko said.

"I am concerned she works too hard. But long past is the time when she will listen to the worries of her father."

Miko's upturned button nose sniffed three times.

Even the way she sniffs is cute.

"Mother, are you making candyfloss?"

"No," Miko's mother said.

"I have the fish fryer drawer on," Auntie Suzu said. Indicating towards the oven. "But I'd be worried if it smelled like that."

"Oh, what a funny thing then," Miko said.

"Babe, we better get moving. To pick up the guys and get there in time to score some good merch," Hattori said.

"Yippee," Miko said, and bounded over to him. Linking her arm through his. "Let's join the thousands of other Aftershave fans across Tokyo leaving their homes right at this very moment."

Her family and Mr. Narita wished them both a happy live show.

Soon Hattori was walking down the apartment's corridor. His arm around the girl he loved. Her warm cheek resting on his shoulder.

2014, without doubt the best year of my life. And soon, hopefully, it will get even better.

❀ ❀ ❀ ❀

Miko drove to the live show with Hattori next to her and Eichi, Nana, and Masumi in the taxi's rear seats.

The five of them talking and laughing together, fueled by excited expectations.

Miko looked around, and smiled—just like her schoolgirl doodles, Uncle Ken's taxi was crammed full with her friends.

After the concert, the five friends emerged from Yoyogi National Gymnasium.

A unique science-fiction-style building with a gray roof held up by thick steel cables strung between two giant towers. The interior was like being inside an enormous two-pole tent, while the outside resembled the spaceport of a futuristic city.

Miko skipped ahead and bounced while she waited for Hattori to catch up.

They linked arms.

The crowd leaving with them were laughing and chatting in the night air. Their voices competing with the metal-sawing sound of a million demented Tokyo cicadas.

"I thought Miyu would win Ace's race," Nana said.

"They dance for hours in heels, and they can run in heels too," Masumi said.

"When it went dark for so long, I thought it was over. But it seemed too soon for the live show to end," Eichi said. "The other fans must have thought the same because the clapping and cheering went quiet. I was so relieved when they appeared on that platform at the back. I was getting worried."

"Don't worry, Eichi," Miko said. "Our three girls were just taking their time to move on to the next stage in their life."

Hattori laughed first. Then the other three clicked and laughed too.

"Oh, I love double meanings," Nana said.

"It's unbelievable," Eichi said. Throwing his hands in the air like a man complaining to the heavens. "How did Hattori, of all people, get a girlfriend who is not only super cute, and smart, and kind, but now we discover she can invent jokes on the spot? It's too much for him. He doesn't deserve this!"

Miko loved how her friends described her as cute or pretty in a matter-of-fact manner, like they were simply mentioning the color of her hair or the clothes she was wearing. Their constant encouragement was a warm balm, healing the wounds from the past.

Sometimes Miko wondered if true friends knew instinctively where you were lacking, and bolstered you without even knowing they were doing you a kindness.

Unexpectedly, Hattori stopped walking.

He faced Miko and took her hands in his.

To Hattori's left, Eichi's face showed panic.

"Wait," he said.

Eichi fumbled for his phone. As fast as he could, he began videoing.

"OK, ready."

"What Eichi said is true. I don't deserve you, Miko," Hattori said. "But it doesn't change the fact that I love you, and I want to keep you forever."

"What's happening?" Miko said.

"This," he said.

He kneeled on one knee in front of Miko.

Revealing in his hand a little red box. He snapped it open. Inside glittered an exquisite diamond set in a thin platinum ring.

Masumi and Nana jumped. Squealing so loud that the passing crowd stopped in their tracks.

Miko's mind was a muddle.

Hattori, the man she loved, was kneeling before her. A sparkly ring sparkling in a most sparkly manner.

But the fact is, that what this seemed to be, was something Miko believed would never happen to her.

This happened only to Akiyo from nursing school, and other girls who deserved it. Not Miko Nishimura.

She glanced around to make sure she was really here.

The crowd had speedily packed into a circle around the five friends. A short man was jumping behind trying to see over the people's shoulders. A sea of faces looked back. Several other phones were out recording.

"Miko Nishimura, will you marry me?" Hattori said.

"Oh," Miko said. She put her hands over her mouth.

This is really happening.

Apart from the incessant cicadas, the night became silent.

Everyone waiting to hear her answer.

Hattori's coffee eyes were fixed on hers. Miko didn't doubt he loved her, it was easy to tell.

Seeing him, her heart was full. A radiant vision of the future was right before her. All Miko needed to do was speak the words and that future would be hers.

She started bouncing.

"Yes, Hattori. I will marry you."

Hattori beamed at her. The crowd clapped and cheered the good result.

He slid the engagement ring onto Miko's finger.

Its metal was a cool and weighty confirmation.

He stood and they embraced.

The crowd cheered that too.

Miko smiled at everyone, and bouncing waved her hand up high so everyone could see her ring.

The crowd loved the gesture.

How things have changed for me, and in such a short time. I don't mind a crowd watching me, just like the girls from Aftershave. And not only do I have friends. Now I have a friend who wants to spend his whole life with me.

"I believe it is a very lucky thing for someone to meet Miko Nishimura," Hattori said. "And so I must be the luckiest man in the world."

"I promise I will be the best wife," Miko said.

"Of that I have no doubt. I'm so happy you said yes. I was scared."

Miko laughed. "You had no reason to be."

As Miko and Hattori raced home to tell her parents their happy news, Miko had a triumphant thought.

So after years of worry, Miko Nishimura will not be Christmas Cake after all.

❀ ❀ ❀ ❀

Miko and Hattori loved cherry blossom season because it reminded them of their wedding day.

They had been married during full bloom on a sunny day at the end of March in 2015.

Since then, many pink-petal anniversaries had come and passed, and during each, they celebrated their love.

Today was the time of *Sakura Fubuki*, or cherry blossom snow—the end of the cherry blossom season when the trees dropped their petals in a fluttering pink snowfall.

Once they had finished shopping at the mall, Miko and Hattori planned to meet their friends at the park so their combined children could play together in the cherry snow.

To the delight of both Miko and Hattori's parents, and Uncle Ken and Auntie Suzu, Miko and Hattori had what in Japan's recent past had been considered a large family.

First, they were surprised with twin girls, and two years later they decided to have one more baby, because Miko knew Hattori wanted a son.

Hattori got his son, but as a bonus it was twins again. They gained a third daughter.

Miko suggested, and Hattori agreed, to name their son Kosuke since they were sure he would be a blessing to their family.

Of their daughters, the youngest was very good at organizing her siblings until her twin brother rebelled and refused to be organized. However, her two older sisters kept going along with her plans.

The youngest talked a lot and was good at making friends.

The middle daughter loved books and read so much she became quite a young intellectual with many theories about things just like Miko. She also inherited Miko's love of animals.

The oldest daughter was full of panache and her endless zest for life was an inspiration, but she also was the one who caused the most trouble.

Miko and Hattori entered the mall. A vast marble and glass cavern of shopping heaven.

"Did I tell you that my retired chairman and that old rock star Jekyll are getting a joint recognition reward today?" Hattori said.

"No," Miko said. Glancing behind to make sure their four children were still in tow. They were, and in the midst of some obvious conspiring. "What for?"

"This," Hattori said. Waving his hand at the expanse of the mall.

Everywhere in the mall children were running, holding their parents' hands, staring down through the glass railings, riding in strollers, eating ice creams, singing to themselves, gyrating on coin-op kiddie rides, or being carried on their parents fronts or backs in nylon carry harnesses.

Today, in Japanese malls and parks and streets, it was normal to see more children than adults.

Toy stores and children's clothing stores were big business. Children's movies packed out the cinemas, and bookstores had comprehensive sections for kids.

Two little boys raced past test driving blue pedal cars.

"I am pleased to know they're good men with good hearts. They deserve their awards for these many happy results," Miko said.

It was telling of Miko's character that she never thought about how her love had changed Japan. She believed she had done what was needed, and anyone else would have done the same. The massive increase in births was how Japan should be. To her heart, the world seemed nicely right.

"Shall we find that cake mixer? We'll have to get it delivered. What was that color you wanted?"

"Cyan. To match the stripe between our kitchen tiles."

At work, Hattori had been promoted three times. Last year, he became a division manager. This, in addition to Miko's before-children taxi income, had allowed them to purchase a large apartment in the same building as Miko's parents.

Miko joked with her parents that they did get to live together in the same house after all.

They were located only a floor down from her parents' apartment, and the kids were adept at sneaking up the stairwell to visit their grandparents for treats.

On Miko and Hattori's living room wall hung a framed collage of pressed cherry blossom petals Auntie Suzu had collected on their wedding day. Miko had arranged the petals into a silhouette of her and Hattori holding hands at the altar.

Also, Miko had kept her promise to little Hanaka, and so the drawing of Hanaka's dream was framed and hung on the wall too.

Now Miko had lots of little people in her life. It was good Miko had such a big heart, because her life was full of people to love.

Fluffy Kitty was not forgotten. He sat in the living room on a prominent shelf watching over Miko's family.

Sometimes, when no one was around, Miko still whispered her secrets to him.

Much later in her life, when Miko was full of years, she made her grandchildren promise to look after Fluffy Kitty and pass him on to their own children.

Miko and Hattori's many descendants would honor this promise, and thus Fluffy Kitty became their expansive family's most cherished heirloom.

Uncle Ken's taxi had been transformed into their family car.

Although only Miko drove the taxi. Because Hattori was too afraid of its power. Ever since his first, and only, attempt at driving the taxi had resulted in spiraling black donuts across a local car park.

Miko often took the car out alone, since driving fast was her best way of relaxing.

In the mall's tidy appliance store the uniformed shop assistant apologized, because a customer had just taken the last cyan cake mixer. Only candy red and apple green mixing machines were left.

"We always have a bowl of green apples in the kitchen," Hattori said.

"I know. And I do love green apples. But I had my heart set on cyan," Miko said.

"Excuse me," a woman with a tartan scarf said. A man stood with her, holding a small squirming child. "My husband overheard that you want a cyan cake mixer. You can have the one I picked. I'm happy to take a red one."

"That is very kind. Are you sure?" Miko said.

"Oh yes. I just took the first box on top of the pile. I don't have a strong color preference."

Miko and Hattori were grateful to the couple. Chatting with them, they went together to the dual counter and stood side by side as they paid and arranged their deliveries.

Each purchaser got a lucky game scratchy ticket that promised special store rewards for spending over ten thousand yen.

Miko let Hattori scratch their reward card.

"We have won a ten percent discount off our next purchase," Hattori said.

"Oh my goodness," the kind woman said. She showed her scratched ticket to her husband before handing it to the checkout operator.

"Congratulations," the operator said. "Between our stores nationwide there are only three top prize tickets. It is good news our store had one."

The other checkout operator and the store assistants gathered around to see.

"Exciting. What did you win?" Miko said.

"A store credit for fifty thousand yen."

"And your purchase and delivery today are free," the checkout operator added.

"I've never been lucky before. I've won none of the many competitions I've entered," the woman said. "Ever since I was a little girl, I've dreamed of winning something, anything. And now for the first time in my life I've won a prize."

"Wait a minute," her husband said. "What about the day you married me?"

Everyone laughed.

After purchasing their new mixer, Miko and Hattori and their four children went walking in the sunny park near the mall. Miko and Hattori holding hands while their children ran on ahead to chase the cherry snow.

They were meeting Masumi and Nana and Eichi and their respective spouses. Their children would play together while the adults chatted.

"So many couples," Miko said.

Amongst the roving gaggles of children, couples walked together or chatted on the bench seats.

"Who says things can't get better," Hattori said. "I suspect we led the way. People saw us get together, and then everyone said, 'what a good idea, let's copy Miko and Hattori'. And that's how we started the trend."

"Like pioneers?"

"Exactly. We are relationship pioneers."

"But we both have married parents, so I detect some temporal flaws in your theory."

"Flaws? No. I'm sure there are none," Hattori said. "Otherwise we'd just be ordinary, and I'm sure we're not."

"I am quite happy that I'm ordinary," Miko said. "When I was a teenager, I believed I was the most insignificant person in Japan. So being an ordinary person is a big upgrade for me."

"Ha, you're definitely not ordinary. Especially to the kids and me. You're the best wife a man could ever have, and the best mother I've ever seen. What's more, your winter soups are amazing."

"You're biased," Miko said. Laughing.

"I don't know if I am. I've noticed throughout our years that wherever Miko goes, good things seem to happen."

"Good things are always happening."

"Eichi admits to us he's pining over a girl at his badminton club, and from his next session he's rostered on each following week for mixed doubles with his now-wife. Masumi breaks her ankle, and mentions a handsome doctor at the hospital, and suddenly he is reassigned to her case and now they're married too."

"Coincidences happen."

"And the way Uncle Ken and Auntie Suzu met? Auntie Suzu didn't even live in Tokyo. The odds of them meeting like that were astronomical."

"Look, here come our little loves," Miko said.

In a rush their four children arrived around their legs, outlining enthusiastically the incredible benefits of being bought ice creams from the pink ice cream van they had discovered.

Now it was pointed out, Miko could hear the distant singing from the van parked on the road across the grass.

"Please forgive me. Please give me time," sang the van.

After feinting reluctance. Miko and Hattori, holding two little hands each, set off towards the musical van to buy ice creams.

"Our lives have turned out well. Don't you think?" Hattori said.

"I do. We both had our difficult times. But it was through those times we found our love."

"Back then, before the Chairman's speech, it wasn't the promise I made, but the hope of seeing you that kept me going."

Miko smiled.

"We must teach our little loves about hope, in case they encounter dark times too," Miko said. "Deep down in the foundations of their beings they must believe no matter how bad things get, that there is always hope."

At that moment, not far away, in a ballroom-sized TV studio. The syrupy awards ceremony had finished. The show would air in a special tonight.

Jekyll remained still as the nervous makeup artist cleaned his face with a cotton pad while the TV company's production team crowded around, angling for an autograph.

The cones of cold brightness from the LED production lights cast oversaturated white patches and stark shadows across their faces.

Years of experience had taught him to move carefully in these environments, to avoid tripping on the thick black cables secured with matte-black gaffer tape to the matte-black flooring.

The makeup removal complete. Jekyll passed his hefty brushed-gold trophy to one of his entourage, so he could sign the CD covers being thrust at him.

The two recognition awards were shaped like fat metal chisels. Each etched through, end to end by a laser, with the graph showing the impressive uptick of Japan's birthrate.

The uptick attributed by historians and social researchers jointly to his release of "My Time, Your Time" and retired Chairman Tarō Ikari's famous corporate policy pivot. The policy that had become Japan's new standard work practice.

Jekyll's bones ached from standing.

How did I end up so old?

"Boss," said his comedian-ugly public relations manager, Ikuya.

"Yeah."

"Chairman Ikari has asked if you would join him in his limousine when you are finished. He has offered to drive you home."

On the other side of the studio, the high executives of the broadcast company and his own entourage surrounded the swarthy old chairman. The great man stood frail and yet dignified.

"Tell him I would be honored."

After the signings and farewells, and listening to people thank him for how his music affected their lives, Jekyll and Ikuya took the elevator down to the basement car park.

The driver opened the door to the Chairman's black stretched Toyota Century limousine.

Jekyll enjoyed cars. Getting in, he could tell this example was coach-built. Full of black leather quality that far exceeded an ordinary Toyota Century limousine.

Fiber optic lighting formed a starfield on the limousine's black ceiling, filling the car with twinkling blue-tinted light.

The Chairman sat in the left rear seat. His face deep with wrinkles.

His matching golden trophy was nestled beside him in the seat's crook.

Jekyll sat opposite, in the rear-facing seat. The door closed with an opulent thunk, and the drone of the outside world ceased.

The limo smelled of leather and thick woolen carpet.

A black velvet divider with a mid-mounted video screen separated them from the driver. The two men were alone. They bowed to each other.

"I thank you for joining me," the Chairman said. "May I call you Hiroshi instead of your stage name?"

Jekyll nodded his approval.

"It is a privilege to meet you, Hiroshi. It seems we are partners in history."

"Thank you for the invitation to join you, Chairman Ikari. I am honored to meet our country's most famous businessman."

"Please call me Tarō. We two iconoclasts should break another tradition together. So let's use first names. Would you like Scotch?"

Jekyll agreed. With a button press on the rear consul it rose, exposing a small bar. The Chairman's hands shook a little as he poured.

Jekyll took a sip out of his heavy square crystal glass.

"So smooth," he said. "What is this?"

The Chairman twisted the bottle around so he could see the label.

That would have cost as much as this car.

Jekyll was wealthy, but his fortune was nothing compared to the truly rich of the world.

The car started moving.

"I must thank you Tarō, for mentioning in your speech that my song played at the start of your formative meeting."

It is unsettling addressing such a distinguished senior by his first name.

"There have been songs about our work culture before. But none with such tremendous persuasive power. Your song softened the minds of my colleagues like an artillery barrage before an attack. It was a most fortuitous event."

Jekyll chuckled. "Sir, I've had my work compared to many things, but never artillery."

"Hiroshi. I must be honest. I have not invited you to join me out of appreciation of your music."

Here it comes.

There was a long silence before he spoke. A pregnant pause, in the manner of wise old men.

"In your acceptance speech. You mentioned that your inspiration for your song came during a taxi ride?"

"Yes."

"Tell me. The taxi driver. Was it a young woman?"

"Yes. Yes it was."

"A fluffy white toy cat on the dashboard?"

Jekyll suffered a frisson at the mention of such a specific fact.

Goosebumps. The hair on the back of his neck stood to attention, and for an instant he was back in that rumbling taxi.

"Yes, sir."

"Ah," the Chairman said, closing his eyes. He smiled with a half-chuckle. Followed with a gentle, knowing nod. Opening his eyes, the Chairman took a long remedial sip from his glass. Before staring out the car's tinted side window with the triumphant look of a man who had found the world exactly as he expected.

"Tarō," Jekyll said. "How did you—"

"Hidden Stealth Ninja Taxi Service?" the Chairman said, still staring out the window.

"Sir, I've told no one that name. And I've never mentioned the woman or her toy cat to anyone. In fact, sir, until this afternoon, I've told no one I was inspired to write that song during a taxi trip. How could you possibly know?"

The Chairman turned from the window.

"Ah, Hiroshi, my friend. I too have a story I've never told. Not to a single soul. Not even to the fish in my garden's pond. Let us make a deal. You tell me your secret taxi story and I will tell mine."

The Chairman listened, as Jekyll told of the night when a taxi driver had prompted him to write the song that became his greatest hit.

Even many years on, "My Time, Your Time" still rotated on the radio and racked up big counts on the streaming services.

The Chairman asked a few questions. Then true to his word, he recalled for Jekyll his own encounter with the woman from Hidden Stealth Ninja Taxi Service.

"She blocked off the road?" Jekyll said.

"The purpose of the road closure was to delay my car, so she would be my sole offer of transport that evening."

"Surely you had security? Cameras? There must be evidence of her closing that road?"

"Yes," the Chairman said. "There was a security camera that overlooked the entrance."

"Wasn't it working?"

"The camera was working. Faultlessly for the entire duration of the event."

"And? What did it see?"

The Chairman chuckled again. He took another long sip. "Before the road was closed, that camera recorded the arrival of a robin. White feathers with a red spot on its smug fat chest. That robin stayed staring and pecking at the camera lens for the next fifty minutes. And when it flew off, the roadblock had gone."

"A robin? Didn't the camera see anything?"

"Of the entrance or the driver? Not a single frame. I have reviewed the entire video. For fifty minutes that patriotic bird blocked the camera," the Chairman said. "I swear to you, Hiroshi, that bird was mocking me. It had a humorous attitude."

"But you had other cameras in your business park?"

"We did. Many others. And they also were working perfectly."

"So? Did you get a picture of her?"

The Chairman shook his head. "Not a single frame. Not when she picked me up. Not of her. Not of her taxi. Not when she, or any accomplices, removed the roadblock. Nothing."

"How can that be?"

"This conversation remains between us, Hiroshi? Swear it."

"Of course, sir," Jekyll said.

"I hired a security forensics team to investigate. To locate that taxi driver," the Chairman said. "Pigeons, Hiroshi. Robins. Sparrows. Doves. Even ducks and grebes. A bird blocked every camera that would have caught even a fleeting glimpse of this taxi driver. Birds hanging upside down. Birds holding out an open wing from the side to cover the lens. Birds hovering in relays in front of the cameras where there was no perch."

"Sir, are you saying she used trained birds to block the cameras in your complex? It is unbelievable."

"In my complex? No, Hiroshi. You don't understand."

The Chairman made strong eye contact.

"Birds blocked every camera in the entire Tokyo Business District."

"No. That cannot be. That's not possible."

"Hiding the view of each road for kilometers in every direction. Especially the cameras on the route she drove me. And those at the railway station too. Many thousands of determined birds of all kinds making it impossible to track her taxi's movements."

What? Is this a trick? Has the man become delusional in his old age?

"Tarō. Sir, with respect. What you're saying can't have happened."

"I know," the Chairman said. "And yet, I have the forensic evidence locked in my private vault. Hundreds of hours of video from that evening. Maps of camera locations with time stamps for each recording. The comprehensive result of a professional sixteen-man investigation team working for eight months at my expense. Evidence I suggest you come and view for yourself. Because Hiroshi, at last, I am relieved to have found someone to share in my madness."

Jekyll swallowed several times.

The implications. They take me to places I have never been. What if he is telling the truth?

And worse, Jekyll was already convinced the Chairman was not lying. He spoke of these events in the same way he would as if affirming the existence of the glass of Scotch held in his hand.

Jekyll crossed his arms in a clandestine self-hug. Massaging his elbows through his suit sleeves to enhance the calming effect.

"Here," the Chairman said. He topped up their glasses with more of the expensive liquor.

"Miko," Jekyll said. "Her first name was Miko. I asked her name."

"Miko," the Chairman said. His voice resonated, savoring both syllables. "Of course that is her name."

"And she called her soft-toy 'Fluffy Kitty'."

"Thank you, Hiroshi. To know her name is a splendid gift. The greatest gift anyone has ever given me. Because in my old age, unless you have not yet guessed, I have become obsessive regarding this single event in my life. Over the years, my meeting with Miko has grown in my mind like one of the expanding water toys we manufacture. In a kind of apotheosis."

Outside, the traffic was heavy. The custom limousine moved in stops and starts. But Jekyll didn't mind the delay. While the implications were unsettling, this was the most interesting conversation he'd had in a long time. Like a spoon stir in long still miso soup, their conversation was churning up the depths of his soul.

"Tarō. When I think back to the other events of 2014, my memory has faded," Jekyll said. "Such is the curse of being a celebrity. So many faces and stages, flights and van trips and events that year, mixed into an indistinguishable mash."

"And yet your memory, Hiroshi. Of that taxi trip?"

"It's vivid, as if it just happened. Every word Miko spoke to me, the smell of her taxi, every turn, every stop and start on the way home. I can replay it in my mind like a film. If I close my eyes when recalling, I am there again in her taxi. In fact, discussing it with you, I realize I have no other memory like it. Nothing from my past do I remember in—"

"Such high fidelity?" the Chairman said. "I have long pondered this question. With great age, your memory leaks like a colander. But I too vividly remember my taxi ride. From the exact moment I first saw Miko standing in front of her taxi at the bottom of the stairs, until the exact moment when she drove out of sight at Tokyo Station. A memory etched deep, like gouges in stone. Like you, I have no other memory equivalent. But, let me ask you a question. Do you remember Miko's face?"

"No," Jekyll said. "I recall I thought she was pretty. But I can see no details."

The Chairman nodded. "I scrutinized her when deciding if to take her taxi, and she turned and looked directly at me several times. But despite the incredible clarity of the overall memory, when I focus on Miko, it's like I'm looking through glasses with a bad smudge."

Jekyll closed his eyes and concentrated as hard as he could. He reconfirmed. In his memory he knew Miko was there sitting in the driver's seat, but her form was only a shimmer of amorphous colors, like a shape viewed through frosted glass.

"Hiroshi. Did you find it strange the way her taxi rumbled?"

"Yes. Once I rode in a race car at Fuji Speedway."

"Indeed. It was obviously not a normal taxi. And in case you haven't guessed, there is no record of a company called Hidden Stealth Ninja Taxi Service," the Chairman said. "After the event, I hunted for clues in every page of that manga. Do you know that Hidden Stealth Ninja fights for those weaker than him and expects no reward? He remains hidden forever to those he helps, while to those who are causing people to suffer, he deals with most firmly."

Jekyll nodded. He loved Hidden Stealth Ninja. Its constant creative genius was inspiring, at the same time making him jealous. Only once in his life had he fully tapped into his own creativity, in those few days after his ride in Miko's taxi.

"I believe this manga's extreme popularity, Hiroshi, is because Hidden Stealth Ninja himself is based on the pattern of the champions of old. There is truth to who he is. An ethereal truth that resonates with us ordinary humans," the Chairman said, loosening his bow tie and tossing the black butterfly onto the seat by his award. He undid his shirt's collar button.

Jekyll did the same. Having his neck freed from the starched collar made their discussion seem more serious.

"It was Miko's words, sir," Jekyll said. "They were like warm honey in my mind. Encouraging me to create. To get the song produced and included in the album. Then, as soon as the song was released, her words turned from firm motivation into a sweet-tasting memory."

"You describe the feeling precisely, with an artist's flair. Even though she was harsh with me, her words did not override my will. Instead, they made me desire with my heart to accomplish the task she set me. What is more, without me suspecting, her words stripped from me my long-constructed businessman's disdain of empathy. I have never regained that callous trait. Since meeting Miko, every time one of my pet fish dies, I weep like a baby because the other fish have lost their friend."

"What has happened to us, Tarō? Are we the victims of a conspiracy?"

"Victims, Hiroshi? Or privileged participants in a historic intervention? In hindsight, what Miko prompted us to accomplish was long needed. But our minds were utterly entangled in a knotted web of tradition and selfish intentions. For us to action those changes, we needed a powerful kick."

The Chairman picked up his metal award. Turning it over in his hand, he began chuckling.

"What is it?"

"Miko appealed to my ego. She made me dwell upon my legacy. She suggested I could be revered as the 'Savior of Japan'. And it worked. She employed not only my sense of doing right and the empathy I didn't know I had, but she also engaged my pride. Masterfully played. Our golden trophies rightfully belong to Miko. Although I know in my heart, she would not care for their prestige."

The Chairman winced, dropping the trophy back onto its leather seat.

"Sir. Are you OK?"

"Mental pain, not physical," the Chairman said. "How do I explain?"

He glanced around the limousine's interior, until his gaze fell on his wrist.

"See Hiroshi, look, we are both wearing wristwatches. They are not jewelry, as we suppose. Examine their metal bands. Do you know what our watches really are?"

Jekyll shook his head.

"They are shackles. Shackles binding us to the chain of time. That universal chain dragging us along without pause, never speeding up, never slowing down. Relentlessly drawing us to our doom."

Jekyll glanced at his own watch's golden band.

"You are not there yet, Hiroshi. But I am. There is no buffer left to soften the terrifying reality when you are close to death. You arrive before the silver mirror placed at the end of your journey, and with every step closer you perceive with increasing clarity who you have become. And yet every step also makes sharper the gut-wrenching reality that there is no time left to correct your faults. You are what you have made yourself to be," the Chairman said. He rubbed his face and sighed. "So truth when it comes, stabs deep. Hiroshi, I am undone. So many years on this earth and I am still a profoundly flawed man."

"Don't be so hard on yourself."

"No. I must face my failure of character. How arrogant I was towards Miko. Assuming I was more important than her. For years, I have considered myself greater than anyone I met. You might see me as an accomplished man. But inside Hiroshi, let me tell you the grim truth. I am merely a messed up teenage boy with too many years. Prideful and arrogant. I have learned nothing. I am ashamed of how I treated Miko. If only I could meet her again. I would beg her forgiveness."

"I too am ashamed," Jekyll said. The Chairman's distress was a crystallization of his own long unease. "I treated her dismissively. I placed myself above her. She was just a taxi driver, while I was a celebrity. I remember thinking what a privilege it must be for her to talk to me."

The old man put his drink down firmly. He leaned forward and grasped Jekyll's arms below the wrists. He pulled Jekyll forward.

"No, Hiroshi. It was the other way around. We were in the presence of greatness, and we were too arrogant to recognize our inferior position."

"Yes," Jekyll said. Nodding his head like a kōhai.

The Chairman let go and leaned back into his seat.

"Since childhood Hiroshi, my gut has told me that the ancient myths are more than just made up stories. I believe they are echoes reverberating on the strings of time. A record of rare visitations by providential heroes. Throughout childhood I often daydreamed about what questions to ask, if I had been one of the few privileged amongst the billions who have walked the Earth to meet someone like Miko," the Chairman said. His shoulders fell forward, and he seemed to crumple, transforming into a derelict old man. "And when I was so honored, I failed to show the proper respect. My selfish life choices have twisted my character crooked. Like the trunk of a badly formed bonsai tree. And so, at the vital moment, my past choices poisoned my actions. I am seeped in regret."

The Chairman's face showed a hollow pain Jekyll feared he too might encounter at the end of his own days.

Minutes passed in silence.

"Maybe Miko is happy with us?" Jekyll said. "After all, we accomplished the tasks she set. And my impression of her was of a kind person. Maybe over time, Miko has forgiven our wrong attitudes."

The Chairman pursed his lips.

"That is a comforting idea. I thank you for that encouragement."

The luxurious limousine crawled in the traffic. It stopped next to a green park filled with parents and squadrons of laughing children.

Translucent pink petal snow fluttering down in the bright afternoon sun.

"We should toast her," Jekyll said.

"Yes!" the Chairman said, slapping his armrest.

He refilled their glasses.

"To Miko. The actual savior of our nation," the Chairman said. "Thank you for choosing us. It was the greatest honor."

"I agree, the greatest. To Miko."

The old men clinked their glasses and emptied them in one draught.

After, they sat lost in thought.

Staring out the window at the sunlit park, watching the multitude of swirling children jumping and giggling as they chased the falling cherry blossoms.

THE END

Author's note on next page

Author's Note

Thank you for reading my novel. I hope you enjoyed Miko's story.

I like feedback, positive or negative.

Please let me know what The Hikikomori meant to you.

Send your thoughts to my private email:
mark@vrankovich.com

P.S. I might have written The Hikikomori to read differently the second time it's read...
Cue mysterious music.

Printed in Great Britain
by Amazon

46187565R00148